W9-BDL-737

JOANNA

A Story *of* Love *and* Betrayal

ENDORSEMENTS

Gene Weatherly has written an exciting, inspiring novel that makes the Bible come alive during the days Jesus walked the earth. This is a jewel of a novel with the heartfelt fictionally embellished story of one of the women, Joanna, who followed and ministered to Jesus. The story's opening hook of the conflict in Joanna's life, the detailed research evident, the first-century setting, dialog, and the deep characterization of the many who surrounded Jesus, as well as Jesus himself, make this a five-star read.

—Elva Cobb Martin, President, South Carolina Chapter, American Christian Fiction Writers

JOANNA

A Story of Love and Betrayal

Gene Everett Weatherly

Elk Lake Publishing

Joanna: A Story of Love and Betrayal

First edition. Copyright © 2017 by Gene Everett Weatherly. The information contained in this book is the intellectual property of Gene Everett Weatherly and is governed by the United States and International copyright laws. All rights reserved. No part of this publication, either text or image, may be used for any purpose other than personal use. Therefore, reproduction, modification, storage in a retrieval system, or retransmission, in any form or by any means, electronic, mechanical, or otherwise, for reasons other than personal use, except in brief quotations for reviews or articles and promotions, is strictly prohibited without prior written permission from the publisher.

This book is a work of fiction. Although based on actual biblical characters, the events as portrayed are the author's imaginings of what may have occurred.

Graphics Design: Jeff Gifford
Editor: Cristel Phelps, Deb Haggerty
Interior Design: Cheryl L. Childers
Published in association with Les Stobbe Literary Agency

Library Cataloging Data
Names: Weatherly, Gene Everett (Gene Everett Weatherly)
Joanna: A Story of Love and Betrayal / Gene Everett Weatherly
358 p. 23cm × 15cm (9in × 6 in.)
Description: Elk Lake Publishing, Inc. digital e-book edition | Elk Lake Publishing, Inc. POD paperback edition | Elk Lake Publishing, Inc. Trade paperback edition | Elk Lake Publishing, Inc. 2016.
Identifiers: ISBN-13: 978-1-946638-36-6 e-book | 978-1-946638-37-3 POD | 978-1-946638-38-0 Trade
Key Words: Bible, Jesus, Disciples, Apostles, Crucifixion, Resurrection, Romans
LCCN: 2017956236 Fiction

DEDICATION

Dedicated to the memory of the late Reverend Russell Duffer, a small-town pastor who saw something of promise in this shy, awkward teenage boy with a stuttering problem, yet encouraged him toward a life of ministry.

ACKNOWLEDGMENTS

This scribe affirms the words of another unlikely individual God used to achieve His purpose: *"My spirit rejoices in God my Savior, for He has been mindful of the humble estate of His servant."* The inspiration of Joanna kept my fingers on the keys in this many years' journey. This is Joanna's story.

I wish to acknowledge the kind, witty, and caring editing of Cristal Phelps. Her help and insight were beyond measure.

I must also acknowledge Edie Melson. I had to drive from South Carolina to Glorieta, New Mexico, to find the encourager who lived only thirty miles from my home. Her words in our critique group, "Gene, you are a better writer than this," made me strive to fulfill her vision for me.

CHAPTER ONE

Late Spring, 32 AD
Sepphoris, Capitol of Galilee

"You've been gone three days to see Jesus, and I only find out through Mariam?" Cuza's eyes burned through me. His face nearly matched the color in his crimson cape. Mariam turned slightly away from Cuza to give me her usual half smirk, half smile. Then, knowing she had achieved her intended damage, got up and strolled out of the room.

I turned to Cuza, "When we put Marcus to bed, I told you we needed to talk." I tried hard to keep a civil voice. "Instead, you insisted on talking to your housekeeper before you would spend time with me." My heart beat out of my chest and flashes of heat raced up the sides of my neck.

Cuza bit out each word, "Joanna, how could you do something so stupid?" His words pierced my heart like a stake driven into my chest. "What will I look like at Herod's palace when word gets back their manager's wife has been running around the countryside to see this Jesus who has everyone in such a stir?" Still glaring, he rose.

"You didn't seem to have a problem rushing to Jesus and begging him to heal your son when Marcus lay near death with the fever," I retorted. "Why is my going with a gift to thank him so awful now?" Tears hovered, blurring my focus. Everything I loved about Cuza—his honor, integrity, his caring ways—seemed to be slipping away.

"That's before we found out about Jesus' connection to that firebrand preacher, John the Baptist." Cuza stalked to the window, his imposing stature and Roman uniform heightened my feelings of insignificance.

"His preaching has Herodias seething. If word of this gets back to her, she'll be livid." He whirled around. "Do you understand that?"

"I didn't know anything about a John the Baptist when I went," I answered, desperately seeking to regain some position in this terribly one-sided argument. "I tried to get you to go and show our appreciation, but you just ignored me." My shoulders shook. "What is this about a John the Baptist that has everyone so infuriated?"

"I did not give you permission to go." Cuza firmly placed both hands on his hips. "You are not to be going out around Galilee without my approval."

"And when did I begin to look like a peasant girl from one of these Jewish villages?" Anger surged within me. "They may humbly follow their husbands around with heads bowed, doing only what they're told, but I grew up here in Sepphoris, just like you did. Even though my parents are Jewish, they had as much standing in this community as your family." I struggled to draw a breath. "Don't you remember what we promised each other before we married, that neither of us would be subservient to the other?" I choked out past the large lump in my throat.

Cuza strode back to the table. "Joanna, if Herod Antipas hears about this, I don't even want to think about the consequences." Cuza forcefully slapped the table. "Hear me carefully—your actions were unacceptable."

I had seen Cuza angry many times in our six years together, but his new sternness and granite-hard attitude since our return from Capernaum had not eased, even slightly. The man I once knew and loved and wedded had disappeared somewhere in the fog of Marcus' fever.

Cuza slammed out the door, startling and shaking me to the core.

I wanted to cry, but my resentment at his condescending manner forced the tears away. The longer I sat, the angrier I became. Cuza and I used to talk. What had happened to those days? His orders to never go out of town without permission enraged my very soul.

I had so looked forward to telling Cuza about my amazing time with Jesus and his appreciation of our gift. I remembered that beautiful day when I listened to Jesus teaching the crowd. I wanted to explain to Cuza the impression Jesus made on me. I wanted him to know how something stirred in my heart when Jesus compared God to a shepherd—one who lost one of his hundred sheep and searched and searched until he found the missing one. I'd never realized God even knew me, much less cared enough to search for me. Growing up under Roman influence in Sepphoris, my parents had taught me so little about our faith. Only through that encounter with Jesus did I begin to comprehend how little I understood about having a spiritual life.

Just as on so many nights, I cried myself to sleep.

The morning dawned bright and sunny, but heavy storm clouds hung over my heart. There had to be more to life than facing Cuza's rejection, more to life than competing with Mariam for a moment with my own little son.

Breakfast was tense. I found myself sitting helplessly forgotten as Cuza and Mariam discussed the important lessons he wanted for Marcus. Their position effectively blocked me from the conversation. Getting in a meaningful word was impossible. Tired of trying, I picked up my tea and slipped out onto the terrace.

Our house is beautiful, but I love the terrace the most. From there we had a magnificent view over the city—the reason we stretched the limits to purchase our home. Sepphoris covers three long hills, and two of them extend roughly east to west. The middle ridge runs more north to south strangely, with the effect the city resembles a bird in flight. From our house on the eastern ridge, I could see the top of the fortress near the city's center. Next to the fortress is the palace of Herod Antipas, where Cuza spent five long days and nights, or often more, on duty every week.

I looked down the street in front of the house. Several streets down, I could see Decumanus Street, the city's main east-west thoroughfare. From that street, Uncle Reuben and I made our journey to take my thank you gift to Jesus. Our trip was the only memory that brought a smile these days.

My time on the terrace helped me beat back the angry tears threatening to surface. I didn't want another fight, but how much longer could I tolerate being cut out of all the decisions about Marcus? I had to do something.

The door opened, and Cuza took one step out. "I'm leaving for the palace. Mariam knows the progress I want from Marcus." He turned back.

"Cuza, please come sit down for a moment." I desperately needed to express my feelings before they exploded into anger I couldn't control. All I wanted was to be a loving wife and a dutiful mother.

That wasn't too much to ask, was it? Both had been stripped from me.

Cuza strode over and stared indifferently at me. "I don't have time. What is it?"

"Mariam does everything in her power to make me feel useless. I hardly feel like a mother anymore." My throat tightened as I continued. "I know you didn't intend—"

"Stop. If you're going into that nonsense of dismissing Mariam, just forget it. Mariam stays."

"Cuza, please—"

"Joanna, I will not tolerate your insolence." Not looking back, he left.

Anger at his rude departure sent hot coals to my stomach where they twitched and burned.

Mariam, emboldened by the trust Cuza placed in her, monopolized Marcus's attention. The harder I tried to spend time with my son, the more necessary activities she planned for him. Clearly, nothing less than Mariam's departure could heal the rift in our family. As with every day in recent memory, the constant struggle left me fuming.

Cuza's reliance on Mariam was the source of our problems—resulting in my constant struggle with him. Being angry with each other certainly did not help our marriage.

Needing to calm down, I thought back to happier moments of our life. That day in Joppa, shortly after our wedding, when we strolled hand-in-hand on the shore of the Great Sea. The sand scrunching beneath our sandals as we watched the salmon-streaked sunset give promise to a wonderful life. I never imagined a time of strife would come in our lives. But strife now governed our lives.

Somehow, I had to recapture Cuza's attention. Somewhere

behind his angry façade was the wonderful man I married. I was certain we could be happy again.

My mind drifted to the day a few weeks earlier when I gave Jesus my offering for healing Marcus. Nothing I had done before seemed nearly so appreciated. The words Jesus spoke brought meaning to my life and hope to my heart. I could not remember a happier, more joyful occasion.

Yet in my own home, Cuza barely deigned to speak to me.

I had to do something—that much was certain. But how drastic a step would I need to make to convince Cuza his attitude was destroying our relationship?

Yes, I knew I overreacted when Cuza discovered the doctor in Tiberius had moved his practice to Caesarea. And I didn't support Cuza when he decided to follow the suggestion of Mariam's sister to seek out Jesus to heal Marcus. I realized I didn't handle myself well when he set out on what seemed such a useless and time-consuming trek. But I had acknowledged being wrong. I had apologized for those mistakes. Why, months later, would Cuza still be punishing me?

Cuza was destroying the few remaining shreds of our marriage by giving Mariam the authority to oversee and instruct Marcus. Cuza wasn't home to witness Mariam's contempt toward me. Even worse, he couldn't see what the conflict was doing to me emotionally. My pleading for him to dismiss her only infuriated him more. Had I reached the place where I could no longer live in the house with Mariam present? Some days the situation was unbearable and many days intolerable.

Would my leaving bring him to realize what his stubborn, vindictive attitude was doing to us, or would I rouse his anger further? What other options did I have?

If I left, where could I go? The only place remotely possible was Aunt Anna's in Cana. She had always been so sweet and understanding. But, I would certainly be a burden to her at her age. If only Mother were still alive. Visiting Jotham and Diana had been wonderful too. Even though Diana and I were only cousins, we became like sisters when Uncle Reuben and I visited on our journey to find Jesus. But to stay for more than a day or two with them would certainly be imposing. And, if Cuza came for me, the retribution on them could be terrible.

As I sat considering my options, my mind again drifted to the beautiful encounter with Jesus. He had said something to me I didn't understand. What did he mean, "I'm looking forward to seeing you again soon?" I had no intention of returning, but that was such a happy, fulfilling day. Another thought floated across the edge of my mind. Had I replied, "I'm looking forward to getting to know all of you a lot better"? Why would I have said that?

I remembered how the younger James's mother appeared entirely dedicated to feeding and organizing everything for Jesus and his disciples. How she did everything by herself amazed me. Her invitation to stay with her and help had seemed entirely farfetched. I wonder?

I had hoped the tension would have cooled when Cuza returned from his five days at the palace, but those hopes were quickly dashed. Except for sweet little Marcus, smiles were non-existent.

The precious little time I counted as ours, Cuza spent meeting with his aides out on the terrace.

"Joanna!"

I jumped, startled. "Cuza, I didn't realize—"

"Just listen. Omar tells me Justus will be here shortly with some palace requisitions. Show him onto the terrace when he arrives."

"Cuza, when can we have time for a civil conversation? I know you have to be at Herod's palace for five days attending your job, but when you're home, I—"

"Joanna, I don't have time for your nonsense." Cuza turned on his heel, his point made by forcefully closing the door.

Was that distant thunder predicting a storm, or the rumbling of my heavy heart? Again, realization hung before me like an approaching enemy. I had to do something. Perhaps recording my feelings would help me better deal with them.

I slipped to the window overlooking the street. Even though I could easily hear a horse arrive on the stone pavement below, I wanted to make sure I wouldn't be disturbed. Sensing everything was clear, I carefully drew the quill and parchment from the cabinet, placing them on the small side table. I stared at the quill for a long moment wondering whether I could explain my true feelings, even to myself.

I finally picked up the quill.

Dear Cuza,

The state of our marriage deeply saddens me. Please hear my heart. We began life together as a team. We knew together we could conquer our part of the world—and you have, Cuza. You have done so much and come so far.

Though I am thankful for the provision of your labor, you must know this. My greatest longing is to be near you. But you keep moving further and further away.

A chair leg screeched on the terrace tile. I froze, then quickly hid my parchment. Beads of perspiration trickled down my neck. I tiptoed to the door. Cuza's assistant paced back and forth. *Good.*

Fear crept over me. *Perhaps I should wait.* Yet, anger over having to write such a note erased that fear. I slipped into the bedroom and among my personal things made a safe hiding place for my thoughts.

The swiftly opening door struck the wall. "Joanna. I asked you to watch for Justus. Can't you even do the simplest thing I ask? He's been standing there waiting."

"Cuza, I came in here only a moment ago. He certainly had not arrived—"

"Don't bother with excuses. It's urgent I personally go to the palace and issue these requisitions for Herodias. I won't be gone long."

Thankfully, he didn't slam the door in my face. It remained half open, and half closed, much like the picture of my life.

Agonizing over the situation obviously wasn't going to solve anything. The time had arrived to do something. But what? The only person I felt comfortable discussing these issues with was Uncle Reuben. Thankfully, Sepphoris provided the security and culture where a woman could walk a short distance without being accompanied by a male family member.

Mariam had Marcus seated for his snack. I summoned a cheery voice as I threw the scarf over my shoulder. "I'm going to a friend's house for a little while."

Mariam, as usual, turned toward Marcus rather than speak to me. I wasn't sure the meaning of her throat-clearing guttural comment, but it didn't really matter.

I leaned around Mariam and kissed Marcus on the forehead, "I'll see you when you get up from your nap. Be ready to recite your alphabet for mommy."

Uncle Reuben was in his backyard helping a young boy fashion something like a rope swing. He quickly finished and came over to give me a hug, just one arm slightly over my shoulder. "Since your Aunt Beth passed away, I'm careful how I greet any woman, no matter how close a relative. You wouldn't believe the gossip." He put his hands on my shoulders. "Stand back and let me look at you. I don't see many beautiful young ladies in elegant silk dresses on this side of Sepphoris."

A small, slender man, Uncle Reuben was hardly taller than me. His sixty some years stayed well-hidden behind his infectious smile. His hair might be gray, but his spryness more than made up for his appearance. We sat down on his little porch with a cup of cool water.

"The conversation with Cuza didn't go well, did it?" Uncle Reuben looked at me a long moment. "Your eyes give you away."

"Oh, Uncle Reuben, it was terrible." I didn't usually talk fast, but my words rushed like a spring flood. "Before I could tell Cuza about my wonderful trip to thank Jesus, Mariam managed to insert a comment about how much more I would know about Marcus's progress had I not been out running around the countryside to see Jesus."

"Oh, I wager that went over wonderfully."

I nodded but couldn't hold my tears. "Cuza completely ignores my feelings. I've warned him repeatedly his giving Mariam control of Marcus is poisoning our relationship. He just won't listen. I can't even bring up the subject without him reacting angrily. I feel so useless, so alone."

Uncle Reuben put a firm hand on my shoulder. He began to speak twice but just bit his bottom lip. His eyes glistened.

"Uncle Reuben, Cuza went way too far, commanding me to never see Jesus again."

The moment those words left my lips I realized I'd said too much. I quickly tried covering by explaining the problems the radical preacher, John the Baptist, was causing Herod Antipas.

Uncle Reuben's eyes remained difficult to read.

"Remember the load James's mother carried, feeding and taking care of Jesus and his disciples?" I pleaded. "I'm thinking of going and helping her for a week, two at the most."

Uncle Reuben's eyes grew large as cups; his mouth dropped, but no words came.

"I'm not talking about permanently leaving Cuza. I'm only thinking about enough time for Cuza to realize what a fool he's being." I wiped the tear trickling down my cheek. "I know the Cuza I married is still there somewhere."

"That's far too drastic a step." Uncle Reuben stood wide-eyed. Then he slowly shook his head. "No, Joanna, don't even ask me."

"Uncle Reuben, please! Don't turn me down before I even ask."

"Joanna, I love you like a daughter, and I was thrilled to take you to Jesus a few weeks ago." He slowly walked the length of the short porch then turned. With sad eyes, he said, "Please don't ask me to do anything that could come between you and your husband."

He returned. "I especially can't go against Cuza." Uncle Reuben placed his hand on my shoulder. "With his position at Herod's palace … the trouble he could cause me."

"I must do something drastic to make Cuza understand." I took Uncle Reuben's hand from my shoulder and held it. "Within a week, two at the most, he'll come begging me to return. Yes, I would like to help Jesus. But most importantly, I want Cuza to come to his senses." Tears trickled down my face. "Please come help me find Jesus again."

Uncle Reuben slowly shook his head. "Joanna. I wouldn't go against your husband, even if he wasn't a Roman officer."

"Then just accompany me back to Jotham and Diana's. I'll ask Jotham to take me to Jesus." I let his hand go. "Your name hasn't been mentioned. I assure you, no matter what, it won't be. You don't even need to know why I'm going to see my cousin."

The long moments Uncle Reuben stood in contemplation seemed an eternity. "Do you think Jotham can find Jesus? We never hear much about him here in Sepphoris."

I gave him my best pleading eyes. "Remember, once out in the countryside, everyone was talking about Jesus. It shouldn't be harder than last time."

"What about Cuza? How is he going to know where to find Jesus and that you will be with him?"

"That's not hard." I managed a slight smile. "I'll write him a long note telling him why I've left and where I will be. According to Cuza, Herod's palace keeps pretty close tabs on Jesus."

"Joanna, I'm afraid there are more holes in your strategy than you possibly imagine."

But ever so slowly, Uncle Reuben's shaking head turned into a single nod. "I'll acquiesce. What's the plan?"

We agreed on the time and place of our rendezvous. I gave him strong assurance that if the situation improved any at all, we would abandon the whole plot.

With Cuza on duty at Herod's palace, Marcus sound asleep, and Mariam in her room, I retrieved my parchment. I looked at it a long moment, took a deep breath, then picked up the quill and forced my hand to continue.

We needed Mariam during Marcus's illness, but now, you find it necessary for her to stay. It is clear you believe only she knows what is best for Marcus. With your empowerment, she easily finds ways to keep me from having a meaningful relationship with my son. Mariam has poisoned our bond and left me feeling completely useless. Cuza, you have neither listened to my hurts nor responded to my needs. Instead, you have consistently listened to Mariam above any opinion I might offer. The two of you have separated me from my own family. I cannot, and will not, live this way.

The only sense of appreciation I've felt in the past six months was in taking the gift to thank Jesus.

Since you and Mariam obviously don't want me here, I am going away, offering to help Jesus in his ministry. This is my decision alone. No one put any ideas in my mind, least of all, Jesus.
The most difficult decision of my life is leaving Marcus behind. But, you have made this drastic step necessary. Please understand. My reason for leaving is to help you realize how you are destroying our marriage, and how I'm losing Marcus.

Should our time apart convince you to make the necessary changes, then come for me. With Mariam gone, I would love nothing more than to be home as a wife and mother again. Please do not come unless my wishes are also the desire of your heart.
Cuza, I love you, but I can no longer bear this rejection. Good-bye for now.
Joanna

CHAPTER TWO

I sat in such a way Cuza couldn't leave without at least acknowledging my presence. He spent half an hour ignoring me while giving instructions to Mariam on progress for Marcus. My determination grew with each passing slight. *You have one last chance to change my mind, Cuza. You had better make it good.*

He muttered a matter of fact good-bye as he brushed past me and reached for the door. A mid-winter breeze chilled the summer air as he strode by.

My legs became like limp rope as I reached the door. With tears, I watched Cuza depart. I bit deeply into my bottom lip as he rode away.

As I turned toward our room, the two conflicting emotions struggled mightily against each other. *Can I leave my own son, even for a week or two?* I can't imagine doing anything so reckless. But if my sudden absence, even so short, could shock Cuza into making changes, leaving Marcus would be worth it.

On the other hand, I simply can't stay and live a useless life where my opinions are ignored, where my husband has destroyed my role as mother. Floods of frustration swept over me like waves of a stormy sea.

Where the strength came from to make the fateful decision I don't know. But I knew I must do something. The agony of departure would be worthwhile if it brought us together again. A gamble for sure, but I could not continue living in this hellish existence.

Pulling my note from its hiding place, I scanned the words one last time. If I hesitated, I knew I wouldn't continue. I tucked my message under Cuza's pillow with the faintest small corner showing. The note would be safe there for only my husband to find.

I dug the money Aunt Bernice left me out of its hiding place beneath the floor tile. Half seemed quite enough. My things were rolled and ready. Meeting time with Uncle Reuben came faster than expected. With the money and my few belongings concealed beneath my shawl, only two doors and Mariam stood in my way.

My heart beating wildly, I leisurely strolled through our main living area. Glancing at the high, ornate ceiling and the beautiful mosaic floor, I lied to myself: *I don't think I'll miss all of these.*

With blood racing through my temples, I remarked casually, "I'll see you a little later, Mariam." I didn't look at Marcus. I knew if I did, I would completely fall apart. Leaving proved far more difficult than I'd imagined.

As I approached our fig tree meeting place on Decumanus Street, Uncle Reuben wasn't there. My heart raced still faster. *He wouldn't forget. Could he have fallen ill?* My eyes strained to look back down the street. Reaching the huge bushy tree, I wondered how to inconspicuously wait for him.

"These are delicious." Uncle Reuben stepped out from the other side with a handful of ripe figs. "Here, try one."

I jumped. "Uncle Reuben, don't scare me like that. No, I couldn't swallow a thing, especially not now."

"Joanna, before we go, take one last look up the street at your house. Make sure this is really what you want to do."

"Oh, Uncle Reuben, I can't. If I do, I'll melt right here. I must keep reminding myself that leaving is my only way to become a wife and mother again."

"Okay then, let's leave some pavement behind us while the morning's still cool."

Near mid-day, I pointed to several tall poplar trees beside a small stream to the right of the road. "Isn't this the spot we had lunch on our first trip?"

"I do believe it is." Uncle Reuben turned toward the trees. "The place looks even more inviting today."

As we rested and munched on the lunch he'd prepared, Uncle Reuben turned to me. "I don't understand why Cuza's so opposed to your going to thank Jesus. Didn't he go to Cana asking Jesus to heal Marcus?"

I nodded. "The reason is all about some wild preacher named John the Baptist. He has the palace in an uproar." I shrugged my shoulders. "Apparently, he and Jesus are closely related."

"What in the world could some crazy preacher do to so upset the palace?"

"All I know is they think John is the Devil and Jesus way too close to him."

A playful coney twitched his bushy tail as he scampered over the adjoining rocks. I tossed him a crust from my bread and another suddenly appeared. As the first made off with his prize, Uncle Reuben remarked, "Isn't it amazing how God provides for these little fellows, even way out here?"

"Hmmm. I can only hope he's looking out for me in this endeavor." A chill tingled up my back.

Thankfully, Uncle Reuben didn't respond. My thoughts kept me quiet as we collected our belongings and started back toward the road. Sometimes, I had found thinking is better when not talking.

Uncle Reuben and I crested a small knoll and the Sea of Galilee suddenly stretched out across the valley before us. Its shimmering blue water reflected silver ribbons across the waves. The lake appeared larger than I remembered. Hills rose from the water on the three sides I could see. A nearly cloudless sky hovered above as we stood a long moment taking in the beautiful sight.

"You know, I so hated those weeks we spent in Capernaum when Marcus had the fever I hardly took the time to acknowledge the lake's existence, let alone its beauty."

A puzzled look covered Uncle Reuben's thin face. "You left your lovely home in Sepphoris … to live in Capernaum?"

"Oh, it was Mariam's idea. Marcus' fever seemed worse on warmer days. Since Mariam grew up in Capernaum, she convinced Cuza the cooler climate beside the lake would help. It did for a while."

A lingering moment of silence passed as the awful memory flashed across my mind. "I'll never forget that terrible night. Cuza returned to find Marcus burning with fever, near death. Cuza rushed to Tiberias only to discover the doctor there had recently moved to Caesarea. We were devastated.

"With every option vanishing, Mariam's sister suggested we find the young Jewish miracle worker named Jesus. Out of desperation, Cuza went. You know the rest of the story."

Uncle Reuben smiled, his eyes glistening.

"With Marcus healed and us leaving for home, I vowed to never lay my eyes on that miserable, smelly little town again." My voice trailed off with the breeze from the sea.

"We need to pick up the pace and get to Magdala." Uncle Reuben's face turned deadly serious. "Now, it is still agreed—I'm only taking you as far as Jotham and Diana's."

A surprised Diana gave me a hug I wouldn't soon forget. "Joanna and Uncle Reuben, come in this house." Although Diana and I were about the same age, she possessed a much stronger image. Her round face, set in curly black hair, contained an infectious smile. Even though she looked nothing like me, with my slender frame and narrow face, she became the sister I never had when we were there a couple of weeks earlier.

The four of us sat down to a delicious dinner. As Diana passed the barley cakes, the look in her eyes indicated the time had arrived for me to reveal the reason for our sudden second visit. I took a deep breath. "Diana, Jotham, I didn't tell the full story last time we were here. Especially about Cuza and me."

An abrupt and complete silence descended over the table. The couple gazed at me while Uncle Reuben sheepishly looked away. Hesitantly I continued, "Our relationship had been complicated, but since I returned from our previous trip ..." The words choked in my throat. "... life has become intolerable."

I felt awkward with such attention directed toward me. But with that much said, I had no choice but to continue. "We desperately needed a nanny housekeeper when Marcus was so sick. But after Jesus healed Marcus, Cuza decided to keep Mariam. She is now the problem. Cuza relies on her judgment for every decision about Marcus. I can't get through to him how Mariam is poisoning our relationship. When I suggest dismissing her, Cuza becomes even angrier. The only way I know to make him understand …" I paused an agonizing moment, "… is to leave."

Shock filled both Diana's and Jotham's faces. Diana's words came slowly as her eyes widened. "You are leaving Cuza and Marcus?"

"Not for long, only a week or two. But I'm desperate." I blinked back my tears. "I left Cuza a long note explaining when he dismisses Mariam and accepts me as a wife and mother, I want nothing more than to be home."

Jotham's eyebrows furrowed even more.

"But, Joanna, what are you going to do while you wait for Cuza to realize all of this?"

I swallowed hard. "When I took my gift to Jesus, he sincerely thanked me. Then as we prepared to leave, he invited me to come help in his ministry. At the time, I dismissed the idea as utterly remote."

Words came hard, and the more I talked, the more ridiculous everything I said sounded. "As things grew worse at home, I knew I had to do something. The image of James's mother appearing so exhausted, working by herself to feed Jesus' followers, kept coming to me." I stopped to gauge their reaction. Skepticism flourished on each of their faces. Swallowing hard, I forced myself on. "I plan to go and offer my help."

"You can't be serious!" Pure astonishment covered Jotham's face.

"Within a week, two at the most," I hastened to add, "Cuza will realize what a fool he's been and come get me." The statement didn't do much to lessen their shock. "I realize this is a desperate move, but

I believe it's the only way."

Diana rose from the table and stood, gripping the back of her chair. "Do you know anything about Jesus' ministry?" Reservation hung heavy in her voice. "Jesus and his disciples travel around the country teaching. You've never been camping have you, growing up in the city?"

I raked my teeth over my bottom lip. "I suppose I'll be learning a lot of things."

Diana looked me over shaking her head. "I'm not going to encourage you. But if you're going, your clothes will be terribly out of place."

I looked at myself. My colorful silk attire did stand in stark contrast to the simple tan robe Diana wore.

After Diana finished dressing me, I probably would have fainted if I could have seen myself. Besides being itchy, the robe was too large. She found a way to tuck and tie it making the garment a little more presentable—but not much. I looked down at myself. *People wear things like this?*

"Oh, you're fortunate in at least one way." Enthusiasm filled Jotham's voice just a little. "Jesus is actually quite close. He and his disciples have made their headquarters in the village of Capernaum by the Sea of Galilee. It's only about a two-hour walk from here."

Did Jotham say Capernaum?

CHAPTER THREE

Just the thought of going back to Capernaum made my dinner do utterly strange things. Somehow, I managed a weak smile.

"What's wrong, Joanna?" A frown crossed Uncle Reuben's wrinkled face. "You look like your best friend just died."

"Oh, no. My mind simply wandered back to some unpleasant memories." Jesus in Capernaum. Sweat formed behind my ears.

"Several of his disciples fish for a living." Jotham's excitement advanced a degree. "But I hear they haven't had much time for fishing lately."

The first serious wrinkle reared its ugly head. How many more are lurking?

I put on the best smile I could muster. "Jotham, could you possibly take me to Capernaum tomorrow? Uncle Reuben desperately needs to return home."

"If we go early," Jotham smiled as he replied. "Perhaps I can actually meet Jesus this time."

As I lay down for the night, butterflies took flight in my stomach. Jesus moved his ministry to Capernaum. How could he do that? Anger crept up both sides of my neck.

Then reality settled in and and shame planted itself firmly between my eyes. I finally spoke to the ceiling and to my wilted heart. "Remember, Joanna, this isn't about you. Jesus can survive with or without your help."

I didn't remember sleeping, but an early morning beam of sunlight rudely awakened me. I squinted both eyes as I sat up.

Uncle Reuben and I hugged before he started home. Shortly after, Jotham and I hurried out the door toward Capernaum. "You haven't had this much confusion in a long time, have you?"

"Oh, it's good for us. Life and work get humdrum," Jotham said as we walked. Then with a coy grin, he added, "And thanks to you, no one suffered boredom last evening."

"Just the two of us talking, heart to heart. Okay?"

He nodded, didn't say anything.

"Do you think all of this is completely beyond reason?"

"Joanna, I can't begin to know your life with Cuza." Jotham slowed down even more and gave a fair imitation of a smile. "I grew up in a home filled with love, as did Diana. I could count the arguments we've had on my fingers." Jotham shook his head. "I couldn't live in a home filled with contention."

"Do you think it will work?" I bit my bottom lip. "To bring Cuza to his senses?"

Jotham stopped dead still. "Well, it will either work ... or make him very mad." His voice trailed off.

I swallowed hard and waited for him to continue. He didn't.

"What about my going to help in Jesus' ministry?" I wanted both his opinion and to quickly change the subject.

"Trying to avoid the question." He started walking again. "Can't really say. Think Jesus could possibly be expecting you?"

"When I gave him my gift, he relayed how few people ever turn to even say 'thank you.'" I smiled remembering that beautiful moment.

As we walked, I continued. "When Jesus mentioned my coming to help, I had no intention of ever seeing them again. But for some reason, I remarked, 'I'll look forward to knowing all of you a lot better.' To this day, I have no idea why I said that."

The early morning coolness retreated, giving way to a summer day's heat. I used my sleeve to dab the moisture forming on my forehead. "I'll never forget turning to leave. Jesus looked directly at me with his deep, dark eyes and said, 'I'll look forward to seeing you again soon, Joanna.'"

I stopped and looked directly at Jotham. "I don't know much about spiritual things, but that day I realized something was missing in my life." I slowly started walking. "I'm not sure exactly what I'm missing, but I want to find out."

We walked in silence many long moments. Jotham finally spoke. "Joanna, I'm not going to say, 'I hope you know what you're doing,' because no one possibly could." His eyebrows furrowed, then a slight smile crept across his face. "All I'm going to say is, I hope you find what you're looking for." Silence again enveloped our space along the road.

The walk from Magdala to Capernaum gave us a sweeping view of the Sea of Galilee. When I came along this road with Cuza, my worry about Marcus prevented me from noticing much of anything. When we left, I had no desire to look back. But as we walked on the road down the hillside toward Capernaum, the view became breathtaking. Tall, spindly cedars lined the road in places. In other areas, vineyards ran up the slopes. But the beautiful blue lake below eclipsed everything.

Having lived in Sepphoris all my twenty-six years, I generally regarded the countryside as some place you suffered through to get to the city—where the nice things were. But the fresh morning air, along with the scent of flowers blooming, combined with the scenery made for an amazing walk. Well, except for the occasional animal pen located too close to the road.

Then we came to Capernaum.

The town still looked like a place the giver of beauty completely forgot. But I did point out the one single pretty thing at the very edge of town. "I don't know whether it's a big bush or a small tree. Look how it's completely covered in red blossoms."

"It's gorgeous."

"I assure you, this is the only attractive thing around here." We started on into town. "And probably the only thing in this town that doesn't smell like fish."

Jotham lifted his nose to the air and frowned. "Think we ought to ask some locals where Jesus is staying?"

I nodded, and Jotham stopped the first two men we met. Both men, as well as others nearby we didn't ask, all said, "Jesus? He's staying in the home of Simon the fisherman down near the market."

"Well, thankfully, Jesus isn't keeping his location a secret." A big smile spread across Jotham's face.

Capernaum, as I remembered, consisted basically of two streets. There were a lot of little side streets crossing, but most of the town lay along the two long streets running parallel to the lake. As we walked, the seagulls swooped and played in the nearly cloudless sky. Occasionally the smell of cooking food mingled with the fresh, cool breeze off the lake. But the fishy odor invaded everything.

As we approached the center of town, I leaned close to Jotham. "Since most of these houses look the same, should we ask which is Simon's?"

"I don't think we'll need to. Look a little further down the street to the house on the left. All those people crowded in the yard tells me Jesus is probably right there."

We stood at the edge of the street watching thirty or so people all pushing to get in an obviously already full house. I looked at Jotham. "This isn't going to be easy. Seems like every time I come to see Jesus, I have to elbow my way in."

The words barely cleared my mouth when four men came charging down the street carrying a sling between them. Had we been three steps further into the street, they would have knocked us down. They reached the back of the crowd, who already couldn't get in, and tried to shove past. The crowd obviously didn't plan to budge.

When they turned toward the side of the house, I caught a good look at the cargo in their sling. He appeared to be the crippled man I remembered begging near the fish market when Cuza and I lived there. I turned to Jotham, "What in the world are they trying to do with him?" He looked just as puzzled.

Most houses were similar to the one we lived in those few weeks Marcus gave us such a scare. Basically, there were three to five rooms, covered with a flat roof that also served as an outdoor living area. Most had a crude set of stairs on the side to the upper roof terrace.

My hand covered my mouth. "They won't try getting that man up those stairs, I hope."

"If that poor fellow wasn't crippled before ..." Jotham's jaw dropped.

"And what on earth for?" My words were hardly audible. Once on the terrace, the four began prying up the roof tiles. "Jotham, that's crazy. I can't believe my eyes." They lowered the poor crippled man down through the roof into the room below.

Jotham shook his head. "If this is what it takes to see Jesus, I might as well go on home."

In about the time it takes to tie your sandals, two men in long, ornate robes stormed out of the house shouting, "This fellow speaks blasphemy!"

One kept repeating the words while the other began shouting, "Who can forgive sins but God alone?" They both waved their arms in the air, "Blasphemy, blasphemy!"

"Jotham, what is blasphemy?"

Jotham's eyebrows narrowed. "It's when you say something contrary to the Scriptures."

"Jesus wouldn't do something like that, would he?"

Suddenly, the crippled beggar burst out the door, through the crowd jumping and shouting, "I'm healed! I'm healed!"

The two men dressed in the religious robes both tried to shout him down. "Shut up, you're just a sinner."

But he kept shouting, "I'm healed!"

"Welcome to Capernaum." The voice came from behind us. I turned, and to my surprise, there stood James's mother, Mary. She wore a big smile as she watched our amazement.

"Oh, it's such a relief to see your face." I grabbed her with a hug. "We were beginning to think we would have to go back home because of the crowd."

"Oh, it's not as bad as it looks." Mary led us a little way from the noise. "You have come to stay a while?"

"Well, if I can be of any help and not be in the way." My heart fluttered. She seemed to almost be expecting me. "When I met all of you beside the lake, you seemed as if you could use a little help."

I quickly added, "But if I'm an imposition, I can easily go back home."

Those last words were far from honest. There wasn't any way I could go back after the note I left Cuza. I struggled to prevent the panic tingling through my body from showing.

"Jesus will be thrilled you're here. Come on to our house while Jesus gets this crowd on their way."

A small, wiry woman, Mary was several inches shorter than even me. Since her son James seemed my age, Mary must be close to fifty years old. Her hair was gray, but her agility reminded me of Uncle Reuben. I loved her take-charge attitude. Her tan outer robe tied over a lighter-colored inner robe looked remarkably like my new clothes.

Mary looked up and down Jotham's lanky frame, then his bushy head of dark hair. "And this nice young man with you?"

"Oh, how rude of me. Mary, this is my cousin, Jotham. He agreed to escort me here. He is quite a fan of Jesus."

Jotham nodded to Mary. "Will I finally have the chance to meet Jesus personally? I watched him clear the money changers from the temple. He was quite impressive."

"I hope so. But he's going to be a while getting away from this crowd," Mary replied.

We looked back across the street. The healed crippled man had left, and the obnoxious religious men apparently decided they weren't getting anywhere stirring up the crowd.

"Jesus looks like he is going for a walk to take the people away from Simon and Andrew's house." Mary turned and motioned for us to follow. "Once he's able to leave the crowd in town, he and the men will be back here, probably starving. Let's get you settled in so we can start lunch."

Jotham stood there, apparently lost in thought. Mary tapped him on the shoulder. "Jotham, would you like to come with us?"

"I'll drop off Joanna's things. But since Jesus won't be returning for a while, I'd better get back."

I had not actually envisioned the moment Jotham would disappear down the street. As my last link with anything familiar evaporated around the corner, serious doubts began gnawing my insides. *What had I done?* I looked down at the brown woolen garment Diana loaned me. *Could I be wearing this?* I wouldn't be caught dead wearing something like this in Sepphoris. Was I really back in the smelly little town I hated so much, wearing clothes I couldn't stand and cooking for a bunch of men I didn't know?

What was I thinking?

CHAPTER FOUR

"It's only for a week," I whispered. Then I whispered my words several more times, trying to encourage my sinking heart. Reminding myself that no one talked me into this didn't help much.

"You can begin the barley cakes, Joanna." Mary woke me from my cloud of self-pity. "We'll need at least fifteen. We never know who Jesus might bring along."

Barley cakes? That's what peasants eat. As the thoughts raced, I glanced down at my ill-fitting brown robe. *Is this really me?*

But the crackling fire and the pleasant aroma of barley cakes baking slowly began to calm my over-anxious heart.

Mary tugged my sleeve. "While things are baking, let's walk back over to Simon's house and see what's happening with his roof."

Simon's home lay across the main street, two houses down. Her son, James, was working with Simon to repair the damage. Yes, for Jesus to take the crowd for a walk was a wise and necessary move. Listening to the men's conversation as they labored, I said, "Simon certainly has an interesting way of putting words together, doesn't he?"

Mary chuckled. "These men came from very rough lives. That's mild compared to what my dear Alphaeus would have said."

Mary called, "James, is Jose up there with you?"

"He's not up here."

"Have I met Jose?" I asked.

"Jose's my younger son. He's nearly six years younger than James." Mary shook her head. "I had James with my first husband, Alphaeus. I was his second wife."

"Alphaeus sounds familiar. Can't quite place him, though."

"Good." Mary turned, and we started back toward her home. "Alphaeus had children with his first wife, but I don't know much about them. Two years after James's birth, Alphaeus encountered a Roman spear."

I didn't realize an expression crossed my face, but Mary asked, "A little confused?"

I nodded. We continued walking.

"You'll be even more so when they return. You won't find nine men more different from each other than these with Jesus." Mary gave a sly quick smile. "Only normal one is my James."

As we reached Mary's door, a young man came running. "Mother, they're on their way, and they have the worst person imaginable with them."

He stopped as he examined me. "Who's this?"

"Hi, I'm Joanna."

"Jose, be kind to Joanna. She's come to help me feed this bunch." Mary placed her hand on my shoulder. "Remember, she brought money to help buy food—while you men forget about jobs."

"Oh, Mother."

"Who's the awful fellow they're bringing?" Mary asked.

"Jesus stopped to talk with one of those thieving tax collectors. Since I'm behind in my taxes, I stayed at a distance." Jose wiped sweat from his face. "When he closed his books and stood, I took a shortcut back as fast as I could." Jose started toward the back room. "I don't want to be around if Jesus brings him here."

Jose reappeared with an armful of clothes. "I'm going to spend some time with Agar." With that, Jose headed down the dusty street.

I hardly caught my breath when James came in tired and dirty from his labor on Simon's roof. "There, that should hold the roof. From the way the clouds are darkening, we'll know pretty soon."

James selected one of my cooling barley cakes and took a big bite. "Goodness, what happened to these?"

"They're that bad?" I ducked my head.

James's eyes shifted to me. "Have we met?"

"James, this is Joanna. You met her a couple of weeks ago. She brought the gift that helped restock the pantry."

A blank expression filled James's face, so I spoke. "Yes, Jesus introduced you as 'the other James.'" I gave him a big smile. "I'm the one whose son Jesus healed." I thought a moment. "Well, I suppose he's done that for a lot of people. My husband, Cuza, was the Roman official who found Jesus in Cana."

James still looked blank.

"Jesus didn't go with him, remember? He only said Marcus would be all right. At that very time, his fever broke. Anyway, I was the one who brought the gift to thank Jesus."

"Oh yes, you had on that fancy silk dress then." James pulled his lips tight. "Cuza ... that name has—"

The door flew open. Jesus and a crowd of men flooded in. I did my best to find a place over at the side out of the way. As Mary predicted, several asked about something to eat as they scarfed up the barley cakes. Thankfully, no one complained—at least not aloud.

Jesus called the men, "I want each of you to get acquainted with Matthew. Don't be too hard on him. He's given up a very lucrative business to join us."

Mathew's fine linen robe stood in complete contrast to the simple brown of the others. He looked as out of place as Diana said I would in my silk dress.

Jesus put his hand on Matthew's shoulder. "Accepting Matthew may be a little hard for some of you, but if you have learned anything from me, it's how to forgive." Jesus looked across the men. "Right?"

Several stood stoically. A few disciples slowly nodded their heads, several only stroked their beards.

"Men." Matthew raised his hand to the group. "I know you have good reason to hate me. I also realize collecting taxes for the Romans has made me a traitor." Matthew's eyes searched for a friendly face. "I can't take back what I did, but I will give you this promise. If I've taken from any of you unfairly, I'll repay you out of my own pocket."

Matthew's eyes turned to Jesus in a silent plea for help. None came. He sucked in his stomach and continued. "This evening, let me enjoy freedom from loving the denarii. Perhaps by serving Jesus …" his voice broke, "I can begin a new life."

That seemed to lighten the tension a little. Some hard looks eased, if only slightly.

Matthew, a small man with a slender face, looked in his late thirties. He wore a neatly trimmed beard, and though small, he did have a well-developed mid-section. He certainly had not missed many meals.

Confusion gripped at me. Did Jesus need followers badly enough to take in a tax collector, someone the people obviously despised? Then another realization began to push into my consciousness. *I'm not that different from Matthew. Matthew collects taxes for the Romans who occupy this country. I'm married to someone the taxes are for. If they have trouble admitting Matthew, they are certainly going to have a problem accepting me.* I whispered, "What have I done?"

Matthew again raised his hand to the group. "Men, I would like to host a dinner tomorrow evening at my house with Jesus as the guest of honor. I would be grateful if each of you would come."

That livened up things. The slightly appreciative opinions I overheard seemed to out-weigh the completely skeptical ones.

Two men huddled close to where I tried to inconspicuously stand. The older one leaned to the other. "Matthew thinks he can stroll in here and just become one of us?" His face hardened. "We've been with Jesus for two years now. I don't think so."

"No need to worry, James." The other tried to whisper. "He doesn't stand a chance."

James? I wonder what he will say about me?

Jesus again called the men. "I see we have another new face today. Joanna returned as she promised." Jesus motioned for Mary and me to come stand beside him. "Mary could no longer take care of feeding us by herself. My Father has sent this lovely woman to help."

Jesus looked at me and smiled, then turned back to the men. "Joanna has contributed generously to our ministry." Jesus looked back at me with his dark brown eyes. "Thank you for returning." I blushed. A big lump grew in my throat. I didn't know whether I should speak. Finally, I said, "I'm glad to be back."

Andrew acted especially thrilled as he introduced himself. I met Philip and liked him immediately. He appeared to be a refined gentleman. Two men, who seemed joined at the hip, came up. The short one with a round cherub face said, "My name's Bartholomew, but you can call me Bart. I'm glad you're here."

The tall and slender man beside him added, "I ... I'm glad you're here too. My name is Th-Th-Thaddaeus, but most people call me

35

Thad." The sight of the two together brought a smile to my face.

All in all, it turned into a rather good reception. But I wondered how their view would change when these fellows discovered who my husband was.

Following the evening's dinner, Mary, the disciples, and I sat around with Jesus and talked about the day's events. Mary leaned over. "No matter what other things the men are involved in during the day, we always gather following the evening meal."

Mary reflected a moment. "Many days are filled with Jesus teaching the crowds and healing the sick. The evenings are his personal time with the disciples." Her eyes glistened. "These times are very special."

There were some brutal questions concerning the addition of Matthew. The men were certainly honest in expressing their feelings.

The older James finally pulled himself up straight. The way he looked at the other eight men indicated he felt some higher level of importance. He spoke directly to Matthew. "We've all come to live relatively simple lives, Matthew. Money's no longer most important." He paused for a deep breath, obviously to emphasize the coming comment. "With your affluent life, how can you possibly fit in?"

I cringed.

Matthew described his changed outlook, but he did have trouble explaining what he intended to do with his lavish home. I suppose he hadn't had time to consider that since his conversion earlier in the day.

Jesus mercifully interrupted and asked Simon Peter about the condition of his roof.

"James and I repaired the damage." Simon Peter didn't say more, but I did notice a redness glowing about his ears.

Through the open window, I heard rain begin to fall, which brought a pleasant relief from the town's usual fishy odor.

As the rain fell harder, Mary rose and covered the window—a frame with a scraped animal skin. Window glass had become relatively standard in the homes of Sepphoris. I would miss the views.

During a lull in the discussion, I looked to Jesus. "This is all really new to me. I'll have a lot of questions, if it's okay to ask."

Jesus' face broke into a smile as he nodded. I continued, "What was happening in the yard today when those two men in the religious robes were hollering blasphemy?"

"Did that seem a little strange to you?" Jesus laughed, as did some of the men.

I blushed but nodded.

"Well, the situation was strange." Jesus rested his elbows on his knees. "You see, Joanna, when I saw four men going to that extent getting their friend to me, I knew there was more to his story than him being crippled."

Jesus gestured with his hands. "This man felt guilty having to beg. He imagined he had done something wrong to cause his condition." He shook his head slowly. "I couldn't heal his body until I dealt with his guilt. So, I assured him his sins were forgiven."

A smile spread across my face.

Jesus continued. "You're probably wondering about the men in the religious robes?"

I nodded again.

"They're called Pharisees." Jesus' comment struck a chord with his disciples. Smirks or looks of disdain crossed many faces. "They are our self-appointed religious leaders."

"Oh?" Confusion replaced my smile.

"Many years ago, when the Romans first conquered our country, some of the more devout men wanted to bring their countrymen back to an awareness of our Father, God," Jesus explained. "The Pharisaic movement began with a noble goal. But over time, they became politically powerful and spiritually intolerant."

I nodded, though I didn't really understand.

"To purify the lives of the people, they created rules on how to obey God's Law." Jesus shrugged his shoulders. "In addition to our Ten Commandments, they have created over six hundred regulations one needs to obey to keep the Law. Instead of teaching love for our Heavenly Father, the Pharisees make rules."

"All they do is try to enforce their rules on the people," Simon Peter injected.

"They make exceptions for themselves," Jesus explained with his hands, "on the very rules they try to impose. They are like a tomb, a beautiful whitewash on the outside, but full of dead men's bones on the inside."

Jesus stood and looked down. "Since I dealt with the crippled man's guilt first, they saw an opportunity to accuse me." A twinkle appeared in his eyes. "They like to do that."

Everyone nodded and murmured approval.

"They are an influential group. Whenever people listen to anyone else, they resent it." Jesus glanced briefly toward the ceiling. "Someday they will probably kill me, but in the meantime—" A twinkle returned to Jesus' eyes. "Aren't they amusing to watch?"

Everyone laughed. So did I. Laughter felt good.

The evening's session broke with the men leaving to go to their homes.

Once in my room, I worried what everyone would think when Cuza came for me in only a few days. I hoped it wouldn't disappoint Jesus—too much.

As I lay there, I thought of Marcus. Oh, how I trusted he would be okay, but I hoped he would miss me. I thought about Cuza. Wouldn't I love to see his face when he reads my note? Could this possibly be only the second evening since I left?

Then, the words Jesus spoke earlier struck my brain like a falling icicle. "My Father has sent this lovely woman to help." What did he mean? Wasn't this my idea to shock Cuza into reality? *Is something going on that I don't understand?*

CHAPTER FIVE

I stepped hesitantly from my little bedroom. "Where is everyone?"

"I'm in the kitchen," Mary called back from somewhere.

I found my way as Mary rose from behind a cabinet. "Oh, Mary, I can't believe I overslept, especially since I don't remember falling asleep." I looked around. "Where are all the men?"

"Quite a storm blew through while we were on our last trip around Galilee. Some of the people's homes need repair. My James is over helping Philip right now."

"Let me assist you with that." I took the jar and lifted it onto the counter. "I would have expected to see Jesus by now. Is he working with the men, as well?"

"Oh, we don't usually see Jesus until mid-morning or later. He spends a lot of time out praying." Mary lifted one of the jars into an upper cabinet. "Hand me the other jar there."

"Umm ... this is heavier than it looks." I picked up a second jar and slid it onto the counter.

Mary began scooping the dried fruit she had been chopping into the jar. "There have been times when Jesus spent a whole day in prayer. The men tell me he goes out before dawn."

With the dried fruit packed, Mary asked, "Help me set this in the pantry."

I handed the jar to her. "I'm afraid I don't know much about prayer."

"I don't claim to know a lot either, but I do know this," Mary's eyes narrowed. "When Jesus prays for something, what he prays for usually happens. Jesus says that's how he heals people."

Mary took off her apron and hung it on a hook. "Another thing. Jesus never worries the least about money. But when the bag is down to the last denarius, money always miraculously appears."

I thought bringing part of my inheritance to help Jesus had been my idea. What don't I understand here? I made a mental note to learn a lot more about this prayer thing.

Mid-afternoon, Andrew and Thomas came to Mary's home. Andrew claimed to be Simon's younger brother, though they were complete opposites. Andrew seemed quiet and thoughtful, while Simon appeared proud and boastful. Andrew's full head of wavy brown hair hung close to his shoulders. His beautiful hazel eyes made me feel at ease. He looked like an easy first candidate to get to know.

I pulled up a stool across from Andrew. "What did you do before following Jesus?"

Andrew looked at me a long minute, then spoke, "Ever since I could pick up a net, I've fished with Simon. Wasn't what I really wanted to do, it's just what we did."

Andrew seemed far more refined than I would expect of a fisherman. He continued, "Simon and I are from Bethsaida. Moved here about four years ago. We heard the fishing was better."

Andrew had a funny way of shrugging his left shoulder when he started to say something. "Actually, I was the first one to meet Jesus. I found Simon and introduced them."

James came in the door and went straight to Mary. "Mother, I'll need some time to get cleaned up for the big dinner this evening."

Andrew stood. "Suppose I need to go get cleaned up for this big event too."

Late in the afternoon, the men began coming in, all cleaned up and in their best garments. They were ready for the big dinner at Matthew's home. James and his brother John, Simon Peter and Andrew, Philip, Bartholomew, and Mary's son James all said they planned to go.

Younger James pulled up a stool. "Thad, aren't you going?"

"I ... I wouldn't be comfortable."

Thomas spoke up. "I think I'll stay behind with Thad."

Jesus' disciples were becoming more interesting. Could Thomas and Thad be just a little shy? Mary was right about not knowing how these—now ten men—could be so different from each other and yet each care so much about Jesus. They ranged from Simon Peter, who had a lot to say about everything, to Thad, who hardly said a word about anything.

Jesus encouraged Mary and me to come along even though we were not actually invited to this men-only affair.

Philip walked over. "There'll be ample provisions, and they're sure to be delicious. I hope you'll go."

As Philip spoke, Simon Peter walked in. "Sara is coming to accompany you ladies." Then he whispered, adding, "She wants to see where all her taxes were going."

Mary leaned over. "Sara is Simon's mother-in-law. She's a sweet woman, but she doesn't get out much. I'm glad she's coming."

That sealed the decision for me. "I think I'll go then. I'll look forward to meeting her."

A sudden desire swept over me to dig out the beautiful clothes Diana convinced me to avoid wearing. I could show them a few things about getting dressed up for a big dinner, but I quickly put that urge out of my mind.

What a disaster if anyone recognized me as the wife of the Roman official who lived in Capernaum a few months earlier. I changed to my other too large, itchy, tan robe and pretended to be all dressed up.

Matthew's home certainly didn't look like anything I had seen before in Capernaum. Impressive! Connected to the main house was an enormous walled courtyard, and the entire area overlooked the Sea of Galilee. The house extended to a large, raised, open porch where a lavish dinner appeared waiting. No wonder tax collectors were the object of so much resentment.

"I'm surprised at the crowd here in the courtyard," I said to Mary. "There're a lot more people here than just us women, and there's enough food prepared to feed half the town."

Mary nodded. "The dinners are planned this way so the host can show off his dinner guests and impress the neighborhood."

I kept my shawl tight around my head. I didn't want anyone to recognize me from my previous time in Capernaum. There were two familiar faces, however—the two religious men from Simon Peter's house were officiously wandering the courtyard.

"Uh-oh," I said to Mary. "What are those two doing here?"

"After a while, you tend to get used to them," Mary whispered back.

I was glad Sara came along. I could finally get to know her. Within a few short minutes, I felt we'd known each other a long time. Her gentle manner seemed much like Andrew, whereas her sturdy frame more resembled her older son. I didn't know how old she was, but what showed beneath her shawl was nearly all white hair.

She nodded toward the porch. "I wish Deborah were still alive to see her Simon all dressed up and attending a big dinner at a tax collector's home. She would laugh herself silly."

I dug into the large pieces of fruit covered with a tasty pudding. "Tell me about Deborah."

"She and Simon married back when we lived in Bethsaida." Sara took another piece of fruit. "Deborah was several years younger, only about sixteen, when they married. Her whole world revolved around Simon."

Sara stopped. I was curious for more but only said, "How nice."

"She had complications delivering her first child." Sara seemed to have read my mind. "We lost both her and the child."

Sara produced a slight, teary smile. "Simon never got over it. That's why we left Bethsaida and moved here. To escape the memory."

Sara looked at me. "I know you can't help but think Simon is loud and brash, and he is. That's his way of hiding the hurt he can't deal with."

I gave Sara my best understanding smile.

She turned back to the display of food. "He became so distraught after her death that I stayed on." Sara's voice dropped. "When he and Andrew decided to move here, he insisted I come too. I had no reason not to."

"I understand." I hoped those words sounded sincere because there wasn't any way I could really begin to understand a loss like that.

Slowly a spark returned to Sara's eyes. "I only hope Simon finds something to live for as he works with Jesus." She paused again for a long moment. "But I worry. He's so ill-suited for life around people. All he's ever known is fishing, just he and Andrew—and that precious boat of his."

As we stood there, a light breeze floated in from the Sea of Galilee and brushed my face. A partial moon kept trying to peek from behind some high clouds. The fresh air smelled a little different coming off the lake. The sea air smelled less like fish than the town did, a welcome reprieve.

Sara tugged my sleeve. "Look, the dinner is breaking up."

The disciples were on the steps where Jesus thanked Matthew. I could only imagine how hard the men worked to be polite to the other tax collectors who were present.

As soon as the group started down the steps, those two religious men jumped in Jesus' face. "Oh, look," the first one shouted. "You and your followers, eating and drinking with tax collectors and sinners."

The second walked around waving his hands. "We fast and pray. But look at you. You go right on eating and drinking."

The first one raised his voice for the benefit of the bystanders, "And you call yourself a religious leader?"

"Do you expect my men to fast and pray while I am with them?" I could hear sarcasm dripping in Jesus' voice. "They'll do that when I am gone. You fellows don't comprehend what it means to love our Father, God." Jesus pointed a finger at them. "You follow the letter of the Law, knowing nothing of its intent."

Jesus and the disciples left the two standing and made their way through the crowd toward us. I leaned over to Mary. "Well, that ought to shut them up for a while."

Mary slowly shook her head. "Don't count on it."

I enjoyed the pleasant walk back to our side of town. The previous clouds had thinned, and the moon glimmered across the ripples on the lake. The cool breeze coming off the water, mingling with the warmer air from the land, filled me with a sensation hard to describe.

Most of the new day's excitement of Jesus teaching and healing again occurred over at Simon Peter's house. I kept wondering what Sara thought when that man came through their ceiling.

In the evening, the men began coming into James's and Mary's home. They must have the largest living area. While others trickled in, I strolled over toward Philip. He appeared older than most of the others, probably in his mid-forties. Philip carried a slender frame but a healthy body. He possessed a square, rugged jaw. His wavy hair and trimmed beard added to his sophisticated appearance.

I found a comfortable place and sat down. "Philip, what brought you to follow Jesus?"

He looked at me rather strangely. "You want to know about … me?"

I gave Philip a friendly smile. "I want to know all of the disciples."

Philip laughed. "I took longer than most. It wasn't a sudden decision." He sat up a little straighter then shrugged his shoulders. "You see, I had a good life, a wonderful wife, and an excellent business." He stopped and pulled his sash tighter. "But still, something seemed missing. I kept thinking there had to be more to life than just keeping the shop I took over from my father."

Philip reached for a piece of the barley bread. He munched a moment then frowned.

I scrunched my shoulders and waited.

He continued, "You see, I'd actually met Jesus much earlier, back when we were going down to hear John the Baptist. Jesus invited me to become one of his followers then. But I didn't see how I possibly could."

Philip seemed a little ill at ease talking about himself. He shifted a few times before continuing. "Several months later, Jesus came to Bethsaida, preaching. The town's people were less than receptive."

Philip looked up, directly at me. "So, I invited Jesus to my shop to talk. He told me my life needed to be like salt on food, like a light shining for others. The more he talked, the more I realized what a useless life I lived, keeping our little shop." Then he stopped.

I urged him, "Do continue."

"This part isn't easy." He scratched the back of his head. "You see, I had a tremendous desire to leave everything and follow Jesus, but I couldn't." Philip gestured with both hands. "I had a wife and a shop to keep going. I needed to earn a living and take care of my family."

Philip stood, and I worried I would not hear the rest of his story. He poured a cup of water, took a long drink and then sat back down. "That night, Rebecca and I had a long talk. Finally, she was the one who encouraged me to follow Jesus, at least for half a year. She said, 'Your father and I can keep this shop going just fine.'"

"The next day I approached my father." Philip leaned back and laughed. "He thought I'd lost my mind. He said, 'I invested everything I had and everything I could borrow to get the business going. I put my whole life in this shop, and you're just going to toss it away.'"

"Rebecca convinced him to help her run the store for six months. He complained his legs wouldn't hold up. That happened a little over a year ago. Dad's a lot healthier, and the shop has never prospered quite as it does now."

"Enough about me." Philip turned his quizzical gaze full on me. "What about you? You don't appear to have grown up around here. Tell me about yourself."

I blushed. The heat hitting my face paled in comparison to the chill running up my back. "I, uh, I didn't … You're right, I didn't grow up in Capernaum." I hadn't anticipated the tables being turned on me. Just as I frantically searched for a sensible reply without revealing my Roman connection, Jesus stepped through the door.

"Suppose I'll have to wait." Philip stood and half turned to join the group. "But don't forget, you still owe me your story."

When Jesus began talking about forgiveness, I had a sneaking suspicion he was addressing attitudes expressed by James and some others about accepting Matthew.

Jesus said, "You must learn to forgive others like you would wish others to forgive you." He explained how human nature harbored a grudge. "But my disciples are to be different. They are to set an example by forgiving."

Simon Peter spoke up, "Master, how many times should I forgive my brother?" He puffed his chest. "Seven times?"

Jesus looked at Peter. "No, not seven times. You are to forgive seventy times seven. You must remove the old 'an eye for an eye' from your thinking."

Mary busied herself in the kitchen, going out of her way to appear as though she wasn't paying attention, like we weren't supposed to listen. I worked alongside her, but I didn't pretend not to listen. I also made a point of glancing toward the older James, watching him squirm.

Jesus concluded by reminding everyone, "Tomorrow is the Sabbath. Be ready to go to synagogue."

A tingle ran up my spine. *Tomorrow is the day Cuza will come crawling, asking forgiveness. I can hardly wait. How hard should I make him beg before I go?*

CHAPTER SIX

"Help me, Mary," I called. "What do we wear? What happens there? Do I have to say anything? I hate to admit this, but I've never been to a synagogue before." I didn't like sounding frustrated, but I was. "I don't have any idea what to expect."

"Slow down, Joanna. You don't have to worry about anything," Mary planted both feet firmly. "Just wear your best robe and look nice. No one will notice us anyway. The whole service is all about the men sitting in the congregation. The women stand at the back and mostly observe. Watch me and you'll do just fine."

Ready first, I had the big room all to myself. But I couldn't sit with so much filling my mind. The Sabbath meant Cuza would come home and find my note. He couldn't lie on his pillow without noticing the parchment. Would he realize immediately how stupid he'd been? *When he comes, should I ignore him? Do I make him beg?*

Mary came in. "No one's here yet? They had better—"

The door opened—James and John walked in. Within minutes, six more arrived. Then Jesus stepped through the door. Before I could get my outer shawl on, the rest crowded in.

The morning sun shone bright. Only a few light clouds floated across the gorgeous sky as we made our way to synagogue. The morning proved interesting, watching the local population as they walked the same direction. Most men walked with their heads held high, talking to other men. Their women walked three or four paces behind, often with heads lowered. Capernaum might only be a long day's walk from Sepphoris, but culturally, existed on the other side of the world.

As we entered the building, I whispered to Mary, "This synagogue is magnificent. Look at those columns at the front. How impressive!"

Mary nodded.

Mary and I found our place to stand near the back while Jesus and the ten disciples made their way toward the front. The leader of the synagogue knew Jesus and indicated their place to sit. From our vantage point, going to synagogue appeared to be a relatively new experience for several disciples as well.

Suddenly, the festive atmosphere changed. The two Pharisees who caused the earlier troubles entered with a man squeezed between them. They held him tightly and made their way down toward the front. As they turned the man to seat him between them, his left arm dangled awkwardly.

I found enjoying the service difficult, wondering what to recite while at the same time wondering what those two Pharisees were up to.

Near the end of the service, the leader of the synagogue invited Jesus to speak. Jesus stood, joining the rabbi at the front. He looked out over the congregation for a long moment. "Is it better on the Sabbath to do good, or not to do good?" Jesus asked.

Many nodded. Some spoke, "To do good."

Jesus turned his attention to the man the two Pharisees guarded, asking him to stand. Jesus spoke directly to the Pharisees. "What do you say? Is it better to do good or not to do anything good because it is the Sabbath?"

A wave of tense silence spread across the congregation, like waiting for the thunderclap following lightning. The Pharisees sat there and said nothing. Their faces grew red till their tanned skin no longer concealed their embarrassment.

Jesus asked the man to extend his right hand. Jesus looked over his hand. "I see nothing wrong with this hand. Is it the other?" The man held out his other arm.

His eyes widened as he gazed at his formerly withered arm. His mouth dropped. "I'm healed!" he shouted. "I'm healed. Look, my hand, my arm, it's healed. Praise God, I'm healed."

The congregation's initial murmur of approval erupted into joy. Except for the two guarding the man, everyone in the synagogue appeared elated.

Both Pharisees rose with defiant looks and stomped out of the synagogue, their robes fluttering behind them. Left standing near the front was one jubilant man. The only other man who didn't appear especially thrilled was the synagogue leader. *I wonder.*

As we left the coolness of the synagogue, I quickly realized how hot the day had become. The sky was exceptionally clear and bright. Younger James remarked, "Ole Hermon is out in all its glory today."

"What's Hermon?" I asked.

James pointed to the north. "There, Mt. Hermon in the distance. Doesn't she look grand today?"

I gazed more closely. What I assumed a distant cloud bank was instead a massive snow-covered mountain. "Oh, it's beautiful!"

"Mt. Hermon is the source of most of the water in our lake," Philip added from behind me. "It's what keeps this land so green,"

"I can't believe I never noticed so large a mountain before, especially with it right in my face."

James added, "Oh, that's not unusual. Mt. Hermon is usually covered in clouds. It's rare to see it clearly—like today."

Doing so little on the Sabbath made the day more like a week. I wished for a way to make time move faster. I had no idea how long Cuza would take to arrive, but I hoped soon.

The afternoon wore on. Every sound from the street caught my attention.

Mary's eyebrows furrowed. "Is something bothering you, Joanna? You keep looking out the window."

"Oh, no, Mary." I shook my head. "Nothing is happening outside."

My words were far truer than I wanted. Too much *nothing* was happening. *When will Cuza get here? He has to come soon.*

The sun began its dip toward the western hills. Anticipation expanded through my chest, threatening to suffocate me. I fought my strong urge to pace the floor.

Being the Sabbath, we ate a light dinner earlier than usual. At least that made time move a little. Still, no Cuza.

Then I realized how fast evening was approaching. *Wait! Give Cuza time to arrive. He's sure to be coming.*

After dinner, Jesus informed us we would soon be going to Jerusalem for the Feast of Tabernacles. I didn't pay close attention knowing Cuza would arrive any moment.

Darkness began to descend, first creeping down the western hills then sliding across the Sea of Galilee. Finally evening inched, block-by-block, across Capernaum. As each length of darkness settled atop the land, my heart sank still further. *Where was Cuza?*

Jesus excitedly talked about the Feast of Tabernacles, but dejection rang in my ears. I fought back tears.

As each small group of men departed, I accompanied them to the door to steal a glance down the street. My mind realized its pointlessness, but something within me wouldn't give up.

Certainly no one in Capernaum would have difficulty telling Cuza where to find Jesus. Since Jesus wasn't a big issue in Sepphoris, I rationalized how Cuza must not have found where to come until too late.

I barely reached my room before the tears started flowing. They just kept coming. *This isn't the way I planned it.*

CHAPTER SEVEN

"You're kidding me!" My eyes grew wide. "We're packing enough food for eleven men and two women for a week? How do we carry so much?"

"On our burro." Mary frowned. "He's strong. Besides the food, he has to carry the cooking pots and the lean-to. We do this all the time, Joanna. Hasn't killed him yet."

The next two mornings, we dragged younger James and Thomas with us to the market. The two afternoons, we packed the food supplies, getting them ready to load. Thomas and Andrew lugged in the canvas lean-to. Finally, by the third day we had everything ready Mary thought we needed.

With the tremendous hustle to prepare everything for our trip, I hardly had time to fret over Cuza's non-arrival. But with the day of our departure upon us, my anxiety level grew immensely. This trip really wasn't fair. Cuza hadn't had time to find me during his first days off. And now, when Cuza was off duty, we wouldn't even be in Capernaum. I had to do something.

Could I tell Jesus I intended to stay behind? If I did, I'd have to tell him why. I knew I couldn't lie well enough to convince Jesus. How would I explain my not being honest in coming to help? That would destroy everything.

Suppose I stayed behind and Cuza didn't come. Shivering, I couldn't follow that thought any further. If I go and Cuza came for me—would discovering we had gone to Jerusalem bring him back? I searched hard, but saw no viable alternative but to act excited about the coming trip.

Early morning mist hung over the lake as they brought the pack animal around to load. Rays of sunlight poked through the haze as younger James and Bartholomew tied on the big lean-to. Mary and I secured the cooking utensils. We spread out the food as evenly as we could, then followed with our sleeping rolls. As the pile grew impossibly high, they brought the smaller lean-to for the top cover. I couldn't believe all this went on one animal.

Never, in my wildest dreams, would I have ever imagined myself tying cooking utensils on the back of a donkey. My luck would be for Cuza to show up at that moment. He would laugh his head off.

With the thought of Cuza, alarm suddenly crept through my stomach. I stood beside the donkey seeing Cuza coming to Capernaum, asking for me.

"What's wrong, Joanna?" Mary's question yanked me back to the present.

"Oh … Uh, wondering where you and I ride," I lied.

John rose from packing the tent poles on the other side of our animal and looked at me with the straightest face. "You get to ride in the cart with Matthew."

I looked around. "Wonderful. Where is it?"

"There isn't one!" John roared with laughter. Blood rushed to my face. But a little voice somewhere deep inside told me to laugh.

I managed a half-decent chuckle. Instantly, the whole group broke into laughter—all except Matthew.

Matthew's face and the sides of his neck began to glow.

My weak smile probably wasn't convincing, but at least I tried.

"Sorry I laughed." Andrew came over and put his hand on my shoulder. "But that was too good. Obviously, there isn't any ride, but I'll help you on the difficult hills. Stay close and you'll make it just fine. It's only a three-day journey." Andrew brushed his long brown wavy hair over his left shoulder. "Just being in Jerusalem makes the trip worthwhile."

With Jesus in the lead, we set out. Behind him were ten men, two women, and one very heavily packed donkey, though not necessarily in that order.

I peered back down the street at my temporary home. Suddenly, the strongest urge hit me to break and run back. But as we turned the corner, my vision of Cuza coming evaporated like early morning mist from over the lake.

Bantering among the men broke the monotony of the long walk. I liked that. This also gave me an opportunity to observe the small alliances. Jesus walked beside James and his brother John, also Simon Peter. Even though I sensed closeness among those three disciples, a strong competition was also obvious. James, being John's older brother, acted so much like an 'older brother,' I found myself laughing. John couldn't express a thought without James correcting or adding something to it. Then James and Simon Peter argued over everything. They didn't seem to argue about big issues; they just never stopped quibbling.

I didn't need to be around James long to realize he considered himself Jesus' number one disciple. John came across as confident but loud. Even though John seemed more a natural leader, James, as older brother, made sure John knew his place—behind him.

No one could ignore Simon Peter. His mother-in-law's earlier explanation helped me to like him despite being hardly able to tolerate him. He obviously also considered himself Jesus' most important disciple. As he boisterously asserted himself in that role, Peter often came across just plain obnoxious.

Andrew and Thomas seemed to be good friends. As they were so thoughtful and considerate, how could anyone not like them both?

Bartholomew and Thaddeus, whom I dubbed my comedy twosome, brought up the rear leading and coaxing the pack animal. The tall and slender Thad alongside the short and chubby Bart always brought a smile to my face.

Younger James stayed close and looked out for his mother while we walked. He and Philip seemed to be friends, even though Philip appeared older. Perhaps James considered Philip more of a father figure. Mary's son, James, had to be the youngest disciple if we didn't count Jose, whom we had not seen since Matthew's arrival.

Matthew hadn't had time to make any strong ties. Since James stayed close to Mary, Philip shared a little time with him. I hoped Philip could help Matthew adjust to the group.

With the sun dipping behind the western hills and the salmon streaks giving way to darkening clouds, a cluster of trees beckoned us to set up camp. The fear I'd avoided successfully all day suddenly came rushing at me. If we were camping out for the night, would I wake up finding some wild animal eating me?

Jesus left us sitting around the campfire after dinner to go out and pray.

Fire brimmed in Matthew's eyes. "I didn't appreciate your lame joke at my expense this morning, John."

Matthew already wasn't easy to like, especially after his comment about not enjoying those scratchy wool garments that *ordinary people* wore. His angry outburst lit the group like throwing dry brush on a campfire. A major problem threatened.

But Philip calmly stood, put his hand on Matthew's shoulder. "Matthew, we all want to like you, but you need to help us some. Your background has us a little on the defensive."

Matthew sulked and said nothing.

Philip dropped his hand and waited a long moment. "I doubt there's one of us who hasn't had a bad experience with a tax collector."

Matthew still made no reply, but moisture pooling in his eyes began to reflect in the fading campfire.

Philip stirred the fire until the embers returned to flames. Several sparks floated aimlessly above the rekindled blaze. "You see, Matthew, if you aren't being teased by this group, then you aren't part of it. That's our way of getting to know you, to see what you are made of."

Matthew's head dropped a little further. "I suppose I was letting my old defensive thinking creep back."

That comment brought Matthew's stock up with me—a little.

Philip studied Matthew. "Tell us about yourself, Matthew. Let us get to know you. Where did you grow up? Who were your parents? What brought you to sell out to the Romans?"

Silence.

Philip continued, "We're not here to condemn you. We just need to know you."

Matthew drew his cloak closer and crossed his arms tight against the sudden attention. "Well … well, first, my real name isn't Matthew."

If Matthew doubted having the men's attention, he didn't need to worry any longer. "Actually, my name is Levi. I realized I couldn't work for the Romans with such a Jewish name, so I adopted the name Matthew."

Matthew squirmed and covered his discomfort by adjusting his robe again. "I was born near Tiberius, though we moved a lot. Well … to be honest, we moved around much more than a lot."

A long, awkward pause ensued. Matthew raked his teeth over his bottom lip. "During most of my childhood, we were on the run from the Romans. My father, Alphaeus, and Mother—"

An instantly wide-awake younger James leaped to his feet, practically landing in front of Matthew. "You are a son of Alphaeus, the Alphaeus who led the second rebellion?"

Matthew's eyes grew large and his mouth dropped. He looked like a scared animal, deciding whether to run or hide.

"I, too, am the son of Alphaeus!" Excitement enveloped James' face. "Mom was married to him until he died. Are you the half-brother father told us about?"

Matthew struggled to his feet. The two men stood gazing at each other.

James grasped Matthew's shoulders. "This is right—Dad told Mother he named his first son Levi. I remember them telling how your mother fled to the other side of the Jordan River to escape the Romans." James wiped big tears from his eyes. "Can you really be my brother?"

Matthew's mouth gaped open, but no words emerged.

James grabbed Matthew's arm. "We have some catching up to do, brother."

Their joyful tears brought real joy to my heart.

I looked around to see Jesus standing near the edge of the campsite. Most of the men probably thought Jesus missed this wonderful reunion. But Jesus' eyes told me he knew of this connection all along.

Mornings certainly came a lot earlier when camped out under a lean-to. I examined myself all over. Nothing had been eaten. I shivered to realize a dozen more nights remained for the wild animals to have their chance.

Following a quick breakfast, we re-loaded our poor donkey faster and certainly in a less organized fashion than the previous morning. As we began walking, I quickly realized my feet weren't recovered from the previous day. The disciples' pace made mine and Uncle Reuben's seem a leisurely stroll. I caught up with Andrew to find out more about this trip. "You men always walk this fast?"

"If we're to make Jerusalem in three days, we need to keep moving." Andrew pulled his shoulder pack to the other side.

"A three-day walk at this pace and I'll only have bloody stumps at the ends of my legs."

Andrew looked at me with his warm, wonderful smile. "Enjoy today, Joanna. Compared to tomorrow, this is the easy part."

"Oh, how's that?"

"We're walking downhill today, following the Jordan River. When we leave Jericho tomorrow, the trip will all be uphill to Jerusalem." Andrew brushed his brown wavy hair back and whispered, "Stay close tomorrow, little lady, and I'll give you a hand in the difficult places."

"Thanks, I'm sure I'll need your help."

Andrew pointed to our left. "See the orange grove near the river? This tells us we're far enough down the Jordan Valley to be where it's warm all year."

"To change the subject," I shifted my load to the other shoulder, "what is this grand festival that requires a three-day forced march to Jerusalem?"

"The Festival of Tabernacles—a really fun time, not like Passover."

I didn't know anything about Passover, so I couldn't imagine this being more fun. "Tell me about the festival."

Andrew shrugged his shoulder. "Remember I grew up in Galilee, fishing. We never had time to do these religious things. I'm kind of new at this too."

Near noon, we crossed a little stream. A sticky warmth had swallowed the morning coolness. A clump of trees to our right provided a large shady area. This must be their usual stopping place because, without a word, the whole group turned toward the trees.

I really felt good sitting down, even on a rock. "Oh, Mary, my feet are so numb I can't feel them anymore."

Mary's look was hardly compassionate.

Not getting any sympathy from her, I hobbled over to where Jesus sat. "Tell me about the Festival of Tabernacles." I felt rather proud at least knowing the name.

Jesus finished peeling a large orange. "That is what they call the feast today. The traditional name of the celebration is 'Succoth.' It's in memory of the dedication of King Solomon's Temple, centuries ago."

Jesus offered me a big orange slice. "There's a lot of symbolism in the activities. In the 'Morning Water Libations,' the priests carry pitchers of water from the Pool of Siloam to the temple and pour them on the altar. This signifies the purification of the temple. In a joyous procession, all the men circle the altar seven times."

A serious look stretched over Jesus' face. "Ordinary men have this one opportunity each year to approach the altar. That is significant."

"How's that?"

"Joanna, my ministry is to bring everyone into the presence of our Heavenly Father. This festival represents that truth." Jesus stood.

I struggled to my aching feet. "But, I thought you didn't get along with those religious people. Aren't they always trying to discredit you?"

Jesus picked up his staff. "You will see there are several kinds of religious people in Jerusalem. Some are sincere and genuine while others are not. Then, there are the outright hypocrites."

All the others were on their feet and Jesus started toward the road. "Our Heavenly Father set aside one of the original twelve tribes to serve as priests. They are the link between God and man. Their life of sacrifice and devotion allows them to lead the worship at the temple."

"Oh, so you like them?"

"My Uncle Zachariah, John the Baptist's father, served as a priest. There was never a godlier man."

As we went back on the road, Jesus picked up the pace. "So far, you've only met the Pharisees who try to be guardians of tradition. In trying to enforce morals, they keep only the letter of the Law, not its intent."

Jesus gave no indication he objected to me walking beside him asking questions, but some of the others certainly did. I received a load of condescending stares from Simon Peter and James.

I started to slink back to my place beside Mary when Jesus added, "I suppose you are wondering why we need to make this long walk for some festival."

I nodded.

"A prophet needs to be among his people. During the festivals, people are in Jerusalem from all over the country. The occasion is an opportunity to share God's love with those I might not otherwise see." Jesus marched on with eyes straight ahead. Never had I witnessed such confidence and knowledge in a person.

A cold chill crawled up my spine. Being so closely associated with the Roman-backed government, I shouldn't even be here. My world of Sepphoris and Jesus's world in Galilee were opposite and competing worlds. *I wonder when they'll collide?*

CHAPTER EIGHT

Following dinner, younger James sat down next to his newly found half-brother. "Matthew ... Levi, I'm not questioning you, so please don't take this wrong." He tilted his head a little to judge Matthew's reaction. "I've wondered about this all day. Tell me about growing up with Alphaeus. What happened to your mother?"

The unbelievable revelation during our previous night's campfire gave us all something to speculate about during the day's walk. There were no inattentive ears around that evening's campfire.

"I was a little over six years old when we suddenly had to flee from the Romans." Matthew pulled his cloak tighter around his shoulders. "There must have been a spy somewhere. After several sudden necessary moves, Father realized how dangerous having his wife and child close by was. He sent several of his men to take us to the region of Perea across the Jordan."

Matthew's voice broke. "Before long, word came the Romans were hard after us again." He swallowed. "Looking back, the Romans must have figured if they caught Alphaeus's wife and son and threatened to kill us, they would certainly have Alphaeus and probably contain a large part of the rebellion."

Matthew idly stirred the fire. Tears filled his eyes. "Mother must have realized how obvious a woman traveling with a boy child would be, especially with the bounty we heard the Romans placed on our heads. She left me with an aunt in Medeba."

Matthew wiped one eye with the back of his hand. "I remember the tears in my mother's eyes. She said she would return soon." Matthew shook his head. "She never came."

Matthew paused, took several deep breaths. "By the time I was twelve, I knew I had become a burden on Auntie. She seemed quite old, as I remember. Within two years, I headed out on my own." Matthew's sigh seemed to indicate he had finished dealing with the question.

Younger James sat up and waited. His eyes turned cold. "What I really need to know is what could have possibly caused a son of Alphaeus—one of the great leaders of the rebellion—to begin working for the Romans as a tax collector?" Uneasiness showed on everyone's face. The crackling campfire reflected the tension.

Matthew didn't reply for long awkward minutes. Even I could feel him bristle.

After what seemed an eternity, he spoke. "Yes, I suppose you deserve to know the rest of the story." Several held breaths released simultaneously.

"The insurrection ended with Herod's brutal crackdown. Thousands were put to death." Matthew's eyes hardened. "The insurrection may have ended politically, but I swore in my heart rebellion would never be over."

Andrew added wood to the fire. The flame grew brighter.

John entered the discussion. "I can appreciate your anger back then, but I still don't understand. How did this lead you to collecting taxes for the Romans?"

"I couldn't fight the Romans alone." Matthew scratched at his short beard. "I realized the only way I could ever repay the agony they caused would be from inside. Becoming a tax collector provided me that way in. I jumped at the chance, thinking of the harm I could cause them."

Matthew's voice dropped. "But as I searched for an opportunity to create havoc, I slowly became accustomed to the luxuries the money provided. I regret to say, my original goal became fainter as the lure of riches grew."

Matthew spoke to the ground at his feet. "I was determined to someday cause all the damage I could—but that time never came. Each year, I became more entrapped and ultimately, more dissatisfied with my life."

Matthew spoke directly to Jesus. "I don't know how Jesus knew of the agony at war in my mind. But when he invited me to become a disciple, I only took a moment to make the decision."

Matthew turned a faint smile toward us. "You can't imagine the heavy burden that was lifted when I made my choice. I have something to live for now." He turned back to younger James. "And that, my brother, is the rest of my story."

We all sat, stunned by Matthew's openness. Nothing was left to be said. I tried not to be obvious wiping the corners of my eyes. The campfire died down to glowing embers.

At the first hint of daylight, we broke camp near Jericho. James reminded us to take special care to reload our pack animal evenly and securely.

For the first mile, I wistfully thought Andrew might possibly have exaggerated the coming climb. But, as the hills we walked toward rose to block the sky, I quickly realized he hadn't.

I whispered to Mary, "I wish someone else would complain so I wouldn't feel so childish." Every step was above the last. Sore feet quickly became sore legs and aching back as everything in me hurt. Each bend in the road revealed yet a steeper hill ahead.

Thankfully Andrew dropped back to give me a hand. "See, this isn't so bad."

My parched mouth, my throbbing legs and the lack of breath in my lungs prevented me from saying what I really wanted to say.

And what a change in the landscape. The lush, green date and orange groves near Jericho gave way to barren, rocky hillsides. The wrinkled stone face of the mountains to the south returned a menacing glare.

Even though there was neither shade nor a place to sit, we thankfully stopped to rest. Philip strolled over. "Look, Joanna, that's the Salt Sea down there." He pointed toward a glimmering expanse in the far distance. "The Jordan River flows in, but it's at the end of the valley so nothing flows out. Over the centuries, it's become so salty that nothing can live in the water."

"Nor anything grow around it," I added. "I don't see any trees near the lake like around our Sea of Galilee."

"You can also see how far we've climbed up this old road." Philip wiped some sweat from his forehead. "The Salt Sea down there isn't far from where we camped last night."

Just as I began to appreciate the view, they were ready to walk again. Neither my lungs nor my legs felt the least bit rested, but I knew I must keep up.

"We don't have too much farther to go." Andrew had hardly

broken a sweat. "In another hour, we'll reach the top. There's a grove of trees where we usually stop for a real rest."

The arduous climb, along with the sun high in the cloudless sky, conspired to make that shady spot one of the most beautiful sights on earth. We sat on several scattered rocks and devoured our lunch. I turned to Philip. "Even the sky seems different up here. It's bigger, clearer, and bluer, if there is such a word. The air even feels different on my skin."

Early afternoon brought us close to a village a little larger than Capernaum. Jesus stopped under a huge date palm. "Let's go into Bethany and see our friends, Lazarus, Mary, and Martha. We can rest and refresh before we go on and set up camp."

The homes of Bethany were mostly of whitewashed stone. They were generally larger than those in Capernaum, but nothing to compare with homes in Sepphoris. Jesus explained to Matthew and me, "The home belongs to Martha. Her older brother, Lazarus, and her younger sister, Mary, live here with her."

After the short walk to Martha's dwelling, we gratefully sat on her patio and enjoyed a cool drink. Lazarus came to the door briefly to greet us. He was a small, elderly man, a little stooped, and rather frail. He quickly returned to the cool inside.

Thomas leaned over. "Lazarus hasn't been well since his wife died a few years ago. He told us that last year."

I only saw Mary through an opened door. She looked much younger and stayed close to Jesus. I wondered about the obvious expanse of years separating Mary and her much older brother. "Their mother must have been an exceptional lady."

Thomas appeared slightly confused. "Why do you say that?"

"Never mind." I shook my head. "If I have to explain, I know you wouldn't understand."

Jesus stood in the doorway explaining to Martha how we needed to go on and set up camp. I supposed Martha had invited Jesus to stay the afternoon and have dinner. I would have enjoyed meeting the two women, but would have especially relished the longer rest. But rest was not to be.

The hour's walk toward Jerusalem proved much more pleasant after the refreshing stop in Bethany.

I didn't see anyone they talked to, but there must have been some prior agreement with the owner of the olive grove. Everyone seemed familiar with the spot as we began to set up camp. Through the low hanging branches of the burly olive trees, I could faintly see other encampments.

The gnarled and ancient looking olive trees were larger and probably much older than ours back in Sepphoris. They also gave off a more pungent odor. From even a foot away, the spiny, low hanging branches had a unique way of snagging clothes.

Near our camp, a chest-high stone wall enclosed several small buildings and an olive press that dwarfed those in Capernaum. Younger James strolled over. "In a few weeks, they'll be busy making olive oil here. Don't know why they think of this as a garden, but they call this place the Garden of Gethsemane."

As I carried the last of the cooking pots from our pack animal to where Mary wanted them, Philip called. I hurried over and he pointed. "Look."

"Oh, that's spectacular!" I gazed across a valley to see a huge wall and a gorgeous temple on the next hill.

"Look directly across the Kidron Valley," Philip said. "The ornate stone opening in the middle of the huge wall is the Eastern Gate.

Now look directly beyond the Eastern Gate. You'll see two distinct courtyards, then the temple itself."

"Philip, it's magnificent. I can't wait to climb those steps and see the temple up close."

Philip blushed. "Joanna … there are some very strict rules about the temple. The first big courtyard is the Court of Women. You're welcome to go there." Philip shrugged his shoulders. "Only Jewish men can go into the next courtyard, the one directly in front of the temple. An entrance sign even says, 'under penalty of death'."

Philip turned back toward camp. "Someday, I hope this will change. But today, those are the rules."

We returned to see Bart and Thad setting up the big lean-to. Peter, John, and James were over in a little group planning something important. Funny how planning always seemed to be their job when work presented itself. Andrew, Thomas, and younger James finished unloading the donkey. Apparently, they were in too big of a hurry trying to put things away. Mary planted herself in the middle, barking corrections. She seemed to be fighting a losing battle.

That night, I lay in my sleeping blankets in Jerusalem, too excited and too tired to sleep. My mind drifted in several directions. Just being with Jesus and the disciples in Jerusalem felt unbelievable. But at the same time, my heart ached to have my life before Mariam back. As great as the time was with Jesus, my greatest desire was still to be able to hold my little boy and know the gentle husband I had before our son's illness.

I counted the days. Tomorrow Cuza would be off again. *Cuza could never find me here in Jerusalem … even if he wanted to.*

I breathed in the cool, dry, early morning air. As I filled Philip's bowl with breakfast, I asked, "Are mornings always this clear and bright in Jerusalem?"

"They are now. But before long the days will be extremely hot and dry." Philip took his bowl. "You don't want to be in Jerusalem in late summer."

As the men gathered their things, Jesus asked, "Would you ladies like to accompany us to the temple today?"

"Let us rest our feet and get this camp into some real order today," Mary replied as she waved her hand over what I considered a fairly well-organized campsite. "No matter how many times we do this, the men can't remember to do any more than set up the lean-to and unpack." She put her hands on her hips. "I'll have this place organized when you get back this evening."

I didn't know how much more order the campsite needed. But I agreed that spot was way too inviting to leave ... for a walk anywhere. I made my way back to the overlook. The morning sun warmed my face. I rested my sore feet and legs and enjoyed the incredible view of Jerusalem. The distant sounds from the city mixed with the gentle rustle of the olive leaves—a beautiful yet unbelievable picture.

My eyes followed the huge, buff-colored stone wall surrounding the temple, first to the right. The wall stretched a distance up the hill, then turned back toward what appeared to be a military garrison. To the left, the wall dropped down the hillside toward another valley. I could see some of the actual city of Jerusalem on the hill beyond the temple. But the temple glimmering in the morning sun remained the truly spectacular sight.

After a short time, Mary and I set to work. There turned out to be a lot more to do to organize a camp for several days than for the simple overnight stop.

As the sun moved toward the western sky, I finally asked, "Aren't we about through?"

"Go on, Joanna," Mary replied. "There are a few more things I need to accomplish."

I strolled back to our vantage point to witness the sun directly over the temple. The temple's stone shimmered, seemingly on fire. The sight made the skin of my arms tingle. I sat there, trying somehow to take all the sights in.

Mary walked up beside me. She shielded her eyes as she surveyed the valley below. "Isn't that Jesus and the men coming off the road onto the path? Looks like them. But they're early."

A stone road crossed the Kidron Valley diagonally and came up the hillside somewhere out of sight to my right. But Jesus and the disciples used a steeper path and made their way directly up the hillside toward our encampment.

The men came into camp talking feverishly. Older James playfully slapped Simon Peter on the shoulder. "What a sight! Jesus really gave it to them today!" He gave a long whistle.

John boomed above the other voices, "Did he ever."

As everyone gathered around our rekindled campfire, I gave James a big smile. "Sounds interesting today. What happened?"

He shrugged his shoulders. "Oh, not much." He then turned and began talking to John.

Quiet fury erupted within me, being dismissed like that.

After dinner, I made a point to sit next to James. He squirmed, scooted a little to the right, turned, and talked to Thomas. I waited patiently for a lull in their conversation.

"James, tell me about today," I asked in as nice a voice as my underlying anger allowed. "Your day sounded interesting. Were the Pharisees up to their old tricks?"

"Oh, just their usual outrage over Jesus healing a man. You know how upset they get over that." James's reply came flat and matter of factly. He must have worked extra hard to not show any emotion.

Knowing there was more, I pushed. "You said Jesus really gave it to them today. What did he do?"

I waited a long, demeaning moment. "I would really like to know, James." I smiled my best smile.

"The Pharisees complained that Jesus didn't have any right to be healing people." James' tone lacked its earlier enthusiasm, but at least he answered my question. "Only religious men like them should be doing God's Work." He shrugged his shoulders. "You know how they are."

I gave James another nice smile.

He relaxed his shoulders a little. "Jesus told them he was doing his Father's work. That's what got them upset. When Jesus added, 'the Son can only do what he sees his Father doing, because whatever the Father does, the Son also does.' they nearly exploded."

My eyebrows went up. "That's amazing!"

Thomas joined in. "If you think you've witnessed angry Pharisees before, well, you should have seen them today." He pulled his sash tighter. "They were ready to stone Jesus on the spot."

"If we had not hustled him out of there, I think they would have," John quickly added, "That's why we're home early."

Intrigued, I slipped over to where Jesus stood. "Since I'm not very smart, I hope you'll explain. What did you mean, 'you can only do what you see your Father doing?'"

Jesus looked at me for a long moment. "Joanna, this is what my work is about." Jesus' voice was low and direct. "I spend hours praying, asking my Heavenly Father to reveal what He wants me to do. I only do what I know our Heavenly Father wants."

Our conversation soon had everyone's attention. "When I do what my Father wants, His blessings are the miracles you appreciate."

Jesus' deep dark eyes reflected the flame of the campfire. "Miracles are simply God blessing *His* work."

Jesus turned directly to his disciples. "Remember, this is how you will carry on my work when I'm no longer with you."

As the last of the flaming embers died to a yellow glow, I climbed into my sleeping roll. Every time I closed my eyes, the excitement of being with Jesus in Jerusalem popped them wide again. I lay there thinking about Jesus being able to talk to God, then doing what God told him. That was amazing.

My mind didn't stop, but continued to Thomas' words, "They were ready to stone Jesus on the spot." My throat tightened as I remembered Jesus speaking on my first night with them. "Someday, they will probably kill me."

I sat straight up. *He wasn't joking—that could really happen. My whole body shook. This isn't Galilee anymore. Jerusalem could prove quite dangerous.*

CHAPTER NINE

I listened closely as the men returned from their second day at the festival. Many exciting events had occurred and thankfully, there wasn't talk of another confrontation. The confusion finally settled, and Jesus stepped over. "We have a special guest coming after dinner."

I glanced at Mary. "Who could be coming?"

She shrugged her shoulders.

As I finished gathering the bowls from dinner, a movement from the side of our camp nearer the road, caught my eye.

A man stepped past our smaller lean-to into view, and my jaw plunged. He wore the blue and white robe of the Pharisees. The tassels around the bottom lightly brushed the ground. *This can't be who Jesus is expecting!*

But he was, and strangely, he and Jesus appeared to be great friends. The cordial attitude displayed by the men indicated they also knew him. I stood completely amazed. How could Jesus be relaxed and smiling in the presence of a Pharisee? *Yesterday they were trying to kill him.*

I walked toward the campfire as Jesus made the introduction. "Matthew, this is Nicodemus. He is one Pharisee who understands God's ways."

With his hand on Matthew's shoulder, Jesus said, "You haven't met Matthew yet. Until recently, he collected taxes for the Romans."

A big smile spread across Matthew's face as he greeted Nicodemus.

As I sat down, Jesus unleashed another surprise. "And this is Joanna. You haven't met her either. She is helping Mary keep these men fed. She's become a tremendous asset to our ministry."

I hope my smile to Nicodemus adequately reflected appreciation for Jesus's thoughtful words.

Jesus swept his hand toward the remaining disciples. "I believe all the others were with me when you came last year."

Matthew spoke to Nicodemus. "It's truly amazing to see you laugh and talk with Jesus. Quite a contrast to what we've experienced from your group." He paused a long moment. "Strange, isn't it? You would be right to say the same thing about me." They both laughed and sat down.

"The story of how you came to be with Jesus is probably as unlikely as mine," Matthew added. "Since I wasn't here last year, I would love to hear your tale."

"Unlikely is an appropriate word, Matthew," Nicodemus replied. "However, I venture a big empty place in our lives is what brought both of us to Jesus."

Me too, I wanted to shout.

Nicodemus was tall, slender, and a bit older than the disciples. His smile revealed white teeth. The age creases in his forehead gave a look of wisdom. He had aged well.

Nicodemus continued speaking to Matthew. "Unlikely, because of my heritage. My father rose to become a leader of the Pharisaic movement. Growing up, I memorized the Law and lived strictly by the Law, making sure I never broke even one command."

Nicodemus impressed me greatly. His tone of voice made clear he wasn't bragging on his past. "I believed my never doing wrong made me holy in the sight of God."

Nicodemus' voice dropped. "But still, a big emptiness described my life. Last Passover, Jesus made quite a stir among the people with his teachings. When he called us hypocrites, his words stung. But deep down inside, I knew he spoke the truth."

Nicodemus stopped while Andrew placed more wood on the fire. John twisted impatiently, "You haven't told the best part yet."

Nicodemus shook his head. "I don't want to take up the whole evening telling my story."

Like a chorus, everyone urged him to continue.

"Well, okay. The next evening, I sent my trusted servant to follow Jesus and find his campsite. He then brought me to this very spot. I stood in the shadows for the longest time before summoning the courage to step into the presence of these men. While they appeared surprised, Jesus seemed to be expecting me."

Nicodemus took a deep, emotion-filled breath. That encounter had obviously become a defining moment in his life.

He continued with a beautiful, self-deprecating smile. "I began by giving Jesus a line of compliments about how he must be a teacher from God and so on. But, he saw right through me. Jesus said something in return that sounded like nonsense. He told me I needed to be born again, like a complete new birth."

"I thought, what under the night's stars is he talking about—a new birth?"

I looked at Matthew, and from the look on his face, I don't think he understood that any better than I did.

Nicodemus continued. "Jesus explained that I assumed God should extoll me because I grew up in a devout Jewish family and lived a holy life. Then Jesus gave me the most amazing truth. He helped me see how everyone must become like a small child to seek God with all their heart."

Nicodemus' words stirred something deep in my heart. I had never really thought about seeking God and having a relationship with Him. I didn't even know that could be possible. But evidently, this man had found a special connection with God.

I listened intently as Nicodemus talked. "All this time, I imagined God had an obligation to love me because of my sinless life. I was shocked to realize my pride was a sin and stood in the way of my coming to God. I needed to ask God for forgiveness instead of asking Him to bless my good life." Nicodemus paused.

I think I stopped breathing until he continued. "When I did this, I felt as if I'd been born all over again. God's love swept over me like a warm spring breeze. I learned more about our Heavenly Father's love in that one hour with Jesus than I did in all my years in rabbinical school." A big smile spread across Nicodemus' weathered face.

He sat up straight. "I've taken way too long. I'm anxious to hear your story, Matthew."

Matthew started twice, but both times stopped short. He finally collected his thoughts. "I came to Jesus from a totally opposite direction. You see, I felt I had gone so far away from God, selling out to the Romans, that God could never forgive and love me again."

I felt both sympathy and a little pride for Matthew as he continued his story. Nicodemus' eyes glistened as Matthew finished. My face awkwardly contained both a tear and a smile.

Nicodemus turned to me with a deep courteous voice. "So, tell us your story, Joanna."

I froze! Chilled blood filled my veins. Cuza had warned that my presence in Jesus's company could destroy his standing at the palace. There I sat, face-to-face with one of the top religious leaders of Jerusalem. I couldn't possibly reveal my identity. I tried to speak, but a shiver tingled down my spine.

Halting words finally emerged from my clenched throat, "Oh, it's too long a story to begin this late."

I excused myself and retreated to the back corner of our lean-to. My hands would not stop shaking.

Nicodemus departed shortly thereafter. Within moments, Jesus came to stand beside me. He saw I couldn't control my quivering hands. Not telling Jesus the whole truth had come to haunt me.

I finally contained my emotions enough to talk. "I know I should have told you long before this, but I didn't. I left Cuza because he forbade me from ever seeing you again. He felt threatened by what my being associated with you would do to his career." I wiped the tears as they pushed through. Jesus didn't speak, but his understanding eyes spoke volumes.

I knew I had to tell him the rest. "What I've told you is bad, but there's so much more."

I took a deep breath. "Do you know who my husband is, besides being the Roman official who came to Cana asking you to heal our son?" The questioning look on his face compelled me to continue. The cool, clear evening air added some needed strength. "Cuza oversees all the palace affairs of Herod Antipas in Sepphoris."

Jesus raised one eyebrow but said nothing.

Starting my story had been hard, but with the barrier broken, words flooded out. "Cuza is personally acquainted with the affairs of state. He's told me clearly, King Herod has a personal vendetta against John the Baptist. He plans to have him arrested, and he knows your ministry is associated with John's."

I couldn't control my shaking hands, but I owed Jesus the truth and had to continue. "Cuza spoke often about Herod saying your closeness to John places you high on their enemy watch list."

My quickly beating heart swelled into my throat. "Should information get to Herod that the wife of the manager of *his* household is with Jesus in Jerusalem, I find hard to imagine the trouble the news would cause." I could barely hear my own voice as I forced out the last words. Sobbing, I turned away. I didn't want to face Jesus.

Patiently, Jesus waited.

Finally, I composed myself. "That's why I became so distressed when a religious leader from Jerusalem asked what he thought was an innocent question."

Jesus gave me a sympathetic smile. "I understand."

I appreciated Jesus' words, but dejection still swept my heart.

Andrew and Philip had come over. I begged them, "Please don't relay any of this to the others."

They both nodded.

One thing seemed more than certain. Jesus would send me packing the moment we returned to Capernaum. Knowing I really deserved to be dismissed made the imminent parting hurt even more. I made a point to avoid everyone as we spread our sleeping rolls for the night.

I looked up at the thousands of brilliant dots illuminating the night sky. *Tomorrow will begin Cuza's next two days off. Will he come looking for me in Capernaum? How can I know? He certainly would never find me here in Jerusalem. What if Jesus dismisses me, and I return to find Mariam still fully in charge?* I shivered at the thought of that cold reception. Again, I gazed at the crossroads of my imperfect past and my improbable future.

During breakfast, most of the men avoided me as if I had a smelly dead fish tied around my neck. My hands still shook from the previous night's trauma. I didn't experience relief until the disciples departed for the last day of festival. Even then, the cloud created by my heavy heart blocked the new day's sun.

I started preparing my mind for the three-day walk back to Capernaum. First, I had to get my emotions back under control. Then, I could tackle getting everything ready for our return trip. Finally, mid-afternoon, I stole a few minutes to rest on my favorite rock. I would still have time before Jesus and the ten hungry disciples poured back into camp.

Several groups of men were already leaving the temple. Glancing at the road below, I noticed people following someone who looked like Jesus. I counted. The man couldn't be him because there were too many men. But when that group left the road and started on the path straight up the hill, I stole a closer look.

"Mary," I called. "Jesus is coming. And there're more men with him than left this morning."

The two unfamiliar faces with the disciples couldn't be strangers from the way they all talked among themselves.

These two appeared completely opposite from each other. The taller, more refined man wore clothing reflecting the business class, nicer than the disciples wore. The shorter, battle-hardened looking man carried a noticeable scar above his right cheek. He seemed to be someone you wouldn't want to challenge.

Jesus stepped to where Mary and I were preparing dinner. "Joanna, Mary, I want you to meet Simon and Judah." Jesus placed his hand on the shoulder of the taller, nicer looking man. "Since

Judah is such a common name, he goes by the Greek, Judas. He has finally made a way to come and work with us full time."

Judas smiled the kind of smile designed to win over any doubtful mind. "It's a pleasure to meet you two ladies." He bowed ever so slightly toward us. If I had to choose between the two, Judas would certainly get my nod.

Jesus turned to the smaller, wiry man. "Simon wanted to come with us last Passover, but he had several obligations to fulfill. He is ready now."

John spoke up. "We've known them since John's baptizing in the Jordan River. They're both good men."

"Can you handle two more mouths to feed?" Jesus asked, then gave a smile that removed any doubt.

"Don't the men call Thaddaeus 'Judas' also?" I forced a smile and hoped Jesus wouldn't sense my lack of enthusiasm.

Jesus laughed. "To make sure, we'll call him Judas Ish Karioth."

Philip turned to Judas. "Oh, Man of Karioth. I'm not sure where Karioth is."

"It's a small village near Hebron." Judas tilted his head slightly upward, "Surely you know where Hebron is?"

I winced.

"I would expect every self-respecting Jew to know where Hebron is, wouldn't you?" Philip wasn't curt, but his previous cordiality certainly dropped a few notches.

Judas intrigued me. Not only did he dress more nicely than the other disciples, he obviously took pride in his grooming. He trimmed his beard much closer than most Jewish men and his hair had style.

Jesus placed his hand on Simon's rugged shoulder. His weather-beaten face spoke of many hard days out of doors. He appeared in his mid-thirties and his brown beard seemed a bit ragged. "You'll never mistake Simon for Simon Peter. Simon is as quiet as Peter is loud." Jesus paused. Simon acknowledged the two of us, but didn't speak.

"Simon was once part of the Zealots." Jesus made the statement as casually as if saying, Simon had been a farmer.

I hope my shock didn't reflect in my face. My legs trembled. Even I knew the reputation of the feared Zealots. They were a shadowy group who carried out "strike and disappear" attacks on the Romans. They considered anyone supporting the Romans their enemy. A chill ran through me. *What happens when Simon finds out whom I am married to?*

Then an even greater chill raced up my spine. What happens when Cuza discovers Jesus's movement has a Zealot follower? I rubbed gooseflesh on my arms. Jesus's most recent choice has the potential to cause more problems than I cared to imagine.

The disciples now numbered twelve. Judas, for the most part, seemed a good pick. But I certainly questioned Jesus's choice of Simon. I hoped the more charming Judas could balance out the secretive Simon.

As Mary and I started dinner, I confided my concerns to her.

"I've never known Jesus to make a bad decision." Mary didn't even look up from working as she spoke.

"I thought the same about Matthew." I shrugged my shoulders. "But he's fitting in well now. Hopefully, my fears are false. But, it's going to be hard getting past the potential trouble Simon's presence might cause."

The words hardly cleared my mouth when I noticed the older James tugging Matthew over to the edge. "Matthew, what do you think about having a Zealot along?" James had a sly look in his eyes.

Matthew's shoulders sagged. "I'm not sure."

"You know about their reputation for assassinating tax collectors?" The tone in James's voice made his statement anything but a question. Matthew slumped a little further, looking like his soul had been sucked from his body.

I felt a cactus roll up my back.

Jesus concluded the evening. "We will need to get up extra early in the morning to start back home."

I need that long walk home to sort out everything ... and contemplate my imminent departure.

Strangely, the controversy concerning my reaction to Nicodemus' visit never came up again. Arriving home in Capernaum, I fully expected to be dismissed from the group. But seemingly, in their minds, the event never happened.

My first chore was to find out if Cuza came while we were away. Asking Peter's mother-in-law seemed far too risky. So, while the men caught up on neglected work, I made a discrete visit to the older widow lady living two doors away. Not revealing any more than necessary, I asked, "While we were away, were there any unusual visitors looking for Jesus here or over at Simon's home?"

She eyed me rather strangely. "You know there're always a lot of people looking for Jesus."

"But, did you see anyone ... unusual?" I insisted.

"Well, after a couple of days, the word got around that Jesus had gone to Jerusalem, so most quit coming."

I couldn't think how to rephrase my question without being obvious. Smiling, I thanked her.

I didn't know what to think. A part of me was pleased Cuza hadn't come while we were gone, but a larger part of me began to worry how long before he did? I loved being with Jesus. This had become the greatest experience I could ever imagine. But I need to return home the way I'd planned, and hold my little Marcus as a mother should. *My strategy has to work. Cuza, get over your obstinacy and come get me.*

CHAPTER TEN

I had no idea where Peter kept his boat when not in use, but wherever, the craft still smelled like fish. Jesus wanted to take all the men to a secluded place where they could have some meaningful time together. Apparently, sailing was the best way to accomplish this, even if going by sea would never receive my vote.

Quite an effort went into loading all our camping equipment, food for a couple of days, cooking utensils, thirteen men and two women in a boat the size of Peter's. I whispered to Mary, "If Jesus adds any more disciples, someone going to have to hang on the side."

A gentle breeze caught the single sail when we were a few arm lengths from the shore, and off we went. I had never been out on the lake. As a matter of fact, I had never been in a boat on a large body of water. I didn't realize waves and wind would rock and sway the boat from side to side.

Andrew noticed first. "Joanna, don't look down at the water or you'll get seasick." He shouted from his place tending the sails.

His call came almost too late. My breakfast already had begun doing strange and unusual things.

"Look across the water at the shoreline," Philip added.

Mary splashed cold lake water on my pale face. I held my breakfast in—barely.

I breathed deeply and fixed my sight on the shore until my queasiness gradually faded. Despite my embarrassing near disaster, the light summer breeze of fresh cool air off the water began to give me an appreciation of the lake.

As Capernaum faded to a distant speck on the shore, Philip pointed over the rail. "We're sailing east, toward Bethsaida. That's where I'm from—see it there in the distance?"

I couldn't see much more than a spot on the shore, but I answered. "Philip, your town must be beautiful."

"Look to the right of Bethsaida," he pointed. "See those steep hills? Those are the Golan Heights."

They were unusually dark and high. "Those look menacing. I hope we aren't going there."

"No, I'm sure we aren't," Philip replied. "The province of Syria lies just beyond."

As we sailed, Jesus directed Simon Peter's attention toward a barren stretch of shoreline. I looked at the desolate spot and nudged Philip again. "We walked for three days to get to Jerusalem, because Jesus needs to be where all the people are. Now we camp out on the edge of nowhere to get away from all the people? Help me."

Philip only smiled.

They selected a campsite away from the shore but still close enough to keep an eye on the boat. The soothing breeze against my face brought a surprise—a pleasant absence from the fishy smell.

Andrew and Thomas, along with Simon, set out searching for firewood. As the sun sank behind the distant hills, our campfire roared to life. That always felt good. During the evenings on our walk to Jerusalem, I so enjoyed the additional closeness of the group. Everyone seemed a little more relaxed out under the stars. Even James and Peter didn't argue quite as much.

Following dinner, everyone gathered about the campfire. I'm sure I wasn't the only one who felt a keen sense of anticipation as Jesus began to talk. But after only a brief discussion, Jesus dismissed the group.

I whispered to Mary. "I'm a little disappointed. After all the effort to get out here and set up camp in the middle of nowhere, I expected something more. I'm not sure what. But certainly, a little more than what we just experienced."

"His talk was rather short." Mary dug her sleeping roll out of the pile and handed me mine.

Jesus threw his heavier outer robe over his shoulder and whispered to us close by, "I'm going out for a while to pray."

John scrambled to his feet. "I'll grab my wrap and go with you."

"Thank you, John, but I especially need this time alone."

John's countenance displayed a hint of hurt. Jesus slipped out of camp.

I awoke to hear John and James urgently organizing the men for something. I stumbled over. "What's happening?" I asked of anyone who might respond in their near frantic effort to go somewhere.

Philip finally turned toward me just enough to spit out, "Jesus didn't come back to camp last night. We're going—"

"Shush! Be quiet," the Zealot firmly ordered. "I think I hear him."

Simon didn't normally say much and talked hardly above a whisper when he did. His forceful command caught everyone's attention. Silence dropped over the campsite like a stone falling in quicksand.

"Hello," came a faint call.

The sound of Jesus' voice sent a thrill surging to my heart.

Simon pointed toward a rocky outcrop high on the barren hillside. "Up there."

John slowly shook his head. "How in the name of heaven did he climb up there last night in the dark?"

As we strode in that direction, Jesus began descending from his rocky ledge. He'd lowered himself down onto the last huge boulder by the time we gathered in front. "I trust I didn't frighten anyone."

"Well, thank you very much. You scared us half to death," I replied, but certainly not loud enough for anyone to hear.

"I needed to make certain of my Father's will." Jesus found a place to sit on the boulder and motioned for us to gather in close. "You men have followed me, and I trust you have learned God's way of doing His work. But time is growing short, so we must be even more diligent about my Father's business."

Jesus looked across the faces of his twelve men. "John, James, Simon Peter, Andrew, Philip, Thomas, younger James, Bartholomew, Thaddeus, Matthew, Simon, and Judas—I commission you twelve to be apostles. As disciples, you were to learn. As apostles, you will now *proclaim*. You will declare to all people the coming of the Anointed One of the Lord."

Jesus had everyone's rapt attention. "I am sending you out like sheep among wolves. Be on your guard against men. They will hand you over to the local councils and flog you in their synagogues. On my account, you will be brought before governors and kings. You will be my witnesses to them and to the Gentiles."

I could see the challenge reflected in the eyes of the men. My only question—would they be up to the task Jesus laid out before them?

Jesus continued, "When they arrest you, do not worry about what to say. At that time, you will be given what to say, for you will not be speaking but the Spirit of your Father will be speaking through you."

No one moved. I hardly breathed. It would be hard to find twelve men more in awe.

Making our way back to camp, Mary nudged me. "Looks like Jesus did have a good reason to bring us out here."

"Don't you get tired of always being right?"

As we re-entered our campsite, Simon spoke, again in his whispered voice. "Many people are coming."

Everyone strained looking. Most shook their heads in disbelief. Suddenly, Thad shouted, "Look! A dozen or more people are coming this way."

"Only because you're a foot taller than the rest of us," Bart replied.

Simon picked up firewood, carefully placing the wood on the dying campfire. "There're many coming behind them."

Philip shook his head. "They're coming from the direction of Bethsaida. That's strange, considering the feeble reception they gave Jesus while I lived there."

Mary and I quickly set to work. "We need to hurry and eat breakfast before all those people get here," Mary urged.

All too soon, people meandered into our camp area. James took charge, directing them down to the edge of the lake. "Jesus will speak when everyone gets here," he told those gathering.

Jesus motioned Peter and Andrew over. "Position the boat in such a way that if we need to leave quickly, we can." Conspicuously absent was the usual broad smile on Jesus' face.

The smile suddenly dropped from Andrew's face as well. He glanced toward Simon Peter then back to Jesus. "Expecting trouble?"

"These people are from Bethsaida," Jesus shook his head. "Need I say more?"

Jesus' tone concerned me, and I turned to Mary. "What about all of our camp equipment? What about that?"

A grimace crossed Mary's face. "We'll worry about those things if and when we need to."

Peter said to Andrew, "Find Thomas and younger James to come give a hand." then hurried toward the boat.

The crowd grew to several hundred, while many others were still on their way. As the sun reached its highest point in the near cloudless sky, the last stragglers dragged in. Jesus moved toward the water's edge, in front of where the disciples attempted to gather the huge crowd.

Mary tilted her head toward the crowd. "I didn't think there were this many people in all of Bethsaida."

Jesus began by complimenting the crowd for coming to seek a better relationship with their Heavenly Father. "Don't do your acts of righteousness to be seen of men," he said. "You should do these in secret. If you do these to be seen, you already have your reward. Done in secret, God will reward you far more."

Jesus stopped and firmly planted his staff directly in front of him, holding the wood with both hands. "When you pray, do not be like the Pharisees. They like to stand in public places and pray so people will consider how religious they are. Instead, go into your room and close the door. Then God can hear your heart. Your Father in Heaven knows what you need even before you ask."

"Here is how you should pray: Our Father in Heaven, holy is your name. Your kingdom come and Your will be done on earth as it is in heaven. Give us the bread we need for today. Forgive us our debts in the same manner we have forgiven our debtors. And do not let us be led into temptation, but deliver us from the evil one."

Jesus paused for a long moment. He leaned on his staff and looked over the crowd. "If you forgive men when they have wronged you, then your Heavenly Father will forgive you when you sin against Him."

Jesus paused again. The moving and shuffling in the huge crowd completely stopped. "Enter through the narrow gate. For wide is the gate and broad is the road that leads to destruction, and many enter through it. But small is the gate and narrow the road that leads to life—and only a few find it."

As Jesus concluded, one by one people began coming forward. With each shout of joy from healing, more people clamored to reach Jesus. The single line became two lines, then five. The disciples struggled mightily to keep a semblance of order. Even Judas dealt with a few people trying to push ahead in line. Somehow, the disciples managed to maintain order.

As the last few stood waiting for healing, Jesus suddenly staggered to one of the big rocks nearby. He sat, propping his head in his hands with his elbows on his quivering knees. Peter and John were at his side in an instant. Several others rushed over. Philip, more wisely, brought him a barley cake along with some dates while Thad hustled water to him.

Philip walked over to Mary and me. "No wonder he's exhausted. Jesus did this all day with no sleep last night."

Jesus finally gathered a little strength. "This crowd is larger than at home. There's little reason to stay here."

A quick conference among the four followed. Peter announced to the rest of us, "Since it's this late in the afternoon, we'll sail home first thing in the morning."

Mary stood and stretched. "I'm going to organize things a little better before we start dinner. You don't need to come for a while."

As Mary walked away, Thomas strolled over and slid into her previous place. "I might as well keep this rock warm ... see if it hatches."

Philip and I both chuckled. Philip looked past me. "Thomas, do you miss Jerusalem and all the excitement of living there?"

"It wasn't exciting living there. It was just plain hard work."

I turned to Thomas. "You're from Jerusalem?"

"My family has a small farm near the edge of town. We had a hard life coaxing anything to grow in the rocky soil. I don't miss *that* part at all."

I picked up on the inflection. "What part *do* you miss?"

"I miss my brother, Timothy. We were twins, you know."

"No, I didn't," I replied. "Was he a lot like you?"

"Growing up, I had another one of me to talk to." Thomas shook his head. "We were so much alike people couldn't tell us apart."

"Where is he now? Why isn't he here?" I asked.

"That's the difficult part." Thomas shrugged his shoulders. "Timothy and I agreed on almost everything. But we didn't see Jesus the same way."

"Timothy didn't believe Jesus was the Messiah?" Philip asked.

"Oh, way worse than that." Thomas stood and studied the ground. "I didn't understand why Timothy couldn't see how Jesus must be the Messiah. Timothy, on the other hand, called me a fool for leaving the farm and following this peasant preacher. He didn't spare many words in expressing his feelings, either."

"Oh, I'm sorry." I meant the sentiment from my heart.

"Someday, he'll come around." Thomas sat back down. "But it's hard until then. We haven't spoken since I left." A misty glaze appeared in his eyes.

All three of us must have individually decided enough had been said for the moment. In an understanding silence, we gazed out over the blue lake.

In some locations, the Sea of Galilee's banks are lush with meadows, trees, and orchards. In other places, the shores are rocky and barren. Sitting there, I realized rocky and barren could also be beautiful.

"Well, time to get dinner ready." I stood and started toward our camp. "Mary's motioning to me."

Sea birds circled in the crisp early morning air waiting for the intruders to leave. The men loaded the cooking pots into the boat as fast as Mary and I could wash them. With the sun hardly cresting the eastern hills, we pushed off and a breeze caught the sail, which flew open with a pop. I found a small spot to sit and turned to Philip right beside me. "Think maybe the crowds back home might have forgotten us, since we've been gone a couple of days?"

CHAPTER ELEVEN

"Uh-oh. Looks like trouble," younger James called. "Some kind of delegation is coming down the street."

I dropped my load from the boat on the counter and wheeled back for a quick peek from the edge of the door. A tight group of a dozen or more men were striding straight toward the house. James was right, this wasn't a casual gathering coming for inspiration.

Jesus stepped past us and out the door as the men entered the yard. A big man in a religious robe led the crowd. "Thomas," I whispered, "is that one of those Pharisees? He looks familiar."

Thomas peered over my shoulder. "Oh, no. That's Jairus, the leader of our synagogue. He gave us a little grief the way Jesus healed that man's withered arm, but he's not a bad person."

Thomas slipped past me into the doorway to hear better. "They're asking Jesus to go to the home of the Roman Centurion in charge of local security." Thomas repeated to the rest of us. "... They want Jesus to heal a servant who's near death."

"Well, isn't this some turn around?" I shook my head. "They get upset with Jesus at the synagogue for healing a nobody on the Sabbath. But when someone important needs healing—who do they run to?"

Jesus stepped back inside. He didn't appear at all cynical like I was.

"John, James, Simon Peter," he called, "gather your robes and come with me."

"Where're we going?" John asked as he grabbed his outer garment.

Jesus briefly explained as he slipped his on.

James walked up to catch the last words. "We're going *where?*"

"Yes, we're going to the home of a Gentile." Jesus gave him a stern look. "Now, come."

Jesus and the three walked beside Jairus as the crowd followed.

Less than an hour later, the four walked back through the door. "What happened?" I asked. "You're back so soon."

John swaggered over toward the kitchen. "We didn't even get to the centurion's home when this servant comes running up and says, 'my master says he isn't worthy to have Jesus come to his house.'" John paused, apparently for effect.

James broke in. "The servant tells Jesus, 'my master says that if you just say the word, I know he'll be healed.'"

John glared at James.

Jesus held out his hand between them. "Please." He looked to the rest of us. "You know I don't believe I have seen faith this great even among the Israelites. Our people always seem to need a sign. Amazing! This centurion simply ... believed."

Jesus led the men on into the living room. But my feet wouldn't budge and my mind failed to function.

Mary nudged me. "What's wrong, Joanna?"

"Oh, Mary." I sat down, my elbows on the table and my chin in my hands. "Why? Why couldn't that be my husband? If this Roman centurion can believe, why can't Cuza?" Resentment swelled within me. "It's been almost four weeks. I'm afraid Cuza just can't bring himself to admit being wrong." My resentment slowly skidded into a good case of self-pity.

Mary patted my shoulder. "When you find a man who'll admit being wrong—let me know."

I tried real hard to not crack that small smile. But I also wondered, *what if Cuza doesn't come? I was so sure he would, I don't have a back-up plan.*

"It's about time the two of you get in here." Mary stood, her hands on her hips. "Dinner's hot and we're waiting for you."

"It's Thad's fault," Bart said as he slid into his place at the low table. "We had to clean up after we fixed his broken door, but he takes so much longer to get ready for dinner now—since Joanna came." A teasing grin spread across Bartholomew's face. "He's even started trying to comb that mop of hair!"

Thad's face turned crimson beneath his dark tan. "T-t-that's n-n-not true."

The front door burst open. A handsome young man appeared in the doorway, totally out-of-breath. Andrew jumped to his feet. "Nathaniel, what's wrong?"

Nathaniel's face looked contorted as he searched for breath. His hands were on his thighs. Finally, he straightened with a deep breath. "Jesus, I have terrible news. Herod Antipas has arrested John the Baptist. The Roman garrison is ordered to crack down on all 'the troublemakers' in Galilee. He's even banned large gatherings."

Jesus climbed to his feet, put his arm on Nathaniel's shoulder, and called John, James, and Simon Peter. The five huddled in serious talk.

I turned to Andrew. "Should I remember Nathaniel?"

"You wouldn't." Andrew's face carried a heavy, worried look. "Nathaniel was part of our group until his wedding. A newly married man needs to be home with his wife."

"That's understandable." My stomach twitched considering my own absence.

"His was the big wedding up in Cana we talked about."

The five returned and everyone gathered in close. "Seems the old animosity is forgotten and there's now some special alliance between Herod Antipas and Pilate. They don't want dissidents being able to hide in the other's territory any longer." Nathaniel spoke low and soft. "This could spell real trouble."

Jesus rose. "This confirms the warning we received earlier." I felt a slight smile inside as Jesus obviously referred to the information I gave him in Jerusalem. "I planned another tour of Galilee shortly. We'll postpone that trip just a little while."

"You haven't condemned Antipas in any way." Philip frowned. "We should be okay."

Suddenly, everyone had an opinion.

The strong hand of the Romans had always been my comfort, knowing they would keep order. What a difference now seeing this from another perspective. The Roman world I knew and trusted and this rural Jewish world seemed headed toward collision.

"Men," Jesus called, "We're letting our concern over what we should do overshadow the enormity of what has just happened. A great prophet is in prison. His call for righteousness is silenced. This is indeed a sad day."

When the crowd finally began to dwindle for the evening, I slipped over to Andrew. "Help me understand things. I thought John the Baptist was a troublemaker, out to discredit Herod." I didn't intend for anyone but Andrew to hear. Jesus and Nathaniel were still talking on the other side of the room.

"Joanna," Jesus interrupted, "John the Baptist prepared the way for my ministry." His eyes glistened. "A great spiritual darkness hung over the land of Israel. There had been no prophet speaking from God for hundreds of years."

Jesus drew a deep breath. "John the Baptist suddenly appeared as the person Isaiah the Prophet spoke of, the one calling in the desert to prepare the way for the Lord."

A broad, yet tearful smile spread across Jesus' face. "John preached a gospel of repentance. Throngs of people went out to the desert along the Jordan River to hear him. He brought a great spiritual awakening."

"John baptized me then too." Andrew broke in with a wide smile.

The emotion in Jesus' voice generated a lump in my throat. "I had no idea." Shame swept over me. "Everyone at Herod's palace referred to him as a troublemaker." I shook my head. "Of course, from Herod Antipas, what else would one expect?"

Jesus' dark, penetrating eyes focused on mine. "As I stood in the Jordan River, John lifted his hand above me and announced to the crowd, 'I baptize you with water for repentance. But after me comes one who is more powerful than I, whose sandals I'm not fit to carry. He will baptize you with the Holy Spirit and with fire.' My ministry began at that moment."

I slipped over close to Nathaniel and Jesus. "Thank you for setting the record straight. Remember now, Herod strongly believes you are also a likely threat. You are high on his enemies list. Be careful."

"Thank you, Joanna." Jesus slipped on his outer robe and left with the others.

I can't think I imagined it. The feeling was too real. Something inside me whispered, *could my being with Jesus mean more than I realized? Could it be part of some greater plan of God?* The feeling swept over me unlike anything I'd ever felt previously. Never had I considered the possibility of God knowing me personally, much less having a purpose for me. The hair raised on my arms.

Alone in my room, I strained to sort things out. Cuza was certainly right about Herod taking actions against John the Baptist. *But where is Cuza? He certainly would have known of Herod's plans to arrest John and therefore know the danger that would place me in. Why hasn't he come? Has he completely rejected me? Have I lost my home and family forever?* Emotions threatened to yank my heart completely out of my chest.

The walls of my little room began closing in on me. Fear imprisoned me like an ugly fog. I needed to breathe—I had to get out.

My racing heart made locating my heavier shawl a challenge, especially in the dark. I finally threw the cloak over my shoulders and crept softly to the entry door. I knew a woman going outside at night wasn't wise, but this excursion was necessary. Dark cloudy skies made the walk difficult, but the lake's shore drew me relentlessly.

As I looked out across the dark, ominous body of water, my tears flowed. I didn't deserve Cuza's rejection. I had done nothing wrong. Through my swollen eyes, I threw my resentment and anger toward the God I had only begun to understand. *If He could use me to warn Jesus, why couldn't He change Cuza's heart?* I stood absorbed in my pity.

Suddenly, an even stronger realization slapped my face. I realized how wrong I had been in leading Jesus to believe I had come to serve, when I only wanted to use him to wake Cuza from his stupidity. My overwhelming desire to be a real mother again brought me to manipulate Jesus for my own selfish ends. Guilt welled up, my whole body quivered. I had been so self-centered, so wrong.

A nearly full moon broke from behind the dark, heavy clouds. The comforting reflection of the moon's bright rays rippled across the empty Sea of Galilee. A cool breeze floated against my hot skin. A difference I couldn't explain began to happen inside me.

Without warning, the heavy clouds again slid across the moon, casting darkness everywhere. As the heavy blackness enveloped me, a sensation of being all alone crept up from the sand, across my sandals and into the pit of my stomach. In the blackness, the lake and the surrounding hills grew more ominous with each passing moment.

As suddenly as the heavy clouds had covered the moon's glow, they parted and the comforting rays returned.

Something began to emerge from my troubled mind. The moon's gentle, comforting light seemed so normal and expected I hardly noticed the glow—until it wasn't there. Could this be what I was missing? That God's love is so real, so encompassing, I didn't realize its presence until my selfish ambitions clouded his love out?

A resolve began growing within me. *I'm not going to let Cuza's lack of action destroy me. I have a reason to be here. God has a purpose for me.*

Stooping down, I cupped cool lake water in my hands and splashed my face. I did it again, then again, until my bitter tears washed away.

I looked out over the moon-drenched lake and knew my heart wasn't the same. Even though I couldn't explain, I knew something was definitely different. *Will I ever know the reason all this has happened? I doubt it. But, thanks to God's love, a reason no longer matters.*

CHAPTER TWELVE

My late-night experience at the lake lifted an enormous burden, and I wanted to share my new feelings with someone. But everyone seemed to be dealing with the trauma of Nathaniel's news about John. That horrible revelation certainly eclipsed my personal episode. I decided to hold talking about my encounter for another time and enjoy its afterglow by myself.

The shock from the terrible news of John the Baptist's arrests left feelings much too raw for the men to be able to talk about. A quiet hush replaced their usual raucous bantering.

Mary asked, "How do you think Herod's crackdown will affect us?"

"We haven't seen any unusual Roman patrols." I sat down, "But they know where we are, and they have a way of showing up when you least expect them."

During our after-dinner session, Jesus lightened the mood considerably by informing us that Simon, one of the leading Pharisees in town, had invited us to dinner two nights hence. The previously pensive evening exploded into an uproar.

"Simon's never shown any concern about what Jesus is doing," Andrew argued. "Why is he suddenly interested in us now?"

Thomas shook his head. "He's going to invite other Pharisees there. You know there'll be trouble."

When the furor waned slightly, I tugged on Philip's sleeve. "Is Simon one of the Pharisees who gave Jesus a hard time at the synagogue?"

"Those two really obnoxious Pharisees are from Jerusalem, sent down by the authorities." Philip spoke over the ruckus. "But even if Simon hasn't been a problem, his sympathies are certainly with those at the temple."

Bart, who usually never said anything, shook his head as he announced, "This won't come to any good."

"You two usually have a strong opinion about everything." Thomas looked at John and James. "What are your thoughts on this?"

James' face slowly turned red. John squirmed but didn't say anything. Slowly, one by one, all eyes turned and focused on the two. Under the intense gaze of ten men, John hesitantly rose to his feet. He cleared his throat then shuffled his feet a long painful moment. "Uh, Zebedee and Simon are good friends. Father thought it would be good for both the community and Jesus if we all got together and buried our differences over a nice dinner." John studied his feet. "Simon agreed, and … uh … well, that's the reason for the invitation."

I whispered to Mary. "So, his father Zebedee is behind this, trying to improve Jesus' image around town."

"I don't trust either of them, Zebedee or Salome," Mary whispered back. "About a year before you came, Salome was over here fussing at Jesus for not giving her boys as important a place in his ministry as they deserved. Now this! My guess is Salome put Zebedee up to it."

"Must run in the family," I added with a sheepish grin.

"I'm not going, not even to Simon's courtyard, to be humiliated." Mary crossed her arms in the most matter of fact way I had seen from her. "Bound to be trouble."

As far as I was concerned, that settled it for me as well. A quiet evening at home looked far more inviting than a confrontation on a rich Pharisee's porch.

Jesus planted his staff on the floor with a heavy thump. One by one the disciples quit arguing and turned their attention to him. "We are going. You may not enjoy the evening, but I need your support. I would like all of you to go with me."

Some were more reluctant than others, but finally all the men agreed to go.

The disciples trickled in late on the afternoon of the big dinner. All the men had on their best clothes, which except for Judas and Matthew, didn't look much different. Judas always dressed a little nicer and wore more expensive sandals. Matthew apparently couldn't resist getting out of his brown woolen robe and dress a little more like his previous life—comfortable.

Mary left the big room to help her James finish getting ready. I was putting away the remains of our small dinner when I noticed Judas motion Matthew over near the kitchen.

"Well, it is good to see at least two of us know how to dress for an important occasion." Unfortunately, Judas whispered loud enough for me to hear. "Thankfully, we don't appear to have just fallen off a fishing boat."

"I didn't quite know what to wear." Matthew's face began to glow. "I've had a few confrontations with Simon in the past. Knowing him, he will be sure to make some comment about how poor I look since I began following Jesus." Matthew's voice grew increasingly flustered. "I don't want to shame Jesus, but I didn't want to dress too nicely either."

"Easy, I'm not trying to embarrass you." Judas put his hand on Matthew's shoulder, "I'm just complimenting you on appreciating the nicer things of life."

I didn't like the tone of the conversation or the direction it was going. The more they talked, the more I tried blending into the cabinetry.

"But that's not what I'm trying to do." Matthew's shoulders shook. "This change from rich to poor isn't easy. Like tonight, I don't really know how." Matthew shuffled his feet searching for the right words. "Same is true in selling my house. I know I should, but it isn't easy to sell a big house ... especially in Capernaum." Matthew's voice trailed off. Judas' eyes lit up.

I felt silly, acting busy while overhearing their conversation, but I knew I would call more attention to myself if I suddenly left the kitchen. So, I stayed and tried to appear invisible.

"Matthew, don't sell your big house." Judas clenched his teeth. "We'll need it for our Galilee base when Jesus takes over the government."

"I didn't know Jesus intended to take over the government." Matthew's eyes grew wide. "Where did you come up with that?"

"Come on, Matthew, can't you see the obvious?" Judas' voice raised a level. "The people are crying for a king who can free us from Rome. You know that."

"I know Jesus is popular with the people." Matthew ducked his head still further. "But I'm not—"

"Look, Matthew, Jesus has power to heal the sick and wounded. He can feed thousands with practically nothing." Judas gestured with his hands. "If he can do that, think what he could do for an army. What could stop him?"

At this point, the gleam in Judas's eye could have burned through leather. "I know this much; this whole thing is about to take off. I don't know about you, Matthew," Judas poked his finger at Matthew's chest, "but Jesus is my ticket to somewhere important."

I could not have been more uncomfortable pretending to not hear. As my insides seemed ready to burst, Jesus came through the door, followed by John and James.

Matthew and Judas moved to join the group. I wiped the perspiration from the back of my neck. All the men, and thankfully no women, left for the big dinner at Simon's home. That was one event I gladly missed.

Younger James pushed the door open. "I knew it! I knew it was going to happen." Andrew waved his hands. "Sometimes you can be too accommodating to people like that."

I jumped up. "What happened at the dinner?"

"Oh, Joanna, you won't believe …"

"Well, I might if you would tell me."

"Okay, I'll try." James sat on his usual cushion. "We sort of knew Simon wanted to show off Jesus to the important people of Capernaum even before we went. As usual, lots of people were in his courtyard sampling the food. As we were eating, this woman snuck up behind Jesus and stood crying her eyes out." James twisted uncomfortably relating the events. "Simon tried to hush her and had servants escort her out."

Andrew threw his outer wrap across a chair and added, "I was embarrassed, I know that."

James continued. "Then suddenly she was back and crying harder. As she knelt behind Jesus, her tears were running down onto his feet."

"You're making this up!" I shook my head.

"No, Joanna, I'm not." James' eyes were wide as saucers.

"Then she pulled a small bottle out of her robe and poured this expensive perfume on Jesus' feet."

My mouth fell opened but words wouldn't form.

Andrew broke in. "It was all downhill from there. Simon frowned at Jesus and said that if he were a real prophet he would have known who this woman was."

"But Jesus handled it well," James added, "He began telling Simon about two men owing some moneylender a lot of money, one ten times more than the other. Since neither could repay their debt, the moneylender forgave both debts. Then Jesus asked Simon which of these two men would love him more for his act of kindness.

"Simon looked perplexed, clearly wanting to get the woman out. But finally, he replied to Jesus that it was probably the one who had the larger debt cancelled."

James continued. "Jesus told Simon that he loved little because he had so little forgiven. She loved much because she has had much forgiven."

"Good. He got what he deserved," I said. "But what happened to the poor woman?"

"Oh," Andrew inserted, "that's when the big uproar began."

"It got worse?"

"Oh, yes," Andrew continued. "Jesus looked at the sobbing woman and told her her sins were forgiven—to go in peace. Simon and his other guest jumped to their feet and began demanding how Jesus thought he could forgive sins. Since everything had fallen apart, we decided to get out of there."

James picked up some dates from the counter. "The worst part—we missed dessert."

An early morning knock on the door startled me. I opened it to see two women standing with bags in their hands. The taller of the two announced, "We are here to follow Jesus."

My eyes grew wide. My ears were obviously playing tricks on me.

Younger James stumbled into the room and took one look. "Oh … you're the woman from last night."

My better judgment warned me, but the only decent thing to do was to invite them in and to send younger James to find Jesus.

I introduced myself and Mary, who had just come in the room. The taller woman had long auburn hair. Her light skin contrasted with her once-elegant jade robe. But her brilliant green eyes would capture anyone's attention.

She spoke with a flourish. "I am Mary. I'm from Magdala. Since there are so many Marys around, most people call me Mary

Magdalene. This is my dearest friend, Susanna. We are here to follow Jesus."

I wanted to say, *yes, you already said that.* Instead, I tried being diplomatic. "I understand. What brought you to this decision?"

With her emerald green eyes sparkling, she said, "Oh, Jesus has made a tremendous difference in my life. I've struggled with anxiety and depression. I've even contemplated killing myself." At the rate she started, she could easily continue for an hour.

I had obviously asked the wrong question. "Yes, yes. I'm sure Jesus will want to hear your entire story … when he gets here." *Oh, Jesus, my heart pleaded, please come quickly. We have far too much facing us to deal with this.*

The thought struck me to turn the conversation to the other woman. "She said you were Susanna? What brings you here?"

Susanna looked younger than the taller Mary, probably in her late twenties. Her almond eyes and slender face complimented her darker complexion. Susanna had deep brown hair, dark eyes, and a gentle demeanor. Both of their robes appeared, at one time, to have been several cuts of cloth above those usually worn around Capernaum.

In a quiet, modest voice Susanna said, "I worked for Mary in their fabric business. We imported fine cloth from the east and resold to the merchants in Jerusalem, Sepphoris, and the Decapolis. That is, until the break-up of her last marriage. She lost the business in that awful affair."

Susanna seemed to possess a calm inner beauty.

Jesus, followed by John, James, and Simon Peter, came through the door … not a minute too soon.

Mary Magdalene grabbed Jesus' hand. "Oh, thank you, thank you for coming to my defense last night against that awful man. He kept trying to keep me out, but I had to see you and thank you for healing me." Mary Magdalene paused the slightest as she brushed her long auburn hair over her shoulder. "Please forgive me if I became a little emotional last evening."

Last evening? I didn't like the way she gazed at Jesus, but I knew he would deal with the situation and send these two on their way.

The look on James's and John's faces reflected my feeling—the sooner Jesus sent them along, the better.

Jesus listened intently as Mary Magdalene again told her story.

Finally, Jesus held up his hand. "Traveling with us will not be easy and certainly won't be the adventure you imagine." Jesus motioned toward Mary and me. "Joanna and Mary work very hard to take care of these men. Our many travels will be arduous. Single women in the company of so many men will be viewed with suspicion."

Jesus stood. "But I assure you, if you decide to come with us, you will be treated with kindness and respect by each of my apostles."

I sat, stunned. No!

Jesus turned to John. "I can tell from the look on your face you're not convinced this is what I should do."

This caught John more than a little off guard. He finally stammered, "Well, I just don't know what all of the people who come to hear you are going to think."

John's lame, half objection sank like a rock in a lake.

With John ruining his objection so badly, James passed on making a comment—I'm sure for only a very short time.

Simon Peter began by stating his strong objection. But in a long ramble, he managed to talk himself in a complete circle, finally concluding, "I guess having two more women to help won't be bad."

Younger James and Mary said that they were for whatever Jesus wanted.

Jesus turned back to James and John. "Keep this in mind, I am not here for popularity's sake. I have come to seek and to save those who are lost. Remember, whoever calls on the name of the Lord will be forgiven. Should it be any different for these two?" Jesus paused long enough for that thought to soak into any but the thickest skull. "If anyone wonders whether God could possibly forgive them, they need only look at my followers. James, were either you or John a pillar of virtue when I called you?"

Something very interesting seemed written on the floor between their feet. They both studied the area a long time before John, then James, shook their heads. I was too numb to know how I felt. I kept thinking I was having a bad dream from which I would soon awaken.

With their acceptance seemingly assured, Susanna spoke. "Jesus, we did come out of that difficult time with a little reward. We want to share it with you." She withdrew a bag from her long garment. "We don't want to be a burden. This should help your ministry grow. The gift's from both Mary and me."

Despite how I secretly felt, a tear rose to the corner of my eye. No, I didn't want their help. I didn't need the exuberance Mary Magdalene brought to every conversation. But I couldn't help being touched. On the other hand, four women competing in the small space of Mary's kitchen? Mary spoke up. "Since Jose's found work for the time being down in Tiberias, you ladies are free to use his room. The space will be a little tight with a second bed in there, but I'm sure there are times when you've made do with less."

Jesus stood and gathered his things. "Don't get too comfortable. We are leaving for a tour of Galilee soon."

I can't wait for them to ask where they're supposed to ride.

CHAPTER THIRTEEN

Dreary rain always makes me want to crawl back in bed and pull a blanket over my head. Dark clouds rolled across the lake and crashed into our little town. The huge raindrops predicted an impending downpour. And this was the morning we were supposed to leave for our tour of Galilee. Hesitantly, we started preparations. I searched for reasons to hesitate more, but could find few.

As Mary sat yet more stuff down to load on our pack animal, I finally admitted, "It's awful hard to get excited about leaving in weather like this."

Mary spoke over her shoulder as she headed back for more. "Jesus assures us the rain's only a passing shower."

"If this is a passing shower, it's sure missing a great chance to be a real rain." I called after her. Susanna brought out her load of kitchen items. She practically dumped them to dart back toward the shelter. "Come on, Susanna," I called. "Help load. Haven't you ever been wet before?"

"How in the name of Abraham do you get all this on him?" Her eyes protested as much as her words. A smile didn't warm Susanna's face as she returned to pick up the wet pots.

"Not you, it's we who gets all this on him. To be honest, I asked the same question on my first trip. Somehow we do." I gave Susanna a reassuring smile. "Now throw that rope over to me."

"Was it raining like this when you made that trip?"

I ignored her question and motioned to Thomas and Thad to bring the big lean-to.

Jesus came out followed by several disciples. He said with a confident smile, "First, we're going up on a special hillside." He pointed to a mountain off in the distance. "I have some important things to share with you before we begin visiting the villages."

The pack animal was finally loaded. Despite the threatening weather, everyone gathered to set out. With two additional women, it took me a minute to realize there were too few men. I grabbed Andrew. "Where are Simon and younger James?"

"Jesus didn't want to alarm the women," Andrew whispered. "With the threat Nathaniel reported, Jesus sent James and the Zealot ahead to scout for Roman patrols." He ducked his head closer. "Remember, the authorities have banned large gatherings."

My eyes grew wide. Not only was I now physically separated from Cuza, but an ever-growing chasm seemed forming between the person I had become and the government my husband stood for. My insides quivered.

As the edge of town sank behind us, suddenly, a bright ray of sunlight broke through the heavy overcast. More clear sky appeared as we reached the first crossroads. Soon, the remaining clouds followed in hasty retreat.

Warmth from the sun felt good on my face, but beneath my heavy rain garment, I began to bake. Thankfully, we stopped to repack our rainwear.

As we walked, Mary and I fought to hold our laughter at the comedy playing out in front. Mary Magdalene assumed there was a special place reserved for her to walk beside Jesus. This wasn't sitting well at all with the three. James would give her *the stare* while either John or Simon Peter walked in a way to cut her out. Mary Magdalene obviously wasn't one to give up easily. Finally, she dropped back and walked with Susanna.

We passed through one small village without stopping. Entering a second village, Simon and younger James suddenly stepped from a corner and walked beside Jesus and the three. Their heads tilted first toward one, then another. The rest of us couldn't hear the conversation but could see concerned looks on their faces.

The two disappeared as suddenly as they appeared. "Where did they go?" I asked Mary as my eyes searched all around.

"To keep us safe." But Mary's smile said a lot more. Mixed feelings pounded my heart. My long-held concept of Roman patrols insuring my safety began showing ever larger cracks.

The closer we came to Jesus' hillside, the more the hill looked like a mountain that became even steeper as we started up. About halfway, the two women pleaded to stop and rest.

Might be good having them along after all.

As we sat, Susanna remarked, "It's absolutely beautiful up here."

"Look, Susanna, you can see completely across the Sea of Galilee," I said, proudly pointing. "See the hills on—"

"What I see are the people coming behind us."

Susanna's comment turned everyone's attention back toward the path we had just traveled.

"I'll never understand how word spreads so fast in these small villages." I shook my head. A steady stream of people was following us a distance behind.

We continued up the mountain to a somewhat level area. There we established ourselves near a rocky outcropping. The disciples began the difficult task of organizing the throng and getting them seated on the grassy area. So much for our special time alone with Jesus.

When most had arrived, Jesus climbed onto the rocky ledge and raised his hands. Incredibly, everyone hushed. Susanna, Mary, Mary Magdalene, and I found a place to sit near one side of the huge gathering.

Jesus thanked the crowd for coming and said he wanted to share some special thoughts his Heavenly Father had for them.

"God blesses those who realize their need for a special walk with Him," Jesus explained. "The kingdom of heaven will be theirs.

"Know that you can be happy even in your sorrow, because your Heavenly Father gives special comfort to those who trust Him.

"Blessed are those who are gentle and kind. You are the ones who will inherit this world.

"God will truly bless all those who hunger for justice," Jesus continued. "They, in turn, will see justice come to pass.

"If you show mercy to others, you will receive mercy yourself."

Mercy? I wondered how much mercy the authorities would show, considering the edict against large crowds. Fear crept up the back of my neck as I surveyed the crowd of several hundred. I glanced back toward the trail we had climbed, half expecting Roman soldiers. Instead, younger James and Simon were slipping quietly toward us. *Maybe this is the best place for a crowd after all.*

"Do you truly wish to see God?" Jesus stopped and looked over the crowd. "You will be able, if your heart is pure."

Jesus held his hand out toward the people. "Remember, if you work for peace in this world, you will be called the children of God!

"Don't worry if people say all kinds of bad things about you, because you stand for what is good. In the end, people will see what is right, and you will be part of the kingdom of heaven on earth.

"You ask about keeping the Law." Jesus stretched out both arms, as if encompassing the whole crowd. "I have not come to do away with the Law. Instead, I want to teach you how the Law can be fulfilled in your lives. The teachers of the Law want you to obey the letter of the Law—but they ignore the intent. My friends, if your righteousness doesn't exceed that of the Pharisees, there isn't any way you will enter the kingdom of heaven."

After an hour of teaching, Jesus concluded by saying, "This is the rule you should live by. Do to others only what you would have them do to you!"

Jesus reached for John and Simon Peter to help him down from the ledge. People began surging forward. The disciples held the crowd so Jesus could take special time with every person. Joy erupted as each received healing. A tremendous amount of rejoicing took place on the mountainside that day.

As the last of the crowd departed, Jesus said, "We will go on for a while, then set up camp."

Within a couple of hours, we encountered a grove of trees beside a small stream that beckoned us to stop. Setting up camp came none too soon for my aching legs, but I kept my lips sealed and enjoyed hearing the two newcomers complain as they hobbled about.

During breakfast, Jesus explained, "Simon and younger James have been out checking the area. Men in several villages report activity from Roman patrols in recent days. Therefore, we will go further north, out of Galilee. This will be our opportunity to visit Caesarea Philippi."

I strolled over to Philip. "I thought Caesarea was down on the coast of the Great Sea."

"This is a different Caesarea. Caesarea Philippi is a good bit north of here, actually in the province of Syria." Philip scratched his short beard. "I understand leaving Galilee, but I have no idea why we're going to such a pagan place as Caesarea Philippi."

"Pagan?"

"Yes, they're known for the worship of the goat god, Pan. Young women are the focus of their temple, and they're certainly not there for worship, either."

"Oooh?" I'm not sure which was wider, my mouth or my eyes.

All too soon, our trek began. Younger James and the Zealot again appeared out of nowhere and huddled with Jesus and the three. We stopped for those few minutes. When we started on, Jesus picked up an even faster pace. Even though our journey wasn't like the climb from Jericho to Jerusalem, still my legs told me were walking a good incline.

Younger James joined his mother and me. "Looked like a serious discussion," I said. "What's happening?"

"Simon and I checked the Galilee-Syria border ahead," James whispered to avoid Mary Magdalene hearing. "Only the usual border guards. Looks safe to cross."

Late afternoon, we finally reached Caesarea Philippi. On a knoll just outside of town, we set up camp. The spot revealed just how far we had climbed. The whole of Galilee stretched out below us.

Thomas strolled over while we were preparing the evening meal. "How are you doing, little lady?"

"I've got you figured out, Thomas. You only want to see what we're fixing for dinner."

"You notice Jesus acting differently today?" The humor disappeared from Thomas' face.

"Well, he sure seemed focused on getting here, my legs can attest to that." I thought a moment. "I guess you're right. He hardly said anything today."

Following dinner, James and his mother strolled over to the campfire. The sun's last glow caressed the valley below. Salmon-streaked shadows capped what were our western hills when at home. From this height, we were looking down on them. A deep blue sky grew darker by the moment. Mary looked out over the vista. "This is certainly a beautiful spot."

James sat beside his mother. "Yes, it's kind of like looking down from heaven on our part of the world."

Silence followed.

Finally, Thomas spoke. "Somehow I don't think Jesus brought us all the way up here to enjoy the scenery."

Jesus finally stepped over and called us together. We sat there … waiting. Something obviously was troubling Jesus. After several long awkward moments, Jesus asked, "Who do people say that I am?"

John sat up a little straighter. "Well, I have heard some refer to you as another John the Baptist." John smiled as if he won a contest.

Jesus' expression didn't change. He looked off, out over the valley below. Then he looked back at the men. Silence. Several squirmed.

Philip looked uncomfortable, but raised one finger. "Well, many I have talked with seem to think you are like Elijah or Jeremiah, another great prophet."

Another long, awkward pause ensued. Jesus looked over us. "What about you? Who do you say that I am?"

Another uneasy silence swallowed the group.

Simon Peter suddenly blurted, "You are the Messiah, the Son of the Living God!"

A smile replaced the troubled look on Jesus' face. "Blessed are you, Simon, son of Jonah. This wasn't revealed to you by your fellow man. It came directly from my Father in Heaven."

A big, pleased smile grew across Peter's face. He sat straight and proud.

Jesus' face looked halfway between serious and a slight smile. "I'll tell you this, Simon. The name Peter I have given you means 'rock'. On this *Rock*, I will build my church." Jesus swept his arm toward Caesarea Philippi. "And the gates of Hades will not overcome it." Everyone sat speechless. Jesus planted his staff, grasping it with both hands. "What I have told you is for my disciples—and you alone. You are not yet to reveal to the world that I am the Christ. That time will come very soon."

I sensed a thousand questions filling the air. Thomas started, but Jesus raised his hand for us to listen. "Soon enough we will be going up to Jerusalem where I will suffer many things at the hands of the chief priest. I will be killed and on the third day be raised to life again."

"Never, Lord!" Simon Peter jumped to his feet. "This can't happen. We won't let it happen."

Jesus looked toward Peter shaking his head. "Get behind me, Satan. It still amazes me how quickly you can become a stumbling block."

Jesus picked up his staff and outer robe. "I am going out for a while to pray. Keep watch here."

The instant Jesus stepped out of camp, the contentious discussion began. As more than one vied to be heard, we gradually spread into several small groups. Thomas expressed the first intelligent thought in the group I joined. "Simon Peter might have actually said something important this time."

Older James shook his head. "If anybody said anything impressive, it certainly wouldn't be Simon."

"I'm not taking his side because he's my brother." Fire filled Andrew's eyes. "Most of the time, Simon gets things wrong, but this time he got it right. Remember, Jesus said heaven revealed those words through him."

I asked to speak. "Who said it isn't the most important point? Think about what Peter said." My hands began shaking. "I know Jesus is a prophet with his wonderful teachings and unbelievable healings. But how am I supposed to understand him being the *Son of the Living God?*" I gave a pleading look to the others. "Do you comprehend what that means? My mind simply cannot fathom ..." Further words failed to materialize.

Philip placed his hand on my shoulder. "I'll have to work on that thought, as well." He turned to the others in our little group. "But what did Jesus mean when he referred to the *Rock* upon which he would build his church? Did Jesus mean he would build his movement on Peter or on the truth Peter revealed?"

"It couldn't possibly be on Peter." James nodded his head toward Simon who remained in a different group. "Anything built on Simon Peter will surely crumble."

Thomas pulled Andrew back down.

After an hour, still no solid answer emerged for what 'his church' could be or for what Jesus meant about suffering in Jerusalem or for what role Simon Peter might play. My head felt ready to explode, but one question would not let go of me. *How could someone I know, someone I consider a friend, be the Son of the Living God?*

CHAPTER FOURTEEN

A gray cloudy morning greeted us. A brief night shower had chilled the air. I rose on one elbow and looked out over the valley below. No valley. In its place were dark, angry clouds. Flashes of lightning cracked through the clouds repeatedly. Distant thunder rolled like mountains dropped from the sky. Totally amazed, I stood. I had never witnessed a thunderstorm looking down on it from above. Somewhere down below that awful mess was the Sea of Galilee and Capernaum.

Following breakfast, we repacked to begin our trek toward Galilee. And yes, toward that awful storm. The scent of coming rain hung heavy in the air. As we started walking, two conflicting emotions continued hammering me. How could Jesus be both the wonderful, caring friend I knew and, at the same time, be the Son of God? Hopefully, time and walking would begin to answer this.

One moment, Simon and younger James were nowhere to be seen, and the next they were walking beside Jesus and the others, their heads tilting back and forth. Each face revealed the seriousness of their discussion. After they talked several minutes, they all nodded. The Zealot resumed a place with the men and James came back to where his mother walked beside me.

"You're learning way too many tricks for my comfort." I nudged James. "You weren't anywhere around until suddenly you were walking beside Jesus. Where were you?"

"That's our secret." James grinned. "And believe me, you really don't want to know."

"At least, tell me where you've been," I insisted.

"To the Galilee border. It's raining heavily there," James nodded in that direction, "but that's a good thing—"

"How can that be a good thing?"

"Patience." James gave me one of those parent-to-child looks. "Only two soldiers are standing guard. The rest are huddled in the command post. Ought to be an easy crossing."

We walked on for several minutes, then James added, "We did hear there're several Roman patrols to the west, around Cana, so Jesus decided to go east, toward Bethsaida."

"Oooh." I groaned. "With the weather, I'd hoped we would head home."

"Not a chance." James turned his attention toward his mother.

I was again—left with my thoughts. Before I met Jesus, God had been some far-off figure in the universe, something Mother would mention in passing. But Jesus kept referring to God as 'Father.' Until the discussion the previous evening, I assumed 'Father' was a figure of speech Jesus used. Now the word seemed so much more, like God was his father. What does this really mean, Jesus being the Son of the Living God? Is there a way to comprehend this?

The heavy mist grew into a light drizzle. Dark puddles along the roadside made clear a heavier rain had preceded us. James stepped closer. "The border crossing is just ahead." He shrugged his shoulders. "Just act normal."

Neither soldier seemed particularly interested in searching a group of seventeen in the rain. Good. They would wish they had not tangled with Mary Magdalene if the comments under her breath were any indication of her attitude about walking in the rain. I would rather have messed with an angry Zealot.

Even though the storm seemed to gain intensity further down the valley, it lessened some where we walked. We soon entered a village. "This is Korazin," Younger James whispered. "We were here once before."

We made quite a stir entering the small town—if by nothing other than the sheer size of our group. We were hard to ignore as we made our way toward the well near the town's center.

Several people began to gather, mostly out of curiosity. I had not noticed a beggar until he began calling out, "What's happening, who's here?" He waved his cup. "Alms for the poor, alms for the blind."

Someone from the small crowd admonished him. "Be quiet. It is Jesus of Nazareth and his disciples."

He suddenly became louder and more demanding. "Alms for the blind."

As Jesus walked over, he called yet louder, "Please, alms for the blind."

"Would you rather have alms ... or your sight?" Jesus asked.

This quickly captured the blind man's attention and everyone else's, for that matter. "Oh, please sir, my sight."

Jesus licked his fingers then rubbed the man's eyes. "If you truly believe, your faith will make you whole."

The man's countenance came to life. He raised his hand before his face and moved it to the right then left. His watery eyes cleared as they followed the hand he was seeing for the first time. He jumped to his feet and grabbed John. He examined John's face. Letting go, he began dancing and shouting. "I can see! Praise God, I can see."

Jesus told him, "Go home and show yourself to your family, so they can rejoice with you."

The few people watching the exchange between Jesus and the healed man suddenly exploded into a crowd. Jesus looked over this large group and began, "The Kingdom of God is like a farmer going out to his field to plant his crops." Jesus explained how some of the seeds fell on the hard-packed ground.

Someone from the crowd shouted, "Show us another miracle."

Then several others took up the call, "We want to see a miracle."

Jesus stopped, his left hand cradling his chin. He looked long and hard at the restless crowd. "If you have ears, you would desire hearing the message of life from our Heavenly Father."

"What's going on? Why are these people so disrespectful?" I asked, not really expecting an answer.

Jesus shook his head. "I feel sorrow for you, Korazin! If the miracle I just performed had been performed in Tyre and Sidon, they would have repented in sackcloth and ashes. I tell you this, it will be more bearable for them on the Day of Judgment than for you."

Jesus turned, motioned for us and started walking. As we departed Korazin, the light drizzle grew into light rain. The further we walked, the harder it rained. Low dark clouds envelop us.

Jesus called, "Let's set up camp before it gets worse."

Two trees near a stream became our camping spot. Though far from perfect, it would have to do. As many as could huddled beneath the smaller canvass while Bart and Thad began erecting the big lean-to. The fire younger James and Andrew finally started brought some warming to our spirits, even if it consisted more of smoke than heat.

After digging out drier clothes, Mary, Susanna, and I went to work fixing as much dinner as we could under the circumstances. Mary Magdalene set as her task to cheer up Jesus—even though I didn't sense he need any cheering up.

We huddled as close to the fire as we could while we ate. The blaze was just under the front edge of the larger lean-to. This placed all of us on the backside. An occasional strong breeze flapped the front edge of the canvass, cascading unwanted rainwater on the fire. Acrid steam and smoke drove us away momentarily, but the back and forth to the fire and trying to eat somehow produced laughter. Laughing felt good.

After dinner, Thomas asked Jesus, "What was wrong with those people back in Korazin?"

With a smile to warm anyone's heart, Jesus said, "Don't be disheartened when people are like the folks in Korazin. Not everyone will immediately accept our message."

Jesus pulled his outer garment over his shoulders. "Believe me, in the days to come, we will experience much worse rejection than today."

I sat there waiting. Someone had to ask about Peter's declaring Jesus as the Son of the Living God. I couldn't summon the courage myself. As the evening grew later, it became apparent no one else could either.

This had not been a pretty day, either in events or weather. But, I realized sitting around a campfire with friends I loved, and with Jesus, hearing rain drop on the canvas, still made it an evening many would envy.

Morning light revealed no improvement in the weather. One moment, the clouds seemed to be breaking up, but the next, dark clouds rolled in and began to pour again. Over a couple of hours, Jesus and the three would periodically look at the sky and talk about getting on to Bethsaida.

Late morning brought a welcomed break from the hard rain. When it slowed to a drizzle, Jesus uttered the most beautiful words I'd heard in several days. "Let's head for home."

When we began this journey, only the animal was wet. Trying to pack our soaked supplies on the slippery back of an agitated burro proved an even greater challenge. The disorganized pile looked twice as big. But the fact we were heading home made packing a joy. We just might make it.

When we were within an hour of Capernaum, the storm hit—rain so hard, the road literally disappeared from beneath our feet. We grabbed anything we could find to get under and stumbled on toward town.

Just as we reached its edge, bright rays of dancing sunlight broke through to welcome us. Everything glistened from the rain. I never imagined dirty, smelly Capernaum could look so good.

Near the close of our time following dinner, Jesus said, "The stormy weather now seems past. I still want to go to the region beyond Bethsaida." He turned to Simon Peter and Andrew. "If the rain is indeed over, make the boat ready in the morning. That area will be much closer sailing."

I thought about looking down on the storm and lightning over the Sea of Galilee as we left Caesarea Philippi. *I sure hope we are never caught out on the lake in a storm like that.*

CHAPTER FIFTEEN

"It's a gorgeous day," I called to younger James as I stepped back inside. "Looks like we might sail after all."

James wiped the sleep from his face, then shielded his eyes at the door, "I guess so." He sleepily turned toward his mother. "I suppose we might as well start packing."

Mary shook her head. "Kitchen's packed, ready for you to start loading."

Mary may have been twice my age, but she was always three steps ahead of the rest of us.

Bright sunlight glimmered across the silver-tipped waves of the Sea of Galilee. A near cloudless sky appeared deeper blue than usual. Sea birds soared high overhead, rising on the currents of fresh air, screeching calls to each other. Yesterday's storm seemed to have even washed away some of Capernaum's pervasive fishy smell.

Simon Peter strode back from the lake's edge. "Only problem, the wind seems to shift directions every few minutes. Sometimes, that means the weather can change pretty quickly." Peter hiked his outer robe and retied his sash as his eyes scanned the shoreline. "But sailing sure beats walking. Let's sail."

With Peter's approval, Bart and Thad dragged the lean-to out while the rest of the men began hauling our supplies to the boat.

"Where's Mary Magdalene?" I asked Susanna.

"Mary says you'll have to go without us." Susanna bit her bottom lip. "Her stomach's bothering her again. It's happened before."

Joy sprang in my heart like a young colt frolicking in its pasture. Fifteen people in Simon Peter's boat already made it crowded. Two more? I whispered toward their door, "Thank you," then felt horrible about my attitude. I was being too hard on Mary Magdalene, but …

On the way to the boat, a voice came from behind me. "I loved the look on your face when Susanna said they weren't going."

I turned. "Oh, Andrew, was I that obvious?" Andrew sheepishly nodded. Then I felt even worse.

Once on board, with clean, clear air filling my lungs, I felt better about everything. Bright sun reflected off the waves as several of our men pushed the boat away from shore.

"A beautiful day for sailing," Andrew called. His voice sounded almost like a song. Even though fishing was surely hard work, being out on the lake on a day like today would probably make any man miss it.

As we sailed peacefully out across the lake, I kept my eyes glued on the shore line. I had learned that lesson quite well enough.

The low hills to the west hung heavily draped with orchards and vineyards. To the north, snowcapped Mt. Hermon hid behind its ever-present heavy clouds. Off in the distance, the Golan Heights rose high and menacing.

A breeze did seem to come from a different direction every so often. Peter and Andrew were kept busy changing the sail to stay with the wind. But, with their expert hands, we were sailing nicely.

Time seems to slow down when on the lake. Even crowded on Peter's little boat, we found relaxing easy. After a good hour of bright sunlight and gentle rocking, Bart began snoring. Thad's big yawn prompted several others. Soon Jesus found a soft canvas roll tempting and laid his head down. I remember yawning ...

"What was that?" I sat up startled and looked down at my drenched robe. Before I could figure what happened, another huge spray of cold lake water splattered the side of my face. Bewildered, I looked around to see heavy dark clouds and Andrew desperately trying to pull the sail in from a howling gale.

A crack of lightning struck the lake—way too close. My ears stung from the thunderous impact. Then the rain came in sheets. Dark clouds hovered barely above the top of the mast.

I glanced to the right. To my horror, another wall of water was coming, higher than the boat.

Terror filled Matthew's voice. "We're going to die!" The look on his face matched the fear in his voice. He clung to the side rail. Our little boat rose with the huge wave. Then, like the floor being yanked from beneath us, we dropped into another deep trough. Judas stuck his head over the side, just in time.

My insides urged me to follow. Desperately I choked it back. At that terrifying moment, just staying alive was the most important priority.

Mary frantically tried to cover our supplies with the lean-to canvas. The wind threatened to snatch the cover from her hands. Thad almost lost his outer garment trying to catch the other, violently flapping, end.

As the next huge wave rose above us, my thoughts turned to Marcus. *Will he ever see his mother again? So young—will he even remember me?*

I was so concerned about staying alive, Jesus didn't cross my mind until Thomas and younger James crawled up to where he still slept soundly. I looked in disbelief. How could anyone sleep through this?

"Master, Master, we're going to die!" Thomas shouted as they shook him. Jesus awoke, then sat up and looked toward the sky. Another wave crashed over the boat, soaking anything not already drenched.

Despite the boat rocking violently and waves crashing over, Jesus rose to his feet.

Like everyone else, I clung to the nearest thing that appeared remotely solid. Jesus stood on the rolling deck and looked toward the heavy wind-blown clouds. As a gust of rain swept over us, Jesus called, "Peace! Be still."

What happened next simply did not fit in the realm of possible. The raging wind slowed to a breeze and the towering waves settled back to a blue sea.

I sat drenched, my jaw hanging. Matthew and Philip gradually released their death grip on the side of the boat.

Jesus smiled as he shook his head. "Where is your faith?"

A single beam of sunlight peeked through.

Where was my faith? I couldn't imagine ever beginning to have faith enough to stand against towering waves and howling wind threatening to dispatch us to the bottom of the lake. As the heavy clouds broke, then scattered like sheep fleeing a hungry wolf, I sat bewildered. I had seen Jesus do lots of things through faith, but my wildest imagination could not possibly produce what just happened.

My mind revisited our evening in Caesarea Philippi. The profound answer bumbling Simon Peter gave slapped me in the face, again. *The Son of the Living God.* I didn't know enough Jewish history to recall what the ancient prophets could and couldn't do, but I felt certain calling for heaven to calm a raging storm wasn't something that happened on a regular basis. Healing blind and crippled people wasn't either; however, Jesus did these on such a regular basis, we almost came to expect them. Jesus seemed so normal to be with and talk to. *Could my friend Jesus truly be the Son of God?* My insides trembled.

Andrew let out the sail and caught the now gentle breeze. Peter steered the boat toward the nearest shore.

"I have no idea where we are after the awful storm," Simon Peter called to Jesus. "If we walk to the top of the hill, maybe we can get our bearings."

From the water, I could only see a rock-strewn shoreline with several rocky outcrops jutting into the lake. Peter spied a small sandy beach and expertly sailed toward it.

"This looks like the most inhospitable stretch of shoreline ever," I said as I crawled off the boat. I planted my feet on the beach. "Inhospitable or not, sand scrunching beneath my sandals feels mighty good right now."

Jesus took James and John, along with Philip and Simon, to walk toward the top of the hill. Huge boulders, as though scattered by giant children, littered the slope in front of us.

"What on earth was that?" Matthew jumped like he'd been stung.

A horrible screeching sound, unlike anything I had ever heard, echoed from the rocks and sent a chill through me. "It sounds like someone's being killed—a little piece at a time."

Younger James' eyes grew wide as saucers. He craned his neck looking toward the area of boulders. "Some of us better go see if Jesus is in trouble."

My heart skipped a beat. Simon Peter jumped to his feet. "Thad, you, Bart, and Thomas go. Andrew and I better stay with the boat in case we need to leave in a hurry."

The three quickly headed up the bank. Suddenly a naked man with long unkempt hair and beard leaped onto one of the boulders. He jumped from one boulder to another, shrieking an awful cry.

Thad, Bart, and Thomas froze in their tracks. I searched for a way to get back on the boat. James grabbed his mother's arm and started in the same direction.

Catching a glimpse of Jesus trying to talk with the wild man brought me hesitantly to a stop. Like a back and forth tug, Jesus tried reaching out to the man only for him to screech in retreat. Suddenly the man's eyes grew wild, and he charged at Jesus. The disciples fell back. Whatever this encounter was about, it didn't appear to be going well.

An ear-splitting shriek twenty times worse came at us from another direction. With my heart pounding in my ears, I scanned for its source. "Look, James," I shouted. "Those pigs! They're squealing and running like they've lost their minds."

The whole herd ran as one, first one direction then another. Finally, the herd made a wide sweep and ran straight toward a rocky ledge overhanging the lake. "Oh, no!" I screamed.

Wide-eyed, Andrew half-asked, "Did you see that?"

"I'm sure I didn't see what I think I saw." A sense of disbelief shivered down my body.

I stood shaking, until the group started walking back toward us. The first thing to catch my eye was Philip's outer robe now covered the naked man walking beside them. I retrieved my bottom jaw. "James, look. That wild man is now calmly talking to Jesus."

When the group came close, I pulled Philip to the side. "What on earth happened up there?"

"The best I can understand, demons must have possessed the man." Philip slowly shook his head. "I've heard people talk of such, but I never believed in—"

"What do you mean, demon-possessed?" I gave Philip a hard look, not believing what he just said.

"I can't explain," Philip looked more than a little bewildered, "but hearing all of those different voices coming from that man … I'd have to consider the possibility."

I wished I had not heard Philip say what he'd just said. Unseen forces of evil, able to move into a person, then into a herd of pigs, causing them to kill themselves, was enough to cause nightmares for weeks.

"The man said his demons were called Legion. I actually heard a number of completely different voices beg Jesus to let them go into the pigs." Philip ran his hand through his hair. "And you saw what happened."

I had never seen or imagined anything quite like this, and I never wanted to again.

"People are coming." Simon spoke softly to John and James.

James stretched his neck looking in every direction. "I don't see anyone. You're imagining things."

My eyes scanned the whole area. I didn't want to agree with James, but he was so confident this time.

Before long though, a head popped out beside a boulder. Then three more sets of eyes peeked at us. Finally, a dozen people emerged, cautiously coming from between the boulders down to our area. Two of them began examining the person they remembered as their village wild man. One even poked at him. He talked to them as calmly as he had with Jesus.

More people stuck their heads around the boulders and soon, the dozen became fifty. Then a large man, flanked by two others, came strutting toward Jesus. The whole crowd parted as the three swaggered to the front.

The big man puffed out his chest. "You will compensate these men for their pigs. You sent them off that cliff. You owe them two hundred shekels."

I nudged Philip. "These men are more concerned about the pigs than seeing this man healed?"

The two men with the village leader began shouting to the crowd. "This was wrong. We want payment."

The situation quickly exploded in an uproar.

Simon Peter gave a loud whistle and swept his arm motioning everyone back on the boat.

With James, John, and the Zealot backing him up, Jesus continued talking to the increasingly hostile crowd. Finally, the four gave up trying to reason with the shouting crowd. As they turned toward the boat, the healed man begged to go with us. The crowd continued shouting, some demanding money, others that we leave and never come back.

I felt a tremendous sense of relief when the sail popped open to catch a nice breeze.

CHAPTER SIXTEEN

Bart and young James burst through the door. "There's an older lady and two men outside." James could hardly get the words out.

"Then she told us who she was," Bart added almost on top of James. "She's Jesus's mother."

James gestured with both hands. "I honestly didn't recognize her. She's aged a lot since Nathaniel's wedding. They're here to see Jesus. Bart pointed to the crowd filling the yard across the street and told them it would be impossible to get through all those people."

Mary glared at the two. "Well, where are they now?" Bart and James exchanged a guilty look. "You didn't leave them standing in the street?"

"We didn't know whether to bring them in here or wait till that crowd dwindled some," James called as the two headed for the door.

Mary called after them, "Bring them in here, then go push through the crowd and tell Jesus."

I called to Susanna, "Important guests are coming."

Moments later, Bart and James helped Jesus' mother, Mary, inside. Then they and the two brothers headed across the street.

Mary's stooped shoulders suggested a life of hard work. Deep lines in her face spoke of experiences I could only imagine. Gray hair peeked from beneath her head covering. She was a small, frail woman. A worried look hid behind her gentle smile.

James's mother apologized again for her son leaving them standing in the street. Finally, Mary introduced the rest of us. "Joanna and Susanna are helping me feed and take care of these men. Then there's Mary Magd—" Mary realized Jesus's mother simply wasn't interested.

Mary didn't say much. We decided to let her rest from the trip. I poured her a cup of tea while Susanna made her a comfortable place to sit. A rather awkward hour passed with the three of us trying to make light conversation. Nothing I said seemed to go anywhere. James's mother didn't fare much better. The longer we sat with nothing meaningful said, the slower time passed.

Jesus, his two brothers, the rest of the disciples, and, of course, Mary Magdalene, finally came crowding into the little house.

With Jesus finally present, the frail, sweet, elderly mother suddenly came to life. And not in the gentle way I expected. Her sudden wrath could have taken on the devil himself—and won. No one was left to wonder how she felt about waiting over an hour to see her own son.

She finished forcefully expressing her displeasure then sank onto a stool. I thought she was finished, but Mary raised herself erect and spoke in a strong, firm voice. "Jesus, you must quit preaching and come home immediately. Your life's in great danger." Big tears began to flow down her cheeks. "Herod Antipas has put your cousin John to death. He's dead ... beheaded!"

Mary's voice broke as she finished delivering the news. She sank into the seat, her hands covering her face and sobbed.

Shock spread across Jesus' face. Everyone, including the stoic Zealot, appeared stricken with paralysis.

My hand went over my mouth. My brain failed to produce a single intelligent word. Cuza's warning of Herodias being determined to do away with John the Baptist flooded my mind. My insides quivered.

The disciples gathered close around Jesus and his mother. But the opposite reaction struck me. I needed space to myself and moved into the kitchen. Somehow, we imagined John the Baptist too popular for Herod Antipas to kill. That assumption certainly has been proven wrong, very wrong. *What else could we be wrong about?*

My shock gradually evolved into a first-class case of resentment. All these years, I had placed my trust in the Roman-supported government. They always made us feel safe. I recalled how we celebrated Cuza's important assignment at Herod's palace. How could I have been so blind?

That flash of wrath grew to include Cuza. He must have known what was about to happen. *If being with Jesus is this dangerous, why hasn't he come for me? Had he now totally abandoned any feelings for me, or my safety? Being with Jesus has turned out to be a lot more dangerous, and seemingly more permanent than I ever imagined.*

In our after dinner gathering, the death of John the Baptist remained the focus. Most of the men vocalized their disbelief and sense of profound loss. The discussion finally moved on to the question of how to proceed, considering the now greatly increased danger. Though Jesus didn't mention my name, several times he referred to what I told him.

No one suggested retreating or even slowing down, for that matter. To my surprise, the whole episode appeared to strengthen the disciples' resolve. As they worked on strategy, even Simon Peter and James found a few areas to agree on. This came as a shock.

The plan that finally evolved would have Jesus staying in Capernaum safely out of sight. The twelve would take a week, traveling in pairs around the countryside proclaiming the coming Kingdom of God.

"This is your opportunity to become true apostles," Jesus told them, "I won't be with you forever, so it's time for you to go on your own." Jesus walked among the men. "You are to travel light, and don't take anything of comfort with you. Instead, rely upon the hospitality of each place you visit. Heal their sick, just like I do. You can do this if you believe in God's power. I will intercede with the Father on your behalf." Jesus sat back down with a twinkle in his eye and whispered to himself, "This ought to confuse Herod, the old fox."

"All this quiet is eating at my nerves." My shoulders shook as I surveyed the nearly empty room.

"Why are you whispering?" Susanna looked at me. "No one's here but us."

Jesus' brothers left shortly after the twelve went out on their Galilean mission. We had not seen much of Jesus either. When not out praying, Jesus spent long periods talking with his mother. Watching the two of them amazed me. After both expressed their initial displeasures, the air cleared and smiles returned. A loving family emerged from what looked to be a complete disaster. Mary wanted to stay on for a few more days, so the brothers promised to come back for her in a week.

While the twelve were gone, Jesus offered the blessing before each meal and prayed for each disciple by name. The connection Jesus held with his disciples became even more evident in their absence.

Finally, on the fourth day of her visit, I found myself alone with Jesus' mother. I couldn't let this opportunity slip by. I didn't entirely know how to phrase my inquiry—I felt a little awkward even asking. Since I couldn't devise a subtler inquiry, I just blurted, "Mary, when did you realize Jesus wasn't an ordinary son?"

"About nine months before his birth," Mary's matter of fact reply surprised me so much I didn't know how to proceed.

I stammered, "Please tell me the story."

Mary tilted her head a little to one side and looked at me. I sensed she wasn't sure she wanted to trust me with those details, but she finally nodded. "I was about sixteen at the time and betrothed to Joseph. Parents arranged Jewish marriages back then. Mine planned for me to marry Joseph sometime in the next year. I lived at home and didn't know him very well. But those were the customs." Mary took a little time to rearrange her cushion. "One day at the local well, I was drawing water for the family ..." She paused another long moment and looked me straight in the eye. "Joanna, have you ever met an angel, face-to-face?"

"W-well, no ..."

"Then this will probably be hard to understand, but here's what happened. Suddenly a tremendous presence—I don't know any other way of describing it—appeared with me in the well chamber. He resembled a man, but he radiated brilliant light."

Mary stopped. The thought occurred to me to close my gaping mouth.

"He spoke directly to me, 'You have found favor in the eyes of God.' Joanna, I was scared half to death."

Mary motioned with her hands. "My water pot lay in pieces at my feet. He could see me shaking and told me to not be afraid. I controlled my trembling enough to hear, 'God's Holy Spirit will come upon you, and God's power is going to overshadow you.'"

Mary furrowed her brow. "Despite my being scared speechless, the angel continued. He said 'God has decided to bless you. You will become pregnant and have a son. You are to name him Jesus. The baby born to you will be holy, and he will be called the Son of God.'

"I didn't know how to answer. The thought certainly didn't come from me, but I told the angel I would be obedient and do what God asked."

It was my turn to be speechless.

Mary continued. "In the same mysterious way the angel appeared, he was suddenly gone."

My words finally materialized. "This actually happened? What did you do?"

"I rushed home, minus the smashed water pot. As I opened the door, the reality of the situation slapped me in the face. 'Who's going to believe me?' Mother will be so upset over the water pot she won't hear a thing I say."

I tried to process Mary's dilemma. I couldn't even begin to imagine something like that happening.

"I couldn't tell whether Mother actually understood or was just treating me like a child with an overactive imagination," Mary continued. "She shrugged her shoulders like, 'well, if you say so.' That didn't help much. At least, she agreed not to tell Father about the water pot."

"How did you deal with something so unbelievable?"

"Oh, that soon was the least of my worries. My big concern became how to explain this to Joseph. A cold chill ran through me as all kinds of doubts swept over me. I even wondered, what if I'm not pregnant?"

"Goodness!" My mouth hung open again. "How did you tell him?"

"The question of whether I only imagined everything answered itself the very next morning." Mary chuckled. "Morning sickness swept over me like a wet slimy blanket. I lost food I never remembered eating." She wrinkled her nose. "As I crawled back to bed, I cried, 'if I've found favor in the eyes of God, why can't He do something about this morning sickness?'"

I laughed. I really didn't mean to, I just couldn't help myself.

"The following Sabbath, I tried talking to Joseph," Mary shook her head. "He became very angry. He didn't exactly accuse me of adultery, but he came awfully close. He shouted that the engagement was off and stomped out of the house. Talk about being devastated."

Mary laughed softly. "Oh, Joanna, the next week was the absolute worst week of my entire life. When I wasn't physically sick, I was crying over losing Joseph. Then the absolute worst thought hit me: Will I have to raise this baby without a father? What on earth had I agreed to?"

I wiped my eyes. "How much worse …?"

"Well, things did improve a little." Mary released a long breath. "The next Sabbath eve brought a knock on our door. An ashen-faced Joseph said we needed to talk. I wasn't so sure until Joseph told me about an unusual visitor in a dream that literally brought him to his knees. He promised to believe all he possibly could, but most importantly, Joseph asked if I would still be his wife."

A smile crept across my face to compliment my teary eyes.

Mary's lip quivered. "I fell to pieces. 'Yes', would hardly clear the lump in my throat.

"Joseph explained that under the circumstances there wouldn't be a big celebration. We would have a simple wedding when the addition to his family's home for us was complete."

"Oh, that's wonderful," I said.

"Well, not quite. Joseph's family seemed to take forever to build our addition. The jobs they were committed to certainly brought in needed money, so those jobs took Joseph and his father away from our important project. My pregnancy began to show. If we didn't move soon, I would be a disgrace to my family. So, I went to visit my cousin Elizabeth for a few months."

My emotions were rising and falling faster than I could handle. "Mary, now I want to cry for you."

"Oh, that pales in comparison to what happened when I returned home."

I looked at her, but couldn't say anything.

"In my sixth month, a Roman delegation came to announce the 'Registration'. Within the next three months, the firstborn son of every family had to return to his ancestral hometown to register."

My eyebrows furrowed.

"Oh, this wouldn't have been a big issue for most people, but not Joseph! He had to be from the tribe of Judah. His hometown was Bethlehem."

Mary noticed my quizzical expression. "Do you know where Bethlehem is?"

I shook my head.

"Bethlehem is another half-day's walk beyond Jerusalem! And you know how far Jerusalem is."

"You didn't undertake a journey that far so late in your pregnancy, did you?"

"Joseph would need to leave for Bethlehem before our addition was completed." Mary sighed. "Our dilemma was the baby could be born while he was gone."

Though obviously uncomfortable, Mary continued. "If it happened, the gossips were sure to spread rumors about my child being illegitimate and suggesting *that's why Joseph left*. Their vicious tongues have destroyed more than one person's reputation."

The twinkle returned to Mary's eyes. "I decided to go with him. I was young and strong ... I had no idea! By the afternoon of the second day, I literally couldn't put one foot in front of the other. Joseph had borrowed a burro to haul our lean-to and supplies for the trip. Hauling me too might kill the poor animal. But the time had come—I couldn't take another step."

"No."

"Oh, yes. Riding on a burro on top of our supplies, eight months pregnant—I wished desperately to feel some 'highly favored before God' right about then."

My sides hurt from laughing.

Mary held out her hand. "Oh—it gets worse."

"Couldn't possibly."

"Oh, it does! After four days, we reached Bethlehem late in the afternoon. A cold drizzly rain had set in. No one ever looked forward to a bath and a good bed more. But there wasn't a single room left at the only inn in town. Joseph spent an hour searching for other accommodations. Nothing was available anywhere."

"What on earth did you do?"

"We had two choices. We could leave the shelter of the stable, go to the edge of town and set up camp in the rain. Or we could find a dry corner there in the stable and wait for morning. That late on a rainy evening, the dry corner looked far more appealing."

"You didn't ..."

"Not only did we, but that's when Jesus made his entry into the world. Right there, that night. Thank goodness, the innkeeper's wife helped. Joseph wouldn't have had the slightest clue. Just as she finished cleaning and wrapping Jesus, some old shepherds came rushing into the stable. They reported how angels appeared and sent them to witness the birth of the Messiah. Joseph and I sat mystified and looked at each other."

"That is truly amazing!"

"Things did improve a little after that. The next day, Joseph found two of his uncles who still lived near Bethlehem. They pitched in and helped us get a little place to stay until the baby grew enough we could travel back to Nazareth. We planned to stay about two months."

"Well, I hoped you wouldn't start right back."

"Other things helped influence our decision as well," Mary continued. "Because of the census registration, people needed to travel. A lot of new building took place. Bethlehem had a shortage of skilled labor. Joseph's uncle desperately needed his carpentry talents. The two months we planned all too quickly turned into six months. Before we realized, six months stretched toward two years.

"Jesus began walking and jabbering like you wouldn't believe. And Joseph's relatives treated us with more love than we could imagine."

"Well, this has truly been amazing. It helps confirm what happened in Caesarea Philippi."

"Oh, what was that?"

"It was just …" I struggled to express the thought. "It wasn't a matter of not believing. It's just … beyond my ability to comprehend, too incredible to understand."

"What was?" Mary interrupted.

"Jesus asked the disciples what people were saying about him. After the usual answers about him being a great prophet, Jesus asked specifically who *they* thought he was. Simon Peter was the last one I expected, but he just blurted, 'You are the Messiah, the Son of the Living God.' Jesus confirmed his statement as coming to him from heaven. I've been struggling with what this means ever since."

Mary's look was difficult to interpret.

"Mary, I'm a simple woman who knows very little of our Jewish faith," I continued. "Sepphoris may be only an hour's walk from Nazareth, but in matters of religion, it's an eternity away. Worse still, my husband is a Roman official."

I paused to search how best to express my heart. "I keep asking myself, 'who am I to even be here? How could I be part of the ministry of the Son of God?' The thought is simply too incredible."

"Joanna." Mary's eyes filled with understanding. "Perhaps it's for the same reason God chose a poor peasant girl like me to bear the Son of God."

My eyes overflowed with joy. My heart felt light. I started to get up.

"Don't you want to hear the rest of the story?"

"There's more?"

"Oh, yes, lots more," Mary replied with a big smile. "Like I said, a year and a half had passed. Then one afternoon the strangest procession showed up at our door. There were a dozen camels carrying supplies, servants, and these richly robed gentlemen. They announced their desire to see the one 'born King of the Jews'.

"Joseph and I looked at each other. We assured them they must have the wrong house, but to no avail. They informed us they had seen his star and traveled all the way from Persia to worship him."

Mary's eyes sparkled. "The men came into the house, set up an elaborate altar, burned incense and then bowed their faces to the floor. Tears filled their eyes as they arose from their ceremony saying, 'We have truly seen God's gift.' The presents they gave Jesus were very expensive. I still have them hidden away at home." Mary's voice grew somber. "The men from Persia warned us, 'King Herod is a wicked man. Be fearful of him.' We had not given so much as a thought of King Herod. What interest could he possibly have in peasants like us?"

Mary took a sip of tea then took time rearranging her robe. "That night Joseph awoke from a bizarre dream. He said an angel appeared and warned us to flee the area, that King Herod considered Jesus a threat and planned to kill him.

"I assured Joseph his dream probably occurred because of our guests' warnings. But Joseph said his encounter had been way too vivid. He instructed me to start packing while he went to his uncles and explained. By noon we were heading south—away from Jerusalem."

"Even further from home?"

"We certainly didn't want to go toward Jerusalem. We traveled into Egypt, made our way east across the wilderness and located the road to Jericho. In taking our time with the young child and staying away from large towns, the trip home took nearly two weeks."

"Two weeks? I can't imagine camping with Marcus for even two nights."

Mary continued. "Our families in Nazareth were thrilled to see us after a nearly two-year absence. Joseph's father had long ago finished our addition onto the family home, so we finally had a place to live."

Mary's smile disappeared. "We had hardly settled in when the terrible news arrived. The day after we left, King Herod's troops came to Bethlehem. They killed every boy child under two years of age."

CHAPTER SEVENTEEN

The fragrance of the wood fire and honey-barley cakes baking filled the room. It was Mary's idea to make the place even more welcoming for the returning men.

With the disciples away on their mission journey, and Jesus's mother and brothers having returned to Nazareth, this left us four women in the house. Jesus wisely spent most of his time praying. Even if he didn't need that much praying, it would still be better than listening to the endless chatter of four women.

Hardly ten minutes passed after taking my fresh honey-barley cakes from the oven, than the front door swung open. James and John walked in. John's huge grin covered his whole face. "Hi. We're home."

"Where're Jesus and the rest of the men?" older James asked without the slightest indication of emotion.

"Congratulations," I replied. "You're the first ones back." Then I added as casually as I could, "As far as Jesus, I'm sure he's out praying you'll be able to find your way home." My smile converted the excellent jab into joking banter. James cracked the slightest grin. Grudgingly, but it was a grin.

"I could eat every one of these." John drew in a deep breath as he picked up two of my still warm barley cakes. A sour look crossed his face. "Who made these?"

"They're that bad?" Deep down, I felt John was kidding; however, I wasn't completely sure. "They're better than they used to be, aren't they?"

He picked up two more and tossed one to James.

Barely a quarter hour passed, when the door swung open again. This time Philip and younger James strolled in. Mary had eyes only for one person. "How did it go, son?"

"Oh, Mother, you wouldn't believe." Younger James wore a broad smile. "I've just experienced the most unusual week of—"

"Tell her about healing the crippled boy," Philip interrupted.

"I actually healed him! Just like Jesus, I asked the youngster if he really wanted to walk again. I told him if he would believe in Jesus and believe a miracle could happen, he would be healed. Mother, he put down his crutch and slowly began to walk. To tell the truth, I was as amazed as his parents."

James hardly finished when the door swung open a third time. Bart followed Thad in. They too shared several great stories. The remainder of my barley cakes disappeared as the rest of the men came through on their way to find Jesus. Somebody must have liked them, at least a little.

Jesus concluded in our after-dinner time, "We need a whole,

uninterrupted day for you to share your experiences, both with me and with each other."

"What about taking the boat to a secluded place on the other side of the lake?" Simon Peter quickly suggested.

I cringed.

Older James shook his head. "The places you've picked so far haven't turned out to be very secluded."

"We had a storm to deal with, remember?" Peter shot back.

"And the time before—?"

"I think Simon will find a suitable place," Jesus interrupted.

Just the thought of another storm … *I never want to go through anything close to that last episode, ever again.*

The early sun struggled against a damp dawn. I handed Susanna the last cooking pot to pack on the boat. "The coolness in the air reminds me it isn't the middle of summer any longer. It's hard to believe I've been with Jesus four months."

"Does that make you worry whether Cuza will ever come for you?"

"Not until you mentioned it." I gave Susanna a reassuring smile despite the knot I felt in my stomach. "Not a day goes by without my thinking about him."

Since Susanna first learned of my heartbreaking departure and my intense desire to see Marcus again, she'd displayed real, heartfelt concern.

"This has been the most wonderful four months of my life," I confided, "but I've pretty much conceded that Cuza isn't going to come. As much as I hate giving up and admitting failure, I'm afraid

I will have to. If I don't go home soon, I may never be able to." My shoulders shook. "I wince at the thought of walking back into that environment."

The rest of loading the boat dissolved into a dream walk as my mind produced different scenarios of stepping back into my home. None appeared even remotely pleasant.

"Everyone who is going, get on board." Simon Peter's call yanked me back to reality.

As we were assisted aboard, my thoughts turned to survival. "Andrew, you aren't going to let another storm come up, are you?"

"I'll try not to, little lady." With a twinkle in his eye, Andrew added, "But you can never be sure."

The last of the fog burned off the lake, and fresh sea air took its place. I leaned back and relaxed, but carefully maintained eye contact with the distant shoreline.

Within a few hours, a secluded stretch of shore loomed not far ahead. I called to Andrew, "This trip sure hasn't taken long. How did we get here so quickly?"

Simon Peter aimed the boat directly toward a sandy stretch of beach and called to Andrew, "Drop the sail."

"You didn't notice the strong west wind because it carried us along with it." Andrew began pulling in the sail. "The wind's been fantastic today—for sailing east."

Andrew finished securing the sail, then added, "But I sure hope it changes before we need to start back."

I scanned both directions. There wasn't a town, or anything for that matter, anywhere within sight. "Well, if you wanted to find 'nowhere', I think you found it this time," I complimented Peter. We began hauling our stuff off the boat.

About noon, I called to the men, "Food's hot, come and enjoy." It always amazed me how much more the men could eat when out camping or on the lake. Fresh air and time on the water seemed to double their usual voracious appetites.

Even after they finished eating, Mary caught a couple men digging through our few remaining supplies. "Thad, James, get out of there!" Mary may appear sweet and humble, but if you mess with her kitchen it's like messing with a mother bear.

"Visitors coming." The Zealot spoke to Jesus in his low whispered voice.

"Where do you see anyone?" Older James strained looking up and down the coast. "How come you always see things the rest of us can't?"

Simon put one hand on James's shoulder; he pointed up and slightly inland. "Look. A hundred or more coming this way."

Thad, standing five inches above everyone, shouted, "Yes, I see them. And there's more behind them."

"It will be at least an hour before they arrive," Jesus said. "Let's spend the time wisely." He motioned them back to their circle.

As sure as fish live in the sea, an hour later a hoard invaded our campsite. The disciples hustled mightily to get them settled down at the water's edge.

After they somewhat contained the crowd, Philip walked over. "Where in the world did all these people come from? Must be close to a thousand." He shook his head. "There isn't a town with this many people anywhere near."

"Suppose they recognize the sail on Simon Peter's boat and know it's Jesus?" younger James asked. "Only thing I can think of."

Jesus strode down to the edge of the lake in front of the huge crowd. He expressed his amazement at their coming out to that desolate spot. As usual, he began telling a story.

"A man had two sons." Jesus stretched both hands toward the crowd. "The younger son said to his father, 'Father, why should I have to wait until you die to get my inheritance. I want it while I'm still young enough to enjoy it.'"

Jesus continued telling the story and then of the son's joyful return and of God's love. Jesus' teaching never failed to thrill me. As he talked, time seemed to stand still.

Jesus finished teaching as old and young, men and women surged forward, clamoring to be healed. Hundreds got in line. The lame walked again, crippled people recovered use of their limbs, blind regained their sight. Tears of gladness filled my eyes as people jumped for joy and shouted praises to God. Heaven surely smiled that day.

The sun slid closer to the western hills. An exhausted Philip staggered over to rest a moment. I nodded toward the huge crowd. "Old Herod Antipas would have a heart attack if he could see what's happening here."

"Would he ever!" Philip replied. Then he spoke to younger James as he walked up. "Let's urge Jesus to send these people on their way. It's going to be evening soon and it's a long way to find something to eat."

"You'd sure better." I spoke up instead of James. "We need to get home. We only planned food for the one meal."

Philip and James walked over to Jesus. Heads nodded. A surprised look crossed Philip's face. Hesitantly they trudged back. "Jesus told us … that we … we need to feed them." This was the first time I ever remembered Philip stumbling over words. "Jesus said we need to feed them before we send them on their way."

"That's impossible!" My eyebrows furrowed. "We couldn't come up with …"

Mary added, "Go back and tell Jesus we have hardly any bread or fish left."

Their trip to Jesus and back didn't take very long. Philip shook his head. "Jesus said to bring what we have."

Andrew motioned to Philip. "This young fellow overheard you. He's offering his basket if it will help."

"This is going to be awfully embarrassing," I whispered to myself.

"Seat the people in groups of fifty or so," Jesus told the disciples. We placed the boy's food along with the pitiful amount we had left on a small blanket and placed it in front of Jesus. I felt embarrassed, secretly wishing some place to hide.

Jesus lifted his eyes toward heaven and blessed that pitiful amount of food. He began breaking those few loaves and passing them to the disciples to distribute to the crowd. Jesus broke them, then broke them some more … and broke them some more. He continued for what seemed an hour, breaking those same loves and distributing the same fish. All twelve disciples kept a steady stream taking more food to the crowd.

Again, this could not be possible, but it was happening as naturally as waves lap the shore. With the crowd fed and beginning to leave, Jesus called Simon Peter over. "We can't leave a mess like this. Food scraps are everywhere. Get the men to gather it all in a pile near the water's edge. The fish will enjoy it." My mouth dropped. The leftover scraps made a pile higher than a man's head.

I needed some time to process what I had just seen happened, but unfortunately the sun began bathing the crest of the western hills. Even though people continuing milling about, Mary decided we needed to gather the cooking supplies and load them on the boat.

Andrew strolled over. "Even if we left right now …"

Jesus interrupted Andrew, "With the wind blowing as it is, I want you to load everyone on board and start toward home." Jesus turned and started back, then spoke to the rest of us, "I will help these people on their way, then I'll need some time to pray."

"We're not leaving you here," James argued. "How are you going to get home?" Simon Peter, then others also voiced strong objections. But Jesus insisted we start back.

I started to express my opinion, but Mary Magdalene shouted over me, "I'm not going anywhere without Jesus." She crossed her arms and stood defiant.

A couple of men helped the three of us women on board. Then the rest of them were required to physically pick up Mary Magdalene and carry her to the boat.

Simon Peter and Andrew climbed aboard, quickly dug out several ropes, secured them to the bulkhead, and threw the long ends over the side. "You'll need to push the boat a lot further out because the wind's blowing directly toward the shore," Andrew explained to the men. "Get us out into chest-deep water, then use the ropes to climb aboard."

"Heave!" Simon Peter called. Hardly had the boat begun to move when a head appeared at the top of the rail. Judas had done his part. Matthew crawled in right behind him. The rest tugged and shoved and finally pushed the boat far enough out for Andrew to open the sail and Simon Peter to point our craft down the coast. Eight soaking wet men scrambled aboard. We secured everything for a difficult sail home.

There was no rain, but the strong wind came from the exact direction of home. This forced us to sail along the shore. Then Peter and Andrew sharply turned the boat in the opposite direction. Each pass up and down the lake took us a little further from where we had been. To make matters even worse, heavy clouds swept in low and darkness descended like a wet blanket. How Peter knew which way to sail was beyond me.

Dark clouds continued to mask the nearly full moon. Hours seemed to pass as we sailed up then down the lake. As heavy clouds rolled over, I could hardly see the others. When the clouds broke for a moment, my eyes didn't have time to adjust. The moon's sudden bright glow would cast a ghostly pale across each face. Mary Magdalene's sobs added to the eeriness of the evening.

Simon Peter's boat wasn't large. With sixteen on board and all our supplies, there wasn't much room left. But the cool lake air, blowing so hard, drove us to huddle even closer. Certainly no one slept. "How late is it?" I wondered aloud to anyone.

Philip's voice came back in the pitch dark, "Judging from the last time I saw the moon, it must be nearly midnight."

A sliver opened in the cloud cover and the pale white face of younger James startled me. While my heart was still in my throat, a cry of pure terror came from the rear, "Oh Lord, save me!"

I jumped, then turned to see Simon Peter at the helm with look of fear covering his face. My eyes swept toward Andrew. His mouth hung open as he pointed. I searched with the others in the indicated direction. Something glowed out on the lake in the sudden moonlight. As quickly as it appeared, darkness again enveloped us.

Long moments dragged in total darkness. The only sounds were of the wind and waves. The clouds broke again, and the white, eerie, glowing shape reappeared in the distance, yet closer. As quickly as I saw it, total blackness swept in and over us again. The blood in my body felt colder than even the chill of the wind. "I don't like this!" I whimpered.

Mary Magdalene suddenly jumped to the rail. "It's Jesus! He's coming to save us. I knew he would."

In the dark, a voice growled, "I wish somebody would knock some sense into that woman."

The darkness enveloped us for long, agonizing moments before another ray of moonlight broke through. There, not two hundred feet from the boat, the ghostly form reappeared. It was Jesus!

As he approached, he called, "Don't be afraid, it's only me."

"It's only me." I repeated through my joyful tears. Like taking a casual stroll on the sandy beach, Jesus walked *on top of the water*.

Never, in all my life, will I understand what Simon Peter did next. He called to Jesus, "If it's really you, Lord, tell me to come to you on the water."

As I urged Jesus to come get in the boat, Jesus called back to Peter, "Come on." He acted as though it were nothing.

With the wind howling and the waves crashing against the boat, Simon Peter let go of the helm, tossed his outer robe to Andrew and climbed over the side. Ever so tenuously, he began walking toward Jesus—on top of the water. Despite the stupidity of his action, we all broke out cheering him on.

Peter turned and, with a silly grin, waved to us. Then he turned back, but his gaze froze on a huge wave coming directly toward him.

"Oh, no!" I cried.

Andrew shouted, "He's sinking! Throw him a line."

Just as his head went under, Jesus grabbed Peter's one arm still above the water. Effortlessly, he pulled Peter onto the surface again. Jesus put his arm on Simon Peter's shoulder, and together they walked toward the boat.

We were again in total awe. But Jesus would have none of our praises; instead he told Peter, "Let's head home."

CHAPTER EIGHTEEN

The previous night's windstorm produced an additional chilling effect. Hot summer days were gone. The abrupt coolness sparked a sudden anxiety to twist my insides. A great deal more time had elapsed since leaving my home than I, in my wildest imagination, ever intended. I had to decide—and soon. But oh, the dilemma.

Being with Jesus, Mary, and the disciples had become absolutely the most wonderful, exciting, and fulfilling time of my entire life. Just the thought of leaving them left my insides quivering. At the same time, the image of my little Marcus hovered in my mind. I had been gone far too long. Oh, how I wanted to see him and hold him in my arms. But each time I entertained the thought of returning, the awful confrontation of the days preceding my departure flooded through like waves from a violent lake storm.

Jesus' teaching rolled across my mind. 'Unless a man is willing to leave his mother and father and truly follow me, he isn't worthy of me.' Would I be unfaithful to Jesus if I left? Jesus certainly wouldn't have me forsake my child, would he? I felt pulled apart in both directions.

I had been so sure that when Cuza read my note he would see the error in his attitude and come for me. I even envisioned him begging me to return home. Was I ever wrong about that. *Has Cuza written me off? Has he simply gone on with his life?*

"I'll talk to Jesus," I said aloud. "He'll understand and tell me what I should do."

Our time together that evening seemed to be winding to a close. I reached down deeply within myself and summoned the courage. Just as I confirmed my decision, Jesus made one more comment. "I will be taking James, John, and Simon Peter on a short trip tomorrow. There will be no need to take camping equipment. We shouldn't be away more than three days so we'll travel light."

A barrage of questions followed. With that, my plans for a quiet discussion with Jesus evaporated.

Early the next morning the small group set off. An awful, sinking feeling swept over me as I watched Jesus and the three disappear down the street. My heart followed them long after they passed from sight.

I wasn't the only one at loose ends. No one seemed to know quite what to do with Jesus gone. Disciples strolled in, milled around and strolled back out. We all seemed a rather helpless bunch.

The next morning Mary Magdalene bopped into the room. "We're going shopping," she announced in a cheerful voice. "Mary, Susanna, and I."

"We're taking James with us," Mary added as she pulled her shawl around her shoulders. "We'd love for you to come along."

"Oh, no. Four is quite enough." I put my cleaning cloth down and admired the group. "Go on and enjoy yourselves. I'll keep things under control here."

Younger James rolled his eyes.

Seeing Mary Magdalene going with Mary thrilled my heart. So often they seemed at odds with each other. Perhaps this time together would help. I finished putting away things from our breakfast.

Startled, I jumped.

"Sorry, Joanna, I didn't mean to surprise you. Are you okay?"

"No, Judas. Give my heart a minute to settle down. I didn't hear anyone come in."

Being alone with Judas shouldn't make me uncomfortable, but suddenly I was. Maybe his leaning close caused the tingling on the back of my neck.

Judas had given a great first impression. He seemed a little more sophisticated than the rest. But as time passed, he struck me as someone who thought himself entitled to special considerations. He made a point of dressing better but doing as little work as possible. Judas seldom missed an opportunity to remind everyone he came from Jerusalem. But his comment to Matthew, 'Jesus is my ticket to somewhere important,' bothered me the most.

"I just didn't realize you came in the room." I continued to settle down from my initial fright.

"Joanna, you're not like the rest of them." Judas leaned a little closer.

The back of my neck stiffened. "Oh, how is that?"

I faked putting pots away to unobtrusively move a little further from him.

"Your hair, for one thing." He closed the distance. "It's grown out some now, but I can tell it has been cut … and quite nicely, I might add."

He was correct on that point. I still missed having my hair cut. "Oh, where I come from, most women have their hair cut." *Uh-oh, I shouldn't have said that. Now he'll want to know where I'm from.* I tried to open the distance between us, but the extra space kept disappearing and at an alarming rate.

"Then I've watched the way you wear your shawl when we're in public." Judas faked a smile. "You aren't used to wearing one. You use the cloth more to hide behind than cover your head."

I blushed. He had been watching me more thoroughly than I realized. My discomfort level rose—from both the direction of the conversation and the direction Judas kept moving. I had run out of back-up space. *He has more on his mind than complimenting my hair.*

"You're sophisticated, you know the importance of power and culture and that impresses me, Joanna." Judas's smile hid something sinister. "You're like me, you really don't belong among these fish-catchers."

I needed to change the subject or go into full panic mode.

"Well, Judas, since you're not a peasant like the others, why are you one of Jesus's disciples? Especially if you don't really belong here."

"Joanna, Jesus is going somewhere … somewhere really big. I feel it. I know it. When he does, I'm going to be a part of it." Judas paused. His eyes narrowed, "After all I have been through, I deserve having something come my way."

I grasped at the straw. "Oh, and what have you been through?"

"You don't know how the Romans came to us in Jerusalem and demanded our shop space for another outpost."

Anger floated in his eyes. "I found out, all too late, that my partner had cut a secret deal with the Romans. He received a fair sum for our shop, and I got nothing. Abner disappeared, and the Romans took possession of what had been our clothing business."

"Oh, I'm sorry. But what does that have to do with Jesus?"

"Nothing, unless I become part of the new Jewish government. Then watch out, Abner."

Sudden as a striking snake, his hand clenched my wrist. "We can go places, you and I, Joanna."

I struggled to free my arm, but to no avail. I didn't want to scream, but I was getting very close.

"Release her. Now." The low hard voice hit like a Roman spike striking pavement. I couldn't see the voice, but I recognized it immediately. With what seemed a single leap, the Zealot landed at Judas's side.

Judas threw up his hands in an attempted show of innocence. "Listen, we were simply having a friendly conversation."

"You make advances toward Joanna—any of the women—ever again and I'll cut you in little pieces and feed you to the fish. Even Jesus won't find you." The look in Simon's eyes made abundantly clear he would do exactly what he said.

The quiver in Judas's voice gave the distinct impression he received the message. With a look of fear, he moved toward the door. Then he stopped. Now out of immediate danger, he straightened his clothes, tilted his head up and walked out like he owned the world.

My legs turned soft. I struggled for a stool. "Thank you, Simon! From the bottom of my heart."

To think, I first imagined Simon as one to fear and Judas as the charming individual. How could I have been so wrong?

"Women will be safe. I make sure." Simon didn't use many words, but the few he did were more than adequate.

"Since nothing 'really' happened, I don't think it's necessary to bother Jesus with the matter." I brushed at the back of my hair trying to slow my racing heart. "And I sincerely don't think I'll need to worry about Judas … as long as you're around."

Simon picked up one of my barley cakes from the dish on the counter. "If that is your wish." He nodded and walked toward the door.

"At least you like my barley cakes," I called behind him.

Simon raised one eyebrow but made no reply as he stepped out the door.

Mary, James, Susanna, and Mary Magdalene walked in and each sat their basket on the counter. Susanna and Mary Magdalene continued to their room without saying a word. James didn't speak either. He turned and strolled back outside. Mary sat down and propped her chin in the cups of her hands.

"Things didn't go well?"

"I tried to explain to Mary Magdalene how the men are Jesus's disciples and we are the helpers," Mary mumbled. "She considers herself one of the men."

"Oh?" I replied. "And you really expected to convince her otherwise?"

Mary shook her head and motioned me to sit. She leaned over. "I get the distinct impression Mary Magdalene imagines Jesus is going to fall in love with her and make her his bride."

I nearly fell over. This had to be the first gossip Mary ever uttered in her entire life. "Oh, Mary, I wouldn't put it quite that strongly."

I sat back. "Older James will make it his life's work to keep ample space between Mary Magdalene and Jesus."

I wouldn't admit it aloud, but Mary was probably more right than she imagined.

"What's the commotion?" I straightened up, startled.

We both hurried to the door.

"Oh my, it's Jesus!" I exclaimed. "Look at the crowd following him."

The big discussion after dinner centered on where Jesus and the three disciples went and what they did for three days. Everyone pressured them for details.

Simon Peter would only say, "We went up on this mountain to pray, and we saw things I couldn't explain."

"I wanted to stay there," John added to the already vague answers. "But we were sure glad to get home."

James was as tight-lipped as I had ever seen him. Even Jesus evaded our questions. John shrugged his shoulders. "We did hear some rather depressing talk in one village on our way home."

"I thought you holy men weren't supposed to engage in gossip." Thomas laughed. "Isn't that what old women do?"

"It wasn't gossip." James' voice was stern. "It's what really happened to John the Baptist." Several laughed at James for failing to catch the jest in Thomas' comment. James's face rivaled a summer sunset.

"You fellows need to hear this." John spoke up. "The palace tried to keep it quiet, but the word's leaked out. It all happened at Herod's big birthday party."

Suddenly the rest of the disciples realized the seriousness of the issue. Quiet descended like a morning fog.

John continued. "You know Herod Antipas. His birthday could only be a wild, lavish affair."

While listening, I could hear Cuza complaining weeks in advance about the mountain of details for such a party. He wouldn't let it be done any way but right.

John gestured with both hands. "Herodias' daughter Salome did a dance for Herod. It must have been something spectacular, because it totally pleased the crowd. Herod, who probably had too much to drink, told her she could have anything she wanted, so Salome ran to her mother."

John stopped. Dead quiet filled the room. He cleared the emotion in his throat. "When she returned, she asked … for the head of John the Baptist on a silver platter."

I gasped. My supper wanted to reverse course. I gazed around at the others. Thomas looked stunned. Shock filled Andrew's eyes. He bit his lower lip.

"Since he promised Salome in front of all his guests," John ever so slowly continued, "Herod apparently felt he must comply. The guards returned with John's head on a silver platter."

My hands trembled as I tried in vain to regain my composure.

"We heard that most of the guests were horrified." John forced himself to continue. "They tried to act lighthearted and continue the party."

Realizing what Cuza surely went through at that moment hit me next. He would have been mortified.

One by one, the group gradually shifted their eyes toward Jesus. He slowly rose to his feet. "Remember what I told you when we first learned of his death? Among those born to women, there has never been a greater prophet than John the Baptist."

Jesus picked up his heavier outer cloak. "So, listen carefully to what I'm about to tell you. I am also going to be betrayed to the religious leaders who desperately want to put me to death."

With my senses already overloaded from the news of John the Baptist, I couldn't react to what Jesus just said. Bewilderment also spread across most of the disciples' faces.

Philip hesitantly spoke, "Master, who—"

Jesus gently interrupted the question by extending his hand. "I need time to pray right now." Spreading his cloak over his shoulders, he left.

Philip tried to shake the puzzled look from his face as he walked over to Thomas and Andrew. "We've been afraid of Herod Antipas. Did I hear Jesus right? Did he say, religious leaders?"

"The Pharisees may be hypocritical and overzealous," Andrew shook his head. "But I have a hard time believing they could … actually murder someone."

"What did he mean, 'betrayed?' Thomas added.

My hand quivered as I raised it to ask, "One of you must convince Jesus to tell us what he means by that."

Thomas looked around. "Who's going to ask him?" No hands went up.

The emotion of the evening had taken its toll. "You'll have to figure this out." I stood. "I can't handle any more, I'm going to bed."

The emotional swings had me exhausted, but inner turmoil kept me from sleeping. The more I turned in that little bed, the more vivid the picture grew of Cuza at Herod's palace witnessing John the Baptist's head being brought in. Yes, I was angry at him for not coming for me, but perhaps assuming he had forsaken me was still premature. He couldn't have known in advance of Herod's promise to Salome.

Despite our months of awful disagreements, I still cared for Cuza. I hurt with him for what he surely went through. Deep down, I also knew Cuza still needed me.

Enough time had passed for Cuza to act. I promised myself I would talk with Jesus tomorrow about returning home.

But the situation at home, how would I deal with it? *I guess I'll just have to figure that out when I get there.*

CHAPTER NINETEEN

The sky cast a pale blue glow on the street stretching before me. The stone house looked expensive and strangely familiar, yet different from anywhere I could remember. Nothing appeared quite right.

I felt drawn toward the house. Yet when I tried stepping forward, my feet seemed clad in lead shackles. Struggling with all my might produced only inches of movement.

The eeriness sent a coldness like frigid winter rain flowing through my veins. Shivering, I pulled my thin silk garment closer around me. How could I have on my favorite summer dress? It was back home in Sepphoris.

My stomach, sensing something terribly wrong, began to gnaw and twist. My mouth was desert dry.

As I stood there wondering, the front wall of the house began crumbling away. Little by little, chunks fell then disappeared. As they did, a sudden realization swept over me. "This is my house!"

My startled expression generated no audible sound. There I stood in front of my home in Sepphoris, looking through the front—as though inside.

I tried yelling, "Hello, Hello," but my words sounded more like a dying croak. Clearing my throat, I tried calling quietly, "Hello." The results were the same. "Cuza, are you here? Marcus, can you hear me?" The same low dry croak.

I'll go find them. Yet the heavy sandals held me to only inches of progress.

I became aware of distant music. An elegantly dressed woman entered the main living area, completely oblivious the front of the house no longer existed. Why was she in my house? As she placed a vase of flowers on the table, she looked directly toward me but gave no expression of recognition. Rachael! Why was Cuza's sister here?

Others came in who looked strangely familiar but whom I couldn't quite identify. Smiling and laughing, they visited among themselves. Everyone's clothing looked as if they were attending a big party or … a wedding? No, that can't be.

Panic struck my heart. Cuza couldn't be getting married. My head began to sway as a cold sickness swept up within me. I called to the group, "I'm here, wait, listen to me." But my cry produced no response.

Cuza walked through the door in his full-dress uniform, looking magnificent. My heart sank even further. Everyone in the room turned toward the handsome figure and applauded. He gave a slight bow to the group. As if on cue, a young boy ran into the room and grabbed Cuza's hand. He looked to be five or six. He turned directly toward me, but he did not respond to my presence in the least. This child looked so much like Marcus, only older.

What is happening?

Then she appeared. She looked strangely like Rebecca, my childhood friend, but also like Mariam, the hated housekeeper. How could she look so much like both? Who was this woman?

Her identity might be a question, but the events about to take place were not. Her attire could only be fit for a wedding. This must be stopped. I'm still here, still alive, still Cuza's wife. I tried to call out as I threw myself against invisible chains. My feet failed to budge, my dry throat delivered only a raspy cry.

I awoke with my heart racing out of my chest. My aching legs would hardly respond. I crawled out of my small bed and clung to its side for the longest time. Could this really happen?

My whole body shook. Rubbing my arms, I stood and gazed out the little window. Rays from the moon glistened across the ripples on the Sea of Galilee. That sight always brought comfort to my troubled heart, yet that night fear continued to grip my insides. I was too frightened to close my eyes again. Finally, I lay back down and anxiously awaited the comfort of dawn. I awoke again to the low-morning sun sending a shallow beam playing across the ceiling.

The vividness of that dream sent shivers crawling through my spine, haunting me. I couldn't even contemplate the thought of going home, let alone talk to anyone about it.

Those awful images slowly began to fade throughout the day. Mary, Susanna, and I, as usual, found our hands full taking care of a bunch of always-hungry men. Of course, Mary Magdalene had her hands full—trying to circumvent James to get closer to Jesus.

During our evening time together, Jesus explained that under these present and more dangerous circumstances, he wanted to utilize those who followed and helped when they could. A good-sized group of around seventy or so men had become dependable followers. Jesus said, "I want to send them out in all directions for four days. They will announce the coming Year of the Lord. With so many spreading the word that I will be coming, the authorities will have no idea where to look."

Excitement filled Jesus' voice. "When they return, we will set out on our tour of Galilee. We will first go north, then west, around to the south, and finally on to Jerusalem in time for the Festival of Lights. This will, of course, take us through Samaria."

An audible groan arose from several men.

After the meeting broke, I tugged Philip's sleeve. "Talk to me. I thought younger James and the Zealot did a wonderful job of keeping us away from Roman patrols on the last trip. Why all the groans?"

"Oh, it isn't about the patrols." Philip tilted his head to one side. "It's going through Samaria."

"That's my second question. What is this place called Samaria?"

"First, Joanna, Samaria isn't exactly a place." Philip looked a bit more serious. "It's an area where people called Samaritans live. Since Jews and Samaritans don't get along, we usually avoid going there."

"I can't imagine you not getting along with anyone." I gave Philip my best smile. "Tell me the story."

"Okay. Back about seven hundred years ago, the king of Babylon conquered many countries, including Israel," Philip began. "He took the best and brightest leaders from the conquered countries to Babylon. This left behind those who weren't very important. Soon, these remaining Jews began to marry the foreigners who came in."

I had a strong urge to ask if that was like now, with so many of us marrying the Romans. Instead, I nodded for Philip to continue.

"Years later, a new king came to power who realized the calamity this policy caused." Philip gestured with both hands. "Thousands of exiles, practically a whole new generation, were allowed to return here to Israel."

I sat up straight. "So, the people left behind who intermarried with the foreigners, were their children still Jewish?"

"That's exactly the point, Joanna," Philip continued. "A great animosity developed between the 'real' Jews and the 'part' Jews. Those 'part' Jews congregated in the ancient province of Samaria. That's why they're called Samaritans."

Jesus and the disciples had quite a challenge to organize seventy men into pairs and map out thirty or so routes. But, they finally completed their preparations, and Jesus gave a compelling send-off.

Within minutes after the yard emptied, Jesus turned to us. "In four days, they'll be back. We'll need to be ready for our journey through Galilee and on to Jerusalem."

The twelve followed Jesus toward the lake.

"We need to begin getting food together for the trip." Mary stood and stretched. "I'll get things ready for us to go to market."

"Shouldn't we wait nearer the time?" Susanna furrowed her eyebrows as she looked up at Mary. "It's four days until we leave."

"Well, I have to do something. I can't just stand here."

The three of us looked back and forth at each other. "She's something else," I said and sat back down and we talked a while longer. Suddenly, I realized I was having a normal conversation with Mary Magdalene.

Mary burst back out the door. "Where have you moved the money?" Her panic-stricken eyes pleaded for an answer.

CHAPTER TWENTY

"The money isn't where I always keep it." Panic filled Mary's voice. "I've looked everywhere. It's not there."

"We'll help you look," I called. Susanna and I jumped to our feet.

Mary showed us the well-hidden basket where she kept the moneybag. For half an hour, we literally tore that little kitchen apart. We looked in every jar, every basket, and every conceivable place money could possibly be hidden. The money simply wasn't there. Mary shook. I tried comforting her as big tears ran down her cheeks.

Mary Magdalene clasped Susanna's arm. "We need to go find Jesus and tell him what's happened." Not waiting for an answer, she tugged Susanna toward the lake. Mary crashed to a seat, her head in her hands, sobbing.

"Our money's gone," Mary explained to Jesus. Tears streamed down her face.

"Well, if I kept the purse—" Judas puffed out what little chest he had, "the money would always be safe. I don't lose money."

I gave Judas an angry glare. Of course, he ignored me and went on telling Jesus how he should be the one responsible for the purse. Since he had been a businessman, he knew how to take care of money.

Had Mary not already felt devastated, Judas's crude comments would certainly have accomplished that task. Instead, she did a beautiful job of not overreacting.

In our after-dinner time, Jesus made only a brief mention of the lost money, which we needed to do the shopping. Mary whispered to me she was weary from the day's ordeal and retired to her room.

Matthew offered to make an additional contribution, but after being on several shopping excursions, I knew his donation wouldn't last long. Exhausted from the day's emotions, I also decided to turn in before the men left.

No matter how large the problems, with Jesus around, each morning seemed like a new beginning. The cool fall air, the whitecaps flickering the morning sun across the Sea of Galilee, and Jesus' reassurance his Heavenly Father would provide, helped us to smile again, if only slightly.

"The seventy will be back tomorrow, and we still haven't completed our shopping." Mary walked toward the kitchen with a rather determined look. "Let's get what we can with the money Matthew gave." Mary climbed up and began dragging baskets off the top shelf.

"What is this?" she exclaimed, climbing back down. Secure in the second basket lay a familiar bag. Ever so slowly, Mary pulled open the strings. The missing money smiled back at her.

I looked over her shoulder. "It can't be. We tore this kitchen apart. I looked in every basket myself, at least twice. This bag wasn't there."

Tears rose in Mary's eyes as she tenderly clutched the bag. "It's a miracle." A huge smile crept across her face.

"I'm not so sure it's a miracle." I shook my head. "Looks more like a guilt-laced thief returned the money."

Soon after we returned from market, Jesus and the men came in. Excitedly, we related the good news. Jesus smiled at our report. Judas placed both hands on his hips and cocked his head to the left. "If I'd been keeping the money, it would never have been misplaced to begin with."

Misplaced? Had Jesus not been standing there, I would have told Judas what I really thought of him. I just seethed and kept my mouth shut. Apparently, keeping the purse is what Judas wanted all along. Judas being responsible for our funds closely resembled asking a wolf to guard the sheep pen.

The seventy men Jesus had sent out trickled in throughout the day. They reported all kinds of miracles and many wonderful events.

As the last departed, Jesus spoke to us. "Hopefully, this will have spread our message—and completely confused old Antipas. Tomorrow, we'll leave on our tour through Galilee and Samaria, and then on to Jerusalem. Plan to start early."

The reality of the moment struck hard when Jesus called the Zealot and younger James over to the side.

Remembering the soaking rain of our last tour of Galilee, I hesitantly tiptoed to the little window. The early sun struggled against a damp dawn. But not a cloud was in sight. Good.

With everything securely packed and loaded, we set out. The fields we passed hid beneath a floating quilt of morning mist.

We visited one village after another. Most of the people were receptive. Jesus made his teaching and healing all seem so natural. By the afternoon of the second day, the little villages began running together, looking all the same.

I became alarmed when crowds began following us from one village to the next. They could easily attract the attention of a Roman patrol. But the Zealot and younger James, occasionally slipping in and out of our group, told me we probably knew the location of the patrols better than their commanders.

The whirlwind of walking and setting up camp and cooking and taking down camp and loading and walking drew every ounce of strength from my body. But seeing the joy in the hearts of the people and seeing so many lives transformed replenished my weariness with new strength.

In one village, a rather well-dressed man interrupted Jesus by asking, "What must I do to inherit eternal life?" I braced as this sounded a lot like the trick questions we came to expect from religious teachers.

Surprisingly, Jesus treated this as an honest question. "What does the Law say? How do you read it?"

"You must love the Lord your God with all your heart, with all of your soul, all of your strength, and with all of your mind." Then he added, "… and you must love your neighbor as you do yourself." His unhesitating response sounded like he knew the Law.

"You have spoken well." Jesus nodded. "If you do these things, you will live."

Apparently, the man ceased to be satisfied with his own answer. He held out his hand again. "But, Master, who is my neighbor?"

Jesus paused, gave a broad smile, then motioned for the crowd to sit. "A Jewish man was traveling from Jerusalem down to Jericho. Along the way, bandits attacked him. They stripped him of his clothes and money, beat him and left him half dead beside the road."

Jesus looked out over the growing throng. "By chance, a Jewish priest came along. But when he saw the bloodied man, he crossed to the other side and passed on. A temple assistant also happened by. He even stopped to look at him. But not wanting to get involved, he hurried on as well." Jesus paused.

"Then a Samaritan came along. When he saw the man lying bloody beside the road, he had pity on him."

Thanks to Philip, I knew why Jesus used a Samaritan to show compassion on the Jewish man.

"Kneeling beside him, the Samaritan dressed his wounds. Then he lifted him onto his own donkey and took him to a nearby inn." Jesus continued, "There he stayed, taking care of him all that day and night. The next day he gave the innkeeper two pieces of silver and told him to continue to take care of the man. 'If the bill runs higher,' he told him, 'I will pay the difference when I come back this way.'"

Jesus looked straight at the man who'd asked. "Now which of these three was a neighbor to the man attacked by bandits?"

The man didn't look up. He spoke in a hoarse whisper. "The one who showed mercy on him."

Jesus looked out over the crowd and then to the man. "Yes. Now go and do likewise."

There were no signs or town markers. We simply came to a village where all the homes appeared many times poorer. Some houses were like one might keep goats back in Capernaum. Instead of the usual tan woolen garments, the women wore darker brown robes. But most disturbing were the suspicious eyes. They appeared to peek around every corner. Even the children disappeared as we came into a village.

Finally, in one town enough people gathered for us to stop. Jesus talked to a crippled man. But suddenly shouting erupted. The mood could not have deteriorated more quickly if Jesus had said everyone there was stupid and their children were ugly. They became hostile, ordering us to leave. We did.

A little way out of town we regrouped. Thomas asked, "What in heaven's name happened back there?"

Peter's face glowered. "It was my fault. I forgot how much they hate Jerusalem. I'm sorry."

"Just mentioning going to Jerusalem caused all of that?" The words exploded from my mouth.

"The hatred goes back hundreds of years, Joanna," Jesus explained. "The Samaritans believe the only true place to worship is Mt. Gerizim near Sychar. They hate the hypocrisy of Jerusalem—the very things I am trying to change." Jesus turned to the rest of the men, "Remember—don't mention Jerusalem while among the Samaritans."

Things improved a little after that. A woman lived in the next Samaritan village whom Jesus apparently had made quite an impression on earlier. She gathered half of the town—all by herself—to hear Jesus.

"Brrr, I need another blanket!" I called as the first light of dawn crept over our campsite. The cold foggy morning air cast an icy mist over everything.

"I ... I don't think there are any m-more." Mary's teeth chattered. "Get the canvas covering the cooking utensils and spread it over both of us. I'm freezing too."

I hated even thinking about crawling from beneath what cover I had. Frosty breath spread before my face as I jumped, half carrying my blanket to grab the canvas. We huddled and shivered.

Mary stuck her head out. "Bart—Thad." Bart stirred a little. "Bart, get up. Get a fire going." Bart rose on one elbow, saw his white breath and promptly covered his head.

Mary reached for a small piece of firewood and heaved it at the pile of covers. "Come on, Bart. We need a fire—now."

"Ouch." Bart acted crippled by the little stick as he limped over to revive the embers. Soon flames began dancing.

"Did Hades freeze over?" Matthew shivered. He wore his blanket to the revived campfire. "What happened to the weather?"

"Looks like the cold moved in overnight," Older James said with his usual analytical expression.

"Well ..." Thomas spoke ever so slowly. "I don't think I would have figured that out."

The roar of laughter at James' expense made the cold morning almost worthwhile.

Mary Magdalene made a dash for the campfire dragging her blanket. "No amount of fire will ever thaw me out."

"We'll need to get on the road early if we're to make it to Jerusalem today," Jesus called as he approached the camp. "The days are a lot shorter than when we come in the spring."

Barely dawn, freezing—and Jesus had already been out praying?

We made fantastic time, but only because we walked extra fast trying to stay warm. Our making good time, however, ended on the approach to Jerusalem. Simon Peter strutted around waving his hands. "Roman checkpoints are usually a formality. What's causing this long line?"

The Zealot spoke just above a whisper. "Romans now check for weapons on every road to Jerusalem."

Simon Peter turned and started toward our pack animal. "Don't!" Simon ordered, and not in a whisper. "They're watching—to see if you hide anything."

They did find Simon Peter's little sword. As the soldier held it up, the other soldiers laughed. "Planning to start an insurrection with this?"

"It ... it's for personal protection," Simon Peter stammered, red-faced.

"Maybe you can protect yourself from some old women." The lead soldier laughed and stuck it back.

We finally cleared the checkpoint and I asked Simon, "They didn't find your dagger?"

The Zealot smiled back. "Never. If they had, there'd be three dead soldiers."

"I'm glad you and I are on the same side," I said, and ... I meant it.

We walked on. The reality of my comment played back to me. A Zealot and the wife of a Roman official—on the same side? Totally impossible. *This will be extremely hard to explain someday.*

We reached the Mount of Olives as evening's dusk spread stillness over the hillside. The lost time at the checkpoint made us late to set up camp properly. Tempers grew shorter as the temperature dropped further. The firewood fought Andrew's attempt to provide warmth and light. We tried to piece together some semblance of a meal in the near dark. I slipped on a stone and brushed against older James. "You're one of them," he grumbled. "You like the Romans being in charge, making our lives miserable."

"Don't try to pit me against my husband." My anger boiled. I felt the urge to lash back at James. If only I could only come up with a perfect reply. But my hesitation provided me a gentler answer. "You wouldn't want an armed insurrection," my voice cracked, "and neither would Cuza."

"That's exactly what we need!" A different voice had chimed in. I turned to see a scowl on the face of Judas.

CHAPTER TWENTY-ONE

Frosty morning air hung over our campsite like a cold, wet blanket. Facing the campfire overheated my front but left my backside frigid. That kept most of us continually rotating front to back. I'm sure we looked silly, but the technique worked. As we finished what breakfast our nearly numb fingers allowed us to prepare, Jesus spoke to my big concern. "We can't leave you women here in this cold. There isn't enough firewood on the Mount of Olives to keep you warm all day."

"Thank you," I replied. "Otherwise, you'd have expected dinner tonight from four frozen corpses."

Jesus laughed and called Mary Magdalene and Susanna over where we huddled. "There's a family in Jerusalem who has a warm home where you can stay today. Get ready to go with us."

He wouldn't have to ask me a second time, and Mary Magdalene certainly set an all-time record for getting ready.

Jesus didn't take their usual path directly down the steeper west side of the Mount of Olives. Thankfully, we went back and took the longer, but safer, road that diagonally crossed the Kidron Valley.

Huddling against the cold, we followed the road up the Jerusalem side, past the temple's Eastern Gate, and on into the city proper. This older part of Jerusalem appeared thrown together with little thought and no planning, unlike our modern city of Sepphoris. Animal pens sat next to shops. Houses and market stalls intermingled. The odor of goats and donkeys mixing with the scent of unusual foods cooking nearly overwhelmed my senses. Confusion reigned. Seventeen of us were trying to make our way through a congestion of people and animals, all trying to move in every conceivable direction at the same time.

After passing a seeming endless area of stalls and stores, we finally left the mad chaos behind and entered a section of nicer homes. The further we walked, the more expensive the homes became. I had almost forgotten how nice a stone home really looked.

Jesus greeted the servant girl answering the door by name. Rhoda obviously recognized Jesus as well. She quickly returned with the lady of the house. "Oh, Jesus, how wonderful to see you," the attractive lady said. "All of you, please come in. You must be frozen."

Most of us completely forgot any semblance of manners as we pushed into the warmth. Jesus introduced our host. "This is Mary Lois, a true believer. She and her husband, Mark, have a large room on the next level. They graciously allow us to observe the Passover meal here."

Jesus then introduced each of us by name.

"You ladies must be frozen." Mary Lois motioned toward an ornate leather bench. "You can lay your heavier robes there as you begin to thaw."

"I'm keeping mine on until next summer." Mary Magdalene pulled her shawl more tightly. "I've been cold for a week and I haven't felt my fingers in two days."

Mary Lois appeared taller than me, but not as tall as Mary Magdalene. Her well-kept hair was light brown, almost the color of mine. I quickly noticed her attractive dress, and I longed for my real clothes. She seemed around ten or more years older than me and possessed a refinement I had not seen in some time.

Mary Lois told Jesus, "I will enjoy the company of these ladies while you and your men go to the temple, especially since Mark and our son won't be home until late afternoon." Assuring her they would not be late, Jesus and the twelve left for the Festival of Lights, or Hanukkah, as Mary Lois said many had begun calling the celebration.

The high ornate ceilings reminded me of my home in Sepphoris. The light off-white stone used in construction took on a salmon hue in the morning sun. The furnishings reflected a meticulous eye for details, and the mosaic floors radiated warmth. Her glass windows were the first I'd seen since leaving Sepphoris. I was certainly impressed.

Over a cup of delicious hot tea, our hostess said, "Since you already have two Marys in your group, you can shorten my name to Lois to save confusion."

"Do tell us your story," I insisted. "How did you come to be here and to follow Jesus?"

"Oh, it's not that unusual." Lois seemed to blush at the attention. "I married a handsome and dashing Roman soldier who grew up here with his family. Mark's father came to Jerusalem as an officer during Herod the Great's rule. He fell in love with a young Jewish beauty, whom I might add is still beautiful today. She taught Mark to respect our beliefs, and he embraces them as much as a centurion can. Mark thinks highly of Jesus and his disciples."

Cuza's heritage so resembled Mark's—his mother being Jewish and his father a Roman officer—that I sat dumbfounded. I was listening to my story, but with such a different outcome. My chest tightened. The more she spoke of how well her family situation worked, the closer my heart came to bursting. I turned away from the conversation more than once to struggle with my emotions. *Why couldn't Cuza be like Mark?*

With the image of my little Marcus weighing heavily, I forced myself back to the present. "How old is your son?"

"John Mark is sixteen. He's beginning to look just like his father back when we first met." Her smile reflected a happy memory. "We named him after Mark and my father John, to blend the Jewish and the Roman sides of the family together."

"I remember John Mark from last spring," Mary interjected. "How is his schooling progressing?"

"Oh, it's going beautifully." Lois rose and poured another round of tea. "Actually, he spends the morning in class and the afternoons in an intern position as an aid to one of Pontius Pilate's staff."

My heart stopped. I had thought of sharing the story how Cuza went to Jesus asking him to heal our desperately ill son, the resulting miracle and then how the palace influenced him against Jesus. The words about Cuza's position had been poised on my lips. But John Mark working in Pilate's office—a chill ran up my spine. *What if John Mark just happened to mention something about meeting Cuza's wife?* My insides trembled.

Mid-afternoon, young John Mark came home. After introductions all around, I stepped over to meet him personally. "Tell me about your work with Pontius Pilate."

"Oh, it isn't very exciting, at least not most of the time." John Mark seemed very grownup for sixteen and completely at ease among adults. He selected a muffin from the table. Between bites, he shared, "Pilate spends most of his time at his palace in Caesarea saying it's cooler by the Great Sea." A boyish grin emerged on his face. "But all the staff knows he hates Jerusalem. Pilate only appears when trouble is likely."

John Mark went on to relate, "I didn't really understand Passover until Jesus came. He made the feast a lot more interesting."

I stood totally amazed at how he could float so easily between the official Roman world of Pilate's office and the Jewish Passover, like crossing a seamless bridge. *Why, oh why, can't Cuza find this connection?*

A knock on the door halted my selfish agonizing. Jesus and the twelve were ready for us to return to our encampment. Oh, how I didn't want to leave the warm comfort of this home.

Mary Magdalene expressed our thoughts more vocally. "Do we really have to go? Why can't we camp in their upper room?"

I felt such a warm, kindred spirit with Lois. Saying good-bye came quite hard. Even though I concealed my background, I felt she also realized a special connection.

The return of milder weather made for a pleasant walk back toward camp, especially after we passed the offensive odors in the market section of Jerusalem.

"How did everything go at the festival today?" I asked as we finally entered our campsite.

"Uh ..." Andrew started.

"Let's just say it was—unusual," Philip filled in.

"Don't expect me to read your minds. Tell me."

Mary slipped up beside us as Andrew finally overcame his loss for words. "So many things happening at the same time made everything a little confusing. The confusion started as we were walking past the Treasury. The usual beggars were pleading for alms. Jesus gave the blind one a coin and we walked on."

Andrew gave Philip a curious look, then continued. "John asked Jesus if the man had been born blind because his parents had sinned. Jesus stopped and spoke directly to John, 'He was born blind so God's power could be witnessed.'" Andrew continued looking a little puzzled.

Philip interrupted. "To be honest, I didn't understand what he meant either. Jesus realized our confusion, turned back to the beggar and asked if he would like to have his eyesight. You can imagine his answer."

I nodded.

"Let me tell this part," Philip said to Andrew, "then you relate what happened after that."

I looked at Andrew, then Philip. "You're confusing me."

"Knowing how easy that is ..." Philip grinned, then continued, "Jesus stooped and spit on the ground making a little mud that he rubbed on the man's eyes. Jesus then instructed him to go and wash in the Pool of Salome."

"Well—" I shrugged my shoulders. "What's unusual about that?"

Andrew cleared his throat. "You'll see. We walked on to where Jesus wanted to teach. Soon a whole group of Pharisees marched up directly in front of Jesus carrying this woman. I sat dumbfounded, because women are not allowed in that part of the temple. They dropped her right in front of Jesus."

Andrew continued. "One of them puffed out his chest and announced, 'This woman has been caught in the very act of adultery. The Law says she should be stoned to death.' The Pharisee looked around to the crowd making sure everyone heard. Then he asked Jesus, 'What do you say?'"

"They knew they had Jesus. Whatever he said, they could use his words against him." Andrew gestured with both hands. "Oh, the smirks on their faces ..." Andrew left the narrative hanging.

"Well, what did Jesus do?" I finally asked.

"He didn't say anything ..." Andrew again left the sentence in midair.

I wanted to kick him. "Come on, Andrew!"

"Jesus made them wait, just like I'm making you," Andrew finally said. "As they clamored for his answer, he stooped down and wrote something in the dust. Just when the lead Pharisee seemed about to have a stroke, Jesus stood up. He said if the Law says to stone her, they should go ahead and stone her. Then Jesus looked at each Pharisee, his voice hardening, 'But make sure the one of you who is without sin throws the first stone.' Again, Jesus calmly stooped down and continued writing in the dust."

I looked at Andrew. "And?"

"Two Pharisees at the back slipped away, then three more followed," Andrew related. "When four others started for the exit, the rest almost ran over them. No one wanted to be last to leave."

"And the poor woman?"

"That's the best part," Andrew said. "Jesus lifted her to her feet, told her he didn't condemn her, and she should go and sin no more."

"That's beautiful." I wiped the corner of my eye.

"Joanna, there must have been five hundred people watching by that time," Philip added. "So, right as Jesus finished talking to the woman, the beggar returned and called out, 'you're the one who healed me. I recognize your voice.' He pushed his way through and knelt at Jesus' feet. 'Bless you, I can see.' When Jesus lifted him to his feet, the man added, 'You wouldn't believe what's happened to me.'"

With a look of pure pleasure, Philip continued. "The beggar suddenly became the center of attention as he related how he could suddenly see and started shouting his joy. He said his friends insisted he go and show the Pharisees this wonderful thing that had happened.

"With even more excitement in his voice, he told Jesus, 'I thought the Pharisees would be thrilled, but they began questioning me like I'd done something wrong. They asked me how a common sinner could heal someone's sight. I told them he must be a prophet of God.' The beggar stretched both hands in the air. 'Oh, they didn't like that.'"

"The beggar became even more excited." Philip continued by imitating the beggar. "'They decided I couldn't have been born blind, so they questioned my parents.'"

"The beggar turned directly to Jesus. 'You know what? Them Pharisees accused my parents of lying!'"

We laughed, but more at Philip imitating the beggar. "The beggar continued, 'They started all over saying Jesus couldn't have healed me, because Jesus was a sinner. I told them I didn't know about that. All I know is, I was blind and now I can see.'"

"The crowd gave the beggar a roar of approval. With the applause, he became even more excited as he related, 'you know those Pharisees cursed me, said I was born in sin and asked what was I doing there trying to teach them? They picked me up, four of them did, and threw me out of the synagogue.'"

Mary and I were both holding our sides laughing. A festive mood surrounded the evening campfire.

Being the center of attention at the temple excited the disciples. But as I surveyed the situation, Jesus seemed to be making bitter enemies about as fast as he was making joyful converts. The more the men talked about confrontations, the more I wanted to get back to Capernaum.

"Someone's coming!" Simon dropped his bowl and vanished in the shadows. No one else had time to react before a young man burst into our encampment.

"It's John Mark," Peter exclaimed. "What are you doing out in the dark at this hour, young man?"

"Jesus!" John Mark's hands were on his knees. He struggled to catch his breath. "Jesus, there's a plot to arrest you tomorrow."

Simon slipped back, returning a deadly looking dagger to somewhere in the folds of his robe.

John Mark rose, still breathing deeply. "Religious leaders were in Pilate's office this afternoon. I overheard them asking the Roman guard not to interfere and let their temple guards arrest you tomorrow. They said you were a blasphemer and a troublemaker. They could take care of the matter quietly if the Roman guard stayed away."

Jesus put his arm on John Mark's shoulder. "You have risked a great deal, young man. Thank you."

"Do the temple guards know where we're camped?" Simon Peter's hands shook. He tried not to look frightened.

"What I overheard is they know you're camped on the Mount of Olives, but they don't know exactly where." John Mark drew another deep breath. "But that's not all. They asked the guard to alert the Galilee border patrol. They said if you somehow avoided capture in Jerusalem, they should arrest you at the border. It sounds bad, Jesus."

Bad didn't begin to describe the situation as far as I was concerned. Jesus walked John Mark over to the side. "Tell your mother to let my followers know that at first light, we will journey to Bethany across the Jordan. We'll be out of Pilate's reach without crossing into Galilee."

Everyone thanked John Mark for bringing his warning, some of us two and three times.

"I need to get home before I'm missed." John Mark slipped out of camp toward the trail.

"Bethany is where Lazarus lives," Mary Magdalene exclaimed. "They're sure to find us there."

"Oh, stop worrying." Older James shook his head. "This is another Bethany, across the Jordan River in Perea. We'll be safe there."

I didn't know about the others, but I knew I wanted to sleep where I could keep one eye on the Zealot. *If he so much as moves tonight, he'll think I'm the hem on his garment.*

CHAPTER TWENTY-TWO

"It won't be daylight for another hour." Mary Magdalene pulled her blanket tightly around her neck. "We can't pack in the dark."

"Jesus said to be on the road at first light," I called back, "not *starting* to wake up." I pulled my outer robe close against the cool, early morning air. "Come on. You can sleep while you walk."

A foggy mist hung over the Mount of Olives compounding the semi-darkness. Trying to pack under a sense of urgency made everything drag like in slow motion. "No time for a campfire this morning," older James barked as he stamped out the remaining embers. "You and Mary pass around some food the men can snack on while we pack. We'll eat more after we pass the Bethphage checkpoint."

Had the situation not been so urgent and the circumstances so dire, I could have made a great comment about James helping pack for once. But I thought better of my statement. "I tried to forget that checkpoint. You think they'll already be looking for us there?"

"With one more day of festival, I doubt it." James tilted his head to look down the ridge of his nose. "But, we only get one chance to be wrong."

Mary and I passed out dried fruit to the men while they took down the lean-to. I came to James. "How are we going to get seventeen people through a Roman checkpoint without them realizing who we are?"

"We're working on that."

"When you figure it out, you'll share it with us, right?"

James always knew more than he let on. Keeping the rest of us guessing probably made him feel important. But with so much to do, I didn't have time to analyze the deficiencies in his character.

Suddenly the thought of being stopped and contemplating the resulting confrontation at Herod's palace hit me—*Cuza, your wife was arrested with Jesus in Jerusalem. Would you care to explain?* I blew a pent-up breath from the deepest part of my lungs.

As the approaching dawn sent golden-pink streaks across the eastern sky, we set out.

A short distance before we reached Bethphage, older James addressed us. "Obviously, to approach the checkpoint together is too dangerous. Younger James, you take your mother and our pack animal. Matthew and Mary Magdalene, you'll accompany them. Leave a little space, then Judas, you can take Susanna, and Andrew will take Joanna. Travel like couples so you don't arouse suspicion. Simon will lead the rest of us over a secret trail through the hills. Walk slowly. We'll catch up with you in an hour or so. Everyone understand?"

We all nodded—except Matthew. He looked caught in the dilemma of choosing between crawling over a rocky mountain path or having to escort Mary Magdalene. The eight disappeared toward the hills to our left.

The checkpoint took time, and we walked slowly. Well over an hour had passed, and we still didn't see Jesus and the other disciples. "Do we stop, or do we keep walking?" Younger James' voice actually shook.

"We would look a little too suspicious just standing beside the road," Matthew hesitantly offered.

"We don't want to get too far ahead." Even more anxiety crept into James' voice.

"Let's keep walking slowly," Andrew responded. "If we absolutely have to stop, Mary can act sick or something."

Acute anticipation does weird things to the passage of time. The next few minutes dragged on like hours. Finally, Andrew spotted eight shadows emerging from a rocky area off in the distance. Seeing them walk our way brought something deep inside welling up. My bottom lip quivered. As they joined us, I said, "I can't tell you how good this feels, all of us back together."

We struck a wide swath around Jericho, then headed east to the Jordan River. I took one long, fearful look at the flowing waters. "We're going to cross that?"

As usual, older James took charge. "Thad, you're the tallest. Go see how deep it is." That's why we love James. He always knows just who to volunteer for the difficult assignments.

"S-so, I'm t-the expendable one?" Thad said as he handed the halter rope to Bart.

The river wasn't all that deep, at least not on Thad. Of course, waist high on Thad meant chest deep on me. I must admit, having Andrew half carry me across felt good. I only got wet up to my waist.

With half of us safely on the other bank, next came the job of encouraging our supply-laden donkey across. At the water's edge, he planted his front hooves in the ground as firmly as tree trunks. The men finally posted lookouts while they unloaded half our supplies and hand carried them across. Pushing and pulling that stubborn animal across the river still took five men. Reaching the other side, the soaking wet men collapsed on the sandy bank.

"We're safe here." Andrew finally sat up and heaved a big sigh. "Pilate's jurisdiction ended right there on the other side of the river."

"You'd better be right." Mary Magdalene stared daggers at Andrew. Jesus and the three decided a clump of trees several hundred feet from the water would shield our camp from sight.

"It isn't noon yet, but is anyone hungry?" Mary's invitation suddenly activated a dozen ferocious appetites.

Later in the afternoon, when the camp finally met Mary's strict set up specifications, Andrew and Philip strolled over. Andrew tilted his head toward the way we had come. "Would any of you like to walk down to the river?"

Mary shook her head. "Why would I want to even get close to that water again?"

"You're looking for another chance to drown me, Andrew?" I rose from my work and gave him my fake glare.

Andrew started to answer but wisely thought better.

I looked at Susanna. "An afternoon stroll down to the river might be pleasant, especially after all we've been through. How about you?"

With Susanna's nod, the four of us set out on our way.

The sandy soil crunched beneath our sandals as we ambled alongside the greenish-blue waters of the Jordan River. "Hard to believe we were freezing to death only four days ago," Susanna said. "It's almost hot."

"Remember the first time you walked from Jericho up to Jerusalem?" Philip kicked some sand with his sandal. "We looked down when we stopped and the Jordan River seemed so far below? They simply don't get winter down here."

"You can talk about high ground and low valleys, but I'm just happy to feel warm sun on my face and smell the dry air." I swept at the back of my robe. "Look, I'm almost dry."

The four of us sat on a couple of large rocks for several long minutes just listening to the sound of the flowing water. Sometimes words aren't needed to enjoy the beauty of a place. This area was so different, with the stark rocky mountain walls rising in the distance on both our east and west. Beyond the scattered trees drawing life from the river, the area appeared practically a desert. Andrew broke the long silence. "This is where it all began."

"What began?" I turned to look at him.

Andrew eyes seemed to envision another world. "This very spot. This is where John the Baptist preached and baptized."

"You were here when John the Baptist preached?" Susanna looked at Andrew with her brow furrowed. "We heard about the excitement, even in Decapolis."

I shook my head. "You and Simon Peter came all the way down to this desolate place to hear John the Baptist preach?"

"Oh, no, not with Simon Peter. He wasn't the least interested in hearing some religious man." Andrew let out a soft laugh. "He told me flat out, 'You're a fool going down there to hear that wild preacher.'"

Andrew paused for a long moment. "John also wanted to check out the excitement, but James was like Simon. Neither wanted anything to do with a fire-breathing preacher. Anyway, John and I came down together. Something pretty special happened here." Andrew gazed from one end of the lonely riverbank to the other. "It seems so empty now."

Andrew's eyes glistened. "People came from everywhere to hear John the Baptist preach and be baptized. John and I became his disciples. We helped him baptize people right there in the Jordan."

Andrew pointed to almost the spot where we crossed. "John the Baptist didn't mince words. He told the people their hearts were sinful, how they needed to repent and prepare for the coming One, the Lord."

"So, if James and Simon Peter didn't come with you, how did they become the two big leaders?" I asked.

"All that happened later. Things really became exciting here. I sent word back to Galilee for Simon." Andrew stopped to look at Susanna and me. "He was only Simon, son of John, back then. Anyway, I sent word to Simon telling him to take a break from fishing and get himself down here."

Andrew paused, then added, "The Pharisees also came down to check out John the Baptist. They gave him the same hard time they give Jesus now."

"Why do I find that hard to believe?" I said half laughing.

"The Pharisees hounded him, asking if he was the Messiah. John told them, 'I'm the voice calling in the desert, making straight the way for the Lord.'" Andrew's voice broke with emotion. "John didn't claim to be the Messiah. He said he was the one sent to announce the coming Messiah."

"All that was with John the Baptist?" Susanna crossed her arms. "How did you meet Jesus?"

Andrew took a deep breath. I could feel the emotion in his voice. "John and I were there in the river helping John the Baptist. A young man waded out to be baptized. John stopped—something like a trance came over him. I'll never forget that moment. In a deep strong voice, John the Baptist announced, 'Behold, the Lamb of God!'"

"Suddenly, my world stopped. John's words struck me like a lightning bolt. Could this be the Messiah John had been preaching about? As Jesus climbed back out of the water, I felt the strongest urge to follow after him." Andrew stopped. His gaze relived that moment.

"Well, did you?" I finally asked.

"No, we stayed there assisting with the baptisms. Later in the day, John and I searched for him. When we finally found him, John and I spent most of the afternoon talking with him. From the very first, I knew Jesus must be our coming Messiah."

Philip stood, looked at Andrew, and slowly shook his head. "You don't remember me from those days, do you?" Philip obviously enjoyed Andrew's blank stare. "After you and John took up most of his afternoon, you were too excited to notice me. I talked with Jesus right after you left."

"You were here?" Andrew's eyes grew wide. "You recognized Jesus was the Messiah, too?"

Philip hunched his shoulders. "Oh, it took me a little longer. My skull's a little thicker than yours."

We laughed. Susanna and I stood and stretched.

The four of us started walking again as Andrew talked. As much as talking to us, he was reminiscing about that special time. "The next morning, to my complete surprise, I ran into Simon. I assumed he would ignore my message as he usually did. After the previous afternoon, I now had a lot more to tell him and immediately took him to Jesus."

Andrew gazed up the river. Then he continued, "Here it really gets interesting. Before I could introduce my brother, Jesus said, 'You are Simon, son of John,' like he had been expecting him. For the life of me, I didn't remember mentioning our father's name. Turns out, this didn't surprise me nearly as much as what Jesus said next. He looked at Simon straight on and told him that from then on he was going to call him Peter, like 'the Rock'."

I stopped in my tracks. My eyebrows knitted. "Jesus gave Simon the nickname, Peter? All this time I've assumed 'the Rock' was a nickname somebody sarcastically gave him. Jesus is way smarter than that."

We all laughed. "You took the words out of my mouth," Andrew came back. "I thought a rock was the last object you would ever compare to Simon. But that day he and Jesus talked in a way I had never heard Simon talk before." Andrew had a sly look on his face. "I'm still not certain about the 'Rock' part." We all laughed again.

Andrew continued. "Now, here's the funny part. When Simon tells this story, you'd be convinced he was the first one who found Jesus."

"Amazing." Philip stopped and just shook his head. "When Jesus invited me to become his disciple, you know what I did? I searched for my friend Nathaniel and practically dragged him to see Jesus. He became a devoted follower, at least until his wedding."

The two men stood looking at each other.

We started walking again. I asked Andrew, "If Jesus grew up in Nazareth, and you met him way down here in Perea, how did all of you end up in Capernaum?"

I didn't give Andrew time to answer. "I've never told this, so please don't repeat my story to anyone. Cuza and I spent a horrible three weeks in Capernaum when little Marcus nearly died of the fever. As we left, I swore I would never set foot in—I won't repeat what I called Capernaum— ever again. Imagine my reaction when I discovered Jesus had moved his ministry to the one town I most hated."

The three enjoyed an even bigger laugh than I anticipated. Andrew gave as serious a look as he could fake. "I'm sure Jesus planned it that way."

When we finally stopped laughing, seriousness filled Andrew's face. "After Simon's wife died, we had to get away from Bethsaida. Capernaum didn't seem like such a bad place, especially since we could fish from there as well. Anyway, time went on. Simon and I caught up with Jesus whenever we could—and still make a living."

Andrew kicked some small pebbles into the flowing water. "One day, about four months later, Jesus came to Capernaum. We were cleaning our nets in the late morning after the worst night of fishing ever. Both of us were tired and completely frustrated.

"Jesus came walking down the beach with a crowd following him. He tried to teach, but the people crowded him so much they almost pushed him in the lake. Jesus asked Peter if he could teach from his boat. Even though Simon thought the world of Jesus, he wasn't thrilled with Jesus tying up his boat the rest of the morning. All we wanted was to go home and sleep off the lousy night.

"When Jesus finished teaching, he nudged Simon awake and told him to go out into deep water to catch some fish. Peter wasn't in his best mood and sort of told Jesus what he thought of that idea."

Andrew chuckled. "But Jesus insisted, so I hoisted the sail and Simon steered the boat out a little way from shore."

A broad smile spread over Andrew's entire face. "That's when the miracle happened. The jerk on the net about yanked both of us over the side. We struggled just to hang on. Finally, James and John heard us calling. All four of us had to drag in the net, which held more fish than we would usually catch in a week."

I stopped and looked around. "You've had us so engrossed, I didn't notice how far we've walked. We'd better start back."

We turned and started strolling back up the river toward camp. Andrew continued his story. "For once in Simon Peter's life he was speechless. We secured the—Oh-oh. Do you see what I see?"

"Don't make any sudden moves," Philip ordered. "Andrew, take Joanna's arm. I'll do the same with Susanna. Don't rush, act like a couple taking a stroll. Then, I hope, they won't suspect who we are."

I gazed at the distance to the safety of our camp and almost froze. Six months ago, Roman soldiers on patrol would be comforting. Their presence insured my safety. Fear tingled up my spine as Roman soldiers on the opposite side of the river marched in our direction. *Oh, how much has changed.*

CHAPTER TWENTY-THREE

"Act like you aren't concerned about them and walk leisurely toward the tree line." Philip's tone of voice expressed more experience than I wanted to know about. "Susanna and I will amble a little further. Then we'll head that way. Hopefully, they'll keep marching … on their side of the river."

My heart beat out of my chest until when we were out of the patrol's sight. "I don't think I'll breathe normally for a week." I exclaimed.

"They could be scouts for a larger detachment," Philip warned as he and Susanna reached us in the trees. "This doesn't mean we've seen the last of them. The authorities in Jerusalem realize by now we've escaped. So, they're patrolling the border."

"Thanks to John Mark, we're already safe." Andrew's eyes sparkled. "That was still close."

"Closer than I care for." I brushed the perspiration from the back of my neck. Once we trudged back into camp, Andrew shared the event with Jesus and the others. Only Thomas believed a Roman patrol might cross the river border to come after us.

I hope Jesus summed things up correctly when he said the Romans wouldn't go out of their way to do the work of the religious authorities, not without a vendetta of their own.

That comment helped ease my concerns as we prepared for the night. I lay in my blanket roll, looked up at the myriad of stars in the yet moonless sky and reflected on the day's swing of emotions. First, there was our near frantic escape from Jerusalem at dawn, followed by an almost comical crossing of the Jordan. We enjoyed a peaceful stroll along the river only to be interrupted by the sudden fear of an approaching Roman patrol. It was almost too much. I closed my eyes relishing the image of Andrew and me strolling arm-in-arm.

We were putting lunch away when James rushed in and called to John. "You're not going to believe this, but we have a crowd gathering down at the river. Go find Jesus."

I followed Thomas and Andrew as they hurried toward the people meandering up the riverbank. "This isn't good," James said with a deep frown. "The authorities are sure to follow any crowd leaving Jerusalem. They'd give anything to know where we are."

We waited by a small clump of trees while Thomas talked with several from the crowd. Our usually skeptical Thomas returned. "I could be mistaken, but I believe these folks are sincere. Word has quietly spread that we fled Jerusalem to hide here. I told them to wait, Jesus would be down soon."

Jesus, Simon Peter, and John appeared from the grove of trees near our camp walking toward the river. The other disciples started that direction to join them. All except Andrew. He lingered in the shade nearby a little longer. "Well, I suppose I'd better get on down to the river ... since they can't start without me." We both laughed. Andrew looked at me a long moment. "You're staying here in the shade?"

I nodded.

Andrew turned and started toward the gathering crowd.

What was that? A crazy sensation surged from the pit of my stomach as Andrew walked away. I shivered slightly even as perspiration popped on the back of my neck. What on earth was that bizarre emotion? Why did my heart suddenly beat fast? Why did I want Andrew to stay? I hadn't had a feeling like that since I was a teenager.

Jesus began teaching the small crowd about the Kingdom of God, but something quite different swirled around in my head. The picture of Andrew and me in our arm-in-arm stroll flashed across my mind. *This isn't right.* I strode back and forth trying to erase the guilty pleasure that lingered much too strongly. *I'm still married. I can't allow myself to have feelings like this.*

"Isn't this amazing?" Mary spoke from close behind me.

I jumped. *How did she know?*

"You suppose Lois told these people Jesus would be here?"

My legs suddenly weakened. Heat radiated from behind my ears. "Sh-she must have." I hastily composed what I hoped was an intelligent thought. "From the way people are dressed, they look to be from Jerusalem." *Had I adequately masked my guilt?*

Around the campfire after dinner, almost everyone speculated on the day's events. "It's a half-day's walk from Jerusalem," James explained. "When they leave in the afternoon, there's hardly time to return home before dark."

"If they do keep coming, it's going to pose a big problem." Thomas looked around the group. "This many people can't possibly leave Jerusalem without the temple authorities suspecting something. What do we do when the Pharisees show up?"

They talked, but my thoughts kept jumping somewhere else. I compelled my eyes to look in a different direction. My emotions had to be brought under control. I had to erase the image of Andrew and me walking together.

While preparing my blanket roll for the night, I decided to concentrate my thoughts on Cuza. I was distressed that my effort to think about my husband produced only a dull ache.

"I can't believe this." Thomas quickly stuffed the rest of his lunch in his mouth. "You know Pharisees are going to be right behind all those people crossing the river."

Soon, an even larger crowd than the previous day emerged. Again, the disciples hustled down to handle the throng crossing the Jordan.

The afternoon passed with wonderful teachings, joyous healings—and surprisingly, no Pharisees. Jesus' words brought hope to many hearts and his healings brought joy to countless lives. Despite our fears, the day turned out to be wonderful.

As we gathered for our time around the campfire that evening, Jesus asked for our undivided attention. "Peter and John received distressing news from some who came today. Our dear friend Lazarus is very sick. Martha and Mary are extremely concerned."

Older James shook his head. "You're not thinking of going back there? We'd be arrested before we got halfway to Bethany."

The men didn't often agree with James, only this night they did.

As much as I hated to admit it, I also agreed. Going anywhere near Jerusalem would be suicide.

Simon Peter spoke up. "If you want to go see Lazarus, I'll go with you."

Andrew supported his brother, but most of the men expressed resentment at Peter's pious offer. The evening was not peaceful.

A chill ran through me. I realized Jesus would never forsake a friend, no matter how dangerous the situation. But, I also couldn't imagine him taking us back facing certain arrest. Sleep did not come easily that night.

The beautiful dry and crisp mornings in the desert along the Jordan River continued to amaze me. Each morning, the barren rocky area came to life with songbirds calling in the cool breeze. Philip assured me this area was unbearably hot in the summer, but during this time of early winter was fresh and invigorating.

As we prepared the noon meal, all the disciples kept glancing toward the river. Like me, they wondered if the crowds would show up again. We weren't disappointed.

"Where are all these people coming from?" John asked as even more people than the previous day arrived. Again, the day unfolded with a large, joyous crowd and thankfully no religious authorities.

Again, the evening's discussion focused on Lazarus' illness. Jesus had not said anything about going to Bethany. But more disciples began to feel guilty about not going—while at the same time, they didn't want to face the obvious risk.

"If we go, what about these crowds?" Thomas spoke up. "More people are coming here than you ever spoke to in Jerusalem."

I became amused. No matter which side of the discussion someone presented, most of the men nodded approval. Then when someone expressed the opposite viewpoint, they, again, seemed to agree.

Jesus stood, and silence gradually descended upon the group. "Lazarus' sickness will not end in death. His illness is so God's Son will also receive glory."

That sounded good enough for me. Lazarus must be getting better. I could finally put my fear of walking back into that viper's nest of Pharisees to rest.

But the very next morning, the mood around breakfast appeared strangely different. After about an hour of gloom, I finally asked the few men still lingering around, "What's wrong with everyone today?"

"It's Jesus. He's bothered terribly by something," Thomas replied. "And he seemed so positive last evening."

Again, about lunchtime, a crowd started developing down on the river bank. Andrew strolled over to pick up his outer robe. "Getting to be like the old days, back when we were here with John the Baptist."

"Better hurry on down. You know they can't start without you." I gave him a flip of my hair.

He gave me his cute smile in return. *Oh, no.* My heart turned into a soupy liquid. *I must get these feelings under control, and I will.*

I forced my thoughts in a different direction. "Come on Mary, let's go watch. We can clean up later."

I made myself concentrate on Jesus. When he healed a man disfigured by leprosy, his joy brought restoration for both that man and me. For the next several hours, everything seemed back to normal and so wonderful again.

Around the evening campfire, everyone—even Thomas—expressed excitement over the day's events. The old enthusiasm had returned. I was relieved in more ways than one.

As the discussion time wound to a close, Jesus stood. He looked over the men until all were completely attentive. "Tomorrow, instruct the crowds not to return. We will be leaving."

Simon Peter erupted. "Why? What's happening? It's Lazarus, isn't it? Is he worse? Are we going back to Bethany?"

Jesus' face grew more distressed. "Lazarus is sleeping." He paused a long moment. "I'm going there to wake him."

"He's sleeping? Isn't that good news?" John called above the din of other questions. "Means he's getting better. Why would we need to go?"

Jesus gazed at the campfire's embers, watching the sparks swirl up from the flames. "Lazarus is dead."

CHAPTER TWENTY-FOUR

James' eyes narrowed. "What do you mean, no?" He placed his hands on his hips. "I said, come on. Let's go!"

Mary Magdalene planted both feet solidly on the raw earth, flung her long auburn hair over her shoulder and pointed a finger at older James. "You're not going to let Jesus cross that river and get arrested. You can stop him. Talk some sense into him—please!"

"Jesus is going to comfort Martha and Mary. You can stay here if you like. Nothing would make me happier," James stomped away calling over his shoulder, "But Jesus is going, and I'm going with him."

Jesus finally walked over to her. "Mary, gather your things. We are going."

He turned back toward the river and motioned us to follow. Mary Magdalene wiped her face, grabbed her belongings and caught up as we reached the Jordan River.

Again, our biggest challenge came equipped with four legs. Even though the men had already ferried most of our camp equipment across, the pack animal still balked at the water's edge. Two men pulled and two pushed him halfway across. A sudden well-placed kick caught Bart on his thigh. With a loud scream, he went under. Thad dragged Bart out of the river spitting and sputtering. We laughed so hard they could probably hear us in Jericho.

Bart crumpled on the bank, half crying from pain and half trying not to laugh with the rest of us. As he wiped his eyes, they suddenly lit up. "No-Jordan. That's it! We've always said that stubborn animal needed a name." Bart hobbled to his feet. "We ought to call him No-Jordan." A glance around showed he didn't need a vote, we were unanimous.

We reassembled everything to begin the dreaded journey. I quickly noticed two men absent from the group. *Good.* Near Jericho, Simon and younger James magically appeared and led us on back streets most people probably didn't know existed. The two stayed with us as we trekked up the steep road to the plateau that cradled Jerusalem, Bethphage, and Bethany. The slope seemed to grow steeper every trip. Panting, I caught up with younger James. "Get Jesus to slow down a little. This pace is killing me."

"When Jesus sets his mind, there's no slowing him down." James shrugged his shoulders.

I thought back to how weak and out of shape I was the first time we made that climb. The image of Andrew taking my arm on the difficult places floated across my mind. A swoosh of emotion swept through me. I tried in vain to shake off the feeling.

A most difficult hurdle soon loomed before us. Would Bethphage and the Roman checkpoint be our undoing? Jesus decided we didn't have time to divert part of the men on the secret trail through the hills. So, we divided into our four smaller groups and prayed for the best. As we moved beyond their hearing, Matthew called. "Wonder why they're checking those leaving Jerusalem so much closer than us going in?"

"Don't get cocky," older James spit back. "Remember, we have to return through that checkpoint to get home."

Shortly before noon, we approached Bethany. Jesus stopped us beneath a large date palm within sight of Martha's house. "Enough people are around who know us to take word to Martha and Mary," he said. "We will wait here."

"And enough Pharisees are around to start a synagogue." Thomas rubbed his jaw as he surveyed the area.

"They're still in the official mourning period. I'd be very surprised if they make a scene today." Philip scuffed his feet in the dirt. "But tomorrow—anything could happen."

We'd stood there only a short time until Martha flew out of the house and hurried down the path, tears filling her eyes. Pain hung like weights on each word. "Lord, if you had only been here ... our brother would not have died."

My heart sank.

Jesus bit his lip. His eyes filled with tears.

I knew how much Jesus wanted to be there. I hoped someone would explain to her the threat we faced, because I knew Jesus would never make excuses. Jesus gave her a fatherly hug. "Martha, your brother will live again."

Martha's eyes welled up with tears. "Yes, I know he'll rise again in the resurrection."

Jesus placed a hand on each of Martha's shoulders and looked in her eyes. "Listen to me, Martha. I am the Resurrection!" He dried her eyes with the sleeve of his garment. "The person who believes in me will live, even though he dies. Martha, do you believe this?"

Martha looked up at Jesus. "Yes, Lord. I believe you are the Messiah, the Son of God." Hope began radiating from her eyes. "You are the One promised to the world."

Martha suddenly spun toward her house. "I must tell Mary."

Very shortly, Martha came running back with Mary struggling to keep up.

A man passing nearby whispered to another just loud enough we were sure heard, "He opened the eyes of the blind. Why couldn't he keep Lazarus from dying?" I harbored an intense urge to hurt him.

Jesus ignored the comment, instead focusing on the two women. "Martha, show me where you have laid him."

A thin, round stone across the face of a rocky ledge marked the entrance to the tomb. A small crowd followed us. We stood there several long, awkward moments. Tears again filled Jesus' eyes. Emotion choked his voice. "Have the stone rolled away."

Two men in religious robes both immediately exclaimed, "No, you can't." The eyes of those in the crowd grew wide. Martha gradually recovered from shock. "But, Lord, he's been dead four days. There's sure to be a stench."

Something impossible to explain began happening. Though nothing appeared visible, two great forces seemed locked in battle. The perception silently, but forcefully, grew. I wasn't imagining the sensation. The wonder of the feeling captured my very being.

Then Jesus spoke. "Martha, did I not tell you that if you only believe, you would see the Glory of God?"

With a slight glimmer of confidence, Martha turned to several friends. "Roll the stone away."

Jesus stepped to the open tomb, lifted his gaze toward heaven then looked directly at the tomb. He called out loudly and strongly, "Lazarus, come out!"

What happened next far exceeded anything my mind could comprehend. A man wrapped in burial clothes walked out of that tomb. Jesus ordered the clothes removed from his face and hands. Lazarus stood there alive, looking quite healthy. The sorrow and shock of the onlookers suddenly became joyous pandemonium. People were shouting. Others ran spreading the news. Never had I experienced such unabashed joy.

Martha didn't take long to organize a celebration dinner to eclipse anything seen before in Bethany. People from the community brought food. The whole town appeared to come to celebrate. Even a number of Pharisees were there acting happy for Lazarus' return.

Considerably after dark, the celebration died down and people returned to their homes. Using lanterns, we made a makeshift camp on Martha's patio. "What do you think now?" Thomas asked John. "Imagine it's safe to return home?"

John unrolled his several blankets. "The Pharisees wouldn't dare touch Jesus now. The people of Bethany would string them up."

James came out to give us the official word. "We'll start very early in the morning for home—in Galilee."

Well before the sleepy celebrants of Bethany were awake, we were packed and on the road. As the sun peeked over the eastern hills, we again approached the Bethpage checkpoint. Only two soldiers were finishing their long night of duty. They waved us by.

We didn't stop to celebrate or rest. We hardly ate along the way. Everyone seemed extremely anxious as we made our way toward Galilee.

We had an hour's advantage leaving from Bethany, but the much shorter days of early winter left us well short of our usual camping spot. No beautiful pink sky announced the approaching evening. Instead, before we found a suitable place to camp, nightfall settled like a dull thud.

The damp wood thwarted Thomas and Andrew's attempt to kindle a decent fire and thus made cooking dinner a challenge.

I took my small meal and sat as closely as I dared to the smoky campfire. Though hungry, I sat for the longest time looking at my bowl.

I didn't plan to say anything, and I certainly didn't intend for my voice to break. I felt more like I was standing outside the circle, listening to myself. "I don't know about the rest of you, but I don't understand. I'm not used to seeing people raised from the dead." I turned to Jesus. "Please explain what really happened in Bethany yesterday."

Jesus stirred the growing campfire. "Although dangerous, we could have gone to Bethany earlier. Then I could have healed Lazarus." He stopped for a long moment. Tilting his head to one side, he asked, "But what would have been different from any other healing?"

Jesus waited for a response.

"Well …" I was caught for a loss of words. "Nothing, I guess."

Jesus looked deep in thought. "People have seen me heal to the point they take the miracle for granted, like that person who remarked if I could heal the blind, why couldn't I keep Lazarus from dying."

Jesus rose to his feet. "I raised Lazarus from the dead so you will know for sure that I am in the Father, and the Father is in me."

Jesus paused another long moment. "We will soon be going to Jerusalem where I will be handed over to the religious authorities, killed and on the third day, will rise again. I want you to understand and be ready, even though I know you cannot really be prepared."

Jesus' comment sparked a thousand questions. He brushed them aside. "In the morning, we will cross the border into Galilee. We don't know what to expect. We will spread out into our usual four groups and trust in our Heavenly Father."

One more chance to be arrested and hauled to Jerusalem lay before us. Capernaum will have never looked so good—*if we make it.*

CHAPTER TWENTY-FIVE

Despite the cold, sullen sky and a dampness that permeated everything, we were happy to be back safely in Capernaum. A fire burning in the kitchen over an hour helped, but the rest of the house seemed to still needed squeezing, like a soaked sponge.

"We've never been gone this long in winter." Mary tried excusing the dampness to both herself and anyone who might be paying attention.

Susanna walked over to the kitchen. "Winter isn't very exciting anywhere. I'm afraid it is going to be even less so here beside this lake. The air's so thick and the fish odor … it's awful."

"Even with the weather and the odor, I'm still happy we're home." I stretched. "These past several weeks were about all the excitement I can handle, at least for a while."

"Speaking of excitement," Mary looked around. "Where is Mary Magdalene?"

"Mary said she needed to sleep for at least a week," Susanna said. Then she sat down across the table and looked over at me. "Joanna,

I'm worried about you. Something happened on that trip—more than just running from religious authorities. You're different."

"I'm that transparent?" I innocently blushed. Meanwhile, my inner defenses jumped quicker than an army could answer a trumpet call.

I did need to unburden to someone about my unwanted emotion concerning Andrew. But I couldn't share my feelings with Susanna. She might breathe a word to Mary Magdalene, then everyone would know and my days with Jesus would be finished.

"You've figured me out pretty well." I struggled for an alternate dilemma. "Yes. I'm in a quandary. My planned two weeks with Jesus has stretched into seven months. I doubt if I can even go home now. If I stay much longer, there won't be a way to ever return home. I still have feelings ..." My mind hit too sensitive a spot and simply stopped functioning. To cover, I got up and poured myself a cup of water.

"Feelings for ...?" Susanna questioned.

"Oh, feelings for Cuza and for Marcus." I prayed Susanna couldn't see what I was really grappling with. "Working with Jesus has become my life. As much as I want to go home, I can't imagine not being here, listening to Jesus."

I stopped again. Thinking one thing and trying to talk about another grew harder by the moment.

"So, you're saying you still don't really know what you're going to do." Susanna looked at me like she was reading something written inside me.

"I think I can speak for Mary Magdalene. We are here, period." Susanna's voice choked on her next words. "There isn't any place for us to return to."

Susanna paused to regain her composure. "But what worries me is something happening to Jesus. He talks so much about being betrayed and killed." She wiped a tear. "If that were to happen, I'm afraid James and Simon Peter would load us on the first cart leaving town."

I heard voices outside the door. "We'll finish this conversation later."

Philip and Thomas shook off the dampness as they stepped in the door. *They'll never know how much I appreciate their coming in at this moment.*

Philip slipped off his rain garment and hung the cloak on a peg beside the door. "Jesus wants us to meet here. We can't do much else in this awful weather. The others will be along soon."

There wasn't much to do in the kitchen, so Susanna and I joined the group as they assembled. Jesus's voice had another unusual effect. Mary Magdalene appeared in her doorway.

When all of us found a comfortable spot, Jesus spoke. "My great concern is someday, when you have become leaders in my church, you will begin to think you are important. I fear you will look down on people who are still searching for the truth. I don't want your righteousness to ever resemble that of the Pharisees."

Several shook their heads. Simon Peter sat up especially straight. "No. That just won't happen. We're not like that."

"Listen then." Jesus' brow furrowed. "Two men went to the temple to pray. One was a Pharisee and the other a dishonest tax collector."

James and Simon Peter, almost in unison, stole a quick glance at Matthew. Jesus stopped. He gave the two a look needing no explanation. Then he continued, "The proud Pharisee stood off by himself and prayed, 'I thank you, God, that I am not a sinner like everyone else—especially not like that tax collector. I never cheat, I don't lie, I don't commit adultery, I fast twice a week, and I give you a tenth of my income.'"

Jesus paused a long moment. "The tax collector stood at a distance. He could not even lift his eyes toward heaven. Instead, he bowed and prayed, 'O God, be merciful, for I am a sinful man.'"

Jesus looked around the group. "Which of these returned home justified before God that day?" Everyone obviously knew the answer. "Remember this," he added, "the proud will always be brought down, and our Father God will always honor the humble."

Something very interesting must have been written on the floor in front of James and Peter. Matthew sat up a little straighter and flashed a small grin.

Jesus continued. "If a shepherd has one hundred sheep, and one wanders away and is lost—what will the shepherd do? Won't he leave the ninety-nine in the sheepfold and go out into the hills and search for the one? And when he finds the lost one, will he not rejoice over that sheep more than the ninety-nine who are safe?"

I felt as if a knife were in my side. *Why do I feel more like the lost sheep than those safe in the sheepfold? I've done nothing wrong.* Yes, I had feelings I couldn't explain or understand. But why did I feel guilty like I did?

"In the same way, it is not my Heavenly Father's will that anyone should perish but all have eternal life." Jesus nodded. "Do not forget this, ever."

Jesus seemed finished, then added one additional thought. "Keep your faith strong, and it will carry you through the trials in the days to come."

As the men rose from the discussion group, Thomas remained seated, his bottom lip trembling. "What trials, Lord? You keep mentioning these but never explain. Tell us what you mean so we can be ready."

Each previous time Jesus expressed a similar thought, he'd dismissed their questions and moved on to other issues. Apparently,

Thomas' distress proved enough. Jesus motioned the men back. "Before long we will go to Jerusalem for Passover. There, everything written about the Son of Man will be fulfilled. I will be handed over to the authorities. They will mock me, spit on me and kill me. On the third day, I will rise again."

"That cannot happen!" Peter looked ready to thump his chest. "We won't let them kill you."

John spoke up, "Last week did give us a scare, but we evaded their plot, didn't we? We can do it again." The remaining disciples joined in the pledge to protect Jesus. After that, no one seemed ready to leave the room.

I slipped over to Philip. "Jesus said we would be going to Jerusalem for Passover. I hope that isn't any time soon."

Philip's eyes widened. "You know when Passover is. It's …"

My face obviously revealed my feelings of utter stupidity. Redness raced up the sides of my neck. I felt like a kid stuck in a deep hole. "I'm sorry. I don't know when Passover is." I turned to hide my embarrassment.

Philip quickly caught on. "Oh Joanna, I apologize. I'm sorry, I didn't remember you were not raised observing the traditions."

I smiled the best I could.

"My surprise only showed because Passover is our most important observance." Philip took my hand. "Let me tell you about Passover."

"It's awful to be ignorant, Philip. But to display it so obviously …" I dried my eyes. "I've heard of Passover, but I don't know much more."

"Come, sit down." Philip pulled a stool out for me. "The story is long but a very important one."

"Okay, but only if you promise you won't tell anyone I didn't know." I tried a weak smile again.

Philip nodded and drew a deep breath. "It all began a little over two thousand years ago. God promised this very land to Abraham—the father of our people. Abraham and his family lived here, then his son Isaac and his family after him. Isaac's son, Jacob, continued and had twelve sons."

"That's a lot of sons." I twisted on my stool to get comfortable. "Didn't he have at least one daughter?"

"I don't know about any girls, but let me correct myself. There were ten sons. Joseph was born several years later to make number eleven. As so often happens, a son born much later becomes the father's favorite. The older brothers resented their father's preference toward Joseph, so they hatched a plot to kill him."

"Oh, no!" My hand went over my mouth.

"But greed got in their way. They sold young Joseph as a slave to a caravan going to Egypt and convinced their father a lion had killed his favorite son. Jacob was devastated."

"I can certainly see why."

"Several years passed, and Benjamin was born. His birth finally brought relief to Jacob from losing Joseph."

I felt a little perplexed. "So, he was number twelve?"

Philip nodded. "Now the important part. Several years later, a severe drought swept over the land, and people everywhere ran out of food. Jacob sent two of his sons to Egypt, where they heard they could buy food. In the meantime, the supposedly dead Joseph had risen to a high position in Egypt. He recognized his brothers. Joseph forgave them and brought the whole family to Egypt to live during the famine. The family grew and prospered in Egypt, so much so, they just stayed."

I inadvertently yawned. "Sorry. I know this is going somewhere."

Philip shook his head. "I warned you this was a long story."

"Go ahead. I dislike being so uninformed."

"Okay. Three hundred years later, the family had grown to probably ten thousand people, who still lived in the luxury of Egypt. Many pharaohs came into power, passed on and the story of Joseph faded from history. Then a pharaoh came to power who perceived the thousands of foreigners as a security threat. He decided to control these Israelites by making them slaves to build his great cities."

"Oh. I see where this is going."

Philip nodded. "The slavery continued over a hundred years. Each succeeding pharaoh increased the workload. The people cried out to the Lord for deliverance and God sent Moses to bring the Israelites out of their slavery."

Philip's voice dropped lower. "But Pharaoh wasn't about to let all his free labor just walk away. A huge contest of wills ensued between Moses and Pharaoh. God sent one plague after another on the Egyptians, but Pharaoh refused to let the Israelites go free." Philip stopped.

"Don't stop. My curiosity is boiling now."

"This brings on the final showdown. Moses warned Pharaoh if he didn't let the Israelites go free, God's Death Angel would take the life of every firstborn child. He again refused."

Philip's voice slipped slower and deeper. "Now, listen carefully to the most important part. You see, the Israelites were not immune from the Death Angel just because they were Jews. Only one thing would cause the Death Angel to pass over the Jewish families and spare their children. They were to slay a lamb and spread its blood on the doorpost of their homes. When the Death Angel observed the blood of the lamb on the doorpost, he would pass over that home."

"Pass–over." My eyes grew wide. "I get it. Passover!"

"Yes, Joanna. That night God's Death Angel spread his wings over the land of Egypt. The Egyptian people were so enraged over the deaths of their firstborn children, Pharaoh had no choice but to free our people. That very morning, thousands of Israelites began a march to return here, their promised homeland. So, the Death Angel passing over the homes with the blood of the lamb on the doorpost is, as you said, Passover."

I sat there with tears in my eyes—joyful tears. "And I have missed this all these years."

CHAPTER TWENTY-SIX
Three Months Later, Galilee, Early Spring

The cold damp days of the Galilee winter gradually gave way to sunshine and warmer temperatures. We certainly welcomed those, but I didn't welcome the renewed talk of Jerusalem and the coming Passover celebration. Mary Magdalene and about half of the disciples embarked upon a campaign to persuade Jesus not to go. Older James, John, to a lesser extent Simon Peter, and a few others talked piously about supporting Jesus whatever he decided. To say we were of a divided opinion grossly understated the situation.

Just when those who opposed going seemed to be gaining, Jesus announced we would be going to Jerusalem. And not only were we going, we would leave a week earlier than usual.

With his decision expressed, everyone quickly fell in line. Our departure would be the day after the Sabbath, one week hence.

"I know it's still a week, but we need to start preparing for the trip." Mary looked agitated sitting on the front edge of her chair. A long moment passed. "It galls me having to go to Judas for money to buy supplies. He always complains about how much we spend. We ought to make him go and help."

I shielded my eyes from the morning sun. "Oh! You'd want him along to ruin an otherwise perfect day?"

Mary cracked a slight smile. Susanna laughed aloud.

I continued, "Think how he'd get his sandals dusty."

"It's about time he gets something dusty." Mary returned to her defiant tone. "He doesn't do enough to be worth the food he eats."

"Aren't you being a little hard on Judas?" She surprised me. Expressing animosity was so unlike Mary.

"Joanna, I won't accuse anyone of anything." Mary shook her head. "But I'll tell you this. Each time I go to him for money, I make a note of how much is left. Each time there's not as much left as the time before." A dark cloud seemed to hover above Mary's head.

A cold, steady rain halted Jesus' plans to start toward Jerusalem. Finally, late that afternoon, the sun peeked through a little. Spirits soared as we anticipated leaving early the next morning.

Large puddles dotted the roadway as we started, but the morning sun shone brightly and soon burned away the dampness. Spring filled the air as soon as Capernaum's fish odor dissipated behind us.

I tugged on younger James' sleeve. "Aren't you and the Zealot supposed to be out scouting for Roman patrols?"

James shook his head. "Not till we get closer to Judea."

The men ahead continued bantering among themselves like there wasn't a problem in the world. The subject of possible arrest didn't even come up around the campfire that first night.

Again, we split into four groups to blend with the many traveling families as we passed through the Roman checkpoint at the Galilee-Judea border. We viewed the lack of a full search as a positive sign. But it was still difficult to ignore the dire threats against Jesus just three months earlier. Could the animosity of the religious leaders in Jerusalem have evaporated like a morning mist? Not likely. Our simple plan involved remaining anonymous and blending with the many pilgrims on their way to the celebration.

Andrew dropped back to visit with James. I nudged him. "That's Jericho ahead. See, I'm beginning to know the way pretty well."

"Good girl." Andrew stretched 'good' into three long syllables.

As we walked past people beside the road, I overheard a man answer someone, "It's Jesus of Nazareth and his followers."

That started the clamor. "Jesus, Son of David, have mercy on me!" a beggar called. Then he called yet louder, "Jesus, have mercy!"

Several onlookers shushed him.

His call became almost hysterical, "Son of David, have mercy on me."

As Jesus stopped, Judas said, "Give to one beggar, and you'll have ten more sticking a cup in your face."

Jesus ignored Judas, called for the men nearby to bring the beggar and asked him, "What do you want from me?"

"Lord, I want to see." He slumped to his knees. Big tears coursed down his cheeks.

Jesus placed his hand on the beggar's shoulder. "Receive your sight. Your own faith has healed you."

"I can see!" He jumped to his feet. "I can see!" The area erupted. People came from every direction. Our hope of remaining unnoticed disappeared like a whiff of smoke in a strong breeze.

There on into Jericho became a huge celebration. People followed, lined the streets, and called out to us. All that attention was the last thing we wanted. If a Roman patrol were anywhere around, they would have no doubt of our presence. The once blind beggar led the procession shouting and rejoicing.

The strangest sight greeted us. Sitting on a low branch was a short, overweight, balding man dressed in clothes far too nice for tree climbing. Andrew leaned over. "Jesus just told him to climb down. We're going to his house for dinner this evening."

"I don't have a problem with that. Any dinner we don't have to cook is a good dinner." I looked at Andrew a long moment. "How does Jesus invite himself and sixteen followers to dinner?"

An onlooker from the crowd called to Jesus. "With all the respectable people in Jericho, why are you having dinner with a tax collector?" Several others added their objections.

The man clambered down the tree. Jesus introduced him to us as Zacchaeus. The little man acknowledged us, then quickly held out his hand to the increasingly hostile crowd. "Look, I know you have reason to hate me, but a man can change."

The crowd greeted his comment with ridicule.

"Look, here and now I pledge to give half of my possessions to the poor," Zacchaeus continued. "If I have cheated anyone, I will repay you four times over."

Jesus stepped onto an embankment to address the crowd. "Listen. Today salvation has come to this house. Know this, I have come to seek and to save those who are lost."

This comment, along with the man's pledge to repay four times over, placated the crowd somewhat. Jesus instructed the formerly blind beggar to go home and show himself to his family. Most of the crowd followed that joyful man.

Way too much excitement occurred, considering our absolute necessity to maintain a low profile. Nevertheless, we hurried on to our usual spot just outside of town and quickly sat up camp. We cleaned much of the road dust off, then walked back into town for the dinner. How he came up with a spread like that on such short notice, I'll never know.

The light, dry evening air, the nearly full moon, and the great meal made the walk back to our campsite delightful. Although I still had my concerns, I decided to enjoy the moment with the others. So much for getting through Jericho unnoticed. Hopefully we were far enough from Jerusalem. We would know all too soon.

The evening's lightheartedness conspicuously vanished the next morning. We broke camp and prepared for the difficult climb to Jerusalem. Everyone apparently saved their gloom for this last leg of the journey. Even the sky seemed ominous, delivering heavy dark clouds and a strong buffeting wind.

"Well, let's get on with it." Thomas' words expressed the mood as we departed the campsite for the long uphill road.

We stopped at our usual place near the top. A cool, gentle breeze replaced the heavy, gusty air of the Jordan Valley below. I tried to break the awkward silence with a cheerful exclamation. "Isn't the difference in temperature amazing?"

My observation fell as flat as most of my barley cakes.

Nothing tempted a smile out of the men. We walked on.

"Since the excitement of Lazarus is past," John whispered aloud to Jesus, "do you think we ought to break into our four groups to blend with the others? The Bethphage checkpoint's just ahead."

Jesus nodded. No one appeared inclined to give directions. But having completed that routine so many times, no one needed to.

Spread out among several other groups, the checkpoint delayed us an hour.

"When we reach Bethany, we'll go by to see Lazarus, Mary, and Martha," Jesus said as we re-gathered into one group. "I want to see how they are doing."

"Don't you think the Pharisees will be watching for you?" Thomas hesitantly asked. "They could almost know you would go there."

"We'll be in and out before a Pharisee even knows we're around," older James spoke confidently. "We're several days early. They won't be expecting us yet."

If James' comment was intended to instill confidence, it didn't come close.

As we resumed walking, younger James whispered to his mother, "I just don't understand. If there's any place they'll watch for Jesus, it will be at Lazarus's home." Mary lifted her head high. "Now, James. You know Jesus isn't going to run from any Pharisee." She seemed the strongest person present. "Remember what he did during the storm on the lake?"

She had a point. I wished I could absorb her confidence.

We did manage to make it quietly to Lazarus's home. But, as we prepared to trudge on, Martha wouldn't have it any other way. We were to stay for dinner, and that was that. She was adamant.

I nudged Susanna. "So much for slipping out of town unnoticed."

During the drama and celebration of our previous visit, I failed to appreciate Martha's house. Although nothing to compare with the homes of Sepphoris, her house did seem a good bit larger than the typical home in Capernaum. Their walls of stone had been whitewashed many times. The home's sloped roof rose higher than most, giving the main room of the house a spacious feeling. Since she wasn't feeding the whole community like last time, she placed three low tables over a number of soft carpets in her larger room.

With dinner ready, we left our sandals outside and reclined around the low tables, all twenty of us. It was my first time to eat in that fashion. I liked the style.

Near the end of dinner, Martha's younger sister Mary slipped away from our table. I didn't think much about it until she reappeared and slipped quietly to where Jesus reclined at the table with Martha and others. As she stood for several long moments, I detected soft, tearful emotions. Her eyes glistened as she drew a small container from the folds of her robe and opened it. A wonderful fragrance spread across the room like a light mist covering the lake at dawn.

She stooped and poured the contents over Jesus' feet. Joy filled Mary's eyes as she pulled the ivory pin from her hair. She let it fall then used her long hair to wipe the feet of Jesus. Surprise and wonderment swept over me.

I was still captivated by the incredible event, when Judas whispered to Matthew, "That perfume was worth a small fortune. Shouldn't it have been sold and the money used to help the poor?"

Mary Magdalene sat up fully, and she didn't whisper. "He doesn't give a hoot about the poor. He just wants the money in the bag so he can get his hands on it."

Oh, that started a commotion. Judas looked set to go for Mary Magdalene's throat. Several men appeared ready to drag Judas out.

But Jesus intervened. "Do not make light of what she did. It was for my burial. You will always have poor people to minister to, but I will not be with you much longer."

I bit my bottom lip and glanced toward Philip. "I could tear Judas apart myself." I struggled to hold my emotions back. "I've tried to put my worry for Jesus out of mind. Why did he have to ruin everything?"

Lazarus saved the day. He raised a goblet of wine and offered a toast to the special evening and to the gift of life. Soon Judas' crude comments were overlooked, and we had occasion to laugh again. Times of lighthearted laughter had proved hard to come by lately. That night became a beautiful exception.

CHAPTER TWENTY-SEVEN

Dusk settled over Bethany as dinner ended. Not long after, John stepped out to announce we would set up a semblance of camp by lamplight on Martha's terrace. I made a point to spread my sleeping roll close to the Zealot's. If anyone could sleep with one eye open for the temple guard, Simon could.

The brisk walk toward Jerusalem the next morning proved to be a lot nicer than arriving in the evening, all tired. But following close behind the excitement of arriving was also a strange sense of dread. The air radiated a tingle of thrill, yet our concern for Jesus' safety placed a heavy damper over everyone's attitude.

We had intended to keep a very low profile, planning to blend with the crowds. In every way, we would avoid advertising our presence. But the reception we received in Jericho, and then our special dinner in Bethany, certainly destroyed that cover. We could be certain the religious authorities knew of our presence. More than few disciples glanced over their shoulder as we sat up camp. To be truthful, so did I.

Even though we had not encountered a visible threat, everyone knew one could lurk around the next turn. The situation obviously weighed heavily on the men as they left for the temple. That is, on everyone except Jesus. He, again, was his usual happy, smiling self. I couldn't understand. Jesus had spoken many times about being betrayed to the religious leaders and then killed. But here in Jerusalem now, he seemed not worried in the least.

Jesus wore a broad smile as he gathered his outer robe. "Since today is the Sabbath, there will not be many important events. The Pharisees would have to violate their own strict Sabbath rules to attempt anything."

"It's a good time to gauge the mood of the people," Simon Peter added. "The crowds always seem to sense when something big is about to happen."

James called, "Come on men, let's go." James always made sure Peter didn't get the last word.

Conflicting emotions flooded my mind as the disciples disappeared down the path. I felt pride being in Jerusalem with Jesus. But fear clutched my heart as I recalled fleeing this very spot last winter. I couldn't imagine life without Jesus, should anything happen to him. I clutched my shoulders while my insides quivered.

Mary continued to rearrange the things we'd placed where she instructed only moments before. Susanna finally put her hands on her hips. "We're never going to get it completely right. Let's go over to your rock and see what's happening at the temple."

"I wish it were my rock," I replied as I followed her over. "Do you think I could convince Thad to carry it back to Capernaum for me?" We both laughed.

Susanna's dark eyebrows furrowed. "The dire warning John Mark reported last time still worries me. Beyond that though, we haven't actually seen a threat.

"I don't know whether we've just been successful in evading danger, or whether we overreacted to an unfounded threat." I stopped to reflect for a moment. "But I would say this; when we do see a threat, it will probably be too late."

"Joanna, you always have such a wonderful grasp on things."

"Well, not really." I let out a weak smile. "Actually, I overheard Philip say that last evening."

As Jesus and the disciples returned to camp that evening, their upbeat mood relieved some of my worries. There had been no confrontations to speak of. *If it can only last.*

The early morning blast of the shofar, announcing the start of the week-long celebration before Passover, startled me. I rose on one elbow to observe Andrew also disturbed by the sound. An anxious look swept his face.

Mary was already rolling up her blankets. I sat up and rubbed the sleep from my eyes as she left for our special area.

Mary came trotting back about as fast as her small legs would move. "Why are these people coming to our campsite? We can't feed all of them."

I stepped to the edge of our lean-to and saw at least fifty people gathered. More were coming behind them.

James shook at the sleep in his eyes. "I don't think they're here for food. They're probably looking for Jesus."

At that moment, Jesus walked back into camp and called, "Thomas, Thaddaeus, I have a task for you." The two quickly deposited their sleeping rolls on the pile and hurried over.

"I need a young colt donkey for our trip into Jerusalem this morning."

Thomas' brow furrowed. "Master, you want us to bring No-Jordan around?"

"You don't understand. Today, I need a colt from a donkey, a colt no one has ever ridden." Jesus pointed in a direction. "You and Thad, go to the village over there. You will see a donkey tied to a post and beside it, a colt. Untie the colt and bring it."

Thad shook his head. "Won't we get into trouble taking someone's colt?"

"No. Tell the person who questions you the Lord needs it."

Thomas' and Thad's sandals flapped as they took off toward the nearby village.

The crowd caught sight of Jesus and began shouting to those along the road, "Jesus is here!"

Older James came around the corner with fire in his eyes. "We need to get these people away from here. They're going to reveal our location to the authorities." James' protest proved useless. The crowd of fifty quickly swelled to several hundred.

Jesus called to the rest of the disciples. "The people are here for me. They will proclaim who I am. All of you, including the ladies, make ready for our trip into Jerusalem."

Thad and Thomas came trotting back with a young colt in tow. They both wore smiles as big as all outdoors.

John's booming voice echoed, "Come on, everyone. We're going to Jerusalem."

Thad threw his outer cloak over the colt's back. Then with Thomas' help, they lifted Jesus to sit sideways on the animal. As they came into view, the crowd erupted, "Jesus! Jesus! Jesus!"

I called to Mary, Susanne, and Mary Magdalene. "I'm not sure what's happening, but we need to get moving."

A glad celebration continued while we made our way over to the road leading across the Kidron Valley. When our procession turned onto the road toward Jerusalem, pandemonium broke out. The several hundred people quickly grew to a thousand or more. Many cut branches from the palm trees and waved them in the air. Others threw their cloaks on the pavement for the colt's path. The throng sang and shouted, "Blessed is the one who comes in the name of the Lord. Peace in heaven and glory to God in the Highest." I had never seen anything like it. A visiting king would be envious of such a celebration.

This wild, loud, beautiful spectacle continued all the way down the Mount of Olives, across the Kidron Valley, then toward the temple's Eastern Gate. Everyone around joined in the festivities. I shouted until hoarse.

Some in the crowd began singing, "Hail King Jesus, Hail to the King of Israel." Ice crackled through my veins. *What on earth are we doing? We're supposed to be entering Jerusalem in quiet obscurity. What about the religious authorities?*

And, there they were. The dour looks on the Pharisees' faces could have cracked stones. But even their presence couldn't dampen the celebration of the throng praising Jesus.

Our boisterous procession made its way right up to the steps of the Eastern Gate. Philip slipped back and motioned to us. "It's okay for ladies to enter the first court. Come on."

Jesus walked halfway up the huge staircase, turned, and raised his hands toward the shouting multitude. "The time has come for the Son of Man to enter his glory." Jesus strode to the top of the steps, then turned again toward the crowd. "When the Son of Man is lifted up from the earth, I will draw all men to myself." The crowd again cheered and shouted.

Jesus stood for several minutes and acknowledged the crowd and their praises. Then, he turned and led us through the gate into the temple's first courtyard.

The experience was overwhelming. We had seen crowds of thousands hang on every word Jesus spoke. We had seen the celebration at the raising of Lazarus, but this jubilation exceeded anything we had ever seen or could imagined.

While crossing the Court of Women, a dozen Pharisees met us, all adorned in their religious robes. They spread out apparently to block Jesus' path. "By what authority do you parade like a king?" a leader demanded. "Who gave you such authority?"

Jesus looked at the ornately robed men as a parent might look at a misbehaving child. "When a man believes in me, he does not believe in me alone. He also believes in the Father who sent me." His voice carried a tone of authority like the day he called Lazarus from the tomb. "I have come into the world as a light. What I say is what the Father has told me to say."

Jesus led us around the stunned group of Pharisees, and we proceeded on. I looked back to observe pure anger steaming from their eyes.

The courtyard was enormous, but people filled it from wall to wall. Jesus stepped to where Mary and I stood. "It's impossible to teach here. Soon we will go over to Solomon's Colonnade. You won't be able to go there. You are free to stay here in the Court of Women as long as you like."

The four of us put our heads together. Three felt it best to return to camp. Mary Magdalene, of course, wanted to stay. When she realized her single opinion wouldn't carry, she gushed, "Oh, Jesus, be careful."

Thad tugged my sleeve. "S-since Thomas and I need to return the colt, would you ladies like to walk back with us?"

"Thad, you're a gentleman. By the way, where is the colt?"

"W-we left it with Thomas back at the Eastern Gate. I-I'm sure he's miffed we left him so long."

Thomas was upset. But after Thad's third apology, he finally said, "It's okay, forget it. Let's go get this colt back home."

We returned to camp, and Mary Magdalene began her campaign. "I'm tired of us not spending time at the temple. We might never have this opportunity again. Let's ask Jesus to take us tomorrow and explain everything."

"You saw the crowds today," I argued. "You really want to be in that mob when we have a great spot to watch everything here?"

"I want to be there. I want to tell my grandchildren how we went to the temple with Jesus."

"You have grandchildren?" I asked.

"No, silly. When … I have grandchildren." Her voice dropped a level. "If I don't do something soon, I'm never even going to have children."

After dinner, Jesus responded to Mary Magdalene's request. "We would be honored to have you women accompany us. In addition, if you would like to make an offering at the temple, you can do that tomorrow as well." The easy victory left Mary Magdalene beaming.

I asked Jesus, "How did things go at the temple after we left?"

"We hardly saw the Pharisees after that encounter." Jesus sat down with us in front of the campfire. "The only interesting thing today happened with the Sadducees. They disagree with the Pharisees about the resurrection."

The Resurrection? A golden opportunity had just presented itself. I asked, "What do we believe about the resurrection?"

"That was the subject of my discussion with the Sadducees today. They wanted to prove their point about there being no resurrection, so they proposed a hypothetical question. 'A man died and each of his several brothers, in succession, married his widow until they each died. Whose wife will she be in the resurrection?'"

Jesus laughed. "I told them they missed the point completely. Marriage is for people here on earth. Those raised again at the last day will never die again. They will be children of God raised up to a new life." Jesus stopped and looked at me with his beautiful smile. "Joanna, you will be like the angels in heaven."

I felt Jesus' eyes look into my heart. "But you don't need to worry about this. You only need to trust in God and trust in me."

I smiled back through my glistening eyes. "I do … I do the best I can."

"The good news is there are many dwelling places in my Father's house. You can be sure of this … because I told you." Jesus paused for a long moment, then added, "I'm going there to prepare a place for you."

By that time, our conversation had drawn everyone's attention. He looked around the circle. "I will come back and take you to be with me so you may be where I am." Jesus stopped, then nodded. "You know the way."

I am sure there were several other perplexed looks besides mine. But Thomas voiced what several of us were thinking. "Lord, if we don't know where you're going, how can we know the way?"

Jesus stood. He looked in each of our anxious eyes as if he had been waiting for that very question. "I am the way." He emphasized each word. "I am the truth, and I am the life." His voice dropped lower. "No one comes to the Father except through me."

Not one of us stirred. Jesus gathered his heavier robe and left the warm campfire to pray. We sat silent for the longest time.

The day turned out completely different than we planned or expected. We had determined to stay unobtrusive and not attract unnecessary attention. But the complete opposite just kept happening. *Either Jesus will win his battle with the religious authorities, or it will be a week to end in disaster.*

CHAPTER TWENTY-EIGHT

Even though I felt excited about going to the temple, the previous threats on Jesus' life had also planted their own kernels of fear. But since Jesus seemed completely upbeat about being in Jerusalem, and I had never witnessed Jesus being wrong about anything, I decided to, at least, act thrilled about a trip to the temple.

"Everything's almost ready to eat," Mary Magdalene called as I approached the cooking area. "See how much faster things go when they *let* me help."

Rather than create dissention, I only mentally rolled my eyes.

Jesus stepped back into camp from his morning prayer time. John asked him, "What about entering through the Sheep Gate today? They probably won't think to watch that direction."

Jesus considered this for a moment. "The Sheep Gate isn't far from the Treasury. Yes, and we can make our offering while passing there."

My offering, yes. I began to feel even better about the coming day.

Mary Magdalene assumed a place at the front of the group as we prepared to leave. "I feel so honored that Jesus planned this day around us." She spoke to Susanna, but the inflection of her voice made clear she intended it more for the rest of us.

My excitement grew as I recalled the people waving palm branches and praising Jesus the previous day. I would put the dour looks of the Pharisees out of my mind.

Again, we made our way along the main road down the Mount of Olives and across the Kidron Valley. However, instead of continuing toward the Eastern Gate, we turned right onto a stone walkway. On what must be the north side of the temple, we passed through a much smaller gate and entered a huge area covered with large paving stones. Several tall spindly cedar trees lined the edges. A good number of people moved about in the area, but it wasn't as congested as the Court of Women had been the previous day.

I slipped close to Philip and whispered, "Tell me about this area. I want to, at least, know more about it than Mary Magdalene."

A sparkle filled Philip's eyes. "See those huge pots over where the people are lined up? One pot goes to maintain the temple and the other is to support the priesthood."

I called to Susanna and Mary Magdalene, "Come on! Let's get in line so we can put in our offering." Then I said to Mary Magdalene, "Is this what you wanted to tell your grandchildren about?"

"Exactly!" she said as she stepped to the front of the three of us.

I did feel a thrill to drop in my offering. Several of us started to move on when Jesus motioned to us. "Watch for a moment."

The procession continued past the pots, each person depositing his or her offering. Most were ordinary people just like us. Then I noticed three men a little further back in line that stood out from the rest. When the three, wearing their ornate robes reached the offering pots, they stopped the procession. Each held his offering toward heaven then offered a blessing. With even greater ceremony, each placed far more in than all of us put together.

"They're disgusting to watch." I turned to leave.

"Wait." Jesus said.

The three departed with grand flair and the procession of the ordinary resumed. A frail, older woman with a makeshift crutch hobbled toward the offering containers with such difficulty I considered going to help her. She dropped in what looked like two small coins then hobbled on.

So caught up in that scene, I failed to notice how many people had gathered. Jesus lifted his hand toward the crowd. "I tell you this truth, this poor widow lady has given more than those three together. You see, they gave a little out of their abundance, but she gave all she had."

Tears welled behind my eyes. I leaned close to Susanna, "Jesus is so right."

Jesus looked out over the growing crowd. "How terrible it will be for these teachers of the Law in the coming judgment. They are very careful to tithe even the smallest part of their incomes, but they ignore the important part of the Law—justice, mercy, and faith. Should one tithe? Yes. But do not leave the more important things undone."

I shook my head. "No wonder people come from everywhere to hear Jesus."

"And no wonder the Pharisees want to kill him," Philip whispered back. "Speaking of Pharisees, here come two more."

Jesus didn't miss their appearance either. He stepped onto a small raised area. "It will be terrible in the judgment for you Pharisees. You are careful to clean the outside of a cup before you use it, but inside you are filthy, full of selfishness and pride. You are the worst hypocrites."

The crowd looked like they wanted to erupt in approval. Instead, most gave a wary glance toward the Pharisees and let the awkward silence spread. The two turned quickly and left.

Jesus stepped down, and with the two Pharisees safely at a distance, the crowd erupted in shouts of approval.

It happened in an instant. Mary crumpled like a damp cloth. Younger James reacted before I even realized the problem. His arm slipped beneath Mary's small body before she reached the pavement. He sat her down, her eyes weak and unfocused. We all gathered around. Thad elbowed his way in to deliver the water he carried. Philip diplomatically suggested we move back and give her air.

Mary took a couple of long drinks and several deep breaths. "I feel better now."

I recalled how we had walked for over an hour, stood in a packed crowd, and experienced anxiety as Jesus confronted the Pharisees. I stepped over to Philip. "No wonder Mary nearly fainted, it's hard to remember she's twice our age."

Mary finally sat up. Color gradually returned to her face. Jesus stooped and put his hand on her shoulder. "Our camp is too far back across the Kidron Valley. Taking her to Mary Lois' home would be closer. She can rest comfortably there."

Thad volunteered to accompany James to take her.

I only thought a moment, then spoke to younger James. "I'll go along and stay with Mary so you and Thad can return to the temple."

Young James looked relieved. "I appreciate this more than you can imagine." Sincerity filled his eyes.

As we turned to leave, Jesus motioned to me. "Inquire of Mary Lois if we might celebrate the Passover meal in their upper room again this year."

Mary Lois was surprised but pleased we chose her home. After Mary assured us she was fine, she agreed to stretch out in Lois' guestroom. James and Thad left to rejoin Jesus at the temple. I slipped back into the room to see if Mary needed anything, only to find her sound asleep.

Lois and I sat down in her spacious living room with a cup of delicious tea. Lois asked, "How did it go after your hasty departure last winter?"

I laughed. "Jesus could only imagine what you were doing here in Jerusalem. Hundreds of people began to show up down at the Jordan River. We were totally amazed as the crowds increased each day."

"Oh, I didn't do much, Joanna. A good number of people here in Jerusalem share our belief that Jesus is the Messiah. I spread the word to a few and they did the rest."

I related the situation about Lazarus and not being safe to return to Bethany. "But Jesus raising Lazarus from the dead changed everything. The people of Bethany started that tremendous reception on the way to the temple yesterday."

"Oh, everyone in Jerusalem heard about Jesus bringing Lazarus back from the dead," Lois related as she poured more tea. "It was the talk of this whole town for weeks."

"How is Mark doing with the thousands of people here for the Passover celebration?" I asked.

"Quite good, actually. They brought his contingent in from the countryside to help in Jerusalem during the festival. It's nice having him come home earlier than usual."

We talked on about John Mark, his classes, and how well things were going for him. The better things seemed to be for Lois and Mark, the tighter the clamp grew around my chest. Each time she referred to Mark, a picture of Cuza flashed across my mind. As she talked, the scene of Cuza coldly walking past me the fateful day I left flooded my senses.

Lois stopped in mid-sentence. "Joanna, something's bothering you terribly. It's all over your face."

The dam holding my flood of pent-up tears burst wide open. I had no idea so much emotion filled my heart. "I'm sorry. It's so rude of me to cry—and over so little."

"Joanna, it isn't so little." She put her hand on my shoulder. "It's consuming your soul."

"Lois, I'm scared." My insides began to tremble. "I love being with Jesus, but I have left my husband and my son Marcus behind. It's been a year since I've seen them. I don't know whether they even care if I'm alive."

Through my tears I shared the intolerable situation with the housekeeper, Mariam, the awful confrontation with Cuza, the note I left, and his complete lack of response.

"Your husband is Cuza, the manager of King Herod's Palace in Sepphoris?" Lois' eyes were as wide as a doorway.

"Yes, and even though Jesus healed our son from almost certain death, Cuza let the pressure of Herod's palace sway his thinking. Herod considers Jesus a troublemaker, plotting to disrupt the country."

My tears slowed. "I love my time with Jesus and helping with his ministry. I have never experienced such love or felt so useful. But at the same time, I long to be home with my son so badly I can hardly stand it." I had to stop and close my eyes for a moment. "Now, I don't know whether I would even be welcome in my home. If I were, I think Cuza would have come for me long before now. When we're in Galilee, Jesus isn't hard to find."

I wiped my eyes with the corner of my sleeve. "In addition, my heart is heavy because Jesus keeps talking about being betrayed and killed here in Jerusalem. I can't leave in the middle of all this. I don't know what to do."

"Joanna, I can't tell you what to do, but I can pray you will become sure in your heart what you should do." Lois' words and our long conversation brought more peace to my heart than I had experienced in a long time.

"In the meantime," I added, "be very careful how you share this with Mark and John Mark. Should either mention anything about Cuza's wife being in Jerusalem with Jesus to the wrong people, it would cause serious problems."

"I'll be very—" A knock came at the door.

James and Thad stood in the entrance. "We've come for Joanna and Mary."

I couldn't believe the whole afternoon had disappeared. When we went to check on her, we found Mary sitting on the edge of the bed, stretching.

As we left, Lois assured us they would be thrilled to have Jesus observe Passover again in the upper room of their home.

The bright morning sun produced a revived Mary. So much so, she again took charge of the kitchen. I had certainly discovered the evening before I didn't know nearly as much about cooking for the group as I'd thought.

While the men gathered their things for the day at the temple, I lingered in the cooking area with Mary. I had certainly enjoyed what little time I spent at the temple the previous day, but I wasn't at all excited about going again. There was something awe-inspiring about the place, but at the same time the temple frightened me.

Mary Magdalene walked over and looked square at me. "I want all of us to go. We may never get this chance again."

"But Mary shouldn't try to go again," I countered. "The crowds and the conflict with the Pharisees could be too much. I'll stay here with her."

"I will be fine!" Mary answered in her usual testy way. "I'll enjoy a day alone. I love you, but sometimes, I love not having to talk to anyone. Now the three of you go on and let me have a day of peace and quiet."

Even though it was the final day before the actual Passover celebration, I remained hesitant. But Mary robbed me of the only excuse I could exploit, so I gathered my things and joined the group as they set out.

We approached the temple from yet a different gate in the huge stone wall. Simon and younger James went in first to scout out any unseen danger. As we waited from a safe distance, I admired the massive fortification. The light tan stone reflected a beautiful golden hue in the morning sunlight. The wall towered much higher than any I knew and appeared wide enough, even along the top, for several soldiers to walk abreast. A donkey braying in the distance jarringly contradicted the location's majesty.

The Zealot and younger James returned, reporting nothing that might constitute a threat. We entered through a gate larger than the previous day's but not nearly as massive as the Eastern Gate. We crossed a large plaza where many people all seemed heading for somewhere else. Once across we entered another, more crowded, area. We were there hardly a quarter hour when the crowd parted. Eight Pharisees strode directly to our group. One spoke to Jesus in a voice obviously intended for the crowd. "Teacher, we know you are a man of integrity and that you teach the ways of God in accordance with the truth …"

Philip leaned over. "That's quite a line of sheep dung they are handing Jesus."

"Philip!" I blushed.

"It's for the crowd. They're always playing the crowd," Andrew added.

The lead Pharisee continued his announcement. "We know you are not swayed by what men say, because you are not impressed by one's station in life."

"Exactly my point." Philip nodded.

A sly smile crossed the Pharisee's face. "Now tell us your opinion. Is it right to pay taxes to Caesar or not?"

My stomach twitched. "Those guys could make me lose my breakfast."

But Jesus didn't hesitate. "You hypocrites. Why are you always trying to trap me?"

Older James uttered something unrepeatable under his breath.

Jesus smiled toward the crowd, then replied, "Show me the coin used for paying taxes."

The Pharisees resorted to borrowing a denarius from someone in the crowd.

"Whose likeness is on the coin?" Jesus asked. "What inscription is written on it?"

After an awkward silence, one of the Pharisees replied, "Caesar's."

"Then give to Caesar what belongs to Caesar, and give to God what is God's." The crowd expressed its approval. The Pharisees turned away almost as a group, throwing disgusted looks back toward us as they departed.

We three women severely limited where Jesus and the disciples could go. I felt badly, because I remembered how Jesus liked to teach on Solomon's Colonnade … and other places we women weren't allowed. Jesus suggested we go observe the daily sacrifice, from a distance.

As we struggled through the crowd in that direction, yet another group of Pharisees approached. I turned to Susanna. "They don't ever seem to let up, do they?"

The lead Pharisee called loudly to Jesus, "Teacher." Again, he clearly intended the crowd to hear.

The Pharisee stood with a shrewd look on his face. "Teacher, which is the greatest commandment of the Law?"

Andrew leaned toward us. "That ought to give everyone something to argue about for the day."

I wouldn't have the slightest idea what to answer, but Jesus didn't hesitate. He acted like anyone should have known. "Love the Lord your God with all your heart and with all your soul and with all your mind. This is the first and greatest commandment. And the very close second commandment is, 'Love your neighbor as much as you love yourself.' All of the Law and prophets' teachings hang on these two commandments."

The crowd again nodded and voiced approval. The lead Pharisee raised his hand to say more, but Jesus suddenly stepped onto a raised area and spoke to the growing crowd. "The Pharisees sit in Moses's seat. Do everything they tell you."

Jesus' agreement with the Pharisees caught me off guard. But before I could contemplate a question, he added in a much stronger voice, "However, do not do what they do. They do not practice what they preach. They tie heavy loads on men's backs but will not lift a finger to help."

Those near the front of the crowd nodded. Some standing more anonymously near the back even shouted agreement.

Jesus pointed with his staff. "Everything they do is to be seen by men. They make their phylacteries wide and their tassels long. They love places of honor and the most important seats in the synagogues." Jesus' voice rose a level, and the crowd voiced even more approval.

"They love to be greeted in special ways and they especially like men to call them Rabbi."

The lead Pharisee also located a raised area to stand on and motioned to the assembled group. But the crowd's attention failed to turn.

Jesus' voice became yet stronger. "Remember, you have but one Father, and He is in heaven. And you have but one Teacher, and he is the Messiah."

Philip shook his head. "He needs to stop now if we hope to get out of Jerusalem alive." He let out a nervous breath.

Jesus raised his voice even louder. "Woe to you, teachers of the Law. You shut the kingdom of heaven in men's faces. You yourselves do not enter. But worse, you do not let those enter who are trying. Woe to you, Pharisees. You are hypocrites. You travel the world over to make one convert. Then you make him twice the son of hell as you are."

Even Simon Peter became visibly concerned. "James, can't you slow him down? We need to get out of here."

Some of the Pharisees stormed away as Jesus talked, others pushed closer. Some tried in vain to redirect the crowd's attention, but all expressed their disapproval.

Surprisingly, this had no effect on Jesus. "Woe to you, teachers of the Law. You are like whitewashed tombs. You may look beautiful on the outside, but on the inside, you are full of dead men's bones." The last of the Pharisees stomped away.

Everyone in our group gave a sigh of relief. Thankfully, for the rest of the afternoon, the Pharisees stayed out of sight. The crowd's approval gave us some sense of security. James strongly asserted the authorities would have a riot on their hands if they tried to arrest Jesus. I could only hope this was true.

I didn't take a decent breath until we departed the temple walls and started on the road back to camp.

CHAPTER TWENTY-NINE

As we just finished putting away breakfast, Jesus walked over. "Thad and Thomas will return to accompany you women to Lois and Mark's home this afternoon to make preparations for the Passover meal. When they finish helping, they can come and find us at the temple."

Anticipating the evening's Passover made the day both fly by and at times drag terribly. We were dressed and ready for the occasion when Thomas and Thad came hiking up the path.

Lois's home reminded me so much of my home in Sepphoris, less the bitter animosity. The blond stone reflected a golden hue in the afternoon sun that gave an impression of strength. As I stepped through their entry, a sense of warmth and stability swept over me. The high ceilings lifted my thoughts. *If only I could capture the harmony and love contained within these walls and transport it to my home.*

I determined I would not reveal how little I knew about Passover. If I watched closely, followed instructions, and didn't say much, I could avoid showing my ignorance.

Lois began by having us place soft mats around the low tables. "Oh, that's the way we had dinner at Martha and Lazarus' home the other evening," I proudly remarked. "That's such an interesting way to eat."

A questioning look spread across Lois's face. The realization arrived slow but sunk deeply. Somehow, I just gave away my secret. I suddenly felt small enough to walk beneath the lowest table, with plenty of headroom to spare. With the first words out of my mouth, my charade was over. "Lois, I hate to admit it, but I know almost nothing about the Passover meal. My parents didn't follow the Jewish traditions as they conformed to the Roman influence of Sepphoris. This will be my first observance of Passover."

"Not a problem, Joanna." Lois smiled, but her smile still held a small vestige of disbelief. "I will explain the meal as we set things up."

"Philip told me the story of Passover and how our people came out of Egypt," I explained. "Beyond that, I'm afraid I know precious little."

Susanna and Mary Magdalene were suddenly much more attentive. Lois motioned to the low tables. "A very important part of the meal is that we recline around the Passover table. When our people were slaves in Egypt, they always had to stand while they ate—to be readily available to serve their masters. By reclining, we show we are now free people."

The young housekeeper, Rhoda, was setting a number of ingredients on the counter as Lois led us into her kitchen. "The hard-boiled eggs show how we became strong through suffering. You see, everything else becomes soft when it's boiled. Eggs become hard."

Mary, who already knew the story well, moved on to help Rhoda.

The three of us listened closely. "The roast lamb is also very important," Lois explained. "It is to remind us of the blood of—"

"—a lamb, spread over the doorpost of the home." I finished her sentence. "It's so the Death Angel would pass over. Excuse me for interrupting, but I needed to show I knew something … especially after appearing so ignorant."

"Joanna, you have missed so much." Lois placed her hand on my shoulder. "You're catching up now."

We waited a moment as Rhoda laid out nuts, cinnamon, apples, and several kinds of grain. It felt good to learn this with friends, especially when I suspected they didn't know any more than I did.

"We will chop these and mix them with wine," Lois continued. "When mixed together, it's called haroset. It will look similar to the bricks our ancestors made to build Pharaoh's cities."

We followed Lois to her cooking area. "When you look at this bread, you'll think something's wrong. You see, the bread didn't have time to rise that fateful morning long ago. So, this unleavened bread reminds us of the haste in which our people left Egypt."

"When did all of this happen?" Mary Magdalene finally broke her silence.

"Well over a thousand years ago," Mary said from the other side of the kitchen. A slightly satisfied smile filled her face.

John Mark came in first. I slipped over to him. "Thank you for—"

He shushed me with a finger across his lips then tugged my sleeve. I followed.

"I didn't tell Mom and Dad about that," John Mark whispered. "They would have been upset, me going out that far at night. But

I knew if Dad went, he could have been in a lot of trouble. So, I decided to go."

"Your secret is safe with—Oh, I hear someone coming in."

I turned to see a very handsome officer's uniform come into the house, and the man wearing it even more striking. Mark greeted each of us. Following his brief hello, Mark excused himself to change for the evening.

"What a transformation!" Susanna whispered as Mark returned in casual clothes.

"Like he needed a transformation," I whispered back.

I admired Mark's interacting with Lois, even asking what he might do to help. He appeared a gentleman, through and through.

When we finished the preparations, Mark picked up a piece of fruit, strolled over to where I stood, and casually said, "A couple of months ago, our Jerusalem Command met with our counterparts in Herod's Galilee Command. My first time to visit the Palace in Sepphoris."

My eyes grew wide. Anticipation exploded all over me.

"During those three days, I met several interesting people." He continued. "Cuza, in particular, stood out. He managed our accommodations while we—Oh, I hear people coming in."

We turned to see Simon Peter and three other disciples come through the door. "Later ..." Mark shifted to greet his guest.

I felt dangling in midair. What happened then? Did Cuza mention me? What did he say? I had to know more. My heart beat a thousand times faster.

Jesus and the remaining disciples entered in groups of three and four, spaced over a quarter hour as instructed. Mark continued to greet and visit with the men, especially Jesus.

The conversation Mark started would have to continue. I couldn't be left wondering. I had to know.

After all the men properly washed, we made our way up the half-level to the large upper room. As Mark led the way, he spoke to Jesus. "Since we have several new to their Jewish heritage, shouldn't they ask the traditional questions?"

Jesus nodded. "Yes, that would be good."

Matthew, possibly Judas, and which other disciple I wondered?

To my surprise and fright, they briefed Matthew, Susanna, Mary Magdalene, and me on the traditional questions.

We reclined around the tables. The nod first went to Matthew. He asked, "Why, on this night, do we eat unleavened bread?"

Jesus answered, "On this night, we celebrate our ancestors going forth from slavery into freedom. When Pharaoh finally let our people go, they fled Egypt in great haste. They snatched their dough with no time for it to rise. As the people fled, the hot sun beating down baked it into the unleavened bread we call mazzah. We eat unleavened bread only on this night and in memory of that occasion."

The second nod went to Mary Magdalene. "Why on this night do we eat bitter herbs?"

Mark answered, "Because our forefathers were slaves in Egypt, and their lives were very bitter. For this we eat the bitter herbs tonight."

Susanna hands and voice both shook as she began her question. "Why, on this night, do we dip the parsley in salt water and the bitter herbs in haroset?"

Lois responded, "We dip parsley in salt water to remind us of the green that comes again in the spring. We dip the bitter herbs in the sweet haroset as a sign of hope. Our forefathers withstood the bitterness of slavery because it was sweetened by the hope of freedom."

My time. Nervous clutter hung in my throat. "Why, on this night, do we recline around the table?"

John had been selected to answer. "Because reclining ..." He stopped, lowered his voice by half. "Because, in olden days, reclining at the table was a sign of a free man. Since our forefathers were freed on this night, we can recline at the table."

My eyes continued glistening as I participated in my first Passover meal. Few things I might experience in life would ever come close to this experience. In addition, the wine served between the courses highlighted the evening significantly.

Toward the end of the dinner, Jesus said, "Philip will give us the reading from the Psalms." He looked across the group. "Following the Psalms, I wish a special time with only my disciples. I encourage the rest of you to gather around the sides and observe. What you witness will be important in the days to come."

Philip stood and spoke completely from memory.

When the Lord brought back the captives to Zion, it was like a dream.
We were filled with laughter and we sang for joy.
It was said among the nations, 'The Lord had done great things for them.'
The Lord has done amazing things for us, and we were filled with joy.
Restore our fortunes, Lord, as streams renew the desert.
Those who plant with tears in their eyes will harvest with shouts of joy.

As Philip sat down, Jesus nodded to the rest of us. We accepted our cue and moved to the side of the room. Thankfully, Mary had presence of mind to drag our cushions along.

The aroma of cooked lamb mixed with the sweet fragrance of haroset created an atmosphere heaven would have difficulty rivaling. The magic of the moment swept over me, leaving the back of my neck tingling.

A heavy seriousness filled Jesus' voice as he addressed the disciples. "I have looked forward to this hour with a deep longing in my heart. I was anxious to eat this Passover meal with you before my suffering begins." Jesus paused for a long moment and cleared the emotion from his throat. "I will not eat it again with you until it comes to fulfillment in the Kingdom of God."

Jesus took a cup of wine from the table and lifted his eyes. "Blessed are you, O Lord our God, King of the universe, who created the fruit of the vine." Jesus looked at each disciple. "Just as the blood of the lamb was spread on the doorpost to spare the Israelites from death, so my blood poured out will bring you eternal life." He passed the cup to John on his right. "Take this and share it among yourselves. I will not drink wine again until the Kingdom of God comes." Each disciple took a sip and passed the cup to the next.

Jesus selected a remaining piece of the unleavened bread. He lifted it, bowed his head for a long moment, then broke the single piece of unleavened bread in two. Jesus spoke in a voice so serious my arms quivered. "This bread represents my body. It is broken for you." Jesus handed one piece to John and the other to Simon Peter on his left. "Each of you, take and eat. It is in remembrance of me." Thad, on the end, received the last piece.

Questions flowed through my mind like leaves blowing before a north wind. Twice, I caught my mouth open, ready to ask.

Jesus lifted another cup of wine. He looked down the low table, his gaze pausing on each disciple. "This cup is the New Covenant written in my blood. As you drink from this cup, know it represents my blood poured out for you." Jesus handed the cup to John, who took a sip, then passed it forward. Simon Peter drained the last as the cup made full circle.

What did it mean—my body, my blood? When would Jesus explain?

Jesus spread his hands. "Here at this table, sitting among us as a friend, is the man who will betray me. This is part of God's plan. But how terrible it will be for the one who betrays me."

Jesus' last words captured the attention of the disciples. They began whispering among themselves. The seriousness of the moment gradually faded.

Jesus held out his hand again. "This very night, all of you will fall away on account of me. It is like the Scripture, 'I will strike the shepherd and the flock will be scattered.'"

Simon Peter reared his head back. "Even if everyone else abandons you, you know I never will." Peter cast a condescending look toward James.

James shook his head. "Oh, Simon. If anything happens, everyone knows you'd be the first to run."

Simon Peter glared back. "You always think you're so important. Truth be known, you'd be looking out for yourself while I defend Jesus."

Jesus spread his hands apart. "You two argue so much about being more important in my kingdom. I will tell you what being great in the Kingdom of God means. Your leader is to be a servant who supports the others. In this world, the leader sits at the head and others serve him. But that isn't the way in my kingdom. Just as I am your Master but have served you, you are to serve others."

Jesus stopped a long moment. Pain creased his face. He turned directly to Simon Peter. "Simon, I am going to tell you the awful truth. This very night, before the morning crow of the rooster, you will deny that you even know me ... three times."

Simon Peter started to react, but Jesus stood and motioned to the rest of us. "It is getting late. Stand and join in the hymn before we leave."

In a much-needed show of harmony, the men sang a most beautiful hymn. Peter even joined in near the end.

As we expressed appreciation to our gracious host, Andrew nudged me. "Wonder where Judas is going in such a hurry?"

CHAPTER THIRTY

"I wish those two would quit their bickering," I whispered to Mary as soon as Lois and Mark's door closed. "James's and Simon Peter's constant squabbling almost ruined the absolutely wonderful Passover meal." I felt like spanking two unruly children.

A light breeze blowing from the east began to cool my attitude and my body. Even though there were few clouds, the moon's absence filled the sky with an intense darkness. Once leaving the glow of the city, only the Zealot's keen eyes guided us safely back to our camp. Andrew and Thomas were quick to strike the kindling, and soon a nice campfire pushed the deep shadows to a more comfortable distance.

As flames began to rise and the warmth of the fire beckoned us, Jesus called James, John, and Simon Peter over.

"Good," I whispered to Mary. "Jesus will give them the scolding they deserve." My shoulders shook at the thought of them turning the beautiful Passover meal into an argument.

Jesus placed his hand on Peter's shoulder. "I am going over to the Garden of Gethsemane to pray. I would like the three of you to come with me."

Did my ears deceive me? Shaking my head, I looked at Mary. "After the way Peter and James acted?"

The four slipped out of camp like best friends.

With Jesus taking the three with him to pray, the warm fire roaring, the emotional exchanges past, and the wine from dinner, both my mind and body began to relax. The rest of the disciples seemed afflicted the same way. Sleepy eyes adorned several faces.

All except Mary Magdalene. Her voice struck just as I drifted off, "Jesus has been out way too long, we ought to go check on him."

"No, Mary." Philip cracked one eye from where he dozed. "I'm sure Jesus is quite safe with James, John, and Simon Peter along. They're just over at the olive press. If there's a problem, I'm sure we would hear it."

I sat near the warm fire nearly dozing, again. My head bobbed twice I remember.

Jesus and three sleepy disciples slipping back into camp awoke me from my slumber. As I arose to gather my sleeping roll, I noticed Simon peering through the low olive tree branches. "Hard to see through the trees. I think the glow is on the road. Maybe someone's lost."

With Jesus and the three safely back in camp, we settled down for a much-needed night's rest.

Bright torches suddenly appeared, coming off the road, straight toward us. The quiet evening erupted into shouts and shrill commands. Thirty or more loud, angry men invaded our camp. Confusion swirled. James grabbed his mother and disappeared in the surrounding shadows. Simon leaped in front of the three of us women, crouched, ready for action.

Five Roman soldiers leading the procession stepped to one side. Twenty or more temple guards, armed and carrying torches, moved in shouting orders. The disciples huddled behind the campfire unable to budge. I couldn't comprehend the unfolding events. I seemed caught in an awful dream.

The temple guards positioned themselves and their weapons so no one dared move. With our campsite fully under their control, a dozen Pharisees in their tasseled robes paraded in. A crowd followed with even more torches, filling our camp.

Without warning, Simon Peter burst from the huddled disciples wildly swinging his little sword. Someone didn't duck, and a blood-chilling scream erupted. What looked to be a man's ear fell to the ground.

A temple guard drew back his spear. I tried shouting, but it was too late. He thrust it at Simon Peter. Peter turned to take another swing. The spear passed between his legs, piercing his robe. Tripped, he hit the ground hard. In the blink of an eye, two huge temple guards straddled Simon Peter, pinning him face down, spitting dirt.

The injured man screamed in pain. Peter cursed loudly as he struggled beneath the weight of the two guards. Other guards shouted orders. Everything swirled out of control. Confusion reigned.

The only calm person present was Jesus. He stepped from among the disciples and walked to where the man's ear lay in the dust. He picked it up, calmly walked over and placed it back on the side of the man's head. His awful screaming shrank to a whimper.

"Am I some dangerous thug that you have to come armed with swords and spears to arrest me?" Jesus looked hard at the Pharisees. "Do I seem to be leading a rebellion? Was I not with you every day in the temple courts? Why didn't you arrest me there?"

Andrew's brow furrowed. "I don't believe this! That's Judas with the Pharisees!"

The group parted as Judas sauntered up to Jesus. He planted a kiss on his cheek and said, "Greeting, Teacher." Complete disbelief overwhelmed me.

The Zealot growled under his breath. "I will rip that rat apart with my bare hands."

Three of the temple guards roughly seized Jesus. Another barked, "Round them all up."

Simon—I'll never know how—swept Susanna, Mary Magdalene, and me up in his arms and rushed us through the low hanging olive trees faster than I could run myself.

It took several moments for me to force the words out … "No one's chasing us."

Momentum carried Simon a couple more steps before we all collapsed in a heap.

We quickly brushed ourselves off and made sure no bones were broken. Simon announced, "I'm going back. Others need help."

Panic filled Mary Magdalene's voice. "You're not leaving us here."

"Go on, Simon." I said. "We're right behind you."

Simon led as the four of us silently snuck back toward the shadowed edge of our campsite. After surveying the situation, he turned back to us, "They only have Peter. All others managed to flee."

Hiding in the shadows, I could see the Pharisees questioning Jesus. Three temple guards turned him and crudely pushed him toward the road.

The two guards holding Simon Peter face down in the dirt picked him up and stood him on his feet. Another guard barked, "We're not taking only one of them. Want us to look like fools?"

The two guards literally picked Simon Peter up, heaved him into the bushes, then hurried on to join their crowd.

The four of us slipped back into the strewn remains of our camp. Thomas and Thad emerged from the shadows on the other side. Simon Peter picked himself up and brushed off his robes. "I guess I showed them."

We had only begun to assess the situation when John and two other disciples reappeared. From another direction, Andrew and Matthew returned. Andrew shook his head. "I should have suspected something when Judas slipped out."

Younger James emerged from the shadows, leading a distraught Mary.

"Did anyone notice that Judas wasn't with us tonight as we walked back to camp?" Philip scratched his head. "I didn't."

John, with his booming voice, took charge. "We can't waste time on that weasel. We need to find out what's happening to Jesus. If we take the path, we won't be far behind when we reach the road." John stopped and looked around the group. "It's dark and it's dangerous. You women will stay here. Younger James—"

"Don't entertain that thought for an instant." Mary Magdalene jumped directly in John's face. "You're not leaving us behind."

"She's right," I added. "You can't go without us. If you're going, we're going."

"I want all of us to go." Younger James spoke up. "But Mother shouldn't try. I'll stay with her."

Mary protested, but everyone agreed with younger James. She finally acquiesced.

"H—has anyone seen Bart?" Deep worry filled Thad's face.

"He's bound to show up soon," John answered, then turned to younger James, "When he does, tell him to stay here. I'd feel better having two men protecting Mary."

We started down the steep path. In the inky darkness, I managed to connect with every low branch and every loose stone along the way. We reached the paved road and could see the torch-lit group moving not far ahead.

As we regrouped, John spoke. "We need to spread out into several groups so we don't call attention to ourselves."

"Spread out, but stay within sight of each other," James corrected.

As the mob approached Jerusalem, the detail of Roman soldiers broke off and marched in a separate direction. We followed the main group from a distance as they wound through narrow city streets. People along the way gawked at the large group of men carrying torches. They certainly had no idea who the closely guarded man in the center was.

The procession of torches stopped at a huge home surrounded by a formidable-walled courtyard. The Pharisees took Jesus through a narrow gate and about half of the temple guards followed. We waited in the shadows, watching. A man came out and spoke to the guards still outside. As he returned to the courtyard, the remaining temple guards began to disperse. We moved closer. A hubbub of activity swirled around the site.

"Whose home do you think this is?" I asked.

My eyes met only blank stares.

Philip spoke, "I'll take Joanna and inquire of someone as they leave."

We strolled up to a couple walking our way and Philip said, "Nice home. Whose is it?"

They gave us a stare that made me want to crawl under a pebble. "You can't be from around here. Everyone knows this is the home of Caiaphas, our High Priest."

We gathered back in the shadows. Philip reported, "Since this is the home of the High Priest, access is going to be a lot more difficult."

"But we must find a way in," I insisted, "We've got to know what's happening."

"John!" Andrew called in a loud whisper. "While we've been standing here, I've noticed something. Couples don't seem to have trouble getting through. It's groups of men she keeps turning away."

John didn't take terribly long to realize the obvious. "I hate to leave the rest of you out here, but we only have three women to help us get in."

"We only have three women?" I whispered to Susanna. "Yesterday, John didn't care whether there were any women, except when it was time to eat."

"I'll take Joanna and go first," John continued. "Simon, you take Mary Magdalene and follow shortly. James, wait a few minutes, then come with Susanna." John ignored James' scowl. "We'll report back as soon as we know something."

John turned to me. "Come on, Joanna. Let's look like a couple."

Could this be the John who hardly knew I existed? For John to need me felt more than strange. But, desperate to know what was happening inside, I produced my best smile and took his arm. We strolled casually toward the gate while my heart pounded out of my chest. *What if someone recognizes us?*

"I am the son of Zebedee, we—" John started.

"Yes, I know your family," the woman gatekeeper said. She swung the narrow gate just wide enough for one to pass.

John nodded to her in a polite manner. He stepped through the gate first, as a proper Jewish husband would, then turned and took my arm to pass through.

"Well, that wasn't hard," I whispered to John. "I hope the others make it through as easily."

John led the way into the huge courtyard. He whispered, "Don't look back. That could give us away."

We strolled toward the middle of the large area. John leaned close. "Look, I can see Jesus behind all of those Pharisees on the porch. Looks like they're waiting for someone."

The courtyard could easily hold a hundred people. Half that many were gathered, milling about on the stone pavement, all waiting for something to happen. Near the steps to the porch, a large fire pit drew most of the temple guards who came in. Torches hung on the surrounding posts to light the area.

From the corner of my eye, I observed another couple successfully negotiate the gate. "That woman gatekeeper looks tough," I whispered. "Let's make a circle back toward the gate, to see if Peter gets through. They should be coming soon."

We moved beside a tree, directly behind the gatekeeper—just close enough. "There's Simon Peter at the gate now," I said.

The gatekeeper challenged Peter. "You're not one of *that man's* disciples are you?"

"N—no! Of course not." Simon Peter appeared flustered by the challenge. "I—I sure wouldn't be here if I was." The gatekeeper spread to a defense stance holding the latch to the gate.

Mary Magdalene stepped up. "Most of *that man's* disciples were fishermen, weren't they? Amos here wouldn't know how to catch a fish if his life depended on it." She gave a silly laugh.

"Well, okay." The woman unlatched the gate, nodded her head toward the porch. "We sure don't want any of that man's followers in here."

I stifled my laughter. Then the seriousness of the situation yanked my mind back to reality.

Simon Peter and Mary Magdalene nodded, then ignored us and strode on toward the grand porch. We followed as close behind as we could without making our connection obvious.

"Where does he think he is going?" John growled.

"I wish he'd stop," I replied. "He's making me even more nervous. James and Susanna aren't even in yet."

John tugged my sleeve. "Look—on the porch. That's Caiaphas, the High Priest. He just came in. This doesn't look good."

The High Priest wore a most ornate ceremonial robe. We were too far away to hear, but I could see Caiaphas interrogating Jesus. He appeared cruel as he and the whole group shouted and sneered at Jesus.

I bit my lip. "Why can't Simon Peter be satisfied to watch? Look. Now he's left Mary Magdalene standing alone and marched right up close to the porch acting like he owns the courtyard."

John pulled his robe tight. "He's being a stupid fool."

Mary Magdalene stepped back to where we were. "I wish Peter would stay back here in the shadows. Why does he have to get right up front? That's where all the temple guards are."

"It isn't like a thousand people haven't seen Peter's face around the temple these past few days," I said to the three. Then I turned toward Peter and softly pleaded, "Peter, be careful. Get back here." If only Simon Peter could have heard me.

John nudged me. "James and Susanna are in. They're coming up on our right. But don't look." I was so engrossed in Simon Peter's brazen stupidity I hadn't noticed.

They recognized us and nodded. We separately moved closer, hopefully to keep an eye on Simon Peter. Smoke from the large fire pit wafted back and for a moment nearly choked me.

We stopped when one of the temple guards approached Peter. He looked him up and down. "You sure look like one of Jesus's followers."

John looked at me. "Oh, oh. He's in trouble now."

"I am not!" Peter reacted. "I don't even know that man."

His words were anything but an innocent man's reply.

Mary Magdalene's whole body shook. "Get out of there, Peter. Come back here. You'll get us all arrested."

John didn't whisper. "I'm going up there and drag him back."

"No." I grabbed John's sleeve. "It's too late. You'll implicate all of us."

Another guard walked halfway around the fire pit to Peter and examined him closely. "I was on the Mount of Olives when you cut my cousin's ear off. I know it was you. You even have a Galilean accent." He raised his voice. "You're one of that man's followers."

Simon Peter stomped and clinched his fist at the guard. "I don't know what you're talking about. I don't even know him."

Then it happened. The crowing rooster sent prickly chills up my back. As it crowed, Jesus's words flooded my mind. "Simon, before the rooster ..."

At that instant, horror swept Simon Peter's face. He stopped short.

There was sudden movement on the porch. Peter glanced that way just as we did—and saw what we saw. As they led him away, Jesus turned his gaze directly toward Peter. Peter's face turned from horror to disbelief. He broke into a run toward the gate, tears streaming down his face.

"Watch out," I cried. Simon Peter nearly knocked the gatekeeper down as she turned to challenge him. Like a blur, he burst through the gate then disappeared into the darkness.

CHAPTER THIRTY-ONE

"Please. Tell me this didn't happen." I wiped my eyes. "Tell me I only imagined this." I stood, my heart beating out of my chest.

Jesus' arrest was tragedy enough. Now an additional catastrophe like this!

John seemed even more distraught than I did. His shoulders heaved. John tried desperately to choke back his emotions.

James shuffled his feet. "I shouldn't have ridden him so hard about being the first to run. This wouldn't have happened."

The longer we stood in the High Priest's courtyard, the worse everything grew. I spoke to both men. "Shouldn't we get out of here? The men waiting anxiously outside don't know anything yet."

"With Jesus led off to who knows where, there's no reason to stay." James shrugged his shoulders. "Let's go."

Many others in the courtyard also realized the end of the proceedings. They began moving toward the small gate. We turned and started, but I suddenly realized Mary Magdalene had not. She stood—her eyes fixed somewhere in the vacant distance. "Come on, Mary," I whispered loud enough to know she heard me. "We're leaving." Still no response. Finally, Susanna and I took her by the hand and led her toward the gate.

Once outside in the shadows, James called everyone together. John put his hand on his brother's shoulder. "Let me." He choked back his emotions and began the report. As he finished, I realized something conspicuously missing. His older brother had not corrected him, not even once.

John finished and we stood looking at each other, shifting from one foot to the other, anticipating some further word, like waiting for Jesus to tell us what to do.

Philip finally spoke. "Even though it's late, we should alert Lois and Mark. They need to know what's happened. Besides, with their access to the government, they can learn a lot more than we can."

We made our way through dark shadows, down winding streets and through strange neighborhoods until we were at last in familiar territory. James knocked and knocked. Finally, someone awoke.

I recognized Rhoda's voice calling from inside, "Who's there?"

"Rhoda, it's Jesus's disciples," I called to her. "Something terrible has happened. We need to tell Mark and Lois." Precious minutes passed. Finally, the door opened and a surprised Mark invited us in.

James and John huddled with Mark and Lois in the living room, filling in the details. The rest of us gathered around but tried to stay out of the way.

John Mark stumbled into the room. He suddenly interrupted. "Where is Simon Peter?"

Andrew walked over, put his arm on John Mark's shoulder, led him to the side and explained what had happened to his favorite disciple. John Mark sat and cried while Andrew stayed beside him.

Mark stood and motioned to us. "I speak for my whole family

when I say we are truly saddened and we want to help. Make our upper room your headquarters as long as you need it."

He paused, and his face turned even more serious. "But do be careful. Don't come or leave in groups larger than three or four. Give a little time between groups. Your coming and going can't be conspicuous. Also, use the side servant's entrance. The authorities will be looking for a group like yours. Please, don't lead them here."

Lois stood beside her husband. "At least for tonight, the ladies should stay here. It's far too dangerous to walk back to your camp in the dark, especially with all that has happened. Tomorrow, please bring Mary here. I'm sure she's worried sick."

John Mark dried his tears and stood. "My intern position with Claudius might give me access to find out what's happening. I'll make a way to be in the staff meeting in the morning."

The men divided up and began their staggered departure. Everyone urged John Mark to be careful. Lois dragged blankets from an ornate wooden chest. I took mine and collapsed onto the first soft place I found. Mary Magdalene and Susanna weren't far behind.

My body trembled as, in vain, I tried to sleep. The image of Judas placing the kiss on Jesus's cheek floated behind my closed eyes. I wanted to smash it in a thousand pieces. The crow of the rooster echoed through my body. In a short, awful dream the guards placed a rope around my arms and began leading me away. I twisted and struggled, but the rope kept returning, again and again.

A gentle hand shook my shoulder. I didn't remember going to sleep, but Lois awakened me as strong rays of daylight broke through the window. "You might want to wake up, Joanna. James arrived with his mother. We're preparing something to eat."

Susanna awoke easily, but Mary Magdalene didn't respond to our calls. A vacant stare filled her eyes.

Mary came into the room, her eyes filled with tears. At that moment, we took hold of each other and held on.

Lois brought the four of us up-to-date. "Mark is on duty. Pilate brought his command in from around Bethlehem to support the Jerusalem guard. John Mark skipped classes this morning so he can report to Claudius. He hopes to learn what is happening. As soon as he knows something, he said he'd return home with information."

John and James came through the hallway from the servant's entrance, followed by Andrew and Thomas. John spoke, "The others will come in shortly. Is there any news yet?"

"John Mark hopes to bring news no later than noon," Lois assured them.

Minutes passed like hours. The Zealot, Matthew, and Philip slipped in and received the same briefing. Again, we sat, looking at the walls, the ceiling, the floor and dealt with our worst fears. The morning hours seemed as long as the past winter's months all put together.

Andrew paced back and forth to the window facing the street. "Has anyone heard anything from Peter? I'm worried." Andrew appeared crushed. His eyes glistened.

I walked over. "Andrew, have you wondered how Jesus knew Peter would deny ... say those words?" I looked at his blank face. "I don't know either, but because Jesus said it, I believe he'll bring some good from this."

Big tears filled Andrew's eyes. He nodded his head, but with great effort.

The time crept toward noon. We sat there looking at each other, wondering, waiting.

The front door slid open, and in stepped young John Mark. The sixteen-year-old boy held our hearts in his hand.

"Let me tell what I know first, then ask questions." John Mark explained. "It's been an awful morning." The boyish smile vanished from his face. "Since Pilate stayed in Jerusalem because of Passover, the religious leaders came this morning requesting an audience. I wasn't present, but I understand Pilate refused and told them to deal with the problem under Jewish laws."

John Mark shuffled his feet as he related the events. "I understand the religious leaders told Pilate a lot of untrue things about Jesus. They said he needed to be put to death."

John Mark paused for a deep breath. "This caused Pilate to call for his staff. I grabbed my parchment and went right behind Claudius, acting like I was supposed to be there. It worked. Then they brought Jesus in."

John Mark wiped his brow. "Thankfully Jesus gave no indication he recognized me. Pilate waited, then went over to Jesus and asked, 'They say you claim to be a king. Are you a king?'

"Jesus remained calm and asked if this was his own question. Pilate shouted back at Jesus that his own religious leaders brought him in asking for the death penalty. Jesus looked at Pilate and told him his kingdom wasn't of this world."

I listened in amazement as this sixteen-year-old boy was growing into a man before our very eyes. John Mark continued. "Pilate waited. Then he shouted at the guards, asking where this man's accusers were. Two aides rushed out."

Nervously, John Mark continued. "The aides hurried back and explained the Jewish leaders said they couldn't enter or they would be defiled on the Passover. Those religious leaders didn't have a problem asking that an innocent man be put to death, but they didn't want to be defiled by coming into a Roman facility. I couldn't believe it." John Mark slumped to a stool. Tears filled his eyes.

"Pilate shook his head and said if the religious leaders wouldn't come in there, we would go out and get to the bottom of things."

John Mark raked his bottom lip under his teeth. "This is where things really got ugly. Pilate moved the entire proceedings out onto the porch overlooking the courtyard. A hundred or so Pharisees and religious people were there. Pilate stepped to the edge and told the crowd he didn't find anything wrong for the man to deserve death. They should try him under their own laws.

"They shouted back that Jesus tells people not to pay taxes, that he causes riots all over Galilee and even in Jerusalem."

John Mark pushed himself on. "Pilate looked taken back. He walked over to Claudius and asked if Jesus was a Galilean. Claudius nodded. Pilate produced a sort of sick smile and said Herod just happened to be in town. He sent Claudius to tell Herod that one of his favorite citizens was on trial.

"Everything came to a standstill. It wasn't long before Herod and several of his staff made a big entrance. Herod seemed delighted as he went up to Jesus and asked him how he did all his miracles.

"Jesus hardly looked at him. Herod asked a bunch more questions that Jesus ignored.

"Herod strolled back to Pilate and complained that Jesus wouldn't answer him, so he didn't know what to do with him. He walked out saying Jesus was Pilate's problem."

Again, big tears welled up in John Mark's eyes as he struggled on. "The crowd began to call out for Pilate to crucify Jesus. They made it into a chant calling, 'Crucify him.' I thought my ears would burst. I wanted to run to the edge of the balcony and scream at them."

Tears streamed down John Mark's face as he finished.

James stood, but John Mark looked up at him. "No, you haven't heard the worst part yet. Pilate told his guards to flog him and at the fifth hour, to take him out and crucify him."

"The fifth hour is only an hour from now." John looked horrified. "We need to get to the Praetorium. Now!"

My legs went numb. *This can't be happening.*

CHAPTER THIRTY-TWO

"Look, the gate is opening," I cried. It creaked wide enough for a detail of soldiers to march out, menacing spears extended. No protest, no queries—the crowd retreated quickly to the edges of the plaza. The soldiers' shields formed an impenetrable barrier. The double-edged swords hanging from their waists glistened in the noonday sun. Their drawn weapons left few questions.

"I'm not about to give them any trouble," Andrew whispered.

Hardly did the words clear his lips, when a bloody figure appeared, prodded forward by the next group of heavily armed soldiers.

"That can't be Jesus," I gasped. My legs weakened at the pungent smell of blood. Nausea swept through my body. Blood dripped from Jesus's scarred face and oozed from a thousand slashes on his sides and shoulders. His back was a mass of tattered shreds.

My stomach heaved. I had seen horrible things in my life, but nothing came close to this. Thorny branches had been fashioned into a crown, each thorn bringing a stream of blood down his face. Jesus stood, his head hanging.

From behind him, two men emerged dragging a huge beam slung between them by a heavy rope. They dropped the beam at Jesus' feet, removing their sling. Together, they hoisted one end onto Jesus' raw, bleeding shoulder. He struggled to absorb its weight. The two stepped back and laughed, one slapping the other on the back. A crack from a whip exploded the still air.

The procession began a slow plod. The soldier flaunting the whip exited the gate on horseback. Five well-armed men followed. The whip popped again at Jesus' ankles.

The awful scene ripped at my soul. No words exist to express the dreadful events unfolding before us. Susanna's hands covered her grief-stricken face. "How can he drag that huge beam ... in that condition?"

I had no answer. Jesus looked beaten nearly to death.

Mary, her face covered in tears, turned away from the evolving horror.

A vacant stare filled Mary Magdalene's face. Slowly, she crumpled onto the pavement, sobbing. Susanna knelt at her side.

I only wanted to wipe the awful scene from my eyes. If only I could somehow make the sight disappear.

I placed my arm around Mary. "We have to move now. Come on, I'll help you." As I turned her in the direction of the procession, James reached her other side and took her arm.

I motioned to Thad and Bart. "Help Susanna with Mary Magdalene. We can't leave them here."

Our crowd grew to several dozen as we fell in behind the soldiers. As we plodded along the market street of Jerusalem, I realized most in the crowd following with us were women. Except for the remaining disciples, men had all but disappeared.

We turned up another city street and another loud crack of the whip stung at Jesus' legs. Then the cross stopped moving.

Again, the whip cracked at Jesus' legs. He tried taking another step, but instead sank to his knees. Another crack of the whip tore yet more skin from Jesus's back. The whip drew back for still another strike, but didn't have time to strike. Wind must have carried me. Before I knew, my body stretched across Jesus. In the next instant, Susanna's body crowded in next to mine, then others. The whip cracked just above my right ear, but no one moved. I was too frightened.

At least five of us huddled over Jesus until the commander of the whip issued an order. "You, man, come here." I glanced up just far enough to see someone caught in the attention of the mounted soldier. "Come over here. Pick up this cross."

The man shouted back, "I'm not from Jerusalem. I don't know this man."

Fire burned in the eyes of the whip bearer. "You come here and carry this cross, or you will hang on one beside him."

The man's expression reflected his lack of choice. He dropped his possessions onto the stone pavement and walked toward us. We climbed off but stood as a protective arch between Jesus and the whip. The man stepped in and nodded. "I am Simon from Cyrene. I'll help." Simon lifted the rough, heavy beam from Jesus's shoulder, steadied it, and then slipped his black shoulder beneath it.

We helped Jesus to his feet. A crack of the whip announced our company would begin moving again.

Blood stained the street's stone pavement. Many similar processions must have taken this long, torturous route. More turns brought us to a huge fortification in the city's wall, the Damascus Gate.

We paused for a company ahead to pass through the narrow confines. Eerily like our group, two men were dragging heavy crossbeams accompanied by two detachments of soldiers, one leading and the other prodding them along. Following were forlorn friends or family. They came to this fate from different condemnations but obviously were headed to a similar conclusion.

My salty tears began at the first sight of Jesus leaving the Praetorium. They had not stopped since. While we waited at the gate, Jesus turned to us, blood running down his face. "Do not weep for me. Weep for yourselves." His voice was hardly a hoarse whisper. "A time is coming when women will pray to be barren so their children will not witness the wrath to come."

The whip cracked. The man from Cyrene struggled to loosen the pavement's hold on the cross. The lead soldiers moved first through the gate and took up positions outside. Next, Simon wrestled the cross through, then Jesus followed by the whip and the rear guard of soldiers. No sense of freedom greeted us as we departed the confines of the city's wall. The only sight before us was three tall beams erected near the intersection of two roads a little distance away. We were on one of those roads.

The soldiers waiting at the site moved with cruel efficiency, their skills honed. By the time we reached the killing place, the detachment had tied the victims who passed the gate before us to their respective cross-members and hoisted the beams to their notches in the upright posts. One vertical post remained that stood between the two writhing men already stretched and dangling by their wrists. Jesus' fate hung in stark detail.

Near the base of the center post, the man from Cyrene strained to lift Jesus' crossbeam from his shoulder. He lowered and let it drop. Mary, her eyes filled with tears, stepped close and thanked him.

The man from Cyrene looked back and forth at each of us. "He doesn't seem a criminal. Who is he?"

"He's Jesus of Nazareth," I answered. "He's a great prophet, both in his words and in his deeds."

I wiped my tears to survey the awful scene. Two men hung from crosses. A third post stood awaiting … no, *calling* its intended victim.

Forming the backdrop to the crucifixion area was a rock-faced cliff rising as high as the city's walls. Cave-like indentions pockmarked its scarred surface. Suddenly, my stomach twisted in convulsions. That rough face of the cliff eerily resembled a skull. I closed my eyes to blot out the gruesome sight.

The cruel and efficient executioners moved into action, pushing Jesus to the ground. Each grabbed an arm and together pulled Jesus' torn body across the gravel onto the crossbeam. With short strands of rope, they secured his wrists to the roughhewn wood. Two more soldiers knelt ready beside him. Each held a heavy hammer in one hand and a spike in the other. "No!" I cried.

I wanted to heave my body across Jesus again. Before I could take a step, their hammers struck, driving the spikes into the palms of Jesus' hands. His chest heaved. I bit my lip until I tasted blood.

With Jesus tied and nailed, four soldiers hoisted the beam up the huge post. The beam slid into its notch with Jesus' body dangling. Another soldier tied his ankles to the post while two waited with more spikes. Jesus cried out in agony as a spike pierced each foot. With each hammer blow, pain pulsed through me.

A soldier running in our direction opened my awareness to those near by. Mary stood with tears streaming down her face. Susanna was trying to comfort a totally distraught Mary Magdalene. Ten disciples stood in a tight group a little distance away. Anguish spread across each face.

The sign the soldier came running up with provoked an angry response from the crucifixion detail. Harsh words flew between them. Finally, a ladder went up the post. A soldier climbed with the sign and another followed with a hammer and two spikes. Only then did we see the inscription: JESUS OF NAZARETH, KING OF THE JEWS.

Pharisees never walked faster than a slow dignified pace, but three were running in our direction. One called to the soldier coming down the ladder, "No, No. It's supposed to say, 'He claimed to be King of the Jews.'"

Two big, burly soldiers swaggered over to the three out-of-breath Pharisees. One placed his hands firmly on his hips. "What is written is written. It won't be changed." Three other soldiers stepped up. The Pharisees slunk back. With that settled, the soldiers selected a place to relax. But they kept a very watchful eye on us.

With the menacing soldiers off to the side, the disciples moved close to where we stood.

I pointed at the center cross. "Is Jesus trying to say something?"

Jesus raised himself on the nails through his feet. He drew a breath. His voice was hardly above a hoarse whisper. "Father, forgive them." He slumped. Then, with great effort, he raised himself again. "They know not what they do."

"Hanging in excruciating pain," I said mostly to myself, "and he asks God to forgive his executioners." I shook my head.

"Would you expect anything different?" Philip asked.

While the executing soldiers were a safe distance, the three Pharisees moved closer. Their true nature revealed itself once again. "He saved others," one sneered. "Look, he can't even save himself." With a haughty air, they wagged their heads.

The Zealot, younger James, and Thomas started toward the Pharisees. Their dignified walk suddenly developed into a hasty retreat. Had it not, I believe Simon might have eliminated a couple of them.

Philip placed his hand on Andrew's shoulder. "Look who's coming." With his head hung low, Simon Peter walked the same road we'd just traveled. Andrew rushed to him and the two men hugged. The father in Jesus's story of the wayward son crossed my mind. John and James also stepped out to welcome him. Then each of the men followed.

Peter choked back big tears as he nodded to each of us. For the very first time, Simon Peter seemed totally unable to say anything.

I whispered to Mary, "Seems different. A humble Peter?"

When Peter's arrival settled a little, I slipped over to him. "You know everyone here loves you. It's in their eyes."

"I know you're right," Peter replied. "But can Jesus ever forgive me?"

I looked Simon Peter straight in the eye. "A little while ago Jesus lifted his eyes toward heaven and asked his Father to forgive those men who nailed him to the cross. Don't you think there's a chance for you?"

Big tears again filled Peter's eyes. He gave me a huge hug.

Thad looked at the sky. "What's happening? It's the middle of the afternoon, but it's getting dark."

We watched Jesus. He struggled to rise a little, caught a short breath and then slumped again. After an hour of increasing darkness, Philip spoke. "I think our Father God is showing displeasure with what's happening."

In the eerie twilight, Jesus raised on his nail-pierced feet once again. His voice was stronger, as though summoning his last bit of strength. "My God, my God," he cried. "Why have you forsaken me?" It echoed against the skull-faced cliff and through my soul.

Mary whispered, "The end is almost here."

Shedding more tears than I dreamed my body contained had weakened me. Mary, however, seemed to grow stronger as the numbing events unfolded. Her strength seemed to hover around me, like a mother's.

We stood there, only feet from the cross upon which our Lord hung. His death couldn't be far away. My heart felt totally exposed as we awaited the inevitable. That cross had destroyed everything I lived for.

Philip pointed. "Listen, he's trying to say something."

Jesus' legs trembled. He attempted to push himself up again. Hardly above a whisper: "It is finished."

Long moments passed. Jesus failed to rise for air again. Agony began fading from his face. His head slumped over.

The reality of his death overwhelmed me. The one whom I had come to believe to be the Son of God had been killed on a Roman cross. The Jesus I loved and followed hung dead. Crucified with him were his wonderful teachings.

With Jesus' death now obvious, I realized the criminals on either side had already died. The soldiers moved up to finish their assignment. One, gripping a heavy hammer, strode to the convict on the left and swung at his legs. The sound of cracking bones sent pain through my side. The victim didn't flinch. The soldier moved to the one on the right of Jesus. The same crack and the same lack of reaction. He strolled back with a calloused face. "These two are ready to come down."

My whole body shook. As the finality of the moment sank in, a strong arm slipped over my shoulder. Its firmness and warmth brought some slight relief. "Thank you," I half whispered. My eyes, swollen from so many tears, didn't focus.

But I knew Andrew must be offering the comfort I so desperately needed. I leaned toward him accepting his support. After a moment, I turned to better express my appreciation.

"Cuza!"

CHAPTER THIRTY-THREE

This simply wasn't possible. Slowly, I realized my eyes were not deceiving me. I grabbed Cuza with an embrace that surely shock everyone. Emotion rumbled through me like a landslide. I held him back to look at him. "Cuza!" My hands trembled. "Oh, Cuza, it's absolutely the worst time ... but it's absolutely the best time you could come."

With strong hands, Cuza gently took both my shoulders. "Joanna." His eyes glistened.

That one tender word from his lips spoke volumes. The horror of the crucifixion, like a giant wave, had flooded my heart. Watching Jesus die swept me to the edge. Cuza's arrival caught me sliding toward the abyss.

The execution soldiers jumped to their feet, suddenly at full attention. Only then did I notice someone on the other side of Cuza. Mark, in his centurion uniform, slowly shook his head as he surveyed the situation. "Jesus was a righteous man." This strong commander of forces stood with tears reflecting in his eyes. "I do believe he was the Son of God."

The arrival of a Roman officer obviously threw a cloak of anxiety over the crucifixion detail. They hurriedly moved to finish their assignment. One soldier grabbed his big hammer and strode to a stance in front of Jesus. He glanced toward Mark before delivering that final insult. Mark held out his hand. The soldier lowered his hammer, stepped away.

Another soldier, surely assuming this officer came to assure they promptly completed their work, quickly grabbed his spear, strode to the spot directly beneath Jesus and jabbed the lifeless form hard just below the ribs. Jesus' body failed to move as blood flowed down his side. "This one's ready too," he called.

My eyes were swollen, almost closed. I know I looked awful, but that didn't matter. I spoke my heart. "Thank you for coming."

The words hardly cleared my mouth when another soldier hauled a long iron bar from the implement bag. I grimaced. "What's that for?" I knew the answer couldn't be good.

Cuza pulled my face into his shoulder and held me tightly as the soldiers pulled the spikes from Jesus' feet. Two ladders were quickly propped against the sides of the upright post and the process of hauling up the crossbeam reversed. The screech of the spikes pulling loose from his hands ripped my insides. Cuza continued holding me through the awful moment.

"Look, here come two more of those Pharisees." Older James spit his words like nails. "Don't they ever get—"

"No, look," Philip called as the two continued to approach. "That's Nicodemus on the left."

Nicodemus's head hung low as he expressed his sorrow to the disciples. The group moved into a semi-circle around the two.

I slipped over closer to hear Nicodemus. "… and this is my friend, Joseph from Arimathea. He also secretly followed Jesus. Again, we both regret we could not prevail against the Sanhedrin to prevent this tragedy. Joseph has something to tell you."

Our eyes turned to the small, stooped, gray-haired man. Joseph spoke in a soft slow voice. "I also believed in Jesus and mourn it ended like this." He paused to dab his eyes. "Not far from here, I own a pleasant garden. There, I recently completed my own family tomb. No one has been laid to rest in it yet. I offer the tomb to you for the body of Jesus. I have secured a writ of permission from Pilate to take possession of Jesus's body. If this meets your approval, my tomb is yours."

John stepped slightly into the semi-circle and looked at his fellow disciples. "I find this a wonderful offer, especially since the Sabbath begins in a couple of hours. Does anyone object?" Grateful smiles were the reply.

Joseph carried the parchment over to the execution detail's lead soldier. While Joseph dealt with them, I stepped in front of the most wonderful people I had ever known. "I'm sure you realize this is my husband, Cuza. Today will forever be the most awful day of my life, but Cuza's coming has also made it a day I will long cherish." I wiped my eyes. "It doesn't seem possible, but I have tears of sorrow and tears of joy at the same time." The disciples greeted Cuza during the next few moments, even older James.

The soldiers, impatient to finish their responsibility, instructed us to proceed quickly with Jesus's body.

Mark stepped over to John and Simon Peter. "I must return to the Praetorium, since I'm still on duty. After you finish the burial details, please return to our home. I'll be there shortly after sundown."

Cuza spoke to Mark. "I must also return." Then to me, "I'm here on state business with Herod Antipas. I'll finish as soon as possible."

The disciples placed Jesus's body on one of their outer robes. Each disciple took hold of an edge. They picked it up, ready to follow Joseph and Nicodemus.

Mark stepped back over to me. "Would you like to go with us? John Mark can take you home from the Praetorium."

"I hate to leave Mary and the others, but, yes, I do want to go with you and Cuza."

The sad procession carrying Jesus' body followed Joseph and Nicodemus.

Mark, Cuza, and I started back toward Jerusalem. Cuza reached and took my hand in his. "Herod asked me to be part of his official delegation. We're working with Pilate's staff to organize security between Galilee and Judea. Mark remembered me from the time he came to Herod's Palace in Sepphoris several months ago." We stopped a moment to watch the disciples with the bloody body draped between them fade around a corner.

"Mark told me much of what has happened with you over the past week," Cuza said. "I'm sorry I'll be involved in official business two more days, but then we can return home."

He said home! That simple word thrilled me, and I wondered how much I could safely ask. How much of the past dare I bring up? The present moment was too wonderful to spoil, but, I had to know, "How is Marcus?"

"He's grown through two sizes since you saw him. His jabbering words are sentences now. He has grown up so much." We walked on for a few minutes. Cuza squeezed my hand. "He can't wait to see you."

Cuza's response is great thus far. But how far do I dare go? The next question had to be the hardest one I ever asked. "And how is Mariam?"

"Joanna, it's a long story, but the short version—Mariam is no longer with us. A nice older lady named Rebecca now cares for Marcus."

Stunned, I stopped short, hardly able to move. Long moments elapsed as I rehearsed the bitter dilemma I'd struggled through of returning with that woman still in charge. "I want to know what happened to her, but I won't be able to understand much until I hear the answer to the question burning inside me." I looked deep into Cuza's eyes. "Why didn't you come for me once you read the note I left under your pillow?" My eyes pleaded for an answer.

A bewildered look swept Cuza's face. "What note?"

"I left you a long note explaining why I had to leave. I told you when you came to your senses, to please come for me." My heart beat faster than I could speak.

"Mariam told me all I knew," Cuza said, slowly shaking his head. "I never knew of a note beneath my pillow. Had one been there, I'm sure I would have noticed it." His whole body seemed to shake the negative response. "All I had to go on was Mariam relating you were adamant, I should not come looking for you, and your mind would not be changed."

We stood there for a long moment just looking at each other. In silence, we began walking again. Cuza stopped in front of the Damascus Gate. "That fits so well with what began to happen after you left."

"I don't understand."

"To say I was angry when you left would be an understatement." Cuza rubbed at the back of his neck. "I found hard to accept that you would leave me and our son without so much as a word of explanation. Mariam, on the other hand, seemed extremely concerned for Marcus and me. She went out of her way doing things to help, even staying some weekends I was off to help with Marcus.

I protested, but she assured me everyone in her family shared her desire to help me through a difficult time."

I started to respond but decided to just listen.

"Then, instead of going home after she put Marcus to bed, she continually wanted to stay and visit. She told me what a poor mother you were, and how you were away almost every day without saying where you were going, practically accusing you of meeting with other men."

"Oh?" I cringed. "Interesting."

Then Cuza's face hardened. "One day, I discovered I had left some important documents at home. I came in to find Marcus sitting on the floor, crying. I heard Mariam yell from the direction of our bedroom for Marcus to stop his crying. I spotted her through the slightly open door trying on your clothes."

Resentment welled up within me; anger filled my eyes. "That—"

"At that moment, all her actions began to fit together. Never had I felt like such a fool. I was furious and ordered her to leave our house immediately."

"Well, thank you for finally realizing what she was up to. She made my life miserable enough."

Cuza examined the pavement beneath his feet as we walked. "In hindsight, it's obvious. I should have suspected what she related about your departure." He kicked at a small stone, "But I didn't."

We walked on through the huge gate fortification and several blocks into the city. My resentment faded enough for me to share my heart. "Mariam's spite and selfishness kept me from you and Marcus for almost a year. I should hate her for it." I looked in Cuza's eyes. "No, I won't hate her. And not simply because Jesus wouldn't want me to. Her evil brought about the most wonderful year of being with Jesus. Because of that, my life is forever changed. Cuza, please understand how deeply I missed you and Marcus. I agonized over being away. But at the same time, understand I would not trade this last years' experience … for anything in the world."

Cuza looked long in my eyes. He didn't reply. I could only hope he would understand better in the days to come.

We walked past many places the paving stones were stained red. Suddenly, the horrid image of that event flashed across my mind. "Right here is where Jesus could drag the cross no further. He slumped to his knees. After the first lash of the whip, a number of us threw our bodies over Jesus." I knelt and touched the dried blood. "The soldiers snatched a traveler named Simon from the onlookers and ordered him to carry Jesus' cross. Someday, I would like to find him and thank him."

We arrived at the Praetorium, and Cuza apologized again. "I hate to return to work after being with you for only an hour. I promise, I'll make it up to you."

Mark placed his hand on Cuza's shoulder. "Joanna will be safe at our home until you are ready to leave." Mark continued. "Now, you will be coming to our home this evening as well, won't you? I'll wait for you until you're off duty."

"I definitely want to come, but I must return to my delegation before late."

Mark left us to find John Mark. Cuza looked down at me. "Joanna, I can't do much to show my feelings here in front of this Roman fortress, but I can hold you. I would like to do that." Cuza, in his military attire, took me, peasant dress and all, into his arms and held me tight. I could only imagine what the Roman officers milling about thought. But I didn't care, not in the least.

CHAPTER THIRTY-FOUR

A huge emptiness filled the room. Jesus had always been there, larger than life, leading, teaching, loving, caring. His absence left a hole larger than the Sea of Galilee.

Jesus' absence also raised the questions I so dreaded. Who would lead? Who will follow that potential leader? And the even greater question—who wouldn't follow him? Would the group gradually fall apart? In a few years, would anyone even remember the wonderful, life-giving teachings of Jesus?

In the first hours back at Lois and Mark's home, something else quite amazing seemed to be occurring. It reminded me of when Jesus healed a crippled man and the man's initial fear when he laid down his crutch for his first step. What began transpiring among the disciples appeared similar to a cripple's first, tentative steps. With Jesus no longer present to be their strong leader, the disciples began to lay aside their clutch of petty rivalries and become the apostles he'd called them to be.

Since that awful moment in Caiaphas' courtyard, I began to see a different older James. He finally realized what his incessant arguing and picking at Simon Peter had caused.

Simon Peter's swaggering bravado was also noticeably absent. Everyone observed his complete failure. There was nothing left to conceal. With nothing to hide behind, a humble Peter gradually emerged.

With his older brother no longer competing with Simon Peter for leadership, the door cracked opened for John to step forward as a natural, gentle leader. James, John, and Simon Peter sat down together, listened to each other and began working together. A completely different tone from the previous night's contentious rivalry filled the room.

Mark and Cuza came through the door. "I'm sorry we're late," Cuza explained. "Herod has no concept of time. Mark had to wait for me."

Mark removed and hung his crimson cape over an empty peg. "Bring us up-to-date. What happened after we left?"

Interestingly, most of the eyes turned toward John. He blushed. "Joseph did have a very nice tomb. They recently carved a burial chamber large enough to stand upright in. It's in a rock cliff at the edge of a pleasant garden. We wrapped Jesus' body in some burial clothes Nicodemus hastily gathered. Then we laid him on the burial platform. The sun was setting to begin the Sabbath when Thad and James rolled the sealing stone across the entrance." John stopped, checked back his emotions.

"As we left, a detachment of soldiers marched up. James asked them why they were there. They said they had orders to guard the tomb." John stopped, grimaced. "We couldn't understand why they needed to guard a dead man's tomb, but we didn't argue."

Mark thanked John then spoke to all of us, "I also have some interesting news. Today, a patrol found a man who had been hung. They assumed foul play until they examined the circumstances. They came to suspect the hanging was self-inflicted. When they brought the body in, the face reminded me of someone, but I couldn't place who. Only later did I realize. I do believe the dead man was your Judas."

Younger James shook his head. "I still can't believe what that traitor did."

Thomas spoke up. "Since the women need to stay here, and Jesus isn't …" He stopped and cleared his emotions. "Keeping our campsite on the Mount of Olives doesn't make sense. I don't even want to go back there. Since Simon and I lived here before following Jesus, we are offering to split the men up between us while we're here. We don't know how long we'll be in Jerusalem, so it might be good to have a roof over our heads. I know it will—"

"I … I have Uncle Cleopas and Aunt Mary," Thad interrupted. "They live only a few blocks from here. They've asked many times why I didn't stay with them when we were in the city. Th … they loved Jesus. I know they would welcome three or four of us."

"Four, four, and three. With the women staying here, that will work," Thomas added. "We can store our camp equipment at my home until we return to Capernaum. What do you think?" Thomas looked around the group.

The disciples glanced back and forth to each other. Then, one by one, they nodded. Thomas continued. "The important thing is, we stay together even though we're staying in separate homes." The men nodded more enthusiastically.

With the evening growing late, Cuza spoke. "I want to thank each of you for taking care of Joanna this past year. Again, I'm very sorry about what happened to Jesus. Under the circumstances, I think it best to take her home with me when I leave three days from now."

Cuza's words caused my throat to swell. I tried to conceal my trembling bottom lip.

"I know you will miss her." The usually stoic Cuza stopped. He cleared the emotion from his throat. "Right now, I need to rejoin my delegation. I'll stay in close touch with you during the next two days."

Cuza and I walked to the front door. He gave me a much-needed embrace, then turned and left. The door hardly closed when the lighthearted kidding began … I loved it.

The clear morning sun and the early spring's crisp air should have produced a glimmer of hope in someone's heart. However, not even the beauty of a new day brought the slightest relief from the horrible reality of what had happened.

For the most part, the men followed the instructions to allow an interval of time between the small groups coming in. That space of time left those already in the house too much time. Most of us just sat and looked at each other. James's pacing scraped a tender layer of my already frayed nerves. The side door crept open and three more disciples slipped in.

More time passed as we awkwardly waited. My anxiety urged me to do something, anything. "I know you've already eaten," I said, "but I feel so useless sitting here. Isn't there anything I can do?"

"I know something." Mary suddenly had everyone's attention. "Yesterday's trauma didn't allow us time. As we rushed to place Jesus in the tomb before the Sabbath began, we were unable to gather burial spices and anoint the body. We should get these and properly prepare Jesus's body, possibly early tomorrow."

"I can help!" Mary Magdalene suddenly jumped to her feet. This was the first time to see real life emerge in her since that gate opened at the Praetorium.

With Mary Magdalene eagerly talking to Mary about spices, Susanna and I moved toward the upper room where John was calling the disciples. Susanna whispered, "I never dreamed I would see Mary Magdalene wanting to work alongside Mary. Maybe now, they'll become friends."

We sat down as Philip entered the ongoing discussion. "How could we have been so wrong about Judas?"

Matthew feebly offered, "Looking back on things, I should have told Jesus my concerns, but I didn't." Matthew told of the conversation Judas had with him about Jesus being his ticket to somewhere important.

"Yes, you should have," Simon Peter inserted.

John shook his head. "Jesus probably knew already. How many times did he say one of us would betray him?"

A slow silence followed.

The thought had burned through my mind far too long. I couldn't wait any longer without an answer. "Help me understand something."

I looked around to each of the men. "Jesus's mother vividly explained how the angel told her Jesus was the Son of the Living God. There wasn't the slightest doubt in her mind. Then in Caesarea Philippi, Simon Peter said, 'You are the Messiah, the Son of the Living God.' And Jesus agreed."

Everyone nodded.

My body shook as I tried to continue. "Men don't have the power to give sight to the blind ... or raise Lazarus and a little girl from the dead. I need to understand. If Jesus were the Son of the Living God, how could they kill him?"

Silent, dejected looks were my only reply.

My bottom lip quivered. "And yet, I saw the spear pierce his side, I know he's dead."

CHAPTER THIRTY-FIVE

Darkness covered the city like a black veil when Mary Magdalene called us to awaken. As the first tentative rays of light peeked between the eastern hills, Mary hastily added oil to the spices she and Mary Magdalene had prepared the previous evening. The sweet aroma of olive oil mixed with aloe and myrrh instantly filled the room.

"Come on, we need to hurry," Mary Magdalene urged.

During the dreadful crucifixion, Mary Magdalene seemed completely unable to operate. Now, the realization that Jesus's body had not been properly anointed for burial brought her renewed life. Mary cradled the bowl of spices in her arms while I held the door, and the four of us slipped out to the darken street. Our sad destination was Jesus's tomb.

The city streets were deserted. A faint glow arched in the eastern sky. As we continued our brisk pace in the early twilight, a cool breeze chilled my face.

The usual detail of Roman soldiers had not yet arrived to replace the two lone guards as we exited the Damascus Gate. Thankfully, Mary remembered the way.

Suddenly, Susanna stopped "Wait." We stepped back to where she stood. Her brow furrowed, "Has anyone thought about how to get the huge stone moved away from the tomb's entrance?"

We looked back and forth among ourselves. One or the other of us must have an answer.

Mary Magdalene placed her hands on her hips. "Come on, let's go. We'll work something out." She started on.

She seemed determined to go with or without us. Hurrying to catch up, I called, "Listen, this is futile. Let's go back and wait until some of the disciples can come with us."

"No, Joanna, come on. We'll figure it out." Mary Magdalene didn't slow.

I waited for Mary and Susanna to almost catch up, then I hurried on. Mary Magdalene only stopped when she reached a crossroads she didn't recognize.

With arms full, Mary tilted her head to the left. "It's this way, then right on the second road."

We reached an ornate gate guarding a beautiful garden. Had the gate not opened easily, Mary Magdalene's yank would have loosened its hinges.

With her hands full, Mary again used her head to point. "The tomb is a little farther—in the cliff side over there."

Rays of light began to seep between the eastern hills. The sky gradually grew bright enough to see without difficulty.

Three-quarters of the way across the garden, we stumbled upon an incredible scene. "Are those soldiers asleep?" I asked.

Susanna tiptoed over to look. "They couldn't have gone to sleep like this."

The soldier on the bottom still had a grip on his spear. He was on his side, with his head tilted back. A second soldier lay partially across his legs. The third lay on his face, his spear also clutched tightly in his fist. Susanna knelt beside the two. "They seem to be breathing. I don't think they're dead."

"The tomb!" Mary Magdalene screamed.

"What?" My focus shifted. A huge round stone lay to one side of an opening in the face of the stone cliff.

Her bowl of spices fell to the ground as Mary cried, "What's happened?"

An eerie, bluish-white light radiated from the entrance of the tomb that eclipsed the growing brightness of the light-streaked sky.

I backed up several steps, preparing to run. Susanna looked ready to retreat as well.

Mary Magdalene, however, started in the other direction. One very slow step at a time, she crept toward the tomb. The glow coming from its entrance reflected off her garment as it shimmered in the early morning breeze. Her starting toward the tomb gave the three of us reason to very hesitantly follow.

Mary Magdalene reached the entrance and paused. We gathered close behind and gazed at each other wide-eyed. Mary Magdalene started in. I swallowed hard then followed. At the same time, I was preparing to flee. Susanna and Mary were as close as the hem of my robe.

Suddenly, seated before us were two imposing figures, one at each end of the burial slab. I shielded my eyes from the radiance of their garments. Their blinding brilliance overwhelmed the entire chamber. The sight stunned my senses. Dazed, I fell to my knees. My mouth opened, but words would not form.

The two radiant men stood in unison, one at each end of the empty burial platform. One angel spoke directly to us. "Why do you look for the living among the dead? Jesus isn't here. He is alive."

The second angel followed. "Do you not remember Jesus telling you in Galilee how the Son of Man must be betrayed into the hands of sinful men, be crucified, and rise again on the third day?"

My heart beat out of my chest. I had never experienced anything remotely close to this. My mouth, completely dry, searched for words. They wouldn't come.

The angel paused a long moment. "Now, go tell his disciples, especially Peter, how Jesus has risen as he said he would." Both angels' gazes penetrated my very being. Even on my knees, my legs trembled.

Then, without a word or warning, they were no longer there. I couldn't explain the experience any other way. They didn't leave. They were simply … no longer there.

With their brilliance suddenly absent, rays of morning sunlight peeked through the tomb's entrance. Several long moments passed before either of us could move.

Mary stood first. "We must find the disciples and tell them."

Susanna and I nodded. I stood and started toward the entrance.

Mary Magdalene didn't get up. Susanna motioned to her. "Come on. The angels told us to go tell the disciples."

"You three go. I'm staying here."

"Staying here?" Susanna's eyes narrowed.

"Yes," Mary Magdalene firmly replied. "I'm staying here."

"Why?"

"In case."

"In case of what?" Susanna asked.

"I don't know." Mary Magdalene didn't intend to give up. "Just … in case."

Mary stepped over to where Mary Magdalene still knelt. "Let us, at least, get you to the entrance. You can't sit in here." We helped her to a spot just outside the stone opening, then the three of us started for town.

As we reached the gate, Susanna said, "I really don't want to leave her there by herself."

I nodded but gently assisted Susanna on through the gate. We walked toward the city as fast as long robes and sandals would allow.

I suddenly stopped short. "I just remembered." The other faces filled with questions. "We didn't check to see if those Roman soldiers were still there." We looked back and forth at each other.

Susanna's eyes glistened. "I have to go back."

"No, Susanna," Mary replied in a confident voice. "If the angels did that to the soldiers, they can easily care for Mary Magdalene. Besides, I would have noticed if they had still been lying there. They weren't twenty steps from the tomb."

I turned to continue, but stopped again. "There's another problem. If we go back to Lois and Mark's this early, it will be several hours before the disciples get there."

Mary thought for a moment. "Thad took us to his Uncle Cleopas's home last year when we were in Jerusalem. Simon Peter, John, and James are staying with him. He said it was only a few blocks from Lois and Mark's home. I might be able to find it again."

"If you think there's a chance, it's worth a try," I said.

As we turned onto what I feared was our third wrong street, I spotted Simon Peter sitting on a front step almost a block away.

"Jesus is alive!" I shouted to Peter when we were halfway to him.

"What do you mean, alive?" Simon Peter stood and drew his head to one side. "He can't be."

My enthusiasm exploded. "The stone's been rolled away from the tomb. The angels' robes were so bright, I had to shield my eyes. They told us not to seek the living among the dead. One said to especially tell you that Jesus is alive."

Each of us excitedly repeated our encounter as the other disciples came out of the house.

Older James twisted his mouth to the side and asked a second time, "Are … you … sure?"

"Do you think we would run all the way here, searching all over this town for you, if it didn't happen?" Susanna settled the issue.

John turned to Thaddaeus. "Think you can find Simon's home in Emmaus? We need to get word to the others, and soon."

"Bart's staying with him, and Emmaus isn't a very big village. I should be able to find them."

"Go and get them as fast as you can," John said. "Tell them to meet us at Lois and Mark's. Then we'll all go to the tomb together and see what has happened."

James said, "I'll go to Thomas's home and get Andrew and the others. The five of you go on." For the first time I could remember, James offered to do more than tell someone else what to do. He paused, a frown crossed his face. "Where's Mary Magdalene?"

Susanna stepped up to James. "She wanted to stay at the tomb for some reason we didn't understand. It seemed more important to get word to you than to argue with her."

Our experience, along with relating it to the disciples, brought a renewed sense of life pumping through my body. With the sudden surge of hope, my feet hardly touched the stone pavement. Even so, the image of Jesus not flinching when the spear split his side flashed across my mind. I believed the angels—but how could someone so dead, now be alive?

I reminded myself how Lazarus returned to life before my very eyes. My words the previous evening … 'How can you kill the Son of the Living God?' … played across my consciousness. I remained elated over what I witnessed at the tomb. But something deep inside whispered, *but … you didn't actually see Jesus … alive.*

As we made our way the few blocks to Lois and Mark's, John asked Susanna, "Tell me again, what did the angels look like?"

We were so excited we completely forgot the 'come in by twos and threes' rule. All five of us barged in at once. Since it was the first day of the week, Mark had already left for duty and John Mark for his classes. Lois joined in our joy as we shared the unfolding events.

The front door suddenly burst open, slamming against the wall. Mary Magdalene stood with her hands on her knees, gasping for breath. She straightened. "I've seen Jesus. He *is* alive!"

CHAPTER THIRTY-SIX

"He called my name!" Mary Magdalene drew a deep breath. "Jesus called my name." Tears glistened on her cheeks.

Simon Peter jumped up and grasp her hand. "Catch your breath. Start at the beginning. What exactly happened?"

"I was sitting near the entrance to the tomb, crying my eyes out. A man came up and asked why I was crying. I supposed he was a worker there and hardly looked at him. I told him I was crying because I didn't know where they had taken Jesus."

Mary Magdalene looked Simon Peter straight in the eyes. "That's when he said, 'Mary.' I looked up, and there stood Jesus." Mary Magdalene looked around to all of us with pleading eyes. "I jumped up to throw my arms around him, but he stopped me. He said, 'Do not take hold of me. I have not yet returned to my Father. Instead, go to my disciples and tell them I have risen.'"

Simon Peter and John both gazed at Mary Magdalene with eyes wide.

"I saw him," Mary Magdalene repeated. "I know it was Jesus. He called my name."

"The rest of you stay here and tell the others. I'm going to the tomb." Simon Peter reached for his outer robe.

"Not without me." John reached the door before Simon Peter. I'd never seen either of them move so fast.

We just began to absorb this incredible information when Andrew, followed by James and two other disciples, came in the side door.

I told them our experience, of the angels announcing Jesus's resurrection and our running to find James, John, and Simon Peter. I explained, "Mary Magdalene insisted on staying behind as we hurried to bring the news. We had just arrived here when she burst through the door shouting she had actually seen Jesus. John and Peter left for the tomb so fast a strong wind couldn't catch them."

Mary Magdalene came back in the room and rushed over. "Andrew, Philip, Matthew—I saw Jesus. He wouldn't let me touch him, but he was there just as real as you're standing there. I saw him. He even called my name."

Philip's eyes widened. "That is truly amazing. I'm thrilled to hear the news."

But I detected something in Philip's tone of voice. It didn't quite carry the same excitement as his words.

Andrew followed as Philip pulled me over to the side. In a soft voice he said, "Help me. Only Mary Magdalene actually saw Jesus?"

"Yes." I nodded. "She's certain it happened exactly the way she says."

Philip shook his head. "You realize Mary Magdalene does tend to dramatize things a bit?" Philip bit his bottom lip.

Andrew looked a little more positive, but I could still sense doubt in both their eyes.

"Normally, I'd agree with you, Philip." I spoke my heart. "But I do believe her. If for no other reason than she wouldn't make up the part about Jesus telling her not to touch him."

Neither appeared completely convinced.

"Besides," I added. "You can't discount our encounter with the angels."

Andrew nervously shrugged one shoulder. "Tell me again, about the angels."

"I realize it sounds incredible, but it happened. The two angels were just like Jesus's mother described when she told of her encounter. Their overwhelming presence took us to our knees. The morning sun couldn't compare to their radiance."

As we discussed this back and forth, John and Simon Peter slipped back in the door. The disciples pounced on them. "What did you see? Who was there?"

John spoke, "Things appeared very much like the women described. We didn't encounter any angels, but then we didn't really expect to. We did find this folded and laying on the burial platform."

Mary jumped to her feet. "Let me see that. Look at the bloodstains on it. This … this is the burial cloth Nicodemus brought for us to wrap around Jesus' body. I know it is. Remember, they were rushing us to close the tomb before the sun set for the Sabbath."

Finally, we had a tangible piece of evidence we could hold in our hands. Mary clutched it like the single most important item in the whole world. I shared the exact same sentiments.

After Mary put the cloth safely away, I pulled her over to the side. "Mary, I'm really bothered by some of the disciples' skepticism. Did we fail to explain what happened at the tomb this morning? I'm not sure everyone really believes us."

"Think about it, Joanna. Would you have a hard time believing our story if you had not actually been there?"

I rehearsed the encounter again. Then I tried to imagine how it might sound to someone not actually present. My mind forced my head to nod.

Before long the disciples staying with Simon, out in the little village of Emmaus, slipped in the side door. Again, we related our story. At least, younger James and Bart seemed more receptive. With everyone there, the group prepared to return to the tomb.

After all the excitement of the morning, I knew Mary would be too exhausted to make that walk again. "Since I have already been there," I said to Peter and John, "and I know what I witnessed, I'll stay here with Mary. She doesn't need to make that journey again."

Mary faintly protested, but with a little encouragement from her son, she gave in.

With everyone gone and Mary resting, I thought through our encounter again and how we told the disciples. The more I thought, the more something bothered me. I couldn't quite put my finger on it.

When the disciples returned, I asked Simon Peter, "Were Roman soldiers anywhere around when you and John went this morning?"

Simon Peter gave me a blank stare. "Oh! I forgot about the guards. No, we didn't see any soldiers. They must have awakened and fled."

Thomas responded to our conversation. "We don't have to wonder what those soldiers reported to the authorities, do we? Now they're going to accuse us of assaulting them and stealing Jesus's body. This is going to cause some major trouble."

Thomas's dire assessment added to my confusion. Deep inside, a thought gnawed at me. Something didn't fit. I reviewed what the four of us experienced, and nothing could ever shake that reality. Mary Magdalene's announcement also seemed genuine. *What could it be?*

Then a thought began simmering to the surface. I called Andrew and Philip over. "I know what's bothering me about all of this."

"Okay," Philip said.

"After what we experienced at the tomb, somehow I expected Jesus to walk through that door and speak to us." I shook my head. "If he is alive, why isn't he here?"

"You had the encounter with the angels. We only heard about it," Andrew added. "So, the feeling you describe is twice as strong for me and probably for the rest of the men."

Philip shook his head. "I agree. If Jesus is alive, why isn't he here?"

But he wasn't. An hour passed. We waited. Then another hour passed. Then another. Still nothing.

Men came and left, bringing brief moments of anticipation, interrupted by long stretches of wondering and waiting. We looked to anyone who came in for news. None came.

We assembled a second visit to the tomb early afternoon. This lifted our spirits briefly, but the long, empty wait scratched away at the marvelous anticipation we'd experienced that morning.

Matthew picked up pacing where Thomas left off. Never in human history had time moved so slowly.

The agonizing afternoon wait increased the doubts floating in my mind. I didn't like doubts. I remained convinced of what took place at the tomb. Somehow, I had expected everyone to instantly rejoice in the news Jesus was alive.

Some welcome relief came when Thad's Uncle Cleopas and Aunt Mary stopped by. We shared our encounter with the angels at the empty tomb. Telling the story again lifted my spirits immeasurably. Mary Magdalene, once again, shared her experience of briefly *actually seeing* Jesus.

Aunt Mary's eyes grew large. "We heard what happened with you women at the tomb, but we didn't know about Mary Magdalene actually seeing Jesus." Aunt Mary clutched Mary Magdalene by the sleeve and led her toward the alcove. "Tell me all about how it happened."

Uncle Cleopas stroked his chin. "I knew they couldn't keep Jesus in a grave."

Simon Peter filled Uncle Cleopas in on many of the details. As he finished, Cleopas pulled him toward a corner. His whisper was just a little too loud. "Why do you suppose Jesus would make all this happen just for the women? Wouldn't he have appeared to you and James first?"

That hurt, but how could I respond? He was right. I would have expected Jesus to appear to James, John, and Peter first. But he hadn't.

After my flash of resentment subsided, I thought back over the past year. A question suddenly stuck out so obviously. *When did Jesus ever do what people expected? Of all the respectable people in Jericho, with whom did we have dinner?*

Thad took his Uncle Cleopas back to the group and took great pains to introduce each disciple and tell something about him. I think Thaddaeus said more there than in the whole previous year I knew him.

He concluded, "I really wanted you to meet Simon and Thomas, but they've gone to the market to buy more food." Thad hesitated then seemed to return to his shy self. "I ... I suppose the four of us have dug pretty deeply into your pantry too, haven't we?"

"Mary and I consider it an honor to feed and house any disciple of Jesus." Uncle Cleopas puffed his chest out a little. "We loved him and his teachings."

Bart stepped over to the younger James. "Simon said he needed me to help him with some chores at his house. I'd like to go back, at least until we hear something more. Could you be ready to go any time soon?"

Younger James hesitated. "I'd rather stay here with Mother, if you don't mind. Besides, we'll all gather back here after dinner this evening."

"Okay." Bartholomew would never push an issue, but disappointment showed on his face.

"I'll go with you," Uncle Cleopas offered. "I need to walk off some nervous energy. If Mary wants to go home before I get back, one of the men can accompany her. It's just a few blocks."

A smile spread across Bart's face. He and Cleopas left for the Zealot's home in Emmaus.

Late afternoon crawled by even slower. Still nothing happened. As I looked out at the sun dipping toward the west, my anxiety increased several more levels. The only encouragement I felt was the anticipation of telling Cuza and Mark about the wonderful encounter with the angels when they came in.

The door finally opened, and in stepped Mark and young John Mark. The door closed. My already long face fell practically to the floor.

Mark gave me a pat on the shoulder. "Cuza sends his love, Joanna. He would really like to be here. He said that if he's to finish so he can leave with you tomorrow, he'll have to work this evening to wrap up the details."

Disappointment hit me like a bolder on a downhill roll; however, the words 'leave with you tomorrow' offered hope to offset the hurt. *Has the time finally arrived for me to return home?*

Susanna and I brought Mark and John Mark up-to-date on all the wonderful happenings of the day. I carefully omitted our many long hours of wondering and waiting.

"Joanna, that's wonderful!" Mark said as he gave me a smile. John Mark gave me the biggest smile I had seen recently.

Mary Magdalene also related her experience again. John Mark took in every word.

I had to give Mary Magdalene credit. In the many times she recounted the amazing event, not one single iota of her story changed. Never had I known her to recount an event even a second time without some embellishment.

I was thrilled by the prospect of finally going home. But there remained one huge problem. Now was the absolute worse time to leave the group. The empty tomb and the angel's announcement thrilled me. But so far, only Mary Magdalene had seen Jesus, and that ever so briefly. While I looked forward to returning home, I could hardly stand the thought of leaving with everything still so uncertain.

As we finished dinner, James, Peter, and two others slipped in the side door.

While we helped Lois put things away, three more disciples slipped in. Andrew announced, "Thomas will be along shortly. He had to go to the market, again. I'm afraid we're eating him out of—"

The side door sprang open. Simon and Bart rushed in. The Zealot sucked in a deep breath. "We've seen Jesus!"

CHAPTER THIRTY-SEVEN

"Give us a minute. We'll tell you all about it." Bart reacted as we practically pounced on them for details. He was clearly uncomfortable being the object of attention, "Cleopas could probably tell this a lot better, but he went straight home to tell Aunt Mary. I'll do my best." Bart motioned toward the Zealot. "Simon was home fixing dinner, so he missed the first part."

"Come on, get to the details," John insisted.

"I am. As Cleopas and I walked to Emmaus, we were discussing the things that happened this morning. We both had a lot of questions." With a slightly guilty look, Bart shrugged his shoulders. "I hate to admit it, but we both had a little trouble with Mary Magdalene's story about actually seeing Jesus."

Bart took a deep breath. "About this time, a stranger who was walking in the same direction asked what we were talking about. Cleopas looked at him as only Cleopas does and said he must be the only person around Jerusalem who didn't know what had happened these past three days.

"The stranger wanted to know, what things? We both told him

about Jesus and how we thought he was the Messiah and how his crucifixion had crushed our hopes. Then we told him about the empty tomb this morning, the angels, and then Mary Magdalene's story. The stranger stopped and just looked at us."

Bart sat down to continue. "Then, it turns out he knew a lot more than he let on. He told us how our hearts were too slow to believe what the prophets had foretold. He went on and explained things to us as we walked. Then he just stopped and asked us, 'Did not the Christ have to suffer all these things and enter his glory?' I looked at Cleopas. Cleopas looked at me. We both looked at this stranger. We were *really* confused. At first, this man didn't seem to know anything. Then, all of a sudden, he was teaching us what Moses and the prophets said about the Messiah."

Bart wiped sweat from his face as he continued, "By this time, we had come to Simon's street and needed to turn. The stranger proceeded on his way, but Cleopas and I both wanted to know more. So, we stopped him and asked if he would come to dinner at Simon's."

Bart squirmed on his stool. "We gathered around the table. Simon was getting ready to ask the blessing, when the stranger just took the liberty of picking up the bread and offering the blessing himself."

Bart drew a deep breath and bit at his bottom lip. "I ... I can't explain why we didn't recognize him before with everything he said. But the moment he lifted the bread and blessed it, the man was Jesus! All three of us could not be mistaken. Jesus blessed and broke the bread." Bart's voice choked. Tears ran down his cheeks.

Simon, the man of few words, finished for him. "Jesus knew we recognized him. Like Joanna said about the angels, he ... suddenly wasn't there."

"Let's go to the upper room where we can discuss these things better." John stood to lead the way and added, "We have a lot to talk about."

As we followed, I stepped up beside Andrew. "I'm beginning to recognize a pattern. I wonder if you've noticed?"

"What Joanna?"

"So far Jesus has appeared to three of our group, not counting Cleopas. He just happened to be there, instead of younger James."

Andrew gave me a long questioning look.

"If Jesus were to reveal himself the way people usually do," I continued, "who would he appear to first?"

"I suppose the top leaders, like John, James, Simon Peter ... and me." Andrew's brow furrowed.

I saw something beginning to click in Andrew's mind. I pressed further. "Instead, Jesus first has the angels announce his resurrection to whom? The lowly women who supported his ministry. Then, when Jesus *does* appear, whom does he appear to? The least accepted woman of the group. When he starts to reveal himself to the disciples, who does he go to first?"

Andrew thought a moment. "Uh ... those furthest from the leadership?"

I gave Andrew a shy smile. "You recall Jesus talking about the first being last and the last being first?"

"That's interesting, Joanna. We need to bring that up after we listen to John."

While each secured a place to sit, John stepped to the front. "Today we've heard of some unbelievable, yet wonderful experiences. The first important thing is those who experienced each encounter are unshakable and sure of—"

John's gaze froze, his words hung in midair. "Jesus!"

I swiveled to look behind us where John's eyes halted. There stood Jesus, just beyond the edge of the group.

"Peace be with you," Jesus said as he walked around us and stood beside John.

Both fright and thrill consumed me. Jesus stood right there with us. There could be no question concerning his reality. Jesus was very much alive, as present with us as John or anyone.

Jesus gave the same coy smile as when he stilled the raging storm, and we all sat on the boat deck in disbelief. "Why are you troubled?" Jesus asked. He looked around at each of us.

Like after the storm, my mouth opened but words wouldn't form. Again, I was experiencing the impossible. It took a long moment for the reality standing before me to become real in my mind.

"You doubt it is really me?" Jesus held out his hands. "Look at my hands. Remember those huge spikes?"

My mind raced to catch up. I knew those hands. I remembered all too well the spikes driven through them. The huge gashes were still torn and red in his palms.

"See, I have flesh and bones," Jesus said as he continued to walk among us. "Does a ghost have flesh and bones?"

No longer did a trace of doubt reside in my mind. I couldn't imagine anyone present having a doubt either.

Jesus stopped and looked down at Mary. "I'm hungry. Do you have anything to eat?"

Mary looked up at Jesus, her face turning red. "You knew I kept a piece of fish from dinner, didn't you?" She unfolded the napkin and handed her saved piece of fish to Jesus.

As he ate, it suddenly seemed like old times around the campfire during our travels. "While I was still with you, this is what I told you to expect. You see, everything written about me by the prophets, the psalmists, and the Law of Moses had to be fulfilled. You remember,

'The Messiah will suffer and die and then rise from the dead on the third day.' I told you this several times."

Jesus paused. The many times he repeated those words trickled across my mind. They were words we didn't want to hear at the time. I remembered how hard I had tried to dismiss them as just reasonable worry. Listening again while Jesus spoke, those same words became very, very real.

Jesus lifted his arm over us. "Now, you are to proclaim my suffering to the whole world. Tell how my death will bring forgiveness of sin and eternal life to everyone who repents and believes in me. This is the reason I called you to be my followers."

Jesus again walked among us. He touched our foreheads and called each of us by name. "You are my witnesses of these things."

How many times during the past year had I uttered, 'This moment far eclipsed anything I ever encountered in my life.'? Yet again, they were the only words to describe what was taking place.

Jesus again strolled to the front of the group. "I am going to send you what my Father has promised. So, stay here in Jerusalem until God's promise is fulfilled. You will receive power from on high."

As Jesus finished speaking, he turned and started to walk. He didn't go anywhere ... he simply was no longer there!

No one moved for the longest time. We sat speechless, staring at each other. How does one comprehend what just happened?

The door opened and Thomas stepped in. He looked around at our stunned faces. "What's happening?"

CHAPTER THIRTY-EIGHT

"I still can't fully comprehend last evening." Susanna said as she walked over. An expression of concern covered her usual smile.

My eyes widened. "You have doubts about last evening, that Jesus is alive?"

"Oh, no." Susanna shook her head. "No doubt at all about what happened. What I'm concerned about is, what does it all mean? Where do we go from here, especially Mary Magdalene and me?"

"It will take me at least another year to figure that out," I replied. "But I'm so glad Jesus came when he did. It would be unbelievably hard to leave with everything so uncertain. Since we all saw him alive, I think I can depart with a smile."

"All except Thomas. He's still having a hard time." Susanna bit at her bottom lip. "But I can understand. If I had not been there, I guess I would have some questions, too."

I walked back over to the bed where I gathered my belongings. "I didn't realize how few things I brought with me until I gathered them. My few nice clothes are hidden back at Mary's home in Capernaum."

I knew it was still too early, but my nerves were all over the place. I returned for another glance out the window, just in case Cuza might have arrived early. The street below contained only the light of early morning. "You're welcome to them, Susanna."

"Welcome to what?"

I shook my mind back to the present. "I know I won't be returning to Capernaum any time soon. I would love for you to have those few nice things I left there." I gave her a smile. "I'm sure the disciples won't have much use for them."

"Joanna, please don't say that." Susanna stopped short. "It'll make me feel a lot better if I believe we'll see you again soon." Her eyes glistened.

I stuffed my few things in a bag. "You think Mary Magdalene will stay with the disciples now that Jesus isn't ..." I paused, searching for the right word. "... with the group every day?"

"I really don't know. Seeing him last night really changed everything, all over again."

I stood and looked at this wonderful, trusting woman for a long moment. "Susanna, what about you? What do you plan to do?"

"I don't know ... yet. The disciples seem to accept Mary better now, especially since Jesus appeared to her first. Even James is treating her like a real person." As our eyes met, we both laughed.

I picked up my bag and started toward the door, then I stopped and looked back. "Should you ever decide to leave, know you can always come to Sepphoris. I'd help you begin a new life there."

Susanna looked straight at me. "I can promise you this— wherever I go and whatever I do, the events of this last year will always—" Her eyes sparkled. "—be the defining point of my life."

I nodded. "I feel exactly the same." Susanna and I exchanged a long, meaningful hug. "Cuza left word he would pick me up mid-morning. I need to be ready."

I looked down at myself. "Looks like Cuza will have to admire me in my peasant attire—at least, until we get home."

"You might be more comfortable in this." I didn't realize Mary Lois had stepped into the room until she spoke.

"Lois, it's beautiful. But you can't—"

"Just watch me. Now, put it on." In record time, I dropped the tan wool garment and slipped into the beautiful silk dress. Lois continued, "We'll say I'm loaning the dress to you. That way I can be sure you'll come to visit to return it."

"Lois, I can't begin to express how much your family has meant to me and to all of us." I spoke from the depth of my heart. "We never would have survived this ordeal had you and Mark not been here. You'll never know."

"Come with me for a moment." Mary Lois led the way. "I don't know how to explain it, Joanna, but something in my heart tells me the events of this past week are part of something ... well, something a whole lot larger than we imagine."

"Thank you for saying that," I replied. "That's the thought I've been trying to find a way to express."

She led me into her bedroom and to an ornately carved chest. "I have something for you."

"Lois, you're being far too generous."

"This isn't about generosity, Joanna." She opened the chest and drew out a small wooden box. "This is about preservation." She closed the chest and sat the box on top. "There are two of these. I will always treasure one."

My curiosity leaped.

Lois lifted the engraved lid from the box, exposing a soft purple cloth. "Should anything unforeseen happen here in Jerusalem, I want one of these to be safe with you in Sepphoris."

Lois lifted the cloth, revealing two silver chalices. "Jesus used two cups of wine during his special time with the disciples at the end of the Passover meal. For your remembrance, but more importantly for its safekeeping, I want you to treasure one."

I gasped. Tears filled my eyes as I lifted and held the cup. Words would not form. With a huge knot in my throat, I simply nodded.

Lois lifted the lid to her chest again, replaced the box with the remaining chalice and drew out a smaller engraved box. "This will keep it safe."

I carefully wrapped the cup she entrusted to me in its own purple cloth, closed the box and held it close to my heart. My throat remained so choked I could hardly speak. "Thank you."

"Come," Mary Lois said. "I know others want time to say good-bye before you leave."

Walking toward the living room brought even more emotion to Lois's voice. "Joanna, I will surely miss you."

Mark joined us. "Cuza will be here soon. We wish you the very best, Joanna."

Andrew and Philip were waiting in the living room. We talked several minutes about Jesus's appearance the previous evening. "What are your plans?" I asked, "What will happen now, after last night?"

"None of us knows what will happen next." Philip creased his bottom lip. "All I know is we're to stay here in Jerusalem, like Jesus said. I don't think we ought to get ahead of that." Then Philip looked down at me with his eyes glowing. "I will miss you."

Andrew broke down and gave me a real hug. "Since it isn't proper to hug a married woman, I declare you family."

"Thank you, Andrew. And yes, we are family. I'll miss you very much."

Philip and Andrew both gave teary-eyed smiles.

Mary Magdalene burst into the room. "Don't you dare leave without saying good-bye." She looked at me a long moment. "I can't bear for you leave. No, you can't go. You have to stay."

"Thank you, Mary." I took her hand. "Listen, learn to make barley cakes a little better than I did. The men will love you for it."

Simon Peter and John came over. Peter took my hand. "You're going to leave a big empty place here, you know that?"

"Thank you, Peter. I assure you, there'll be a big empty place in my life with you not around."

Older James wiped something from his eye as he said his good-bye.

Thad stuck his head in the door. "Here comes Cuza now."

I hurried to the door. "Oh, my, a two-horse carriage." Cuza rode up in a beautiful carriage and pulled over to the stone curb. "Someone's moving up in the world," I called to him.

"Don't get attached. It isn't ours," he called back. Cuza whispered, "Courtesy of King Herod Antipas."

"Don't say that very loud." I placed my things safely in the carriage. "Next to Pilate, Herod is about as far from a favorite person around here as anyone can get."

Cuza visited with Mark while Lois and I hugged one last time.

As I climbed into the carriage, younger James stepped up. "Thank you. You've meant a lot to Mother and me." James pursed his lips. "Mom wanted to say a last good-bye, but she didn't want you to see her cry. She asked me to say it for her."

"Thank you, James." The carriage began to move.

Cuza and I had a lot to talk about—but where to start? So many thoughts were sifting through my mind.

"You actually saw Jesus alive last evening." Cuza's voice broke through the rhythm of the horses' hooves. "Tell me."

"Oh, yes." Blood rushed to my cheeks as the previous evening flooded my mind. "Jesus appeared to all of us. He could not have been more real. He touched my forehead and called my name. I felt the wounds in his hands. He ate with us." I realized I was talking fast, but I could hardly slow my excitement. "He told us how his death was the sacrifice for the sins of all people, and we were to spread his story to the whole world."

My heart beat fast. "Cuza, Jesus may not be physically present like he was this past year. But he's as real in my heart right now as he ever was in life. This isn't a feeling. It's a reality that will never diminish."

Cuza smiled as he tried to digest what must have sounded like an oration. A long pause ensued.

"The three soldiers had quite a story to tell when they returned from their deployment." Cuza again broke the silence. "I hope they don't face execution." He shook his head. "The religious authorities had no idea the position they put those men in."

I looked out the side of the carriage as the trees and hillsides moved by. "This is certainly faster than taking three days to walk home."

Cuza laughed aloud. "Still hard to believe a city girl like you walked anywhere for three days … and camped out along the way?"

"I soaked my feet a lot." I blushed. "The steep walk from Jericho up to Jerusalem was always the hardest part."

Those long walks and the bantering among the disciples and the evenings together around the fire and the bright stars in the night sky all marched, one by one, across my mind. "Crazy as it seems, I'm going to miss those walks." A tear almost came to my eye.

Soon after we passed into Galilee, we stopped at a shady area to enjoy the lunch basket Mary Lois had so thoughtfully prepared. As we ate, a curious smile crossed Cuza's face. "Tell me about your wonderful stay in Capernaum."

"You would have to ask that."

"Seems like I remember your saying something the day we left about hoping to never, ever see that miserable, dirty little town again." Cuza's smile changed to a devilish grin.

"You wouldn't believe how humbling to discover Jesus and the disciples had made their headquarters in Capernaum." I shook my head. "When Jotham told me, I almost turned back. If I had not left you that note, I think I would have."

Cuza gave a big, deep-throated laugh.

"I knew you would laugh."

Rebecca proved to be totally the opposite of Mariam. I paused a moment to look up and thank my Heavenly Father.

I saw little eyes peek around the corner of the hallway. "Here comes the hug I've been waiting for." A boy two inches taller than I remembered gave me the longest hug in history. Afterward, I held Marcus away from my body for a short moment and just looked at him.

"Welcome home, Mommy."

"He's speaking in sentences. I'm amazed."

"Mommy, I four now." Marcus held up four little fingers.

"Honey, I only hope I can make this past year up to you." I choked back my emotions.

⌘

About two months later, I received a letter from Mary Lois. She recalled several precious moments we had together.

Lois went on to relate the progress of the disciples:

> Remember how Thomas missed seeing Jesus the last evening you were here? Well, Thomas finally saw Jesus, as did my whole family. By the way, Thomas asked me to tell you, "Timothy is now in the fold." He said you would know what that meant.
>
> Jesus appeared several more times to his disciples as well as to a great number of followers. According to Philip, Jesus took them out to a place near Bethany where he again told them they were to take his message to the whole world. As Jesus spoke, he began to rise into the sky. They last saw him as clouds moved between them.
>
> The disciples continued to meet regularly in our upper room. I worried about them, though. If they were to spread Jesus's message like he said, they weren't getting very far.
>
> Then it happened, Joanna. One day while they were there praying, this whole house began to shake. Such a violent wind blew through I had to hold on. Even inside, lightning flashed all around. The disciples ran out the front with all this following them.
>
> I have no idea where the people came from, but suddenly hundreds of people gathered across the street. The Lord had to be

present, because it was Simon Peter who climbed on the rock and proclaimed how Jesus's death brought God's forgiveness.

Joanna, it has been amazing. Nearly three thousand people have become followers now. They even have a name, 'The Way.' It's spread all over Jerusalem and literally turned this city upside down. I knew you would be as thrilled as we are.

By the way, I'm still waiting for you to come for a visit. You need to see how these disciples have become real leaders in this huge movement.

Give Cuza my best regards and your little Marcus a great big hug for me.

Mary Lois

I smiled as I finished Mary Lois's letter, rocking Marcus in my lap. I gave him another great big hug. I was home.

ABOUT THE AUTHOR

Gene Everett Weatherly

Gene graduated from Ouachita Baptist University in southern Arkansas, attended the University of Maryland Graduate School, and Southern Baptist Theological Seminary.

Gene's career includes forty years as a minister, pastoring churches in the Baptist Convention of Maryland/ Delaware. He served on the Executive Committee of the convention's General Mission Board. Retiring to the lake in South Carolina, Gene is now fulfilling his dream of writing.

He co-authored the Leaders Guide for the Lay Renewal Emphasis of the Southern Baptist Convention's North American Mission Board and has short stories published in Spoken Moments and Divine Moments.

Gene is a member of the South Carolina chapter of American Christian Fiction Writers and the Greenville chapter of Cross N Pens. In addition to writing, Gene greatly enjoys boating, water skiing, and especially riding his Harley motorcycle with his wife Rita.

Gene Everett Weatherly may be contacted by e-mail: GeneWeatherly@gmail.com He lives in Anderson, South Carolina.

80440555R00196

Made in the USA
Columbia, SC
17 November 2017